Praise for VISIBLE AMAZEMENT

"A wonderful book in every way. Garnett writes with humour, wisdom, and soul, perfectly capturing the voices and hearts of her marvellous, tough, funny, touching characters."
– ANNE LAMOTT, Author of *Operating Instructions*,
A Modern Library Book of the Century

"A fresh and engaging tale . . . wonderfully funny and rich . . . eager, upbeat, boundless."
– GLOBE AND MAIL

"Sneaks into your subconscious and doesn't let go . . . the best orgasm I've ever read . . ."
– MARTIN SHERMAN, Author of *Bent and Rose*

"Garnett is the new tough voice of contemporarory literature . . . unequalled amongst her peers."
– AUSTIN CLARKE, Giller Prize-winning author
of *The Polished Hoe*

"Unlike anything since *The Catcher in the Rye*."
– Donald Free, Author of *The Secret Honor*

". . . unique and touching."
– ATOM EGOYAN

"Energetic . . . forceful . . . hilarious
. . . breathtakingly honest."
– EDMONTON JOURNAL

"Garnett is a thrilling new recruit to the rank of brilliant authors. *Visible Amazement* will go round the world in triumph."
– SIMON CALLOW, Actor and Author

TRANSIENT DANCING

GALE ZOË GARNETT

McArthur & Company
Toronto

Published in Canada in 2003 by
McArthur & Company
322 King Street West, Suite 402
Toronto, Ontario M5V 1J2
www.mcarthur-co.com

The author would like to thank the Ontario Arts Council, the Department of
Foreign Affairs and International Trade, and the Canada Council for financial
support.

Permission to use song lyrics was granted by E.B. Marks Music for "Nobody" by
Bert Williams and Alex Rogers, the estate of Cole Porter and Warner
Publications for "Every Time We Say Goodbye," and Warner Publications for
"Bye Bye Blackbird" by Ray Henderson and Mort Dixon.

National Library of Canada Cataloguing in Publication

Garnett, Gale Zoë
  Transient dancing / Gale Zoë Garnett.

    ISBN 1-55278-369-3

    I. Title.

PS8563.A6732T73 2003   C813'.54   C2003-903782-7

Composition + Cover: *Mad Dog Design*
Cover Image: *David Szolcsanyi*
Printed in Canada by *Friesens*

The publisher would like to acknowledge the financial support of the
Government of Canada through the Book Publishing Industry Development
Program, the Canada Council, and the Ontario Arts Council for our publishing
activities. We also acknowledge the Government of Ontario through the
Ontario Media Development Corporation's Ontario Book Initiative.

10 9 8 7 6 5 4 3 2 1

In memory of
Edwin Louis Battle
and
Andréas G. Papandréou—
Each shared with me
His country, as he knew it.

There is a wanderer child, who is born again and again,
Causing a howling grief in the mother,
Who knows that this stranger-child
Will, one day, wander off,
Looking for home.

Yoruba Legend

Two on an Island
Ydra, Greece, 1995

Theddo Daniels, who didn't feel all that well anyway, was not pleased.

He sipped liquorice Ouzo. An enormous flame-red sunball slowly disappeared into the sea. A sailboat floated between two rock islets. Nonetheless, he was not pleased.

First trip to Greece, he thought—cradle of the Whitefolks' Whole Thing, and what am I looking at? Stepin Fetchit. *Miss* Stepin Fetchit!

Nougat-coloured skinny fool looked to be about thirty. Wore a black domino mask with white feathers and silver glitz all over it, faded jeans, and the top half of a baby blue pimp suit.

Flapping his arms, he was. Batting his eyes. Grinning wide ("So's you kin fine me in de dark, Mista Chan!"). Singing, dancing—making too damn much noise.

Theddo stared hard at the younger man. Yeah, he thought, you got *that* right, Watermelon. Don't even *think* of looking at me. Thaaass right, let the Greek waiter serve me, even though I do seem to be in your section. Oh my goodness. Oh shit, oh dear, you *are* gonna look at me. Go ahead on, Minstrelshow, try the shit-eating grin on *me*. You get to do it but once, Babycakes. Go on. McQueen me just one Butterfly and I will, I swear I will, kick your skinny ass straight into the sea! Huhn! Lookin' away, are we? Well, yeah, I guess! Sick and old as I am, I am still big enough, still strong enough to ROLL RIGHT OVER YOU, SON!

Theddo lowered and shook his head, blowing quick mirthless laughter out of his nose. "Perhaps we are overreacting, Mister Daniels," he muttered. "Perhaps, Mister Daniels, we could butch down a bit?"

Greek Time, and the God of Soulfood

Got to be Daniels, Johnny thought. He'd seen the picture in the paper, and knew Theodore "Theddo" Daniels was in Greece.

It was still difficult for Johnny to read in Greek. Going slowly, with the lexicon at his side, he could decode that Daniels was heading the Africa Group at an international "Diaspora Conference." He had, Johnny read, given a speech in the Greek Parliament. He loved seeing Daniels' name in Greek letters—Θέντο Ντάνιελς. Like the first time he saw Martin Luther King's name that way; it united his past to his present and future.

Soula had asked about taking the Flying Dolphin hydrofoil to Athens to hear Daniels speak. They could stay overnight with her aunt, who'd been wanting to see their daughter, Marilena.

"Can't, baby," he had said. "Gotta work. No time." Years ago, in the States, he wanted, needed, to have Theddo Daniels wait for *him*, Daniels had No Time then. Now he, Johnny, was the one with the No Time. No time for Theddo Daniels, no time for struggling, for diasporating, for defending and proclaiming. All that was the mauling opposite of what life on the Island was about. He was on Greek Time now. He had a Greek wife, a Greek child, a Greek job. He listened to Greek music, ate Greek food.

Funny about Greek food. Rice. Beans. Greens. And *mávromatika*— black-eyed peas. He had been able to keep the favourites without having to cop to the need. Who said there wasn't a God? It was Greece. There were *hundreds* of gods. And, amazingly, one was in charge of soulfood.

Witches

Soula had known that Theddo Daniels was going to visit the Island. She was sure his coming would be important to Johnny. In case it was some sort of *difficult* important, she made a big pot of fish soup.

Marilena did not know, did not care, and hated fish soup. Her baBAH was home from work and had promised to listen to her say the monologue from *Romeo and Juliet*, which she had chosen to present in English class. "Not now, Marilenamou," he said, and then failed to surprise Soula with his newsflash about Theddo Daniels.

Once, before Marilena was born, after noisily tender lovemaking, while holding Soula and floating into sleep, Johnny had asked if Island women had special powers. She had laughed lightly, saying, "Yes, Iannakimou, all Island women are witches! I did not have this power in Athens. Only here. And now you are bewitched!" Then she had laughed again, as had Johnny.

Laughter or no, he believed Island women were witches. Good witches. So-called *white* witches. Except, Soula said, the thin old woman who had come from Spetses two years earlier. This woman had no relatives on the Island, a dark moustache, and one blind eye. After she arrived, many of the donkeys got sick. Then she went back to Spetses, and the donkeys got better. When this happened, this miraculous healing of the unwell donkeys, Soula said, "Now the Island is all good witches again." Johnny knew she was teasing, but still believed what he believed. Having Soula in his life made him feel safer.

Soula did not tell him that it was all singularly unmystical. She had read about Theddo Daniels in the Greek newspaper. And, when you're married to the only black man living on a Greek island, if another black man shows up, everyone you know telephones, shouts across the market square, comes up to you in the port, stops at your house—wanting to know if your husband's father (who was, in fact, long dead) has come to visit.

Telling Johnny about this would only make him feel *exo*—outside, isolated. It had taken more than ten years for him to stop feeling this isolation. Soula, with her reasonably fluent if somewhat formal English (the product of language training in London, in preparation for two years as an Athenian tour guide), had helped carry Johnny from outside to in. Naturally, his uniqueness would always be there. . . . As Michailoulaki was the Island's only *vouvós* (deaf man), Johnny was its only *mávros* (black man).

Mrs. Damanakis, Johnny's mother-in-law, born and raised in the Athenian middle class, had her generation's usual collection of suspicions regarding non-Greeks. She had also, however, grown to love Johnny (mostly because he made her laugh). After moving to her inherited Island mansion—the last home of her own mother—she needed a bit of Athenian energy and craziness. When Soula said she and Johnny wished to marry, she assured her mother that they loved each other, and that she would want to be his wife even without the baby inside her. She said also that they wanted better air for the baby and would like to live on Ydra. Mrs. Damanakis looked into the eager face of her only child. Finally she sighed, smiled, shook her head, and laughed softly, saying, "*Etsi, Marisoulamou,* I would like you to be on Ydra with me. This house is so big. He, Tzonny, is a good person. It's good. It's done. At least it's not Michailoulaki . . . not the deaf-mute of the Island."

Invisible Blood

The non-deaf-mute of the island gulped down two bowls of fish soup, told Soula that Daniels was on Ydra, said he'd had a coffee in *Sto Kéndro*. No, they had not spoken. No, Johnny had not served him. He did not say that he, Johnny, had been doing his performance-for-tips routine, the one that made the black-clad grandmothers laugh and leave money for him under the rim of the metal ashtrays, even though tipping was considered a touristic thing to do.

He did not tell her that Theodore "Theddo" Daniels, one of the most powerful non-family forces of his teens and twenties, had watched him do this, and was, unmistakably, sickened by it. And that he, Johnny, having seen himself in the mirror of Daniels' disgust, felt shamed. And that, even if he continued to work at *Sto Kéndro* forever, he might be too embarrassed to do what it was he did to earn a decent living there—the Pete St. Pierre thing. The *commedia* clown routine.

The clown was still alive, but leaking invisible blood, having been cut by the eyes of one of the most powerful black men in the world. That clown had to get healed. Or replaced. By what, Johnny wondered. What the hell by?

The Greek God of Soulfood Strikes Again

Theddo's hotel, chosen because it had the same name as his mother—Melissa—was small, whitewashed, clean, and, he thought, beautiful. There were gauzy cream-white curtains in his room. Fuchsia and white flowers filled the terracotta vase that sat fatly in the centre of a heavy, dark-wood chest of drawers. Four beams of that same wood cut across the white ceiling. Theddo medicated, then fell onto the bed, wasted, thick as a barrel of mashed potatoes. His sleep was, happily, and unusually, deep and dreamless.

When he awoke it was dark, and he was hungry. He took only those medications that did not kill appetite ("I'm a human being. I'm hungry. I want to know what Greek people eat").

He found a taverna in a tree-filled courtyard with tiny white lights strung in the trees. The Greeky murmurs and sidelong glances (some not so sidelong) did not feel in any way hostile. Curious, only, as local people had been years before, when he'd taken Björn to St. Lucia.

Theddo went inside, to the steam-table kitchen, where he pointed to tomatoes, olives, some sort of lamb with rice-shaped pasta—and a surprise. I'll be damned, he thought, black-eyed peas.

Paréa Means *Group,* *Estía* Means *Hearth*

When Johnny Reed was a teenager, after his father's death, he'd watch groups of black men, *coloured* men, hangin' out in groups. There'd be laughter, teasing, sometimes music from a radio or a jukebox—even "live" guys jamming jazz or blues in a street-corner combo. These sights and sounds were such a hearth to Johnny that he'd almost hold his hands out to warm himself on them. He hoped that, when he was old enough, he would be part of such a group, such a hearth.

As with the good news about the food, this was another local bonus: Greek men hung out in groups. Men "hangin' out" with *women* was not a tradition—in neither Greece nor his North Carolina boyhood. But, for Johnny, the company of his wife and child also warmed him. Soula and Marilena were his *paréa stin estía.*

"*Paréa,*" Soula had explained, just after Marilena was born, "means *group—estía* means *hearth.* We, Marilena and me, we are your *hearth group.* The men at the cafés and bars—they are your *paréa sto limáni,* your *harbour group.*"

This hearth-warmth filled Johnny with so much love and joy he'd become afraid of bringing bad luck by thinking too much about it. At these suddenly anxious times, he'd rub the golden Greek cross he wore, or, imitating Soula, make the spitting sound, *p'toosoo.*

The Night of the Full Moon and Black Men

Men, when they want to un-shame themselves, need other men. After dinner, Johnny said he was going to Fano's. Soula nodded, did the little "yes" tilt with her head, said that was okay. Marilena didn't say anything. She had expected them to work on the Shakespeare together as he'd promised that morning. Johnny said "not tonight." This was a broken promise and a wrong answer. Marilena, therefore, was not speaking to him. Accepting neither hug nor kiss, she went off to her room to whisper aloud the roles of both Romeo and Juliet. "Tomorrow, Marilenamou," Johnny shouted after her. "I promise."

"*Dhen beeRAHzee!*" Marilena shouted back, without turning to look at him. "It doesn't matter."

Apart from Fano, and the man repairing the plugged toilet, there were few people in *To Kósmo Tou Fanóu*: Aryeeri and Tasso, playing backgammon. Maki, in a corner, heading his tiny body into the next morning's booze-riddled muttering shakes. In another corner, a Finnish couple toasted each other in straight vodka and looked as though they'd be hurrying back to their hotel soon.

"Iásou Tzonny."

"Hey, Fano. *Mía béera se párakaló.*"

Fano, a good friend to Johnny, as Viky, his wife, was to Soula, had been away on the neighbouring island of Porto Heli sorting out his mother's access road. Rural Greek real estate always seemed to involve masses of debate about who owned how much road, who could use the well, animal grazing rights, parts of porches. Having spent two weeks with Island lawyers discussing water, goats, and footpaths, Fano was glad to be home and wanted a few laughs. The sulking Johnny, usually a source of levity, was not looking likely to provide.

"Are you good, my friend?" Fano asked in Greek. "*Óla kalá,*" Johnny mumbled—all was good. "All" was strange, Fano thought, but he let it go, let Johnny question him about something that bored the asses off both of them—Fano's mother's access road.

"Big fuckin' drag!" Johnny shouted suddenly, four beers later. "Bein' bummed out is a Big. Fuckin'. Drag!" He then lurched off his barstool and headed for Fano's ancient, upright piano. When he started to play barrelhouse rag, Tasso and Aryeeri stopped arguing about their backgammon score, shouting approval and encouragement.

"You gotta see yo' mama eve'ry night
Or you can't see yo' mama at all . . .
You gotta love yo' mama, treat her right,
Or she will not be home when you call . . .
You gotta love her in the mornin'
Love her ev'ry night,
Give 'er all yo' money, sonny, treat her right . . .
You gotta see yo' mama ev'ry night
Or you can't see yo' mama at aaalll!"

Johnny sang this in his locally legendary Big Mama voice, a completely non-Greek sound. A sound that, because it was coming from the loving husband and father they all knew, liked and trusted, threatened nothing in his Island pals.

When the song ended, Fano, Aryeeri, and Tasso clapped and cheered. Johnny didn't want to need this. He needed this. The second song was another Big Mama Special:

"If I can't sell it,
Gonna keep sittin' on it,
Ain't gonna give it away . . .
If you won't buy it . . ."

Without being all that loud, the unfamiliar voice that cut through the room seemed enormous. Clear. Deep. Filled with muscle and challenge.

"You know 'Old Black Joe?' 'Swanee?' 'Mammy?'"

Oh God, Johnny thought. He didn't have to turn around to know who it was, but he *did* have to turn around. That was the rule with shit like this. Shit like this? Had "shit like this" followed him home, followed him, doing the crawlstroke from hell, all the way across an ocean? He turned. Had to look up. Bad position, sitting, having to look up. It made him littler when he felt a lot littler anyway.

There was no other position available. He looked up at Theddo Daniels.

"Look, Mr. Daniels . . ."

"Know my name, do you? Have we met?"

"No sir, I . . ."

"No sir, yessir, yassa, massa, three bags fullsir . . ."

Oh please, Johnny thought, I don't wanna do this. Why is this happening?

"No sir, we haven't met . . . I know who you are, I . . ."

"And I know who you are."

Try to finesse this, Johnny thought. He stood up, needing desperately to get off his ass, to get on his feet, to get some kind of level with this colossus standing between him and the door. He stood, smiled, offered his hand. Daniels took it, held it, did not let it go.

"You. Are. Steppin'-Fuckin'-Fetchit. Are you not?"

Johnny Reed was six feet tall. Theddo Daniels wasn't much taller. Two, three inches maybe. But he was big. Big hands. Big head. Barrel chest, starting on a gut. He had to be fifteen years older, at least. Johnny had age in his favour. Age and speed. But he was so damn skinny. Always had been. Stringbean, Yellowbean, Beanpole, Scarecrow. Scared crow.

Standing there, unable to free his hand, he felt like the lapel of Daniels' jacket. He knew he was drunk, and, looking into the older man's eyes, saw instantly that Theddo Daniels was also drunk. He swallowed hard, trying to take in as much air as he could without looking as if he were gulping. "My name is Johnny Reed, sir. I live here. Welcome to Ydra." Daniels still had his hand.

"Huhn! You the Greek ambassa-goddamn-dor, are you?"

"No, Mr. Daniels. I just live here." Daniels yanked on Johnny's hand.

"Wrong, son. You do *not* 'just live here,' an' you *are* an ambassador.

We're *all* ambassadors, you unnerstan'? And you need to be *recalled*, because you are *an embarrassment!*"

Recalled? Johnny tried again to free his hand. Who sent Theddo Daniels to recall anydamnbody from anydamnwhere? The U.S. government? The NAACP? The Klan? All this went batflying through Johnny's head. What came out was "Leggo my hand, you crazy old fucker!"

"You make me let go, Snowflake!" was the equally sophisticated response, and Fano, short, round, and loyal, was coming out from behind the bar. Aryeeri and Tasso stood up. Maki did not stand up because he would be falling down well before the next time he would be standing up.

"*Óhee,*" Johnny said "*Avtó éinay dhikó mou.*" No, this is mine. His? How had this mess gotten to be his? Why was his lifelong idol a drunken bully, and why was he, John G. Reed, of Ydra, Greece, gonna have to at least try to take that bully down? Which would be like hitting his father.

And that thought made his eyes fill up, and there was totally no fuckin' way he could be fuckin' *crying*, no matter what hellacious thing he had to be *instead* of crying.

Theddo also, somewhere in the muck of the medication, food, and wine, wanted to go back to before, but the two of them had no shared before to go back to, except the one that had filled him with this rage in the first place. Still, he didn't really know why he should have to *hit* this fool, so it was good that the guy gave him a reason. Skinny little bastard pulled his hand loose and punched him, hard, right in the breadbasket.

The two men pushed and wrestled out of Fano's. Grunting and muttering, they picked up onlookers and followers as they punched, kicked and clung to each other like large magnetised toys all the way across the length of the marble-stoned harbourfront. The full moon shone down as the best explanation for all of it.

They grappled, staggered, fell and rolled. The donkeys that ferried people and things up and down the hillside were wherever donkeys went at night, but there was one lone pile of donkey droppings in front of the bank. Johnny did manage to roll Theddo into it, which filled him with a rush of surprisingly exultant joy.

People were shouting, cheering. Theddo understood none of it, but knew it was for Johnny, the local entry, the homeboy.

Natural and right, he thought; sporting, rather than hostile. He was all right with it. The air and the pump of combat were sobering him up, but he was still a short time away from feeling really silly.

"The Night of the Full Moon and Black Men," as it would become known in the constantly accreting day-to-day mythos of the Island, finally ran out of gas, coming to a clunky, wheezing halt under the streetlamp in front of the Ydra Archives. The exhausted combatants sat like chubby-legged punchy babies in an invisible playpen. They both smelled of donkey, but nobody was really hurt.

Theddo was winded and achy, but felt stronger and happier than he had for a while. He looked at Johnny, who was looking at him.

"Oh my," he said.

"No shit," Johnny replied.

"Oh my," Theddo said again, and they both laughed. Some of those around them, spotting a turning away from the path to broken bones, laughed as well. One or two even ventured into the Sacred Playpen to squeeze the shoulder of Their Guy, then, for balance, of the other guy as well.

Johnny, still laughing in spurts, asked, "What *was* all that?"

"*A difference of political, and philosophical opinion, Ladies and Gentlemen, regarding the role of the African-American male in the wider world.*"

"Yeah, that's what I would've said."

That sent them both into a major laughing jag—holding each other's shoulders, resting their heads on each other's chest, mumbling sillies and "Oh God's," intercut by Theddo's personal expletives, "Terrific!" "Huhn!" and "Oh shit, oh dear."

Like the fight before it, their laughter finally subsided. The crowd hung about, or settled in a nearby harbourfront taverna to both watch and drink.

"Well then. What now?"

"Well, Mister D., you could break into the Ydra Archives behind us here, try to find your family in the files . . . or we can walk up the hill and find mine."

"Your family?"

"Yep."

"I'd be . . . pleased to find yours. Thank you."

"My pleasure." They helped each other up. There was a smattering of applause from a cluster of seated onlookers. Johnny bowed.

"Look at you, carryin' on," Theddo said. "Can't you just hold your head up and walk through a crowd? You're not a goddamn actor."

"I was."

"Was what?"

"An actor."

Johnny had a fantasy, one of many. In this one, he would bring home some Great and Famous Black Person; Sidney Poitier, Maya Angelou— Theddo Daniels. "Soulamou," he would say, "this is my friend Sidney . . . my friend Maya . . . my friend Theddo." He did not, not even in the fantasy, know what Soula, eyes filled with wonder, would say.

"Soulamou, this is my friend, Theddo Daniels."

"Poh, *gaidhouriska TAH!*"

"How do you do, madam. What did she say?"

"Donkeyshit. She said, 'Poh, donkeyshit' . . . Soula this is Theddo Daniels, the man who gave the speech in . . ."

"I know who he is, Iannakimou. Welcome to Ydra, Mister Daniels. You must come with me now."

Theddo had a hot shower. There was absolutely no doubt that this shower had to be taken if he wished to stay in the house. Which was okay with him—the smell that wasn't doing anything for Soula Reed wasn't doing much for him either. It was her house and she clearly had definite ideas about how it, and those within it, were supposed to smell. Having been raised by a small, strong, half-Caribbean mother, who also knew how houses and people were supposed to smell, Theddo liked Soula at once.

The Honoured Guest having been properly de-donkeyed, it was then Johnny's turn to shower. Theddo, wearing Johnny's white Moroccan caftan, was invited by Soula to have pastries and Greek brandy on the Reed's large whitewashed balcony.

Under the full moon, high above the town, it was a fine night, smelling of sea and flowers. Theddo could hear dogs barking, an occasional bray.

"Please, Missus Reed, please accept my apologies for that dreadful smell. There was . . . an argument."

"Ah. *Sto Fáno?* In the bar?"

"Yes."

"Ah. Many people fighting?"

"No . . . It's okay now, I think. Some things to . . . discuss, but no more fighting."

"This is good. Johnny does not like fighting. He does not fight most times. He was fighting for *you*, yes?"

"For *me?*"

"Yes. From the books."

"Books?"

"Yes. Come."

Soula led Theddo back into the house, to the wall that was floor-to-ceiling bookcases. She pointed to a centrally placed and fully stocked shelf. There, alphabetically ensconced between Eldridge Cleaver and W.E.B. Dubois—on the same shelf as Maya Angelou, James Baldwin and Ralph Ellison—were all five of his books, a variety of InterAfrA pamphlets, as well as anthologies that included his essays. She took down a beat-up, yellowing copy of *Brothers: Black Men on Earth*. A first edition. She showed him dog-eared corners, pages of underlined passages. "Iannaki, Johnny, he says your book made people to fight sometimes."

"Yeah. Sometimes it did. Sometimes it does . . . Soulamou. Your name is 'Soulamou'?"

Soula laughed, a rich, honeyed, open sound.

"Ohee. No. My name is 'Soula.' The '*mou*' means . . ."

Johnny stood, cleaned and caftanned, in the archway.

"It means *mine*. My Soula. Not like I own her, just that we care for each other, we're there for each other. We're in the same group. *Soula* is a nickname. Soula's full name is *Marisa;* her mother calls her *Marisoula*. It's a Greek thing. They take the consonant of the last syllable and hang an *oula* or an *itsa* on it. For guys, it's an 'aki.' Like me, Iannaki—*Ianni* is Greek for John—then I get the *aki*."

"Yeah, Theddo's a nickname too. When I was a kid, my mother would get on me about how *Theodore* meant *God-given*, and how I should behave more like a gift and less like a problem. *Theddo* got hung on me at school, playing football, and I felt freer, stronger with it than I did trying to be this perfect church-tied gift. If I was going to pis . . . make folks angry, I figured I should also take the blame—not blame God, who, god or no, has absolutely *no* control over what black women name their children."

Johnny laughed. "That's for sure. We get some *seriously* Not-God's-Fault names!"

"And some that seriously *are* God's fault. My sister Dora—that name suggesting that our mother saw her as a somewhat more *secular* gift—once broke off with a guy she really liked, because his name was Ezekial. When they were . . . in a romantic situation, she couldn't say his name without crackin' up."

"Ohh, EeZEEkial!"

"Egg-Zackel!

"Yeah. I've always been glad my name was just John. My father was Marcus Aurelius."

"Marcus Aurelius? Roman. That goes straight back to slavery. I've a close friend in D.C. who has that heritage. Her name is Calpurnia."

"Hodge? Calpurnia Hodge? The senator? You two are sort of 'together,' right?"

"Mm hm."

Witnessing these two men from the same place, from the same group, did not make Soula feel *exo*. She felt she'd opened a door into an unfamiliar but welcoming room, where she could sit quietly, feeling the room's energy. It was magic. Like Delos or Delfi: You don't know; you feel.

And she did feel. Felt what Johnny had said he felt when she got going with Viky and Fano, and he could watch the joy running through them, happy to witness their happiness.

Moved by the laughter, by Theddo's graceful power, by Johnny's expression of uncharacteristically shy studious wonder, Soula spoke, as they stood at the door saying their goodnights.

"Mister Daniels, can you come tomorrow evening, to have food with us?"

"A home-cooked Greek meal? I would be delighted, Soula. Thank you."

"KaLAH. Good. We would like you to meet Marilena, our daughter. So, can we start more early? Eight o'clock?"

"Eight o'clock is fine. I'll see you both—and Marilena—at eight."

On the outside, Johnny was smiling. Inside, he was a strange combination of warmed and scared.

"Listen, so you don't get lost, let's meet at the taverna, at Fano's bar. I have a sort of band practice there at six. . . . If you promise not to hit anybody, you could come to that and we could walk up to the house together after."

Theddo wondered who made up the membership of this band and whether Johnny would be playing the anorexic Aunt Jemima again. Soula and Johnny, as a couple, felt solid to him. He wanted their company, wanted to meet their kid. Black men doing drag made him uneasy, but Johnny wasn't *doing* drag. The whole drag business was a misreading that he, Theddo, was bringing to the party. Check your guns at the door, he thought. Or at least put 'em in the closet where they usually lived.

So, it was agreed: *To Kósmo Tou Fanóu* at six. Theddo assured Johnny that he could find his way to the Hotel Melissa (same name, he told them, as his mother) and headed down the hill. He made it to his room just before "Shake n' Bake"—the chills and fever—kicked in.

He medicated, turned up the dial on the rectangular heater in the wall, and waited for the shivering and shaking to stop. Then, in his mind, he produced a selection from a life full of pleasing memories. There were, in plenitude, other less pleasing memories, but Theddo's beautythought collection, sought after and fought for, was impressive. It was also the best way he had to get the Monster to lie down, to sleep, so that he, the Monster's hostage, could also sleep. As always, this took a while. Sometimes nothing would get the Monster to sleep, and they, man and Monster, would stare at each other all night.

"Theddo Daniels!" Johnny shook his head. Daniels, so often in his thoughts and those of his father, had now been in his house (not to mention in his face), met his wife, would come to dinner, would meet his daughter.

With an hour to go before his shift at *Sto Kéndro* started, he sat on the café's terrace drinking strong Greek coffee. The harbour cats clustered in front of the unloading fishing boats in the early morning autumn light (one of Ydra's many perfect lights). Reluctantly or not, he felt himself hurtling backwards whence he had come.

Whence

Wetherill, North Carolina, 1954–1971

A too-small, sweaty summer baby, his mother said. A premature arrival who had fought hard to stay on the planet.

He wasn't without help. His father, Marcus Aurelius Reed, almost always called "Big"—Big Reed—or, less politely, but with affection—The Fat Man—was a respected community activist. He taught English at the "coloured" high school.

Big's commitment to black students of all ages sometimes got loud, once even earning him a story, including a picture of his large, bespectacled face, in Wetherill's newspapers. Both white and "Negro."

The flap was about the *Five Little Peppers.* ("Who is this 'Pepper' family? The *"Five Little Peppers and How they Grew?* I'll tell you how they grew. They grew *white!* All five of these Little Pepper children are *white!* Well, a sickly pink, but what this dinky-pinky *means* is *white!* Now, there's lots of black pepper in this world, but not *here.* Not one spicy little bit of black Pepper in this entire Caucasian quintet. They give *this book* to *black* first-graders." Big tapped the book, hard, with his index finger. "*Where,* exactly, are these black first-graders going to find themselves in all this white Pepper?"

"Y'see," Big continued, "by the time black students come to me in high school, and meet Mister Baldwin's people and Mister Wright's people and Miss Hurston's people, and Mister Ellison's people, they probably figure that they, these former first-graders of Wetherill, North Carolina, are among the few black children in the world. Or

18

that black people don't get lives until they are older. This situation is a dumb mess!

"Now, everyone knows I *revere* the great Caucasian literature. I teach my high school students the joys of Mister Aeschylus, Mister Shakespeare, Missus Shelley, Mister Milton, Mister Dante Alighieri, and all sorts of other white authors of great literature.

"But these Pepper-books, they are not *literature*. They are books of daily life. The daily lives of children. They are here so children can see *themselves* in books. And children of African heritage are nowhere in these books. We must find some *black* Peppers, or some black somebody-or-others, so black children can read about how people like us grow!")

There were no equivalent books for black school children, Big Reed was told. Feeling sloughed off, he went looking. Damned if the principal and his board weren't right. In 1960 America, if one didn't want the entire Uncle Tom/Sambo canon, which Big Reed decidedly did not, there truly was 'flat nuthin'.'

A few weeks after his book search, Big stood before Jordan Gillis's first-grade class.

"Good morning! I am Mister Reed. We will be spending some time together when you get to the high school, which is where *I* teach. Mister Gillis was kind enough to invite me here today so that we could do some colouring. Everybody here *like* colouring?"

There was a raggedy chorus of yesses.

"Good stuff. So, let's get to it. Please open up your *Five Little Peppers and How They Grew* books. The ones about those little pink n' white Peppers. Neecee, would you please distribute these crayons? Seven different colours for each student." Neecee Reynolds, the kitten-eyed daughter of Willie Reynolds, Big's oldest friend, went from desk to desk, handing out crayons.

"Now class, you see all these little Pepper-faces. Your crayons have colours from black and deep umber to pale beige and white. That's not enough. 'Black' people, like 'white' people, come in an enormous range of hues. These colours are all I could get. They are a good start.

"What I'd like you all to do now is to colour the faces, hands and legs of these Pepper children. Please have one of them be a 'white' child. That's the crayon called, of all things, 'nude.' After we've coloured our

Little Peppers, we can show our choices and then read aloud. Have fun colouring!"

Big knew that the Five Little Peppers were, for most black kids, *very* white, no matter what colour they were crayoned. But, again, it was a start.

When word got out within the school about what Mr. Reed, the high school teacher, had done with Mr. Gillis's class, the principal, Fred Jackson, called Big to his office. There was a lot of carry-on about "defacing books" and "not teaching vandalism by example." In the end, however, Dr. Jackson was persuaded of the exercise's value. Big, the class, and the books got written up and photographed, and were on the radio and the local television station.

Johnny's mother, Carlotta Dixon Reed, as slim, fine-boned and soft-spoken as Big was burly and booming, taught music and led the high school choir. Johnny Reed grew up believing that black people were a presence in the world, that arts and culture were good things, and that achievement and advancement were possible.

Then there was Uncle Carl. When Johnny was about eleven, Neecee Reynolds told him she thought his Uncle Carl could be, if he wanted to be, a movie star like Sidney Poitier.

Carl Dixon *was* starry. Tall, thin, café-au-lait-coloured like Johnny's mother, like Johnny. He had Indian cheekbones ("We're part Seminole," he said. "We never made no peace with *nobody*"), shiny processed hair, gold cufflinks in the shape of rams' heads, and a suit the colour of his eyes—robin's-egg blue. Johnny loved that suit. Uncle Carl said he'd leave it to him in his will when he died. That suit and *all* the ties.

Dapper. That's what Carlotta called him. "He's . . . dapper, your Uncle Carl," she would say softly. She always paused before saying dapper, as if she were deciding, choosing the exact right word. She always chose dapper, holding the word in her mouth like a chocolate-covered cherry; pursing her lips, looking pleased.

Uncle Carl was a musician—a travelling saxophone player, working with different black bands and combos on what was called the chitlin' circuit—segregated jazz and blues clubs throughout the Southeast. Once, Johnny told Neecee, Uncle Carl was in a band that toured all over Europe.

Carl Dixon was also a first-rate jazz piano player, but did not play that instrument professionally. The thirteen-year-old Johnny, who was taking, and enjoying, piano lessons, asked him how come he picked the saxophone over the piano. Carl laughed and said saxophone players got more girls; that standing was stronger than sitting; that saxophone players *always* got the girls. Johnny nodded, said "uh huh," but he knew, he just *knew* that his Uncle Carl would get all the girls he wanted even if he played the kazoo.

The following year, when Johnny entered high school, Big Reed started the Drama Club, and his son, who would happily sit in the Palace movie theatre all day if allowed, signed up for it. Big was scrupulous about not favouring his son, but it was clear to the whole class that Johnny Reed was a natural actor—the one you watched even when he was just standing onstage thinking.

It was sophomore year, and they were working on the play version of the novel *Look Homeward, Angel,* with Johnny playing the young Thomas Wolfe—a black actor *playing* Thomas Wolfe, rather than a *black Thomas Wolfe*—the play had no references to race. Suddenly, Big made a loud *aah!* noise, grabbed his left arm, furrowed his brows, fell to his knees. Johnny and Delia Farnham stopped rehearsing and ran to him. Big looked into his son's eyes, then pitched forward and died.

There was a funeral at the African Methodist Episcopal church, where Big had been a deacon. Lots of speeches and singing. The whole community came, including little kids who looked sideways at Johnny, trying to see if "dead father" made him look different. Uncle Carl, who'd been playing in Atlanta with the Rex King Royals, arrived in the middle of the service, with a blonde-afro-ed black woman named Bonita (years later, Johnny would think of her hair as yellow dandelion-fluff). Other members of Carlotta Reed's family—the Florida People—came up from Daytona Beach (there were five of them, including his Granny Ruth, and she, plus two other grownups, slept in his bedroom for some days).

That whole time was soupy in his memory. He could remember sleeping in the parlour, with other kids, who did that "looking at the dead-father kid" thing, but didn't talk much. He could remember sitting on the porch with Uncle Carl and Bonita, who had "a beauty salon" on Peachtree Street in Atlanta. Uncle Carl, who said he'd heard that Johnny was becoming this really good actor, called him 'Robeson.' When

Johnny asked who that was, Uncle C. said to look it up, that it was a fine thing to be called.

Bonita smelled of cinnamon and roses. She had long legs, and long fingernails, painted with pale pink, almost white, polish. She said Johnny was "a good-looking kid." Uncle C. said he was "too skinny— just like me." Bonita said he "could do worse for size," and they both laughed. Johnny laughed too. Not because he understood what was funny; he just felt lost and wanted to be part of something.

After everyone went back to their various cities and houses, Johnny asked if he could sleep on the daybed in his father's study for a while.

It was in that study where he first met Theddo Daniels. Met him through what he had written about black people. Big Reed had a lot of books by and about black people: Garvey, King, Lomax, Malcolm, Hurston, Dumas, Hughes. Johnny, a newly fatherless only child, was drawn, knowing nothing about it, to the book called *Brothers* by Theddo Daniels.

It was Easter Break, so Johnny had time to read. Surrounded by the undertone of his father's scent, eating endless bowls of his mother's universal panacea—fish soup—he read, as his father had asked him to, about his brothers all over the world—about what Theddo Daniels called "Black Men on Earth."

Shortly before he died, Big had asked him to do something else, so he also read, aloud, from the works of William Shakespeare—particularly (as requested), *Anthony and Cleopatra, Romeo and Juliet* and *Hamlet*. Daniels, Shakespeare and Big's life and death commingled deep inside him as a long story about race and family, about love and betrayal, about belonging and loss, about indecision and choices. For Uncle Carl, he looked up 'Robeson.' Paul Robeson's story wove itself into the others.

In 1971, Johnny's senior year, Mrs. Donaldson, who'd replaced Big Reed as drama teacher, announced that the senior class play would be *Hamlet*. There were open auditions, but everybody figured Johnny Reed, the best actor in the school, would get the title role.

Which he did. Then, the following month, an unusually cold and damp February, everything went crazy.

Smitty's, a white-owned liquor store, was burned to the ground. Six black men and a white woman were blamed for it, put on trial and found guilty.

In Wetherill's black community, some said the people who owned the store burned it down for insurance money, and then hung the blame on this particular group because they were civil rights workers who had organised the very shaky integration of the white high school.

Johnny, for all his young life, had nested inside a sense of belonging, of being valued, of being essentially safe, at least among his own people. Yes, there was always black and white shit— sometimes *terrifying* black and white shit—the Three M's—Martin, Malcolm and Medgar, school girls being terrorised, being killed.

In Johnny's childhood, about once or twice a month, Big Reed would go somewhere to march and rally. Carlotta and Johnny would wait and worry, listening for Big's name on the radio, looking for his face in the television pictures of water hoses, dogs and death. Mercifully, he always returned from what was called The Movement. Once he had a broken arm (all his students signed the cast).

Such things, however, did not follow Johnny all the way home. Until Smitty's, in February 1971. People got beat up, people got threatened, people got scared, secretive and careful. Johnny, without Big to turn to, and needing to put all the fear and anger somewhere, threw every bit of it into the persona of Hamlet.

"To be or not to be—That *is* the question! ("Yes!")

Whether 'tis nobler in the mind to *suffer* the *slings and arrows* of *outRAGE-eous fortune* ("Go on!")—Or to take arms against a *sea* of troubles ("A *sea* of troubles!")—And, by *opposing, ennnd them!* ("Tell it!!")

The student performance, the "call-and-response" *Hamlet,* became a place for people to come together—to recognize their own story in something that could not get them in trouble by being *proven* to be their story.

Every night they cheered their Hamlet. A Hamlet who was only indecisive because the play said so, who only died because the playwright had him killed. Every night, Johnny saw that the so-called "Wetherill Seven" (whose guilty verdict would take ten years to be overturned) could speak to people through Hamlet's voice ("For *who* would bear the *whips* and *scorns* of time—*The oppressor's wrong—the law's delay?!*"). He also learned that if black men everywhere were, according to Theddo Daniels, his Brothers on Earth, William Shakespeare was, whether he'd known it or not, a cousin to those brothers.

The Next Sidney

The letter came in June. Johnny had been accepted with a full scholarship to the Manhattan Actors' Playhouse in New York starting in September.

Wetherill was still being a good place to get out of. Granny Ruth, eighty-two years old, had died the month before, leaving her Daytona Beach house to Johnny's mother, her only child. Carlotta felt that Johnny's acting school acceptance was a sign. It was decided that she would sell the house, give Johnny some of the money for his stay in New York, and move to Daytona.

Neecee Reynolds, who really wanted him, Delia Farnham, who thought she had him, and Colette Davis, who taught him what little he knew about naked couples, were really sorry to see him go, but each and all wished him good luck in every way they, and he, could handle.

In August 1971, John G. Reed left Wetherill, North Carolina, for New York City, fully intending to become "a movie star, the next Sidney Poitier."

Harbour Cats
Ydra, Greece, 1995

The next Sidney Poitier (aka Johnny Reed) carried his coffee cup into the *Sto Kéndro* kitchen. Yeah, well, he thought, Greece is better than greasy spoon, but it looks like another actor wound up waiting on tables.

Theddo, like Johnny, was watching the harbour cats. It impressed him that they could, simultaneously, swarm and sit elegantly, patiently, tails curled round their forelegs. They knew how to wait and when to pounce. Like Stockholm streetboys. Like Björn.

    He was doing his cat-watching and having a cappuccino on the terrace of *Ydróneira*, at the other end of the harbour square from *Sto Kéndro* having decided his new friendship would fare better if he didn't watch Johnny prancing around hustling tips. He could still see the younger man in the distance, in "that damn pimp-jacket," but at least he wasn't wearing the feathered mask.

Viky & the Rembetiko Brotherz

It was an unusual sight and an unfamiliar sound—though it reminded Theddo of music he had loved years earlier in Tunis.

Lined up against the back wall of Fano's bar, on a small wooden stage, sat five men and a woman. Johnny was at the piano, off to one side. Except for the piano, a guitar, and a sort-of clarinet, the other men were playing instruments Theddo'd not seen before. Fano beat on a powerfully resonant hand-drum shaped like a flat-topped light bulb and another man plucked at a large stringed instrument, which lay across his knees.

In the centre was a short, dark-haired woman in a loose-fitting black dress. She had no instrument in her hands or lap, and looked down at the floor.

Theddo smiled and nodded to everyone. Everyone smiled and nodded back. He figured Johnny'd told them he'd invited "the crazy black guy from last night" to watch rehearsal.

Theddo seated himself at a table near the door. Another man (one of the previous night's backgammon players, he thought) brought him a glass of brandy, saying only, "Metaxa. It's good. Please."

"Thank you very much."

As the brandy hit the inside of his belly, a sound filled the room that he would remember forever after. The woman raised her head, took a breath, opened her mouth. Out rolled an *enormous* voice—merging full-bodied melody, glissando upon glissando, and all the pain and loss in the world. Theddo understood not a word of what she was singing; but he knew, blood and bone, what he was hearing: Greek blues.

As all the instruments played, twisting the yearning fist of some minor key into Theddo's brandied gut, the woman sang: chanting, keening, moaning, belting.

It's universal, he thought, the cry of a people that has been beaten up but not beaten down.

A Famoss Black Man from AmeriKEE
Comes to Dinner

Soula knew there'd be more than four. Iannaki would invite Viky and Fano. Out of courtesy, he'd likely ask *all* of Rembetiko Brotherz. Tasso, Andrea and Mitso would probably have to eat with their own families. Aryeeri would say "thankyou much, no, no, I don't want to make work for Soula," but would be persuaded, which she expected. What she was not expecting were Marilena's classmates: Litsa, Nitsa, Elly and Fofo.

She had told Marilena, before sending her off to school, that there'd be a friend of her father's, a famous and important black man from AmeriKEE, coming to dinner.

"The man I heard last night, with the big voice?"

"Yes, Marilenamou, that man."

"KaLAH!" Marilena said. She had liked the sound of that man, had wanted to come downstairs to see him, but was too sleepy, and, besides, was wearing the ugly pyjamas with the stupid ducks and the torn sleeve. She asked if she could wear her church dress. Soula said no, but that she could wear her new tracksuit from the girl's running team.

"You can also, if you wish, wear your hair loose and picked out with the African comb."

"No, Mana. I will wear the long braids like Litsa's."

She could also practise speaking English, she thought, with someone other than her parents, her teacher (Litsa's mother), and her classmates. Somebody, finally, like her father.

"He's a famous man from AmeriKEE, *mávros*, like my baBAH!" Marilena told Litsa and Fofo.

"Does he have videos like your baBAH? Was he also a star on AmerikaniKEE TV?"

"I don't know. . . . Mana says he's famous but I don't know *why*. If you come to my house, after the school, you can ask him, okay?"

Fofo and Litsa thought meeting the Famous Black Man (who might even have videos of himself being shot by American police, like Marilena's baBAH) was *very* okay. They told all this to Nitsa and Elly, who asked Marilena if they could come too. Marilena, who'd just about used up her brags about the Rembetiko Brotherz band and Johnny's American videos, was pleased to invite her friends home, pleased to be special again.

Macaronia, Soula decided. She'd feed the four girls pasta and mushrooms in tomato sauce, and the pot of rabbit *stifado* with vegetables and rice would be for the adults. She left the girls watching cartoons on the television and went to the *fourno* for more bread and pastries.

After rehearsal, which had also included an instrumental and Johnny singing "Trouble in Mind" (in his male voice, accompanied, sweetly by Aryeeri on the clarinet), Theddo was introduced to the band. Johnny was touched to see him with Viky. Smiling, his voice almost a whisper, holding her hands in his, he said: "Your voice is extraordinary, madam. You're . . . a great artist."

Viky could feel the warmth and intention of what was being said but did not understand the words. Johnny translated.

As with many less-travelled Ydrioti, Viky had learned her smattering of English from listening to waiters, concierges and shopkeepers speak to tourists. She smiled shyly up at the stranger, sincerely offering one of the four words that, along with "hello," "yes," and "please," echoed throughout the island during the summer months.

"Thangyou."

Johnny invited everyone to dinner. Fano and Viky had been asked (and had accepted) earlier. Mitso, Tasso and Andrea said they were expected at home. Aryeeri, recently widowed, said he didn't want to make more work for Soula. Johnny assured him in his sometimes highly original Greek that Soula would be wonderful to see him. Then every-one had another brandy and headed up the hill.

Marilena, usually shy and standoffish with strangers, took one look at Theddo and decided instantly that this big, deep-voiced man was, with or without videos, a kahLOSS AHNthropos. A good person. The most good-person stranger she'd ever seen.

Litsa, whose parents were teachers, had the best English, in which she asked, "Are you reeahlee a famoss black man from Ameriki?"

Theddo laughed, raising his eyebrows. "Now, where did you hear that?"

"From Marilena."

"I see. Then it must be true."

"Do you have videos? Are you a movie star?"

"ArkeTAH," Soula said, "Enough. It is not good to ask so many questions."

"It's all right, Soula, I don't mind. No, little one, I am *definitely not* a movie star. I *do* have some videos. Not with me. They are in America. Actually, there is one from Athens. It's in English. I will try to get a copy for Marilena, and you can all watch it here. Would that be all right?"

Litsa said that Marilena did not have "a VeeCeeAir," but that *she* did, and they could all watch at her house. Marilena said it would be very all right to send it to *her* and that *she* would bring it to Litsa's. Then Soula bundled the girls off to the kitchen for their dinner, while the grownups were ushered to a candle-lit table on the canopied balcony.

During what he declared to be a splendid meal, Theddo, with Johnny translating as necessary, asked all sorts of questions about the history of Rembetiko music, about the four-hundred-year Turkish occupation of Greece.

"That's why you thought the music sounded sort of Arab, Mister D."

"Please, John, call me Theddo."

Theddo continued to praise Viky's voice.

"This remarkable sound should be recorded, should be heard beyond Ydra."

Fano agreed, saying that he, and many others on the island had said

Rembetiko Brotherz should try to record in Athens. Others, mostly Johnny and Soula, thought getting involved with "city bigshots in the crazy music business" would only disrupt everyone's life. It was a continuing discussion.

"We'll see," Soula said firmly, clearly wishing to change the subject, "maybe one day."

Suddenly self-conscious, she softened her tone and smiled.

"Please, Mister Daniels, will you have some more wine?"

Theddo said, "Yes, thank you, Soula," and asked how it was that a band with such an amazing woman singer was called Rembetiko *Brotherz*. Everyone nodded and laughed. It was explained that the group was originally only men, and that, in the coming summer performances, they would be Viky and the Rembetiko Brotherz.

Aryeeri said that his late wife knew someone, a boyfriend of her cousin, who knew important "record people." He felt that the band should at least make a *cassetta* to sell on the Island in the summer when they played every weekend for Islanders and tourists, at *To Kósmo Tou Fanóu*.

Theddo agreed, and offered sympathy on Aryeeri's wife's passing.

"O KarKEEnos," Aryeeri said softly, pressing his stomach twice. "CanSAIR."

"Terribly sorry," Theddo said again.

"Are *you* married, Mister Daniels?" Soula asked.

"No . . . I was . . . with someone for seven years . . . also died. Also cancer."

"I am sorry."

"Yes. I am sorry too . . . but we are all getting too sad."

As he said this, he noticed Marilena peeping out from behind the white sliding door that separated the balcony from the house. She seemed to be looking only at him. Their eyes met. She turned and ran back into the house.

"Soula, John, everyone—this dinner has been, *is*, a generous welcome to Greece for me. Could we possibly have the children join us for dessert? It would be good, I think, to enjoy their . . . *liveliness*."

"Good. Yes. Let us all go inside for sweets, OHlee maZEE. All together."

Fofo, who was Viky and Fano's daughter, lived in Kamini, the small village that was a fifteen-minute walk from Ydra town port. Nitsa and Elly also lived there, so Viky and Fano could see them home. Litsa's house was just down the hill. With the grave self-possession sometimes exhibited by teachers' children, she offered to escort Mr. Daniels to the Hotel Melissa. Theddo, both touched and amused to be protectively escorted home by a gracious bilingual eleven year old, agreed to meet Johnny at *Ydroneira* the following noon (Johnny's day off), and that they would lunch together at *Dina's*, a seaside taverna in Kamini. Cheeks were kissed, hands were shaken, and Soula gave Theddo a plastic bagful of cakes and cookies.

As he and Litsa headed down the hill, with "bye, bye, bye" and a sprinkling of Greek words echoing behind them, Theddo taught his young guide the word *cicerone*, and she translated the friendly farewells:

"'Good night,' they are saying to you, and 'go well,' and 'sweet dreams.'"

Theddo, softly singing "Trouble in Mind" and wishing he knew even a part of Viky's song, took a hot shower, splashed on some lime cologne, and wriggled into his soft, ancient, cream-coloured silk nightshirt. He'd medicated earlier; the proper amount of things at the proper time, and all felt well. He was tired, but it seemed a natural tiredness. He climbed into the satisfyingly hard-mattressed bed, between cool sheets, under a dark blue woollen blanket. "Sweet dreams" seemed possible—even likely.

Just before first light, there were terrible cries outside his window. Two cats, one in the power position, under the belly of the other, were howling, hissing and tearing each other apart. Theddo got a glass of water, threw it on the gashed, bitten and bloodied cats, who howled sharply in protest as they ran away.

Everywhere in the world, Theddo thought, at every moment of the day and night, something is trying to kill something else.

Dina's in Kamini—Mister Daniels Remembers

"John Brandon Reed, right?"

"Grandon. John *Grandon* Reed." Johnny smiled, more pleased than he wanted to admit. "Who told you . . . Litsa?"

"No. Got it on my own. There was a catfight under my window at about four in the morning. When I couldn't get back to sleep, I went for a walk around the port. I was standing in front of the place where you work. Bam! it hit me. You did the Andover Phipps play . . . I had read about it . . . and then you replaced that man in the Broadway musical, the one who did the big drag number . . . the man who . . . died."

"Pete St. Pierre."

"Yes," Theddo said. "There was an article in . . ."

"*Newsweek.*"

"Right. About how it took courage for a 'butch black leading man' to take that role . . ."

"Pete was a great friend, and a mentor to me. He was the star of the first play I did in New York. *Brotherz*—the Phipps play. The Brotherz part of Rembetiko Brotherz is my way of honouring all that.

"Pete also brought me to meetings of the racial equality committee of Actors' Equity, the theatre union. That was when I believed that everything was possible, or at least *could be made possible,* for a serious actor who . . . happened to be black."

"I take it you don't believe that any longer."

"Maybe for somebody else. For me, all that is history."

"It did well for you though, yes? I mean, you have a lovely home, and . . ."

"Oh, our house doesn't come from my savings. Or from waiting on tables. Soula's mom had a huge mansion house here. Inherited. She died when Marilena was three and left everything to Soula. We sold the house, bought our place and started a fund for Marilena's education. We'd love it if she went to university."

"You just quit acting, cold?"

Johnny laughed, a quick brittle sound. "Cold? No, it was more like *hot* when I quit. Too hot for me anyway. I'm good right where I am, Theddo—glad to be done with that whole craziness."

Then, on the terrace of *Dina's*, eating from plates of assorted Greek foods, sharing a pitcher of pink wine and looking out at the bright blue and newly wild autumn sea, Johnny began, for the first time in many years, to talk about That Whole Craziness.

That Whole Craziness
New York, 1971–1976

When Johnny Reed first hit New York—and to the eighteen-year-old Hot Ticket from Wetherill it felt like he *was* "hitting" New York—hitting it hard. He wrote his Uncle Carl, "This is *the best*—I'm *happ'nin'!*"

While Sidney Poitier, Harry Belafonte, Billy Dee Williams and any other "happ'nin'" black actors of the time were neither devising a laurel wreath *for*, nor putting out a contract *on*, their young successor, it was also true that things were off to a fine start for the New Kid.

The natural talent, attractiveness and focus that had made his work so compelling to friends and family in North Carolina held up well against the strangers in the tougher field at the Actors' Playhouse.

Against was the correct word. In high school, classmates moved aside for Johnny Reed. In "New York School," almost every student, of any colour, any sex, planned to be a star, and fought any other student for all available scraps of turf. At least a hundred people auditioned for any available job.

Johnny, who loved improvising, working with whatever and whoever showed up, now had to deal with whole new stage concepts—ambush and upstaging being only two of them.

Dorrie Stockwell, a classmate who was two years older than he, and who, due to a frequently discussed and widely resented social injustice, had managed to be rich, good-looking *and* talented, told him that the competitive upstaging problem at the Playhouse was "well below nothing" when compared to the university where she'd trained previously.

"Aside from an assassin or a buttfreak," she said, "the one thing you most don't want behind you onstage is a Yalie."

The Playhouse had a policy: No professional jobs for the first two years. Some tried to sneak around this. Those who were caught were expelled (unless their sneaking resulted in stardom, which, of course, reflected well on the school, and garnered it more funding).

Tall and thin, Johnny did get some catalogue-modelling work (which was permitted), but played by the rules, not auditioning as an actor, even when he felt he could ace the audition and get the job.

Instead, he threw himself into all the classes on offer —improvisational theatre games; modern, jazz and "world" dance; voice and speech; *commedia*; mask and clown. Bobbie Kreiner, the androgynous beauty who taught voice and speech, praised Johnny's deep and resonant voice as he worked to clean up the lazy Southern speech that Big Reed had called grits-mouth. After a few months, Johnny was speaking standard mid-Atlantic, the shared accent of North American actors, only reverting to his original regional speech when angry, tired or frightened.

He was filling, filling, filling—yet always with room and hunger for more. The performance-related classes, as well as the theatre history he was gleaning from books, all made him feel he was doing something of value—not just for himself, but for his family, particularly for Marcus Aurelius "Big" Reed, the father he still spoke to, in the dark, before sleeping.

"Daddy, this is so good!" he would say "I'm working hard and it's going well."

"I know, son. I know and I'm glad. I'm proud," Johnny would then reply, in his father's voice.

Ethnic Groups

Johnny's success with women had also come North with him—though that too was more complicated than high school. Dating Gina Bellini, for example.

They'd worked together on a scene from *The Rose Tattoo*, about a sheltered Italian girl and a young sailor. In the discussion-critiques, which were held after all scenes, both Johnny and Gina were praised for their concentration and stage chemistry. Their teacher, Ben Eisenglass (the man who founded and ran the Manhattan Actors' Playhouse), said, "These two are an example of really relating—of being *fully committed* onstage."

Quietly, the two had also tried being fully committed offstage. This full commitment came to a complete halt when it was brought to Johnny's attention by a large man he'd never seen before (and intended to endeavour to never see again) that committing to Gina Bellini in any "romantic way, you unnerstan'?" would get him hurt in a manner that could include death. Johnny said he understood fully, fully understood. He and Gina discussed this understanding, and promised to have no further naked, or even mouth-to-mouth, contact. Gina said it wasn't about Johnny's "ethnic group," but that "daddy would prefer my dating Italian boys."

A few weeks later, entirely by coincidence, Gina's father was sent to jail for some tax problem. Mrs. Bellini, Gina's mother, a blonde woman wearing heavy eye makeup, outlined lips and a dark fur coat, was seen on television, saying, "My husband is a professional gambler. He is also in the olive oil business. That is all I know. Now, please go away; the cameras and the lights are frightening my children." Johnny wondered why Mrs. B. was wearing a fur coat indoors (if this had happened in Wetherill—if anyone that he knew in Wetherill even *had* a fur coat—it would mean they couldn't pay the bill and the heat was cut off). He also wondered if Gina had been one of the children inside the house. How the hell was she going to be an actor if she was frightened of cameras and lights?

In his third and final year of study, Johnny was allowed to accept acting opportunities (though only if they didn't interfere with classwork). Casting people, who'd been watching "this good-looking black kid" for two years, began to set up auditions for him. Theatrical agents who would receive commissions if those auditions garnered paid employment, all vied to sign him up. He chose the Golden Group.

Rose Golden, a short, apple-shaped woman with a sharp nose, curly, close-cropped gunmetal grey hair, and huge brown eyes behind gold-framed harlequin eyeglasses, was both friendly and smart. She'd expressed interest in Johnny's work from his first year at the Playhouse ("You're a good actor. And you're special. You have your own quality, your own beauty. I think, with the right breaks, and seriousness and discipline on your part, you could be the next Sidney"). Rose's small "boutique" agency represented some of New York's best actors, and was taken seriously by casting agents and directors.

Professional theatre work was still not possible, due to the rehearsal time required. One off-broadway lead, first offered to Johnny, wound up taking Nick Bartlett, a classmate, to Hollywood (to repeat his role on film). Johnny's decision to complete his three years at the Playhouse earned him the nickname "Hick from the Sticks" among some of his colleagues. He was okay with that—New York seemed to be waiting for him and, he believed, it would wait for a few more months.

Rose lent him the money for what she called a dark New York suit. She said the two hand-me-down Bandstand Specials Uncle Carl had given him for the trip North—a lavender silk shantung jacket and a cream yellow linen suit with slightly frayed cuffs and the echo of a wine stain just above the right knee—would not do.

He was then submitted for five television jobs and got two of them—a drug dealer with one scene and a gang leader with three. He'd already had the conversation with Rose, and with black and Latino actors at Actors' Equity, about "traditional black casting"—dope dealers, gang-bangers and pimps. (He was considered too young—mercifully, he thought—for the pimp parts.) He'd known only the sheltering embrace of an all-black high school and a "colour-blind" New York liberal acting school. In North Carolina, he had personified Thomas Wolfe and Hamlet. At the Manhattan Actors' Playhouse, he'd been praised in plays by Eugene O'Neill, Edward Albee and Tennessee Williams, as well as those of black playwrights LeRoi Jones and Lorraine Hansberry (in whose play, *A Raisin in the Sun,* he played Walter Lee Younger—the role that had made a star of Sidney Poitier).

Now, in the work-for-wages world of the professional actor, he was getting, and taking, roles he had promised himself, promised his father, promised the books and pamphlets of Theodore Daniels he would not take. Roles that Sidney Poitier had *never* taken.

People from the Playhouse saw the two television shows. They said he was good. As the gang leader, they said, he was better than good. They, including Ben Eisenglass, said he had humanized Slick—a father-less, dirt-poor kid with big dreams and few options. They were, they said, moved when Slick was killed in a shootout with police. A reviewer in the *Daily News* wrote that his eyes, in the final close-up, were "filled with bewildered yearning and feral rage"—apparently something more noble and pure than just ordinary rage.

Johnny liked the praise, but when he thought about these roles— thought about who he was being, what he was saying—his heart and mind filled with sadness. Sadness and an unfamiliar and entirely unac-ceptable sense of shame.

He told Rose Golden she could let him go if she had to, but that he couldn't do those parts any more. He reminded her that, when he became her client, he'd joked that he chose the Golden Group because their building was big and black.

Rose said she believed in his talent—they would try it his way and see what happened. She hugged him, accepting an invitation to attend his graduation from the Actors' Playhouse.

His mother and Uncle Carl came North to celebrate.

"You are this family's first professional actor. We are so proud! Your father would be so pleased," Carlotta wrote. "There is no way that Carl and I would miss being there with and for you!"

He read the letter to a few of his classmates. Dorrie Stockwell said, "Lucky old you, Reed. *My* family thinks I'm supposed to marry a banker and stop dabbling in bohemianism."

The graduation ceremony consisted of young people being applauded as they bounded onto a stage, where they received a rolled, ribbon-tied piece of paper, along with a handshake and an embrace from the tireless, seventy-five-year-old Ben Eisenglass. Then everyone filed into the school's theatre to see a selection of scenes featuring the newly graduated actors.

Johnny's scene was from Edward Albee's *Zoo Story*, a two-character one-act play. His scene partner was Terry Cruddy (a name that all concurred would have to be changed). Cruddy, sometimes called *Very Cruddy* because of what Dorrie Stockwell described as "an underperfected hygiene awareness," played the middle-aged, conservative and nervous character of "Peter." The needy, perverse, street-tough "Jerry" was portrayed by the recently renamed John Grandon Reed. (There was already a John Reed in the Screen Actors' Guild. Neither John Marcus Reed nor John Aurelius Reed sounded right. Grandon was the small Kentucky mining town where Big Reed had been born. When they closed the mine, the town and its name disappeared. Big had always hated having his birthplace vanish. Johnny couldn't bring back the town. It pleased him to bring back the name.)

Terry Cruddy was a notorious upstager, frequently forcing colleagues to play whole scenes with their backs to the audience. He also had what Ben Eisenglass called jackrabbit's disease—a tendency to rush, transfixed, towards the brightest light onstage the way rabbits did with automobile headlights.

The scene was supposed to start with Terry, as Peter, sitting on a park bench, fastidiously eating his lunch. Jerry (Johnny) was then supposed to enter, stand downstage and say, facing out towards the audience, "I've been to the zoo."

Terry took his position, started neatly nibbling at his sandwich, waiting for Johnny to enter. And waiting. And eating. And waiting.

Suddenly, Johnny popped up, in one clean move, behind the bench. "I've been to the zoo," he said, but much of the audience failed to hear him because the startled Terry screamed. This wasn't a problem, as the second line, also Johnny's, was, "I said I've been to the zoo."

For most of the rest of the scene, Johnny refused to come out from behind the twisting and turning Terry, who became angry. Then, when Johnny, still behind the bench, wrapped his arms tightly around Terry's chest, nibbling at his earlobe, Terry was genuinely afraid. This guy Reed has gone nuts, he thought. It's my big night and I'm acting with a crazy black guy. At the end of the accelerating scene when Terry stabs Johnny to death, in less a murder than the result of reaching for, demanding, intimacy, Terry seemed at once, horrified, confused and babblingly overjoyed at finally being able to control and slow down his weaving-and-bobbing adversary.

The audience had been completely involved in the scene, frequently laughing at Johnny's playfulness, watching his volatile unpredictability with the cautious wonder of children hearing a ghost story. Their tension released itself in loud applause and cheering when the two actors took their curtain call, bringing them back for two additional bows. Uncle Carl stood up and shouted "Bravo Johnny." Carlotta Reed said he should sit down and not make a commotion, but tears rolled down her cheeks and she was grinning almost beyond the circumference of her face.

Afterwards, backstage, the dressing rooms and corridor were packed; friends, families, actors and tech crew coagulated into a large lump of laughing, praising, story-telling gridlock.

Ben Eisenglass finally said, "People . . . PEOPLE! Can all those who were *not* in the *PERFORMANCE*—PLEASE GO NEXT DOOR to *Teddy's ShowBar?* There's food and drink there. Your geniuses will join you there shortly."

When it was just teacher and performers, Ben, who had already given each student a written analysis of their strengths and weaknesses, as well as a form for setting up one-on-one meetings, congratulated them on their work, saying a few specific words to each actor.

To Johnny, he said, "Your energy, creativity and . . . your *integrity* onstage are a joy . . ." Terry Cruddy, who'd been tangled up inside since the *Zoo Story* scene, could not contain his anger, blurting, "His *integri-*

ty?! He re-blocked the whole scene! He didn't do anything the way we rehearsed it!"

"You're right, Terry. And that is usually a lousy, unprofessional thing to do. But there are many meanings for that word, integrity. Johnny has integrity in the sense that I am using the word. He is honourable *when he is given room to be.* The word also means an ability to integrate—to give an integrity to a scene. To incorporate what is available to you into a character and a story. Johnny does this always. And, in *this* case, kiddo, the integrating, the *integrity* of what Johnny did produced the best, the richest work *you've* done in three years. I want you to think about that. I want you to understand what made that happen. That understanding will decide whether you grow up to be a gifted actor or a greedy show-boating hack. . . . Now, all of you, get into your street clothes and out of this building so we can have something to eat and the doorman can go home to his wife and children."

Andover Phipps—one of the new playwrights who, along with N'tozake Shange, August Wilson, David Hwang and Miguel Algarin, was chang-ing the stories and colours audiences saw onstage—had been attending scene nights at the Playhouse for two years, waiting for Johnny Reed. Three days after graduation, the script for *Brotherz* was on Rose Golden's desk. A month later, following a local-boy-makes-good family visit to North Carolina and Florida, John Grandon Reed was in rehearsal.

Pete St. Pierre was the lead actor. He was also Andover Phipps' lover. They had a loft in SoHo—a huge open space, divided into room-like areas by screens, plants, tables—where Johnny would sometimes have dinner. The three, and whoever else was about, would discuss the play and "just generally shoot the shit." There, Johnny learned that, as he'd added Grandon to his name, Andy Phipps had become Andover.

"Andover's a rich white kids' prep school. Drives Eastern Waspy white folks crazy to hear that name coming out of my black fag face. I just walked into their world and said, 'This is a stickup . . . 'Andover the name!'"

Johnny laughed. Pete St. Pierre said the pun was funnier the first forty times you heard it. Andy said that actors who failed to appreciate . . . and *re*-appreciate his wit could find themselves underemployed.

GALE ZOË GARNETT

Brotherz was the story of Jamie Forbes (Pete St. Pierre), a successful New York painter who returns to his rural southern hometown for a showing of his work at the local high school. He is accompanied by the white man, a composer, with whom he's had a five-year relationship. In the last scene, Forbes is killed by local rednecks in a phantasmagoric explosion of colours, while working on a huge painting of his lover in the makeshift studio that he and his kid brother have constructed in the family shed.

Johnny played the kid brother who tells the story in narration and flashback. He had been playing a narrating kid brother on the day Big Reed died. In the *Brotherz* programme, he dedicated his performance to "my father, Marcus Aurelius Reed."

Johnny, who loved the play and was thrilled to be in it, was nonetheless nervous about going to the Phipps–St. Pierre loft. Before he left Wetherill, Uncle Carl had told him to be careful in New York, that there were "a lot of fruits in the theatre. You're a good-lookin' kid. They're gonna be after your ass."

There were indeed a lot of "fruits" in the theatre—including at the Actors' Playhouse.

As to his ass, Johnny found things calmer than his uncle had predicted. Sure, people sometimes came on—Phil Van Eck more than once (only when he was, as he put it, "pissed to the tips of my godlike amber perm")—but when Johnny said it wasn't his thing, they backed off, remaining, at the least, reliable co-workers.

Dorrie Stockwell said, "You males are such wimps, Reed. Watch women. We deal with unwanted passes all the time. We simply say 'go away.' They usually do. The ones that don't are jerks, and being a jerk has nothing to do with gay or straight. It has to do with being a jerk . . . besides, all it means is that somebody thinks you're attractive, which is better than having them think you're not."

Brotherz, directed by Andover Phipps' usual director-collaborator Jimm Linton, opened off-broadway at the New York Forum Theatre in September 1974. All the critics said "Yes!" Their affirmation included heaps of praise for Pete St. Pierre and "a stunning debut" by John Grandon Reed.

Johnny celebrated by drinking too much wine, singing "Nobody" (his father's favourite song) at Sardi's, and sleeping with Dorrie.

Johnny and Dorrie were not in love, but each had been the other's best friend at the Playhouse. The closeness deepened when they discovered that they could sing well together—jazz tunes and standard ballads, at *Teddy's ShowBar* after classes.

Keeping that friendship mattered to Johnny. He worried about having another Gina Bellini problem. Dorrie, lying closely beside him on his single bed (happy to be gently jammed against his warm body, but also with no other choice, given the size of the bed) laughed.

"Relax, Reed. Bankers don't have people rubbed out—they just take their homes or deny their loans . . . and after tonight, 'Kiddo,' as Ben would put it, you're not going to need any loans. You're gonna be a big old star!"

That Whole Craziness
Hollywood, 1977–1978

Brotherz played in New York for eighteen months. There were newspaper and magazine articles about "Young John Grandon Reed, who, 21 years old and fresh out of drama school, is breaking into the bigtime!"

In the middle of the run, there was a film offer. Johnny, Pete and Helena Lewis, who played their mother, were all signed to repeat their roles. Jimm Linton had only directed in theatre, so despite Andover Phipps' threat at one point to pull out of the deal, it was finally agreed that Robert MacKenzie, who'd had success with two black-centred films, would direct.

In September 1977, Johnny, who had never been entirely sure it was a real place, flew to Hollywood.

Film acting did little to answer the Real Place question. Johnny found it, simultaneously, like being on the moon and the most natural thing he'd ever done. All he had to do was think something, want something—and the camera would capture it. It was as if that machine could see straight inside him, knew his deepest feelings. His job was to let it do that, and to always be thinking and wanting something that belonged to the person he was playing. If he was either not wanting anything, or wanting something that didn't belong to the scene (to make a phone call, have a cup of coffee, take a piss), the camera would see exactly that. So you're supposed to look like "I love you" and you look like "I want to take a piss."

Some directors didn't let actors watch "dailies"—what had been filmed that day. Robert MacKenzie, an avuncular, actor-friendly director, didn't mind, as long as the actor didn't initiate discussions during the nightly screening, or as a result of watching them, become self-conscious in subsequent filming. Pete St. Pierre and Johnny both went to dailies. At first, Johnny didn't like his face on film ("I look twelve. My nose is too small. There's razor-bumps on my neck. My eyes are too far apart"). After a few nights' viewing, Pete, who'd been in two other films, said, "Oh, get over yourself—this ain't about *your face;* it's about your character."

Pete was right. Johnny stopped watching his personal face and started watching the character. And learning the "arc" business. They were, he thought, shooting the film backwards and sideways. They'd shoot stuff from the middle, then stuff from the end, followed by stuff from the beginning—out of sequence, they called it. Watching the dailies let Johnny figure out what MacKenzie called the arc. Seeing what he did in the middle of his character's journey told him what he'd need to do the next day, when they shot something from the beginning or the end.

The deeper he went into film acting, the less he could answer his original Real Place question. Film-making was crazy. You started really early in the morning and people played with your face and your hair and your clothes. There was food all day but it was mostly donuts, cubes of bright orange cheese, or chunks of green and orange raw vegetables that you dipped into white goo. You had to stand in tiny spaces and not move your face or your hands a lot. He loved it. And it loved him back.

In the middle of filming, Dorrie Stockwell showed up on the set.

"Hey, Reed!"

Johnny blinked. The voice and the grin were Dorrie's, but the long blonde hair was new, as was the thinner, smaller nose and the gaplessness between her two front teeth. He hugged her. She felt and smelled the same. Breaking from the hug, he looked at what he called "a new you."

"Same old me, Reed. Except that I've gotten this shiny new contract for a big fat TV series. And Marty, Marty Rachman, who did the deal, said these changes had to happen. What do you think?"

"I think . . . I think you were beautiful before and you're beautiful now. I *did* like the space between your teeth though."

"Yeah, me too. I tried wearing this little filler-inner thingy, but food kept getting stuck in it, which was sort of disgusting, so we did the dental work. Marty says it's not so important for television, but that it matters if I want feature films, which I do."

"Marty Rachman. He's a huge agent. When did that happen?"

"He was at our graduation scene night. Actually, part of my being here is to invite you to dinner with us. He's really interested in you."

"Did you tell him I was with Rose Golden?"

"He knew that. He still wants to say hello . . . and I want us to have dinner together in Malibu—his place is out there. So, cool?"

"So, *very* cool. Let's do it Saturday, when I don't have to shoot the next day, okay?"

"Sure. I'll give you our address. Come in the afternoon and we can hang out in the sun before going to dinner."

"*Our* address? Are you two . . . together?"

Dorrie looked down, then up and into Johnny's eyes. There was . . . something; he didn't know what.

"Yes. Two months now. He's . . . a sweet guy. Really smart . . . and one of the few people I've ever known who isn't afraid of my father. I think you'll like him. I know he'll like *you*."

There were at least twenty agents in L.A. named Marty. Four of them, however, were considered heavyweights. This foursome was collectively known as The Marties, or The Smarties. They were always stealing clients from one another: the joke was that actors had enough lines to learn without having to remember their new agent's name.

Marty Rachman was thirty-seven, the youngest of The Marties. He had the youngest clients and the most hair. Including, Johnny noted as they sat by his diamond-shaped pool, curly black tufts on his back. Johnny reckoned that Marty wasn't going to be doing feature films and didn't have to have them removed. It was good, he thought, that Dorrie, looking terrific in a dark green bikini, didn't have hair on her back.

Dinner was at *Sacco and Vanzetti*, a new *in* Italian place in Malibu. The food was called "Cal-Ital," and was mostly different kinds of overpriced spaghetti, which Johnny now usually remembered to call "pasta."

For most of the meal, Johnny and Dorrie told stories about the Playhouse, while Marty made occasional laugh-noises, looking a bit like a divorced father on a visitation-rights weekend with the kids.

Plates of fruit and Italian pastry were brought, along with espressos and a super-strong colourless liquor. Marty said it was called grappa. Johnny, already full of red wine, laughed.

"Grappa, huh? In Wetherill, North Carolina, this exact same stuff is called moonshine and sometimes makes people go blind."

Marty, making a softly nasal "heh-heh" noise, offered Johnny one of his skinny cigars. Johnny said he didn't smoke.

"Good boy. I don't much either—just one or two of these after dinner . . . or after sex. So. How long have you been out of Washington?"

"Wetherill. About four years now. Actually, my mother moved to . . ."

"And Rosie Golden was your first agent?"

Nobody called Rose Golden "Rosie." Johnny didn't like the "Rosie"; didn't like the "was"—didn't like Marty Rachman.

"Yes, Rose is my agent, since I first went to New York."

"She's a nice woman. Has a heart as big as her ass," Marty said. "Too bad she doesn't have an office out here."

"She has . . . an affiliation with Claude Martin's agency."

Marty Rachman had a smirky mouth anyway, but Johnny thought the smirkometer inched up noticeably.

"Sure. I suppose that's better than nothing, an affiliation between two smallish agencies. *Respected* smallish agencies. But smallish is smallish. In this town, you need a power agent, an agent who can put you into star packages."

"Star packages?"

"Mm hm. The suits at the studio, they want Robert Redford. So we, the agency—an agency with enough clout to do it—give them Robert Redford . . . *if* they take John Grandon Reed—that's you—for one of the other leads or key roles. Star packages. That's how it works out here. That's how *you* need to work out here." He took another sip of his fancy moonshine.

"Look," he continued, "Claude Martin is a sweet old queen, but you've already got too many queers around you. Besides, Claudia hasn't done a major deal since the sixties. Is that *really* where you want to be?"

Where Johnny wanted to be, *really* wanted to be, was anywhere Marty Rachman wasn't. He knew it would be bad if he hit Marty Rachman. He knew it was juvenile and stupid to want to hit

Marty Rachman. He knew it would be good if wanting so much to hit Marty Rachman and not *doing it* didn't give him the shivering fits. He couldn't help it. He shuddered. Dorrie, who knew him well, jumped in, all charm and smiling gapless teeth.

"Hon, Johnny is in the middle of his first feature film shoot. I know you guys'll talk business all night if some woman doesn't suggest something else. Well, *this* woman is suggesting you let the guy concentrate on his work. When *Brotherz* wraps, you two dynamos can have a big old meeting. But for now, why don't we just go down the road and catch Ferdy's last night? There's this super jazz trio. Marty and I are crazy about them, and I think you'll be too, Reed. What'cha think?"

Johnny thought Marty wouldn't talk while a trio was playing. He was wrong, and Dorrie had to jump in, repeatedly, with various Episcopalian versions of shut up.

The trio, two old black guys and an old Italian guy, were riding out their final glidepath making music for what Uncle Carl had called "no-soul turkeys who snapped their fingers on one and three" and who talked through their sets. They played really well. Johnny wondered if they knew his uncle.

Dorrie, who had sung twenties and thirties torch songs at *Teddy's ShowBar* back in the Actors' Playhouse days, sat in with the trio, singing "What'll I Do" and "You'll Never Know." When she came back to their table, Marty kissed her on the mouth and said, "You did good, babe. Halperin from MGM is here. Good."

Finally, the evening was over. While they waited for Johnny's taxi (most of his salary seemed to be going for taxis—when the film was finished, he thought, he *had* to take driving lessons), Marty talked about the deals he was doing. The cab arrived. Dorrie kissed Johnny on the cheek, saying pointedly, "Let's have another meal together soon—no business, just food and gossip, yes?"

Marty handed Johnny his card. "You're at a critical point, pal. Call me when you're ready to move. Good luck with the rest of the shoot."

Dorrie has everything going for her, Johnny thought, as the cab headed down the Ventura Freeway to *Hillside Hacienda,* his furnished West Hollywood apartment—how could she fuck that creep?

The answer turned out to be not well, and not often.

"Marty," she explained over lunch in Johnny's trailer, "sort of puts all his power into his work. He's very affectionate, and says I'm the love of his life, but he has this . . . performance-anxiety thing. He's huggy, and sweet with me . . . does all sorts of other sex stuff, sort of *at* me, which is worse than not doing anything . . . it's like when you shift gears wrong in a car, and everything grinds . . . I do care for him, though, and he's being super about helping me with work-stuff, and . . ."

So the two friends, who were not in love, but loved each other dearly (and never ground each other's gears) started sleeping together again. Discreetly, happily, from time to time.

Apparently

It took almost five months to finish filming *Brotherz* (including some reshooting, due to technical problems). In late January 1978, Johnny was in the middle of postproduction ADR (re-dubbing his voice while looking at his face onscreen) when the guy in the sound booth said, "Phone call, Johnny."

Two Baltimore police officers, both at once, had shot and killed Uncle Carl.

Apparently, they, the two Baltimore police officers, wondered how come a black guy was driving a ragtop Fiat.

Apparently, they pulled him over to inquire about this.

Apparently, he was reaching into the glove box to get the registration, without being asked to do so.

Apparently, they shot him many more times than it would logically take to kill someone.

Apparently, Johnny thought later, it must be harder to kill black people, or other people wouldn't be working so hard at it for so long.

Choices
Ydra, Greece, 1995

Theddo Daniels, in the sharp-edged autumn sunlight of Kamini, listened intently. (That night, Johnny would tell Soula it was "like with Marilena when I tell her a scary story.") As he repeated the word *apparently* with its explosive double-p, Johnny slapped at the metal tabletop with his splayed-out fingers. Having said his piece, having let the blood and smoking stench out of yet another brain-balloon marked "Uncle Carl, Murder Of," he did not so much stop talking as subside and look into Theddo's eyes, his own eyes, years after the event, still filled with puzzled, wounded anger and pain.

Theddo knew this look. Black or white, it was always young—or from the young place in a person of any age. He wanted to hold Johnny, knew Johnny needed to be held. For his own complicated collection of rules and reasons, he could not let himself do this. He put his hand over his mouth, making his grief-sound of blown-out air, "Pwwhhh."

"Oh God, John," he said softly, and then, "Wait a minute. I *know* this case, this story . . ."

"This *murder*. Yes. Yes, you do."

"This murder. Yes, right, the musician. NAACP and the Muslims got involved. . . . The black caucus in D.C. There were rallies. I . . . I spoke at one. It was raining. There were umbrellas and candles . . . a tallish woman, slim woman, she led some young people in singing . . . very well-spoken . . ."

"My mother. Carlotta Dixon Reed. She's a high school music teacher. 'The Musician's' sister."

"Jesus, John. *You* were *there*. The next day we both had our pictures in the paper. I remember the article. 'Young Star Interrupts Hollywood Filming' . . ."

"Actor."

"What?"

"Actor." Young *actor*, not star."

"We met then? Met there?"

"No. By the time my plane got in, you had gone. . . . You had to go to a hospital, they said."

Had to go to a hospital. Now Theddo had the whole night on his inner screen. The rain, the wind, the fierce, shiny-eyed woman holding his large hand so tightly with her little, long-fingered ones, asking him to wait, to please wait. "My son has read all your books. As did my late husband. He is coming from Los Angeles, my son. He is making a film there. He's an actor. Can you wait?"

He could not wait. Björn had decided to leave Stig Hanssons, a born-rich Swedish composer and musician who had periodically attended to his financial requirements and general rescue since he was fifteen. Hanssons owned a large, waterfront mansion in the Swedish archipelago and an elegant harbourview Stockholm flat in which he kept old musical instruments and young Björn.

Björn had telephoned ("Hey Man, it's the Little Bear, it's Lille Björn"), had laughed at "all this romantic stuff," saying: "Well, man, I miss you too. You know that. Stig knows also. I tell him I miss you. I tell him I want to be with you. Stig is a good man. He says he knows before I tell him. That is why I must come to you, must come to America. If you still want me to. Do you still want this? Yes? Yes! Then I come to you!"). A chilly, rainy January night, the same night as the rally for the innocent black man who had been shot, was the night he would arrive. He would need to be met at the airport, would need to be driven to the East Capitol rowhouse of Theodore Daniels where he would have his own basement apartment—a handsome renovation with a fireplace and a high-hedged garden.

This eighteen-year-old blond boy was in every way (if one did not count the Italian gypsy, which Theddo most determinedly did not) a departure from Theddo's usual deeply secretive closeted habits. He was inappropriate, this boy—*beyond* inappropriate. He was too young, too white—and a rent-boy—a boy whose "I want to be with you too" was not likely given to anyone who could not or would not take care of him. Theddo knew this, but the sight, the sound, the smell of this inappropriate boy turned a private and careful man into a loving and grateful devotee. He knew enough to not let Björn know the degree to which he felt this devotion. He also knew that nothing short of a death in his own blood family (and perhaps not even that) would keep him from being there when Björn's bright blue eyes scanned the throng at Dulles Airport.

So, he told Carlotta that he was "terribly sorry," "wished he could" and "certainly would," but that he had a dreadfully ill nephew in the hospital with some sort of pneumonia. It was touch and go, he said, and he had "to be there, for the family."

"Of course, Mister Daniels. I understand. Thank you so much for coming tonight, for . . . speaking on Carl." Theddo assured her that he would continue "speaking on Carl" until his murderers had "accounted for themselves before all Americans." He meant that. He hugged the woman; then, in the sudden fast flurry of such things, he was surrounded by security people provided by his own group, the Inter-African Alliance (InterAfrA). As the young choir started to sing again ("Children go where I send thee . . . *How* shall I send thee? . . ."), they led him quickly to a limo where he removed the oversized buttoned-to-the-neck raincoat that black leaders were urged to wear at large rallies in all seasons. Then he removed the bulletproof vest.

A murdered man. An angry, targeted community. A beautiful boy waiting at an airport. Surely, Theddo thought, as the limo sliced through the cold rain, I have made the wrong choice here. Then he sighed, knowing there was nothing voluntary about compulsion. There was no choice here—there was only Björn.

A Good Person

"Did he make it?" Johnny asked.

"What?"

"Your nephew. Did he make it?"

"No. He died."

"I'm sorry . . . were you close?"

Theddo considered the question: Were they close? The question immediately evoked Björn—his huge blue eyes, the texture of his skin, his laugh.

Were they close?

One truly loved the other. The loved one, wanting and needing the love, would sometimes speak the words, sometimes curl up inside that love with the tranquil sweetness of a sleeping child. For the one who more fully loved, the feeling was new, was nervous-making, revelatory, and surprisingly tender.

For the loved one, it was . . . what? An exchange? Commodity for sanctuary and sustenance. Like a harbour cat being petted, warmed, fed by a tourist. The tourist thinks the cat is delightful. The cat finds the tourist warm, needed—a break from local neglect, from constant hunting, from the always-competitive securing of food and shelter; a respite from teeth and claws. It is, for the harbour cat, transactional.

Were they close?

"We . . . became close over time. He was a remarkable boy. In families, you're not supposed to have favourites. He was my favourite."

"What did he do?"

"He danced. He was an extraordinary dancer."

"Oh. Ballet or modern? Jazz?"

"A bit of everything. He'd taken classes in modern dance and also some Asian dance forms. He started by performing in clubs. He seemed to have a talent for any and all kinds of dance, from ballet to disco and rock n' roll. At the time he was taken ill, he had just started dancing successfully in Europe. In concerts. And he was very interested in American music videos. The ones on television. Wanted to choreograph those. Said there was a clique of people who always got those jobs. I think he would have, could have, eventually broken through that. He saw *all things* as dance. He . . . moved . . . beautifully."

And they looked at each other, Theddo and Johnny, on a Greek island terrace, and, together, knew more than either of them felt free to acknowledge as shared information.

"I'm . . . really sorry he died."

"Thank you, John. And *I'm* sorry I couldn't wait to meet you in Washington, I truly am."

"Well, you've met me now. We were supposed to meet, and now we have, and . . . oh, *damn! Meet!* Soula's doing a pregnancy education thing for the Women's Centre. I'm supposed to meet Marilena at school. She can walk home by herself, but I said I'd meet her. I've been breaking promises to that kid all week! I forgot the time sitting with you, doing Native Son Goes to Hollywood.

"How far is her school from here?"

"About fifteen minutes, if we sprint."

"Let's sprint then, I need the exercise."

"You'll come with me? Great! It'll give me some street cred with my kid. She asked this morning if you'd please come back to the house. She said you were a kahLOHSS ANthropohss—a good person."

Theddo laughed. "Oh yeah? And how exactly does she know this?"

"She knows everything. Don't have to tell her nuthin'. She's her mother's daughter. Her mother knows everything too."

"So did mine."

"Mine still does."

Johnny was right about Theddo's effect on Marilena. The indignation at having to wait for her father (all by herself, friends gone home) burned off in an instant and transformed into an open grin when she saw the large figure lumbering up the hill behind her baba.

The two men and the girl walked through narrow cobblestoned back streets; Theddo singing, Marilena diligently learning the words to "*If I Had a Whistle.*"

"If I had a whistle,
If I had a shiny thing . . . No lie!
If I had a whistle,
If I had a shiny thing . . . No lie!
I'd whistle 'til you found me-ee . . .
Whistle 'til the songbirds sing . . . No lie!"

A "kahLOHSS Anthropohss." A good person. That child, Theddo noted, did indeed go all smiley when she saw him hauling his sorry self up the hill. That dear child had told her father that Theddo Drag-Ass Daniels was a good person.

The Good Person hurt like hell. Achy and shaky. Running uphill was never his best thing, even when he was younger and fully well. Showered and bed-ready in midafternoon, he looked at himself in the long thin mirror inside the armoire door. He saw the large man he'd seen since he was a teenager: his close-cropped wiry hair now almost fully grey, his widow's peak hairline, he said to the mirror, "has become an older and more peak-ed little widow."

He thought he had good eyes—large, almondine, with clear whites and chestnut brown eyeballs. He'd never liked his nose ("too flat," he complained, but mostly to himself). Now, with other things to worry about, the nose no longer concerned him. "Black men—the black men who bitch—bitch about their noses the way black women bitch about their hair," he had told Tafiq when Tafiq, an Arab man who bitched, was complaining that his own nose was too long.

The man in the mirror was also growing a paunch and a double chin, carrying about twenty pounds of extra weight.

Funny though; in the particular illness world to which he secretly belonged, fat was good. Thin was bad. Thin meant you were losing.

Thin meant the Monster was winning.

Before showering, he had turned up the heat machine on the wall. The room was not cold, but he was shivery and understood why. He medicated, more heavily than usual. He knew this would probably knock him out until at least the middle of the night. He'd covered that, telling Johnny he needed to go through some papers and would find a taverna if he got hungry.

He pulled on his sleep-shirt and climbed into bed, pulling the top sheet and two blankets up to his chin.

He thought about young Marilena Reed, who believed he was so good. It wasn't, he was certain, that she found in him an unusual level of goodness. No, it wasn't that he was so good (though he wished to be, since childhood had tried to be). It was that he embodied, for Marilena, good *news*.

Afro-Hellenic. A new word for him; a new concept. This Afro-Hellenic child had lived all her life in Greece. Mostly, Theddo assumed, on the island of Ydra.

He had once before, in the far colder Swedish climate, wondered about acceptance of atypical island children.

Afro-Hellenic Marilena seemed open, vibrant and happily allied with her schoolmates. Had that always been so? For a lone black child at an all-white school, that was not usually the case. Not even for light-skinned black children. Not even in more urban places than a Greek island.

What did Marilena know about her father's side of her heritage— apart from the felicitous fact that he'd been in films and "had videos"? She had likely met her paternal grandmother, but her grandfather and her uncle were dead. Her father was an only child. She spoke a confident English, with some grammatical gaffes and only the slightest Greek accent. Could she also *read* English? Probably. Theddo thought he'd seen an English-language grammar book somewhere at Johnny's. Had she explored the bookshelves, read any of the many books, including his own, handed down from grandfather to father?

She had, he imagined, occasionally seen black men visiting the Island. Tourists. Men she might look at from a shy and polite distance, figuring "if these belong to me, they will speak to me." Did any, ever? Theddo did not know. Had any other black male, family or otherwise, ever accompanied her father home, come to dinner, been celebrated as a guest, met her at school, carried her on his shoulders, taught her a song from his own black childhood?

Most probably not—and *that*, Theddo thought, was what Marilena found so good about him—that there were other black male grownups from America like her father, and that one of these men interacted with her father, with her father's friends, with her mother. With her.

All his life, he had worked for the connection within the Diaspora. His core belief was that it was important, *essential* for black people throughout the world to interweave, to rebuild a collective future through owning and sharing their collective past and present. His sense was that John Reed had run—from his country, from his people. What, exactly caused this flight? *Was* it flight, or had he simply fallen in love with Soula and agreed to live in her country? And what was all that camp carry on he did when he was working? The suit jacket, Theddo now knew, was a loving thing—an homage to his slain uncle. The queeny stuff—was that also an homage? To the black actor who died?

Too many questions. He'd had heavy exertions, followed by heavy medication and heavy pondering. Sleep sank him quickly, sank him deep. He dreamt of Björn.

Björn was naked except for his gold nipple-ring and that glittery red-and-silver scarf he loved wearing to dance clubs; his challenge (or *shawlenge* as he pronounced it, not hearing the grim pun) to "the ghost of Eessadora Duncan!" They were on Ydra in this dream, on the winding oceanside road to Kamini. Björn was running and dancing ahead of him, revelling, as he always did, in the warm bright sun on his body, on his yellow-gold angelsilk hair—laughing, whirling, bending and swaying. "An island dahnce from an island boy," he said, extending one long arm, wriggling long fingers for Theddo to follow. Which he did, with quiet smiling delight. He followed the dancing Björn past cliffs dappled with star-flowered low green shrubs, past windmills, ancient cannons and a promontory bearing one black iron bench. Björn. So young, so healthy, so much alive—exulting in his sun dance. Laughing, leaping, beckoning—until Theddo was awakened by a morning symphony of two donkeys and one rooster. He squeezed his eyes shut, trying to stay in the dream, but the bubble had burst and Björn was gone.

No Lie

"If I had a wheesssell . . .
If I had a shineee thing . . . No lie!"

Marilena, in the grey flagstone road in front of the house, had come home from school with Fofo Papadimas and was teaching her a song. In English. Soula did not think she'd heard it before. Marilena sang loudly, rolling some of the notes like blues music.

Ach, Soula thought, smiling, she likes it, this song. She listened harder. Something about a whistle. Johnny had taught Marilena many songs, but Soula hadn't heard this melody before, or any song-words about whistles. She poked her head through the gauze-curtained kitchen window.

"OHmorfo. Pretty song, Marilenamou. Did you learn it at school?"

"No, Mana, Mister Daniels taught it to me. He came with BaBAH to get me from school. It is a song from long ago, when he was a boy in Ameriki."

"Ah . . . and where is BaBAH now? *Sto Fano?*"

"I think yes. Practising songs with Rembetiko Brotherz."

The Brotherz instrumentation always made Johnny feel Arabic—"Moorish" he said. He didn't know much about Arabic, and only slightly more about Moorish, but when he sang with the Greco-Turkish instruments, he always saw himself all in white—white caftan, white turban with its knotted tail hanging over his left ear. He saw his skin as darker, tanned a deep coppery bronze. He had sandaled feet, finely crafted silver rings on four fingers of his right hand.

He called this alter ego, whom he'd never met prior to singing with the Rembetiko Brotherz, Mister Moor. He loved Mister Moor, loved what happened when songs he'd known all his life, his mother's songs, Uncle Carl's songs, merged with the Rembetiko strings and drums.

The santouri and bouzouki played a fat chord. This chord and the tembeki drum, the one that seemed to go straight to both his heart and groin, made a deep hammock that cushioned him, cushioned them all. And, from inside this Anatolian instrumental cushion came the defiant outcry Johnny called International Up-From-Under.

"Don'cha lie, black girl, don'cha lie to me . . .
Tell me where did you sleep last night . . . ?
In the pines, in the pines, where the sun never shines . . .
An' I shivered the whole night through . . ."

Theddo awoke because he was too warm. Not the fever heat that signalled the bake component of his disease's shake n' bake—just the warm of two blankets and a wall-heater cranked up to broil. He turned on the light that nested in the whitewashed wall, just behind and above his head. He turned the temperature down, and, bone-dry, drank an entire bottle of Greek mineral water.

A barely nibbled almost full moon shone outside his window. He decided to walk for a bit. Dressed quickly. Jeans, cream-coloured cotton sweater, socks and battered black running shoes. On his way out the door, he pulled his shearling-lined brown leather jacket, the one Björn had called his butchy-bomber, from a wrought-iron hook.

It had rained while he'd been in thick medicine-driven sleep. The wet, striated multicoloured marble of the vast harbour square glistened in the moonlight. Elegant, Theddo thought, luminous.

And slippery as black ice, even with the rubbergrip of his runners. He landed on his butt just in front of a two-storey beige brick building whose sign proclaimed it the "National Bank of Greece."

Instead of standing up again, he buttscooted back a few inches and raised himself onto the wide concrete step that, protected by an overhanging awning, was dry. This vantage point commanded a panoramic view of the harbourfront with its shuttered cafés, shops and bobbing boats of various types, shapes and sizes.

The cat was barely four inches long, not counting his tail. Pale orange, with bright blue eyes and a black nose. Discomfited by rainwater on the black pads of his paws, he almost pranced as he jumped onto the dry step next to Theddo.

"Well, hello my friend," Theddo said, thrusting out his large hand to pick up the wet furball. It hissed, showing minuscule fanged teeth.

"Well, look at you, y'little shit. Smaller than my damn hand, an' you already know you're a lion."

He slowly turned his hand palm-up, let the kitten sniff and lick at it.

"Good for you, little lion. Humans are also born knowing that sort of thing. Then, y'see, they train us to forget it, don't they just . . . and *we*, we spend the rest of our lives trying to . . . re-remember."

The kitten was looking at him, just watching him. Theddo laughed.

"Oh dear. I *am* honoured to speak to you this evening. Thank you for attending my lecture."

He laughed again, softly, tried again to pick up the tiny animal. Again, the cat hissed, drawing back.

"Uh huh. Right. I see. Look, I'm not gonna mess with that hissing shit. And if you bite me, my blood could do you harm. I dunno. It could. Anyway, I'm gonna sit here and look at the moon. If you want me, Lion, you know where I am."

And he looked at the moon. The cat sat next to him, curling his tail around himself. Theddo, moving only his eyes, looked down at him and smiled. He felt joy—unmistakable joy. This surprised and pleased him.

"Uh huh," he said softly, smiling, arching his brows. "You lookin' at the moon too, are you?"

After a short while, the kitten climbed onto his lap and arranged himself there, curling up, purring—a startlingly big noise for the size of creature that was making it. Theddo began, softly, to sing.

"Oh, love . . .
It ain't no lie . . .
Oh love . . .
It ain't no lie-i-ie . . . .
Oh love, it ain' no li-i-i-i-ie . . .
This life I'm livin's . . .
Mighty hard . . ."

As he sang, he stroked the animal, finally putting him inside his jacket where he nestled against the body heat, purring like a motorboat.

The kitten was getting warmer but Theddo was beginning to feel cold. He got up slowly, cupping the animal that was still inside his jacket, still purring. They headed up the hill to the Hotel Melissa, one walking, one carried.

Spiro the policeman watched all this from the snake-narrow lane between the travel agency and the souvenir shop. The *mávros* from *Ameriki.* Johnny Reed's friend. The one who had spoken in the Greek Parliament. The one from the Night of the Full Moon and Black Men. Singing to the moon. A very Greek thing to do, singing to the moon. Making speeches to cats, putting a cat in your jacket, this was not Greek. Cats were for killing mice. And for tourists.

In front of the Hotel Melissa's heavy wooden door, Theddo peered inside his jacket. The Lion was asleep. There were many good reasons for not taking him into the hotel, into his room. He felt badly about disturbing his repose, but it had to be done.

"I'm sorry, my friend . . ." he murmured, gently lifting the animal out of his jacket. The cat looked at him, blinked, jumped down and took off down the hill.

"I see," Theddo said, shaking his head. "Cat-love."

Cat-Love

Washington D.C., 1979–1982

Theddo and Björn were very different creatures: different ages, different races, different cultures. In 1978, when Björn first arrived in Washington, there was reciprocal pleasure in exploring these differences.

Then came the arguments—petty little snitfights, usually over banal things.

Theddo: "Where are you going?"

Björn: "Who was that?"

Theddo: "Are you going to wear that?"

Björn: "Why can't I come with you?"

These snitfights diminished with time, tenderness and familiarity.

Until the surge of static arising from the Wet Hair/Hay-Adams Incident. Healing *that* took work, and outside support . . . but heal it did.

Later, in 1982, however, when Björn's Monster Dance arrived in force, old and new fights accompanied the Monster. The largest was about a cat.

Björn had only been out of hospital three days when he brought the cat home. Theddo'd come back from a long InterAfrA meeting. It was early evening, winter-dark. Seeing no lights on in Björn's apartment, he wondered if Björn were sleeping, worried that he might be rushing his recovery, might be in some club, dancing . . . or worse.

As landlord, he had a key, but had been asked not to "just let yourself in."

("This is either my space or it is not. If it is, you must knock. You must not come in without first knocking. And you must not come in if I am away. Yes, okay?" "Yes, okay.")

He knocked.

"Come. It is open."

Björn, barefoot, in faded black jeans and Theddo's old white turtle-neck sweater—always too large for him, now huge—was seated on a red-and-black Persian rug in the middle of the beige-carpeted floor. In his large, elegantly articulated hand he held a tiny ball of fur. He looked up, smiling like a Christmas miracle.

"Look, Thedd-doh. Isn't he perfect?! Look! Black and white, like us!"

It was good to see Björn so delighted. There'd been precious little of that for a fair while. He was, Theddo understood, terrified—and his last hospital stay had indeed been terrifying. He'd contracted some sort of bird-borne tuberculosis only available to people with AIDS. It had rocketed through him, along with various bits and pieces of this and that opportunistic horror. Always slim, he'd lost about twenty pounds in two weeks. He had not yet acquired that El Greco-from-hell gauntness with its beakiness and sunken eyes. He was still, Theddo thought, lyrically beautiful, in some ways more so for the fragility; but he knew that, barring a miracle, Björn was moving faster towards the end.

Björn had already seen what he'd named the Monster Dance. With Per, his best friend in Stockholm. Then with Stig Hanssons, the older man who had loved and helped him—and, of course, with a number of other young rent-boys—boys who would, one day, just not be around, who would then *stay* not around. He knew this dance, knew this monster, knew it far better than did Theddo. He was also fighting hard to not know what he knew.

"I found him, this little baby. Found him in the street. In front of the Hay-Adams Hotel, like you found me in Stockholm, in front of the Grand."

Oh God, Theddo thought, I'd assumed we were done with the Hay-Adams. Surely, he can't be doing the Hay-Adams *now*.

Björn remained seated on the red-and-black rug, looking like a gaunt Nordic djinn, his flying carpet having been slapped to Earth.

He held the Holstein-coloured furball up and out towards Theddo.

"I have named him *Bjeddo!* It is a combination of our two names, yes?"

He can *not* keep a cat now, Theddo thought. If birds had brought him tuberculosis, a *cat* could bring him "toxo," the brain-crazies from hell. Doctors weren't certain about a connection between cats and toxoplasmosis, but considered them a strongly possible source. Many people with AIDS had been told to give away their cats. Theddo knew that Björn wouldn't want to hear any of this.

He sat on the rug. Björn placed the kitten between them. He, not knowing the New Person, clambered back to Björn, curling up in his lap, looking up. Björn laughed, scratching gently behind the animal's ears.

"I am his favourite. He will like you too. I am yost the one who rescued him. You know, like you rescued me."

Theddo shook his head, smiling.

"It was not exactly *rescue*, Lille. You were not living on the street."

"Yes, but you know how Baltasar was . . . and I did not *love* him."

And do you love *me?* Theddo wondered, What *is* "love" for you?

What he said, as softly, as gently as he could, was, "Björn . . . cats . . . cats can carry . . . things that can . . . make you sick." He rested his hand on Björn's shoulder. Björn shrugged the hand away, standing up, holding the kitten to his chest.

He looked at Theddo, eyes wide, both brows arched. "I am *already* sick Thedd-doh. This little fellow makes me happy. Happy is good for me, yes?"

"Yes, happy is good for you . . . but animals, cats in particular, they are not certain, but many doctors feel . . ."

"I do not care what your many not-certain doctors are feeling. He is *my* cat, not yours. He loves me and you are, even of cat, yellous!"

Theddo put his large palms together, prayerfully, in front of his pursed lips.

"Ah yes, yellous."

"Oh TerriFICK! Make mocking of my accent also. DJELLous, okay? DJELLous! DJELLous! DJELLous! He is *my* cat. He is something that *you* did not give to me! As with the watch from Baltasar! So you do not also want me to wear the watch! And you do not also want me to have the cat! He will *not* be *Bjeddo*, then! He is *Björnvehn*. Björn's friend! *My* friend!"

The kitten, a street-animal, now pulsing against the chest of an angry stranger, dug his claws into that chest. Björn cried out and opened his hand. The kitten jumped down and ran out the open door. Björn, barefoot, ran after it, into the January night.

Theddo followed, shouting, "No, Lille! You'll catch cold! Please!" He could hear Björn, who was still capable of sprinting like a gazelle, somewhere ahead of him, shouting, "Bjerrrnn-vehn? BJEHRRnnn-vehn?" Crying out to a probably long-gone creature for whom both the name and the sound meant nothing. Then the shouting stopped, replaced by Theddo's own voice. "Björn! Björn, please! Please come home!" Very bright, Mister Daniels, he thought, Middle-Aged Black Activist Found Bellowing in the Streets of Washington, looking for his lost and dying teenaged white lover. He lowered and shook his head, deciding it would be best to look more quietly.

After about twenty minutes, he found him. Always instinctively aware of how he looked, Björn, even though frantic, had seated himself on the sidewalk under a streetlamp, a few blocks away from the house. He sat in a half-lotus position, shivering slightly, naked feet concealed below the ankles, under his calves. Arms wrapped around himself, eyes liquid with suspended tears, he looked up at Theddo.

"My cat. Is gone. I cannot find him." He almost whispered, his voice broken, tired and honestly bereft.

"Yes Lille, I know." He extended his arm and open hand downward. "Come home, yes?"

Björn grasped the hand, pulled himself up.

Theddo had bought the bed at auction in 1975. It originally belonged to an old South Carolina landowner, from one of "Charleston's better families." The English-voiced auctioneer in New York said the family owned more than a hundred acres and more than a hundred slaves.

The bed, a standard double of solid oak, brown-patinated by time, had an angel's face, framed by open wings, carved in each corner of the high headboard. A rumour, never confirmed, was that the black comedian and activist Max Cullemore, a major collector of "post middle-passage anti-bellum material" (as it said in the auction catalogue), had been bidding by phone for the bed. This rumour had it that when Cullemore found out he was bidding against Theddo Daniels, he withdrew, and Theddo got his bed.

And now, between the two carved brown seraphim, Björn lay, crying, babbling in a polyglot of Swedish, English and North-American-dance-club slang. Legs retracted up fetally, he clung to Theddo's thermal shirt as the kitten had clung to him—frightened, needy, heat-seeking. Theddo, who had given him mint tea, a hot shower and soft flannel pyjamas, lay beside him under the warm duvet, on his back, watching the play on the ceiling of black-leaf silhouettes from windblown tree branches. Björn was still shivering a bit, occasionally sucking his breath in sharply. Theddo petted his silky hair, murmuring, "Its all right, Lille. I'm here."

But it was not all right. And, in the way he had once so completely intended to be, so tried to be, he was not there.

Everything Rhymes with Yearn
Stockholm, Sweden, November 1977

Theddo spent his first afternoon in Stockholm watching the boy from his hotel room window. In the unguarded and completely unfamiliar way of younger, freer men, his heart seemed to be opening in a tenderness that was also, somehow, protective. This feeling was both pleasant and worrying. He was certain his intense attraction was not about the blondness. He had always seen blondness as somehow unfinished. Literally half-baked—not fully pigmented. Blackness, the look and sound of it, in all its variety, was a rich and glorious thing to him. And, as he celebrated this in others, he celebrated it in himself. Indeed, his African roots, his shared heritage, had always been the only thing about himself that he knew he loved. This love encompassed both a sense of world-family, as well as his sexual and romantic desires and impulses.

Billy Witherspoon, his first furtive young love, was as brown-ebony as the masks of Africa's Luba people.

Tafiq al Din (Terrific Alladin), the Jordanian photo-journalist who was taken from him by a desert landmine—the best-looking, the most loving, sexually open and fulfilling man he'd ever known—was, from birth, the rich bronze tan that white people risk carcinoma to achieve.

Björn's version of blondness, shot through with youthful vitality and dancer's grace, was unquestionably attractive, but it was not the thing that touched Theddo. What he thought he saw, even from across the road, and what he did eventually see and hear when the young man engaged him in mannered conversation in front of the opulent Grand

Hotel, was the camera-negative reverse colour image of his own Baltimore boyhood.

The awkward attempts at elegance, the way his eyes would follow his own elaborate hand gestures, the casting about for a style, for a persona, and, yes, the bone-deep need to be acknowledged as someone of consequence. Theddo knew much, well before he was told, about how this fatherless, mother-loved boy had grown up surrounded by homophobic schoolmates and adult male predators.

He'd seen the cluster of teenagers, six of them, slouching, jostling one another, preening or posing with studied casualness in front of the ferry dock across the road. Theddo knew this type of boy from every world capital to which his work had taken him. These were front-of-hotel boys. Neatly dressed well-mannered boys that could be asked into a hotel bar, to dinner in a good restaurant.

The rougher trade—homeless kids, gypsy kids, sons of Turkish immigrants—those were to be found *behind* the hotel, or in the narrow streets of Södermalm, Stockholm's south side, or near and inside the central train station, the cavernous T-Centrallen.

There was something exciting about the wild scruffy boys, reminding Theddo of Caribbean forest flowers, but the dangers were too great—sometimes deadly. He knew a man, a mid-level Kenyan civil servant, who had been stabbed to death by one such boy. And his own singular experiment—an Italian gypsy from Rome's Porta Portese market—had left Theddo with this ridiculous itchy twitchy reflex that would come upon him whenever he saw a similar-looking boy, even though the Roman crab lice were long gone. After Italy, Theddo simply could not look at a feral street boy without starting to itch.

The blatant classism of this made him angry with himself. Reminded him of Phil Greenbaum, the great civil rights lawyer, confiding to him, "You know, when I was a kid in the suburbs of Cleveland, we had a black cleaning woman. I've never been able to look at a black woman of a certain age and type without thinking I smell furniture polish and floor wax." After that, Theddo could not look at Phil Greenbaum without wondering what his white friend might be smelling. It was, he thought, the exact same thing as going all phantom-buggy in the crotch at the sight of rough-trade kids.

He'd come out of the train station, having spent the morning exploring Gamla Stan, the Old Town. "Hallo!" he heard, shouted in his direction. The tall slim blond boy, with his long neck and long-fingered elaborate hand gestures, stood out among his teasing peers—a daffodil in a rock garden.

"Hallo to you! Good Ahfternoon!" the boy shouted again, now accompanied by a smile and a flutter-fingered wave, right arm straight up.

"Are you speaking to *me?*" Theddo asked.

"I am, sir! I wish to wish you a good Al Ifternoon!"

"And the same to you, young man!" he shouted back, before turning and making himself walk calmly into the Grand Hotel, which he felt was more befitting a gentleman of his age and experience than his natural impulse, which was to flee in flustered panic.

After that flirtatious and strangely courtly exchange, Theddo would watch the boys, watch *that* boy, from his hotel window. Even from that distance he was certain the boy was looking back at him, smiling. Once, he even seemed to wave again, then laugh, and abruptly turn his back. Theddo grabbed his beige wool scarf and brown leather bomber jacket, took the elevator, the snakily-named "Hiss," to the lobby, sped through the revolving door. The boy was gone. Two others were there. They looked at Theddo with interest. Embarrassed, he busied himself with a map from his inside jacket pocket, pretended to be deciding something, and then strode off purposefully around the block. There, nose running and ears cold, he waited like a fool for over ten minutes, finally entering a bookshop and buying a British newspaper. Returning to the street, he looked into shop windows for a while. When he returned to the hotel, the boy was still not at his post.

Theddo apologized to the concierge for forgetting his key. His door was opened for him. He took a hot shower, shouting aloud "And what the hell was *that* about, Mister Daniels? Get a grip!"

Then, the day before the *World in Colour* Conference was to begin, the boy appeared next to him, just outside the hotel in the crisp autumn air, regarding his hypermodern oxidised-metal watch with self-conscious theatricality.

"Oh, these Georg Jensen watches! They look sooo fanTAHstic but they do not always tell the time properly. It has died. It needs a new battery. Do you know the time?"

Theddo thought this entire horological cruise-gavotte could be simplified.

"It's five-fifteen. I'm going to have a drink. Would you care to join me?"

"Here. In the Grand?"

"Yes. I'm a guest here."

"Ah, I see. I am not certain I am properly dressed."

Theddo quickly feigned appraisal of the young man's attire—clothes that likely had been acceptable in this same hotel bar many times before.

"Let's see. White shirt, black jeans, leather bomber jacket, boots. You are wearing almost exactly what I myself am wearing. Except that your jacket is black, and my shirt is the colour of your hair. I think we'll both be acceptable. I'm Theddo Daniels." He extended his hand, which the boy shook with grave dignity.

Then he smiled. A big dimple-revealing smile. One slightly angled and overlapping upper tooth, just to the left of his front teeth, agreeably moderated perfection.

"Thedd-doh?"

"Theodore. I have always been called Theddo."

"I am Björn Nilsson. My first name rhymes with yearn, not with torn."

"Yes, I can hear that."

"Good! Good for you! Most Americans are imPOSSible with my name. I say, over and over, *Byearn*, and they repeat, also over and over, *Byorrrn*. This is why I have learned to say that my name rhymes with yearn."

Everything rhymes with yearn, Theddo thought.

"May I have a vodka and tonic as my drink?"

The blurted vodka-and-tonic question made the older man wonder just how young the younger man was.

"Are you old enough to drink, Byearn?"

"Oh yes. I have papers."

Not a grownup answer, Theddo thought, gesturing for Björn to precede him through the revolving door.

Theddo ordered a Swedish beer, and a vodka and tonic. Björn took the same bubbly delight in his drink that small children exhibit when a beverage comes with a Japanese paper umbrella, preferably red.

"Ah. Vodka and tonic! I do really think this is the *best* drink. I have had many different kinds of drink, including one from Fiji, made of pepper. Of *pepper!* Can you imagine?"

"Yes I can, actually. It's called Kava. Were you in Fiji?"

"No. There was a Fijian gentleman staying . . . here in Stockholm. Last year. Attending a conference."

"As I am now. Attending a conference, I mean. Was your Fijian gentleman called Kemuni Rotu?"

"Yes! Do you know him?"

"Mm hm. He was the Fijian minister of culture. We have attended conferences together."

The boy looked ever so slightly nervous, as if there might be some crowding about to happen in his busy young life.

"Were you here last year?"

"No. This is my first time in Stockholm."

"Is *he* here now, Mister Rotu?"

"No. There is a new minister. A woman. I can't remember her name."

The boy took a gulp of his drink. "Strong, this drink!" he said, laughing. Then: "I am a dancer. In a club here. Mister Rotu saw me dance. In a different club. I dance tonight. Would you like to come and see? We could then have a Swedish dinner, yes?" Theddo said yes, that he would very much like to do that. Björn wrote out the name and address of the club. He then stood, a bit uneasily, and said. "I must now do things before my show. I will see you there." That world-lighting smile again. "Thedd-doh! I like so much your name! I am glad you will see me dance! Goodbye until tonight!" He dashed from the bar. Theddo could see him sprinting away, heading south. He looked down at the bill. A vodka and tonic at the Grand Hotel cost about the same as he'd imagined Björn himself would cost. Quite a lot. He looked at the other scrap of paper. *Klubb Kul.* Kul. K-u-l. Swedish for cool, which Theddo was not sure this was. Cul. C-u-l. French for asshole, which Theddo was not sure he was not.

What the hell did a middle-aged man wear to a place called Club . . . no, *Klubb*, Kul? Kul indeed! Shit, he'd just go as A Black Person. He *had* heard that Black People were always considered cool in Sweden. Cool and sexy, he'd heard. So, that was it; he would enter Klubb Kul as the Coolest American Black Person Over Forty Currently in Stockholm.

The newly self-proclaimed CABPCiS showered, and then anointed himself with splashes of West Indian lime cologne. He didn't know if dance clubs still had black light, but he wore a white thermal shirt under his black corduroy jacket, just in case, and black button-fly Levis, because, hell, *everybody* knew *they* were cool. He rubbed some oil in his grey-flecked, close-cropped hair. "Lookin' good, bro'," he said. And laughed. He was acting like a teenager. At least he assumed he was. When he actually *was* a teenager, he was cautious and formal. Senior class president. Academic achiever. A credit to his race, they said (those who said that sort of thing). The devoted and loving son of a doting Caribbean-born single mother. She knew what she knew, his freelance journalist and guidance-councillor mother—particularly after coming upon Theddo and Billy Witherspoon, *literally* in the closet.

They never spoke of it, choosing instead, when not just laughing and joking in the privacy of their cramped but orderly apartment, to dwell on his scholastic accomplishments and social goals.

He was not much less closeted as an adult (more closeted, probably, given his professional situation), but he was also a known personality. A public figure. A spokesman for his people.

A spokesman for his people? Yes, he was that. And what, he thought, brows furrowing, was a spokesman for his people, for *anyone*, doing chasing after a boy who could be fifteen, and was certainly no more than nineteen or twenty? A boy who survived on the attentions and expenditures of older men. Black men knew better than other men did, Theddo thought, that people were not supposed to buy other people.

His superannuated teenage high imploded. He thought of not going at all to *Klubb Kul.* Then the rationalisation mechanism kicked in; the one that gives us good reasons for doing what we were going to do anyway.

"Oh shit, oh dear! Wait a minute! Who said anything about *buying* anyone? I have been invited to see a dancer dance. I find this dancer attractive. If this dancer finds *me* attractive, we'll see what's what. Huhn."

His taxi pulled up in front of an elegant old mansion of cream-coloured stone, nestled among other similar houses, on a street landscaped with large old trees, high bushes and lichen-covered stone walls. The only indication that it was a club, and a private club at that, was the tuxedoed, spiky-haired burly young Asian sentry in front of the heavy wooden doors. In English, he asked Theddo his name.

"Theodore Daniels."

"Theddo?"

"Yes."

The man smiled politely, with a quick nod, check-marking Theddo's name on a list he pulled from his breast pocket.

The door opened and a woman appeared wearing an ankle-length silky black dress draped Grecian-style over one shoulder. She was slim but full breasted, with long straight hair, a bit yellower than Björn's thatch of shaggy shiny straw.

"Welcome to *Klubb Kul*, Mister Daniels. I am Kari, one of the managers. You are Mister Nilsson's guest. At table five."

Theddo, who had been expecting a Berlin-style teen-cave and/or Boy-Bar, felt too casually dressed. He was glad his clothes were freshly washed, and at least black or white, and that at the last moment he'd grabbed his white silk scarf.

Kari spoke again, in a warm, throaty voice. "Björn Nilsson will not be dancing for another hour or so. He has informed us that you will be dining elsewhere together later in the evening. Would you care to go first now for a drink to the bar? You can see the clubroom and stage from there."

Happiest when he could orchestrate events, Theddo was pleased by this suggestion, but wondered if he'd prompted it in any way, wondered if he looked at all uneasy.

"Yes, I'd love to stop at the bar, have a look around. This is my first time in your lovely city." (Oh dear, he thought, now *there's* the chamber of commerce ass-kisser line of all time!) Happily, the glamorous young woman did not look at him as if he were wearing white socks with a tuxedo.

"Ah," she said, "you are enjoying Stockholm, then?"

"Yes. Very much. Of course, I don't have much free time to look around. I'm here for a conference."

"Ah, yes. *The World in Colour,* I believe."

"Yes! You know of it?"

"Oh yes. There has been much about it in the news. And you have conference colleagues here in the club this evening. The party of Doctor Oliver Gwangwe of South Africa, and his wife."

"Oliver and Vuyo? I am *delighted.* They are dear friends. I knew they were arriving in Sweden today, but I've not seen them as yet."

"They are at table fourteen. I can show you from the bar where they are seated. And also show you table five."

"Terrific. That would be terrific. Thank you. *Tack.*"

"*Var sho good.* You are welcome."

The interior of *Klubb Kul,* despite the silly name, was nothing at all like what Theddo had been expecting. There certainly wasn't any black light. Nor a mirror ball. If the place was anything like anything he had seen before, it was those chic discotheque/restaurant/bars the Parisians invented.

The roof bar was extraordinary—circles within circles. A large round glass room that sat on top of the house, like an outsize ship's crow's-nest lookout—curved chrome bar, black leather barstools, couches and chairs, and about a dozen small, round black marble tables. The entire room was encircled by a shiny, curving art deco double-cylinder chrome railing, and, about two metres beyond the railing, thick see-though rounded glass walls of a pale sea-blue. Through these walls and the one-way mirror-glass floor underfoot, one had a 360-degree view of the club-restaurant below. The restaurant, while more Victorian than art deco, also looked like something out of the 1920s or '30s, with linen-clothed candlelit tables, an enormous crystal chandelier, and long windows, draped, swagged and tasselled in an almost-black green velvet. There was a tiny stage, polished as a black mirror, a Corinthian column on either side, each column topped by a miniature potted palm in a bulbous highly glazed cream-white vase.

Kari directed Theddo's gaze down and to the right, to where Oliver and Vuyo Gwangwe were seated, along with another African man in white robes and a woman in a sari. There was no way to call to them from the coolly climate-controlled but thoroughly sealed eyrie—not that calling out to them would have been remotely suitable behaviour

("Hey Oliver! Hey Vuyo! I'm up here! How you guys doin'?!" he imagined himself bellowing. Now, wouldn't that make a splendid impression on our swellegant Nordic hosts and hostessi?)

"Could you possibly take a note to them, Kari, telling them I am here and will see them when I come downstairs?"

"Of course. My pleasure."

Kari got a notepad from behind the bar, along with a cold Swedish beer for Theddo, who had seated himself in a plush black leather chair and was nibbling at cashews from a red glass bowl on a little table.

"*Molweni, friends!* he wrote. *I am above, in the crazy glass bar. I am so pleased that you are both here, and will join you downstairs presently. I'm supposed to sit at another table, but perhaps we can all sit together there.*

Ukuthanda,

UT'eddo Daniels"

He folded the note, wrote "Mr. and Mrs. Gwangwe" on it, and handed it to Kari. The Gwangwe table seemed to have a decent view of the stage. Theddo asked where table five was located.

It was directly in front of the stage. Only one person was seated there. A tall white man with a shaved head and a silvery handlebar moustache. He appeared, from Theddo's observation perch, to be dressed entirely in black leather. Oh shit, oh dear, he thought, asking a question to which he knew the answer.

"Is that gentleman a friend of Mister Nilsson as well?"

"Oh yes, that is Baltasar Axelsson. He arranged for Björn to dance here, and frequently comes to see him. He expects you."

"Does he? Good. I wonder if he would mind if my friends, the Gwangwes, and their party, joined us at table five."

"I don't imagine that would be a problem. Mister Axelsson is a member here for a long time. He often brings others to see the show. Shall I ask him if the Gwangwe party may join you both?"

"Yes, that would be fine . . . but could you first ask the Gwangwe party if they would like to do so, or would prefer staying where they are? I do not wish to inconvenience them . . . or Mister . . . Axelsson."

"Very good. To the left of the bar is the stairwell leading to the Grand Salle. Come down any time you wish. Niklas, the barman, will take care of anything else you may require while you are up here."

They did a bit more reciprocal thanking, and then Kari headed downstairs.

He watched her arrive in the "Grand Salle," walk briskly, threading her way sure-footedly between tables, until she came to Oliver and Vuyo. She handed Oliver the note. He read, looked up towards the glass bar-bubble, and waved vigorously. Theddo doubted that he could be seen, but stood up nonetheless, leaned over the railing, and, with equal vigour, waved back. Now both Oliver *and* Vuyo waved. Theddo smiled, silently translating the imaginary headline in the next day's Stockholm newspapers: "Coloured Folk Have Inexplicable Sudden Spate of Hand-Waving in Chic White Private Club."

He drank his beer, readying himself for the mixed bag of things he had to do next.

"Right," he said and walked to the bar to pay for the beer.

"It has been taken care of," said the too-cool-to-smile Nicklas. "Mister Axelsson has asked to put your food and drink on his account, with his compliments."

Theddo was not comfortable with this. Theddo was, in fact, not comfortable in general. He had felt a bit silly about a possible teen club, more than a bit paranoid about a possible Boy-Bar, but having his drinks bought by a white, cueball-headed leather queen who had some sort of relationship to the boy dancer/hustler who had brought him to this rich people's wet dream of a place was making him damn near crazy.

Damn Near Crazy was definitely not an option.

Christ! he thought, I've been speaking in public for more than twenty years. Spoke at the frigging UN, for god's sake. Faced down rosythroats and bigots all over the world. *And* Oliver and Vuyo Gwangwe are here. MISSter Assholesson is *not* a problem!

Going down the stairs to the Grande Salle, he also thought he might actually try to *like* the man who'd bought his drink. That would be a lot harder to do if the man had also bought Björn, which he knew was highly likely, but he'd do his best. Before he had to do any of it, though, he would see his friends.

Doctor Oliver Gwangwe, the South African apartheid exile who had headed London's Brixton People's Clinic since 1968, was frequently described as "larger than life." Once, on hearing this description, Oliver laughed his deep, perhaps overly booming laugh and said, "Whoever is the fool who said *that* clearly has no idea how *enormous* LIFE is! I am, as are we all, considerably smaller than life, and just doing my best, which is almost *never* good enough!"

That somewhat falsely humble pronouncement notwithstanding, Oliver was one of the most committed and hardworking people Theddo knew. A Xhosa, he missed his country, but felt he was of more value as Doctor to black people in London than he would be as Boy or Kaffir to white people in Johannesburg.

For all his almost sleepless dedication, and a fearlessness in confrontation that had almost gotten him killed on at least three occasions, and had him practically canonised in London's black community, Oliver Gwangwe was significantly unsaintly. He occasionally drank until he fell down where he was, and Vuyo, his partner in life and work, had long looked the other way with regard to various younger mistresses, in both South Africa and London.

"Hello, my dear friend! I see from your note that you remember your Xhosa!" Oliver boomed, rising to embrace Theddo. They were both large men, about the same size and about the same age, yet Theddo felt enveloped and, for a moment, safe as a boy in the arms of a loving father.

"Hello Oliver, hello! As to my Xhosa, I did not have that much to forget in the first place . . . and I had a good teacher. I knew you'd be in Stockholm for the conference, but what a surprise that we should be together in *this* place! And hello Vuyo! You look as lovely as ever!" (There I go again, he thought, sounding like the chamber of commerce. Why do I *do* that?) Vuyo Gwangwe, a tall woman of about fifty with a body both rounded and athletically toned, widely spaced doe eyes, full lips and glorious cheekbones, *did* look well. She always looked well. Theddo genuinely liked and admired her.

What he did not admire in *himself* was the fawning he sometimes engaged in with women. Was it, he wondered, an apology for not wanting to sleep with them? If it was, he was arrogant as hell *on top of* being a jerk. Why would he think that any member of the world's female population was particularly concerned with, or saddened by, his lack of interest? His mother thought he was perfect. She was the only person holding this opinion. And she was wrong.

Oliver introduced Theddo to the others at the table, Doctor Michael Adedidji, the associate cultural minister from Nigeria, and Doctor Nusrat Halim, the newly elected Pakistani education minister. Theddo congratulated Doctor Halim on her appointment, and then, reflexively, looked over at table five. Baltasar Axelsson, who was looking in their direction, nodded and raised his hand in a brief wave. Theddo waved back, amending his news headline to include Swedes ("Black Americans, as They Had Earlier with Blues and Jazz, Popularise Hand-Waving in Stockholm"). Then he sat down between Vuyo Gwangwe and Doctor Adedidji.

"Listen guys, I'd rather stay here, with friends and colleagues, but . . ."

"We know, my friend," Oliver Gwangwe interrupted, producing a business card. "Mister . . . Axelsson has written that you are his guest, and that we are invited to join him as well. Is Mister Axelsson a friend of yours?"

"Does Mister Axelsson *look* like a friend of mine?" he asked mockingly, and instantly regretted the question; Oliver knew Theddo's sexual orientation, but had no idea of his tastes. Could he possibly think it ran to . . .? He went on, quickly. "I've actually never seen Mister Axelsson before tonight. He is a friend of Björn Nilsson, a dancer who is performing here. Björn is . . . a new acquaintance. He invited me to see him dance, and made the table arrangements."

"A front and centre table! We would be fools to refuse. Why don't you precede us to Mister Axelsson? We will take care of our bill and then join you there. Yes, people?" Oliver looked around the table as the others murmured variations of "yes," "certainly," "delighted," etc.

Theddo was pleased. He rose, said his goodbyes and made his way, less uneasily than before, to table five. As he did so he called forth yet another anxious moment, wondering what, if any, explanation Oliver was giving to his tablemates for all this carry-on. Clearly, nervousness about Björn and about Axelsson's relationship *to* Björn was making him even more paranoid than usual.

Oliver knew well how private Theddo was about his sexual life, and, having secrets of his own, had always been an understanding and reliable confidant. He would surely continue to be so. As Theddo reached this pacifying conclusion, he also reached table five.

Baltasar Axelsson stood up and, with a large, slender, multi-ringed hand, patted Theddo firmly three times on his left shoulder.

"Mister Daniels. How do you do. It is good to meet you. Björn has told me so much about you."

He has, has he? Theddo thought. That is truly amazing. I've spent all of about half an hour in the boy's company. He did not say this.

"Well. I hope what he said was positive and that I won't disappoint either of you. Thank you very much for inviting my friends to join us. They are delighted to do so, and should be coming along quite soon."

"Yes, they are coming now."

Theddo looked over his shoulder to see the World in Colour contingent walking towards them; Doctor Adedidji's robes billowed about him, the gold accents in Doctor Halim's emerald-green sari glinted in the light as she moved. Oliver and Vuyo were both in black suits, with only Oliver's orange-black-and-green kente-cloth tie suggesting his African heritage. That, and, as with Vuyo, Doctor Adedidji and Theddo himself, his skin. Were there other black people in *Klubb Kul?* It was neither the time nor the place to attempt a head-count.

There was a flurry of introductions, handshakes and seat-sortings. Axelsson insisted that Theddo sit next to him.

"Here is the best view of the stage."

Theddo did so, trying to decide whether Axelsson was being gracious, perverse, or both.

The lights dimmed, and, amplified by discreetly placed wall-speakers, music filled the room. A Kyrie. The angel-voiced Latinate tones of a full-throated boys' choir. "*Keeereeeh. EhleeAYssson.*" Two pale long-fingered hands parted the black velvet curtains at the back of the small stage. Björn stood there, barefoot, feet together at the heels, toes turned outward. Arms extended, bent at the elbows. He wore only midcalf-length black tights, and was bathed in white light from a single spot hung in the middle of a one-bar grid above the stage. His arms and hands came to rest at his sides, palms turned outward in what felt to Theddo like silent supplication. Then his neck seemed to lift and lengthen as he swayed slightly back and forth, heels lifting off the floor. His large eyes appeared to look out at all and nothing, everyone and no one. Then his gaze turned inward. He dropped to his knees, leaned slightly back, and with a push of his hands on the shiny black floor, slid, in one unbroken move, to the edge of the stage, where he came to a clean stop. There was something so vulnerable in his pale body, the forward thrust of his strong-chinned yet child-soft face. At that moment, Theddo saw the small gold ring piercing his left nipple. To his surprise, he felt he was about to cry. Sheer force of will halted this water before it left the circumference of his eyes. Björn then, in time with the music, slowly raised his arms, hands and chin to the ceiling. Bidden by the combination of this particular music and this particular dancer, Theddo thought, a crucifiable boy. That did it. He made no sound, but one tear broke free briefly, warm on his cheek. He could feel Axelsson looking at him, hated the helplessness of the moment. His anger stopped the eyewater and guaranteed that it would not return in that environment.

As if in support of Theddo's determination, Björn forcefully leapt straight up, a Nijinskian gravity-defying leap that seemed, impossibly, to hold in the air. When he landed, almost noiselessly, the music of the European Kyries changed to the one by the all-black Congolese Boys' Choir, a recording from Theddo's own teens, when the Congo still "belonged" to Belgium. Björn's movements became fast, as multicircularly woven as the medieval Norse runic designs Theddo had studied in preparation for being in this part of the world. The choreography was clearly of Björn's own making, original and personal. Even in the early posture of supplication, and in the "crucifiable" moment, there was strength and pride. No cheapness, no begging, no hustle. The dance was both by and for Björn Nilsson, and, in engaging him, engaged those who were watching him.

Björn ended his dance with a series of antic one leg after the other marionette-like lateral leaps, his powerful thighs and calves reminding Theddo of a Matisse jazz-painting. Facing the audience, he leapt from one side of the tiny stage to the other, each angularly leaping leg led by an extending hand and arm. Then he leapt straight up, legs fully extended, toes pointing, in an airborne split. He landed on the stage in that full split, lowered his chest and head to the ground. He then raised his upper body, followed by his arms and chin as earlier. Holding his arms out, but relaxing his head he stood, bowed, laughed, and bowed again, as his audience applauded with scattered cheering words, sounds, whistles. He bowed again formally, low and from the waist, then backed up in one quick move and, as swiftly, drew the black curtains closed in front of him.

It was said softly, nasally, almost whispering. Theddo would remember it later as a Peter Lorre voice.

"He is, as you say in America, hung like a horse, yes?"

No, Theddo thought, Axelsson's summary of Björn's dance could not possibly be what he thought he had just heard. He looked around the table. The others seemed not to have heard it, and were animatedly praising Björn to both Axelsson and Theddo.

"Theddo, your friend is a splendid dancer," Vuyo said. "Have you seen him dance before?"

"No. This evening is the first time. He was . . . wonderful."

"Did you know he was using *Missa Luba* as part of his music. Had he done that for . . .?"

"No." Axelsson said sharply, mouth smiling, eyes cold. "He has always used the black music as part of the collage of Kyries. It injects a different rhythm, a simpler, more primitive . . ."

And then Björn was there, in his white shirt and black jeans, a long, black-and-white striped silk scarf around his neck, dangling down, fore and aft, to mid-thigh. He had showered, and his hair and pale eyelashes were still damp. He was slightly flushed, looked quietly happy—and about twelve. Theddo introduced him to the others at the table. Led by Oliver, everyone, including a somewhat reluctant Axelsson, stood and applauded, producing a smattering of seated applause from others in the room. Björn stood before Theddo.

"Did you like it, my dance?"

Theddo wanted to hold him; not sexually, but in some way that would give both praise and shelter.

"I loved it, your dance. You are . . . very gifted."

Björn had bent his head to receive this affirmation, as if, Theddo thought, he was about to be knighted. Or beheaded. At the word "gifted" he looked up and into Theddo's eyes.

"Thank you. Your words mean a lot to me."

Why the hell, Theddo wondered, would my words mean a lot to him? Why would the opinion of a stranger, even one who was staying at the Grand Hotel and could pay the ransom fee for a vodka and tonic, matter? Was it said to make Axelsson jealous? Was it simply Björn's equivalent of the flowery nonsense *he* tended to insincerely ooze with women?

Theddo's pull towards Björn had been deepened by the happy discovery that he was a true dancer. He was *not*, as Theddo had so expected him to be, a pretty boy who climbed up and down on a shiny chrome pole to the tune of "Love to Love You, Baby"—a boy who would receive not applause and gracious praise from comfortably privileged Stockholmers, but crumpled bills stuffed into the crotch of his g-string.

Axelsson stood behind Björn, kneading his neck and right shoulder, while looking past him at Theddo.

"Well, we can stay for another drink here if you wish, Mister Daniels, but we should go soon. I have made a reservation for the three of us at a charming little restaurant in Gamla Stan, near to where we live."

Near to where *we* live, Theddo thought. Beg off, Mister Daniels. Run like a thief. Get out of this mess before you're really *in* one.

"Yes, Theddo, the restaurant is called Gata SHAYlleren, the street cave. It is very charming. I believe you will like it very much, and I very much want to know more of your thoughts about my dance, so I think we should go very soon right away now if we may, Baltasar."

As if he could read Theddo's mind, see his impulse to bolt, Björn said this all at a hurried, gulping pace, looking imploringly at him.

Oh my, Theddo thought. All those verys. I don't know why this matters to him, but clearly it does. He gave me an extraordinary dance. I can at least give him my company for dinner at his charming street cave, Axelsson or no.

"Of course, Björn. I am, as I told you earlier, pleased to dine with you both" (there had been no "both" in the earlier invitation he thought, but we will play the hand we've been dealt), "and *delighted* to discuss your wonderful dance."

Oliver Gwangwe, ever the diplomat, stood, anticipating the next phase of things.

"Please! *Salanikakuhle!* Do go on, you three. As you know, Mister Axelsson, my little group has already dined very well, at this restaurant." He took Björn's hand in both of his. "And *you*, young man, thank you again for your splendid dance. All our best wishes in your future career. Theddo, my friend, we shall see you tomorrow at the opening of the congress, yes?"

"That you shall. Ten in the morning. Enjoy the rest of your evening—it was a very happy surprise to find all of you here tonight."

As they were leaving the Grande Salle of the *Klubb Kul,* Theddo turned to look at his friends, and, with the help of Oliver and Doctor Adedidji, added further corroboration to the rumour of a black-driven hand-waving craze sweeping Stockholm.

The *Gata Källeren,* a grey stone and stucco medieval fantasy hidden in a narrow street of the Old Town, was smoky, crowded and noisy. German rock n' roll, all breathy voices and electronic music, pulsed from wall-speakers. Good-looking, artily chic types of all ages and both sexes chattered, laughed, smoked and manoeuvred amiably for space at the old oak bar. The maître d', greeting Axelsson by name, escorted his party of three past the bar and through two large arch-shaped heavy wooden doors to an adjacent, quieter room. People were chatting and dining animatedly at most of the tables and booths. Theddo, discreetly checking his watch, (eleven o'clock), was, as ever, amazed by how late Europeans ate.

They were brought to a large booth in a back corner, against a grey stone wall, under two large candle-holding bronze sconces in the shape of horns. Axelsson gestured for Björn to slide in. He did so, and Axelsson sat next to him. Theddo sat facing them both. A waiter appeared, greeting "Herr Axelsson." A conversation ensued between them, in Swedish.

"We are discussing wine, Mister Daniels. There is a quite nice Riesling, or a Montrachet if you wish the *salmon en croute, Béarnaise,* which is what I shall be having. There is also a first-rate Cabernet, if you want to try their French-style chicken stew, which is a favourite of Björn's. Of course, you can also have a beer. We have quite good beer here in Sweden."

Theddo *did* want a beer, but he also wanted to appear as elegant and worldly as his host. He split the difference, ordering Björn's food-choice, the chicken stew, with a carafe of Cabernet, rather than beer. Björn, of course, would have his stew with the *best* drink, a vodka and tonic.

When the food arrived, Björn ("I can never eat before I dance. I am *staaahrving!"),* attacked his stew with the purposefulness of a hostage recently released into the custody of his mother. Theddo, realising that he had not eaten since early morning, did something similar, only slower, and with what he hoped was a bit more dignity.

"Don't eat so fast, *min barn'* you'll only have terrible cramps in the middle of the night and I'll have to feed you camomile tea," Axelsson said, toying with the puff-pastry enveloping his salmon, as Theddo felt he was toying with him.

Yeah, Yeah, I got'cha, Herr Salmon en-fucking-croute. The two of you spend nights together. We *know* this, chump, all right? he thought.

What he *said* was:

"I don't even have your excuse, Björn. I haven't done any dancing, but I still managed to forget about food all day, except for breakfast."

"Were you thinking about your conference, Mister Daniels?"

"Yes, I suppose I was."

Björn continued fervently eating the aromatic and tasty chicken stew. He also placed his left-booted foot, lightly, over Theddo's right-booted foot.

"And how do you and *min barn* know each other, Mister Daniels?"

Björn withdrew his foot.

"*Min barn?*"

"Yes, *min barn.* It is my what you call nickname for Björn. It means my baby. *Min,* my. *Barn,* baby."

"I see."

Björn had finished his stew and was gulping his drink, eyes wide. Was he frightened or just unsure of how to proceed?

"Well, Mister Axelsson . . ."

"Please. Call me Baltasar."

"Baltasar. Yes. Well, we met at the Grand Hotel. The *World in Colour* Conference has a performance component. Musicians and dancers have been invited, along with delegates from different parts of the non-Caucasian world . . . you know, Africa, Asia, Black America, et cetera. Björn was signing up to view the performances, which are open to Swedish performers and . . ."

"Oh yes, Baltasar! I meant to tell you! This event will be a very good thing for me! I could find new music and new moves if I see . . ."

"Yes. A fine idea. When are these performances, exactly?"

"Thursday afternoon and Friday evening. Did you sign up to watch both sessions, Björn?"

"Yes Theddo, yes, I did! Both sessions! I am very much looking forward to . . ."

"Pity. I must be at the shop on Thursday. I own an antique shop here in Gamla Stan, Mister Daniels, and it is my assistant's holiday weeks. But we could certainly attend the Friday performance together."

"Pity," Theddo said, looking straightforwardly, neutrally, at Axelsson, imitating the tone of his "pity," but not so you could prove it. "Pity, that, because, unfortunately, Baltasar, the sessions are only open to performers. A *cultural exchange*, you understand. With limited seating space. I can try to get you in, but . . ."

"No, no. That is all right. I do not keep the boy on a chain. He can certainly have . . . a *cultural exchange* without my being there."

Björn laughed, a bit loudly. "I can show you the dances, Baltasar, what I remember from them, after I've seen them, yes? May I have another vodka and tonic?"

By the time they'd come to the fruit/cheese/coffee conclusion of the meal, Björn's third vodka and tonic had rendered him a bit giggly. And a bit incautious. He looked at Theddo with mooncalf eyes as he attempted to discuss his Kyrie-dance.

"I make that dance for my *mor*. For my mother. She, *min* mother, loves very much church music. So I make the dance for her. She lives with my little brother and little sister in Gotland, so she has not yet seen it. I will take it to her soon, though we will have to find a place for me to dance it. Our family house is not so big, and also full with too many things. The place my mother lives in Gotland is called Fårö. It has ahMAYSSing beaches with very big rocks from the beginning of time. They are magic, these rocks. They have a music, I think. I always hear music when I look at them."

"Ah yes, music. I am curious, Björn. How did you come to choose the Kyrie from *Missa Luba* as part of your collection?"

"I have a friend who is musician and writer of music. When I tell him I am making a dance of Kyries, he gave me a cassette of this music from the Congo and I thought it was . . ."

Axelsson lit a cigarette, quickly, snapping the Zippo closed with a sharp clang.

"Stig Hanssons? He gave you this music? When did you see Stig Hanssons?"

"Two months ago. Just on the street. In Söder. He asked what I was doing, and when I tell him, he say that he have music from Africa what are also Kyrie."

"And you went to his flat to get this music, yes?"

"Yes. For a moment only, Balti, just to get the cassette."

Björn was smiling, more a tic than a smile, as he answered. As he did this, he started to sway his head from side to side. Like Ray Charles, Theddo thought. Ray Charles did this because he was blind. Björn, Theddo was fairly certain, was doing it because he was frightened. As he had done with the music and dance programme at the Grand Hotel, he moved to extricate Björn from a trap.

"My friends, the others at the table, thought your dance was extraordinary, Björn. As, of course, did I. If you take it seriously, you could have a fine career as a dancer. You know that, don't you?"

Björn giggled and shook his head. "I am not certain of this. I know that I love to dance. I love this very much. But it is hard to get a placement, and I do not belong to a school, and . . . your friends really liked my dancing so much? Truly?"

"Yes, truly. Nusrat Halim said . . ."

Axelsson laughed, a loud metallic sound. "*Who* said?!"

"Doctor Halim. The woman in the green sari . . ."

"And her *Christian*, I mean her *given* name is *what?!*"

"Nusrat."

"Noss. *Ratt!!* How per*fect!* A steering wheel in the nose! A NOSS RATT!"

As he shouted this, he stuck a long index finger into each of Björn's nostrils and sharply turned the boy's head from side to side, saying "Noss ratt *left*, noss ratt *right!* It is funny this, ya *min barn?*"

Theddo stood up.

"No. It is not funny. You are hurting him. Please stop."

Axelsson stopped jerking Björn's head, but did not remove his fingers from the boy's nose.

"Do not concern yourself, Mister Daniels. We are only playing. He likes to play a bit rough. It is fun for him. Is it not, *min barn?*"

Björn looked up at Theddo, to the extent he could with his face being controlled by Axelsson's long fingers and hands. His eyes were shiny, but he was not crying, rather in the same way Theddo did not cry earlier in the evening—by sheer force of will.

"Yes. It is fun for me."

"And it can stop if you ask, yes?"

"Yes, Balti."

"Do you wish to ask now."

"No, Balti."

"Well, I wish to stop. It is boring to have my fingers in your nose." And he laughed. And Björn laughed. Theddo wanted to punch Axelsson until he turned to ectoplasmic invisible dust and disappeared entirely from the Earth, leaving only a slightly perfumed fartlike stench. He held his hands tightly at his sides and spoke softly.

"Well, I do not always understand the amusements of other cultures. No matter. As you know, I have to prepare for the conference, and really must go. No, please don't get up. I hope you enjoy the music programmes, Björn. I believe they will contain discussions of the music and dance forms in addition to the dances themselves. Don't forget to pick up your pass by Wednesday at six in the evening. At the long table in the hotel lobby." He walked briskly from the *Gata Källeren* into much-needed night air.

At one in the morning and back at the Grand, Theddo was still fighting down the dregs of rage and nausea. He was surprised to see someone still at the sign-in table for the World in Colour.

"My goodness, Kimiko! We Never Close, huhn?"

"Hello, Mister Daniels. Actually, once the conference has started, there won't be anyone here after seven in the evening. But now, we still have delegates coming in, some for the first time, and . . ."

"Well, it's fortunate for me that you're here. This evening, along with other conference delegates, I saw a performance by an extraordinary Swedish dancer. His name is Björn Nilsson. Mister Nilsson would like to be an observer for the music and dance programme. If we have space."

Kimiko opened her loose-leaf binder. "Yes. We do still have a few places. A *Swedish* dancer, you said? That's good. There are very few observers signed up from our host country. Please, can you spell the man's name?"

Mister Daniels Fights Himself to a Draw

Theddo took a long hot shower, then put on one of his silk sleepshirts and climbed into bed. After brooding for a while about "that poor boy," "fucking Axelsson," and what one does to get what one needs, he fell into a dreamless sleep. Which was interrupted, some hours later, by an unfamiliar ring. He shook himself awake and picked up the phone receiver.

"Yeah, Daniels."

"Good morning, Mister Daniels. We are sorry to disturb you so early in the day, but we have a young man here at the concierge desk. He says you are expecting him."

"He says? *Who* says . . . Oh yes . . . is it a . . . Mister Nilsson?"

"Yes sir, that is right. Do you wish to speak with him?"

"Yes. No, that won't be necessary. I have some papers to give him before . . . before his train leaves. He has an early train. Just send him up."

Björn's Blake-angel face, under its thatch of choppy hair, looked frightened and anxious.

"I am sorry, Thedd-doh . . . I did not know where to . . . did not know what . . ." His eyes filled up.

"It's all right, Björn. Please . . . come in."

He walked past Theddo, slowly, carefully, limping slightly. He went to the window, drew the curtain to one side, looked out at the ferry slip across the road. His voice was almost a whisper.

"Over there. That is where you first saw me. Where I first saw you.

I waved . . ." He started to sob, still not turning around, his shoulders shaking. Theddo closed the door and, intensely aware that they were alone in his room, was afraid to move.

"Björn, what's wrong? What has happened?"

Björn gripped the windowsill so hard that his knuckles turned a bloodless white. His voice was still barely audible.

"He. Balti. Thinks you are my lover. He thinks this also of Stig Hanssons, who is my friend, and was, at one time, a very short time, my lover. He, Balti, has beat me and put me out in the street." He then turned around, but still did not look directly at Theddo. Eyes downcast, he removed his boots, his jeans, his shirt. His gold nipple-ring glinted in the light from a bedside lamp.

Apart from the odd shiner or split lip, Theddo had not seen heavily bruised white skin before, even though he had, on a few defensive teenaged occasions, done some of the bruising. Naked, Björn turned again to face the window. His buttocks and thighs were covered in purple-blue blotches and striped with welts and dried blood. Theddo, horrified, remained motionless, near to the door of his room. He recognised what he was feeling. Fear. Why fear? *He* was not the one who had been brutalised. What was he afraid of? Of course, he quickly understood. He was afraid of being set up, of being held responsible. Afraid of being busted in Stockholm for beating a white boy.

"Black Civil Rights Leader Arrested in Sweden for Attack on White Boy Prostitute." (The tabloids would not say dancer. They would say prostitute. As Theddo would have said, had he not seen Björn dance.)

"Put your clothes on, Björn. Now please." Björn gathered his clothes, and did as he was told.

"The boots as well. Please."

Leaning against the wall, Björn pulled on his boots, his fancy watch catching the light, as the nipple ring had done. Once dressed, he walked to the door. Then, as under control as a teenager who'd just had the shit beaten out of him could be, or at least look, he put his open hand on Theddo's chest. Instantly, reflexively, Theddo pulled back from the touch. As quickly, Björn withdrew the hand, placing it on his own chest.

"I am sorry. I should not have come. I did not mean to cause you . . . any difficulty."

Theddo still stood motionless, arms at his sides.

"It's all right. I understand. You have not caused me any difficulty. I am . . . truly sorry that this . . . *business* has happened to *you*. There isn't really . . . anything I can do. I . . ."

"I know. I see this. I think, *thought* . . . never mind."

"You should not go back there. Is there someplace else you can go?"

"Yes. I can go to my friend Per . . ."

"Then do that. Please, please go to that place, to any other place. Axelsson is a pig, he . . ."

"He is not always like this. Not always pig. He can be very sweet, he can . . ."

Theddo opened the door before he knew he was doing so. His voice was clear and businesslike.

"I don't want to discuss him, Björn. He is not anyone I wish to know. Do whatever you think best. For the moment, I believe it will help if you see the music and dance programme. I *have* registered you. I think you will find it worthwhile."

"Yes, I plan to attend. Thank you very much." He quickly hugged the rigid Theddo, then left the room, running down the hall and through a door marked "Trappor/Stairs."

Theddo walked to the window. After some minutes Björn emerged in front of the hotel. It was just before dawn. There was not much traffic—a few cars, trucks, buses. Björn crossed the road to the ferry dock. He leaned against an iron grille, alongside a lamp-post, facing the water. After a moment, he turned and looked up. Theddo sharply drew the curtains closed.

Fortunately, there would be no speeches given until day four of the five-day conference. Having not slept more than two hours before Björn came to his room, and not at all afterwards, Theddo was a leaden lump and not worth much as a contributor, let alone a speechmaker. After years of work, he did have what he called his grace-and-charm hologram, and he sent this hollow-centred but well-informed and pleasant copy of himself out among those he encountered on day one of the conference.

He wanted to talk with Oliver about events of the previous evening, but knew he should wait until a more appropriate time—not to mention one when he was more coherent. Which was what he said when, as promised, they saw each other during the morning coffee-cluster outside the primary conference site, the Winter Garden Room of the hotel. Oliver looked at him, somewhat gravely, Theddo thought, and nodded.

"Of course, my friend. Tell me when, and we will make the time. Are you all right?"

"Been better. Not enough sleep," he smiled feebly. Then, concerned that Oliver would read something bacchanalian into his words, he added, "Stayed up all night thinking about things. Can't do that anymore. Not as young as I used to be."

"None of us are, my dear. Don't worry. This starts peaceably. Housekeeping and boilerplate."

There were welcoming speeches, after which the various delegates hived off into an assortment of small rooms for workshops. Each workshop leader would be reporting to all the attendees in a plenary on the fifth day.

As usual, Theddo's workshop was on making linkages between and among those in the African Diaspora. His contribution was reflexive, and only occasional. Being a long-time worker in this area, some of his statements did stimulate discussion. Oliver, as workshop leader, was his usual dynamic self. This was, for the sleep-deprived Theddo, a helpful relief.

Outside the workshop setting, he avoided significant contact with his colleagues, including Oliver and Vuyo, claiming he needed to work on his speech. Mostly he stayed in his room, eating insanely expensive room-service food and demolishing both the beer and snack components of his mini-bar. And thinking about Björn.

"My first name rhymes with yearn," he had said. Theddo was not yearning. In fact, seeing the savagery of the young man's relationship with Axelsson had sickened the desire out of him. What he felt was anger. Much of it was directed at himself, at "me and my damn closet!" Björn was in trouble. He had come to him for help and he, Theddo, had gone stone cold on him, withdrawing into self-protection, as he had since his teens.

"Dammit!" he shouted, pointing an angry finger at the ormolu table lamp, "I *have* to be careful! I head a large successful organisation. The

Inter-African Alliance has been a going concern for thirty years . . . all kinds of black American organisations have gone bankrupt, or lost their relevance, but InterAfrA is alive an' well!" He gulped a swig from his bottle of Swedish beer. "Brothers just don't like homosexuals! Lots of white folks don' either, but I don't care what-all *they* think! InterAfrA is run by, for and with black people. And they don't like faggots. Black women probably don' mind, but black *men* don' like fags." He pointed at himself in the mirror.

"An', you, Mister Daniels, are a fag. A big black closeted fag."

He beat up on himself in this fashion for three days, and when he wasn't doing that, he worked on his speech. He worked *hard* on his speech. It was as though one Theddo was shouting "faggot!" and another Theddo was saying "Get out of my face! I am doing useful work here, you chickenshit homophobe!"

What Have We Got?

A Speech by Theodore "Theddo" Daniels to the World in Colour *Conference, Stockholm, Sweden, 25 November 1977*

Oh my! Look at *us!* So many people, from so many places. So many languages—and thank you to the translators in the booth for translating mine—so many hues. Rich and variegated hues of clothing, and of skin. I cannot speak for all of you, which is fine, as each delegate here will do this most ably. I will try to speak for and about my own group. Black people of the African Diaspora.

So, what have we got in 1977, we of African heritage? After thousands of years on Earth, including hundreds of those years in varying sorts of enslavement and servitude, *what* have we achieved? Here. Now. More than *two-thirds* through this *twentieth century.* What *exactly* have we got?

Well, we've got this conference. Oh yes, we've got ourselves another conference. We've got an expenses-paid trip to a very expensive hotel, in a very expensive city. In a country full of gracious and hospitable *very white people!* And I now wish to thank our hosts here in Sweden for recognizing that "white" is *one* of *many* colours, and for wanting to *exchange* with the *other colours* and *peoples* in the *world* that we *share. Tack så mycket, Sverige;* thank you so much, Sweden!

Now, back to our expenses. For most of us, these expenses are being paid out of the coffers of *our own* organisations! Money that could have been used to provide necessities for those we represent.

Necessities such as college tuition and scholarships for our young people. Literacy programs, food for new mothers, medical expenses in those countries, *amazingly* including *my own very rich country*, which do *not* have a *national health plan* for *all* citizens. Our expense money could also have been spent on *political* drives—not just for *voters*, though we know that many black people, who are finally *allowed* to vote, do not bother to do so. Why not? Because they believe they will only get a rotation of the same old, same old. Only a change of white men, chosen from among the same small group of white men! In fairness, some few of those white men, from within that small group, are actually doing a halfway decent job of remembering, much of the time, to work for *all* of those they've been chosen to govern.

That said, we, Americans of the African Diaspora, want, and need, and have a right to—indeed *must have*—candidates, politicians, and chief executives chosen *from among our own people!*

Oh yes, we now *do* get a smattering of black men and, more recently, black *women*. But the numbers, in white-majority cultures, are tiny tokens, relative to *our* numbers and our needs after years of being kept out and kept down. And even those elected Black, Hispanic, Native-American and Asian officials, more often than not, learn going along to get along. They learn to "think white."

And, in the countries represented here where virtually *all* the people are of non-Caucasian heritage, what have we got *there?* Too often, we've got people who've never had power before, and are dazzled by it, fearful of losing it, fearful of going back to where they came from, down with the poor folks in the street. So they hoard their power, hide their money, buy as many fancy things, and fancy people, as they can, and are themselves bought and sold by those with more money and power than they. Precisely what our former masters always did, and still do, *with* and *to* their *own* people. If it is right for them, our former masters, surely it is right for us too. Is that not equality?

Well, yeah, it is a *kind* of equality. The *wrong* equality. A greedy, hierarchical equality where all in power abuse power equally. That equality continues keeping most people down—people of *all* colours, in fact—though the ones farthest down have farther to travel to get the hell up.

We are, many of us, genuinely committed. Not just in words, but in daily deeds done, and in yearly written promises to both governments and private supporters—as well as to ourselves. Committed to making sure we move forward from old and destructive, corrupt and corrupting privilege games. And we are committed to making sure the money we have is there to assist in providing aid and advancement to our people. Of course, there is never *enough* money. Certainly not in the U.S., where most people remain afraid of being called socialist, or even *liberal.*

So then, *what* are we doing spending much-needed money bringing our fine many-coloured selves to yet another conference? What do we expect to get here that we do not yet have? In order to give you at least this one person's opinion—I ask you first to look at what we *have* got now.

Cultural. Exchange. For years, I have been actively working for international cultural exchange. Particularly, as it is what I know best, as it is what I *am*, exchanges among those of the African Diaspora. That is the mandate of the organisation I represent, InterAfrA, the Inter-African Alliance.

As I look around at this group, many of whom have become friends, invaluable colleagues and co-activists, I see people from all over the world. I see Africans, Black Americans, Latinos and Latinas, people from every part of Asia, from Polynesia, Micronesia, Melanesia. I see descendants of First Nations—people who were named Indians by white folks with no sense of direction. People who have lived in the U.S. and Canada since long before the arrival of the Europeans whose descendants now run the U.S. and Canada. These early Europeans radically reduced First Nations populations through murder and disease. Of those First Nations peoples who remain, there are social warriors and healers at this conference.

I see Ainu from Japan, Sami from Norway, Aboriginal people from Australia, and Maori from New Zealand. Kurds from Turkey and Iraq. People from all over the Arab world, including Palestinians without a Palestine. Black and Yemenite Jews from Israel. Turkish guest-workers who have seen violence and death at the hands of neo-Nazis. Armenians whose ancestors suffered genocide at the hands of Ottoman Turks. There may be others here that I have failed to mention, but with whom I fully align in solidarity. We are, indeed, a *seriously* multicultural group. And, as we always do, we are exchanging!

With each other! It is, as ever, a joy to do this. It is also useful to exchange both information and assistance, so that we won't keep on inventing the same wheel, which will then roll around and around.

Those few with true power, most of whom are quite rich, *and* quite careful not to get their names in the papers, they actually *encourage* these conferences. "Let the children play. Give them bread and circuses, rice and circuses, tortillas and circuses, injera and circuses. Let them play among themselves, feeling strong and proud and productive. And, while the children play, *we*, the money-holders, with our Tri-Lateral Commissions, Clubs of Rome, Bohemian Groves, and all those other "Hadacol" names—wc *haddu* call it *somethin'*—who own the elected leaders, continue to keep the power of the world in our own hands."

Well, we, who are not children at all, have begun to *see* you! Both the *elected* leaders who talk the talk but don't walk the walk—hell, they *don't* walk *at all* when a poorer person can *drive* them, and the *un-elected* powers who work the puppet-heads of those leaders. We don't know all their names, but wc know their style and we recognise their banking-centred events as the meeting places, the *international conferences* where the *real* work gets done because the *real calls* can be made, the calls that bring immediate gratification to those few who run the world.

And we are here, today, together, to tell those secretive hoarders of power, that, while we love the *beauty* and *talent* of our cultures, we are *not* your *theme park!* We are *not* your pancosmic, polyglot Disneyland! We are not an international coalition of strange music and interesting costumes!

It is time, it is *past* time, for *us* to *exchange* with *you!* As equals! With an equal place at your overt and covert tables. With money and power being a key component of what it is we are sharing.

So, while we will meet always with each other—to exchange, to help, to support, we must also pledge to seek out these shadowy people. Then we must call them out. By name. In great numbers.

Some of these folks are like vampires. They cannot live and suck blood in bright light. We must pledge to shed that light! To show up at those conferences, and in front of those buildings! To demand a seat at those tables, on *behalf* of those *we represent*, those who are *like us!* Those who *are* us! If we do not pledge, in writing, in words, in *actions*, to do this, all we can hope for is a bigger circus, a bigger circle in which we go around and around. I am *dizzy*, dizzy, my friends and colleagues, my brothers and sisters, from going around and around. I must, *we* must, all of us, go *forward! Forward! Forward!*"

Exhausted, he looked out into the vast conference room. The applause was strong and long-lasting. Oliver was smiling at him. He left the dais, moved through the group, receiving praise, exchanging business cards and promises. The elevator carried him to his room on the seventh floor, where he opened the mini-fridge, drank two bottles of Ramlösa mineral water and then, after removing his clothes, slept until his wake-up call at eight the next morning.

He was looking for Oliver and found Björn. More accurately, Björn found him, in the pre-workshop cluster outside the Winter Garden Room. He approached from behind, spoke softly.

"Thedd-doh?"

"Hello, Björn."

"I heard your speech yesterday. It was fanTAHstic!"

"Thank you. It was a lot of English. Did you understand all of it?"

"Yes. I had also Swedish earphones, but my English is pretty much good anyway. I liked much the part about true equality and vampires. . . . White people can have white vampires too, you know."

"Yes, I have always known this."

"Me too. Always. Can we have a drink? I can buy my own."

The open longing, the earnest innocence in Björn's face leaned out to Theddo, entered him.

"Buying drinks isn't the problem, Björn. I have a workshop to go to. In about fifteen minutes."

"I see. I went yesterday to the music and dance workshop. Before your speech. There was more workshop, but I left to hear you speak. The music and the dancers of the workshop were, much of them, very fine! I meet and talk with some and perhaps we make dances together. I go back tonight to the workshop. Thank you again so very much for my ticket. Could we, perhaps, meet after your workshop and before mine? I really do need to speak with you. I promise to not make problems."

Theddo looked at the schedule at the top of his sheaf of papers.

"Eighteen hundred hours? That's six o'clock, yes?"

"Yes."

"Well, I could meet you at six. My workshop ends at five and yours begins at seven."

"*Tack*. Thank you. Very much." He smiled, for the first time in the conversation, then turned and did his dancer's dash out of the lobby and into the street.

Theddo thought of inviting Oliver and Vuyo to join them. Of course, whatever Björn wished to tell him would be personal, so he allowed his feelings, and his sense of fairness, to overrule his paranoia.

Björn was already in the bar, drinking a vodka and tonic. Theddo ordered a beer. For moments, they were silent.

"Well, you asked for the meeting" was neither appropriate nor what Theddo wished to say. What *did* he wish to say? Finally, he thought of something that was, if not wished-for, at least serviceable.

"Are you living at your friend's?"

"At Per's? Yes, for now. I cannot stay there long. Per lives with a man who is now away, but will soon be coming home. I shall need to . . . find somewhere else. I will probably go for a time to my mother's. In Gotland."

"You won't go back to Axelsson's, will you? I mean, it is, of course, your decision, but I . . ."

"No. That is finished. I will never go back. There *is* a problem. I lived at Balti's almost one year. When I left, it was very angry, very fast. Balti has my clothes and other of my possessions. He says he bought most of them for me, including my clothes, which is only a little bit true, most clothings I already had from before, but he will not let me come there to get these things, *my* things. Funny, this Georg Jensen watch he *did* give me and the things he will not return he mostly did not."

Björn's story was draining all joy from Theddo. Joy he had felt in giving his speech, and in the response to it. We both live most fully and most productively in front of an audience, he thought. He had not linked the two of them in that way before. He had seen his speech as part of his work. But, as he listened to this recently battered boy who was fighting for his place in the world, he saw them as even more alike than he had thought. No man had ever supported him. He had made his own way, made his own luck, his own place. Yet, like Björn, his private life and public gifts and work were in conflict, and always had been.

"He should return your things," Theddo said, thinking, Well, Mister Daniels, yours is certainly a piddlyassed little contribution.

"Yes, Thedd-doh, but I cannot make him do this. It will come back on me. He tells me this. He tells me if I make trouble for him, he will make it so that I am arrested as t'ief and whore. He has friends who are powerful."

As do we all, Theddo thought.

The thought transferred itself to Björn.

"Do you know anyone who could make Balti give me back my things? These jeans are Per's. Per is shorter than I am. And more fat in the *röva*—in the back-end. The pants are bagging and you can see my ankles." He held out one long leg.

"Yes, I see. You should have your things back. Perhaps if you offered to exchange the watch . . ."

Björn, horrified, wrapped a large slim hand around the watch as if it were his infant child.

"No! I love this watch! It was a gift! Is a gift not belonging to the person it gives to?!"

"Yes, Björn, a gift should belong to the receiver. It would with a normal person . . . but I think your Mister Axelsson . . ."

"Yes! You are right! Baltasar is not normal. He is, how you say, *saddist*. He likes hurting people. In body, in mind, in heart . . ."

"Easy. Don't shout. I do understand your feelings. It is wrong that this has happened to you. Let me . . . think about it a bit, all right? I will not have *anything* to do with Mister Axelsson, you understand, but perhaps I can think of something *you* might do."

"Oh, I would be so grateful. I am so sorry to bring you these problems . . ."

"Don't worry. People bring me problems all the time. Problems are my job. And I like you and want to see you happy."

"Me too, I want to be happy. And I like you too. Very much. From first moment."

"Thank you."

"Did you like me too? From first moment?"

Theddo couldn't help laughing "Yes, Björn. I liked you from the first moment."

"When do you leave Sweden, Thedd-doh?"

"Tomorrow is the last day of the conference. I will leave the following day, in the afternoon."

"For America?"

"Yes, for America. For Washington, D.C., where I live."

"Washington? Is that not where the American president lives?"

"Mm hm."

"Do you know him, the American president?"

"Mister Carter? No, I do not know him. We have met. We don't hang out."

"But you have met him. This is because you are important, yes?"

Theddo laughed again. He was enjoying this conversation more than the one about Axelsson, and felt only slightly guilty about that.

"Not really, Björn. I met Carter because *the work I'm doing* is important. And because if they don't meet with some coloured folk every now and again, it makes the government look even worse than it is."

And he laughed again. Björn finished his drink, also laughing.

"Could we have dinner together, after my dance workshop. I could ask Luz, a girl dancer from my workshop, if you do not wish only me to be there."

Theddo, who wished very much for only Björn to be there, was touched by his thoughtfulness.

"It would be lovely to have dinner with you. And Miss Luz does not need to be there. Here, take this folder of papers. When you finish your workshop, go to the front desk and ask them to ring my room. I will leave word that I'm expecting you to deliver some papers. We can have dinner quietly, in the room. Would that be all right?"

"Oh yes! I will like this very much!"

"Me too. Now go, or you will be late to your workshop."

Theddo asked for a phone and rang Oliver Gwangwe's room. He asked Oliver to meet him in the bar. Without Vuyo.

Mister Daniels Receives

Björn removed his shirt and asked for total darkness.

"Please, Thedd-doh. I am ashamed of my marks. I do not want them, my marks, to be with us. Please. I want to give to you. Giving to you will make me very happy. But I hate my marks. Can you make black the room? Can you do that? Please?"

So Theddo made black the room, and, in that blackness, Björn gave to him. Björn gave—hands and mouth, tongue and whisper, breath and bone—and Theddo, believing himself the recipient of a head-to-toe, inch-by-inch benedictive miracle, received.

Björn was clearly pleased with this new and unfamiliar companion. Nonetheless, the giver determinedly would not be given *to*. ("No. Just let me give to you. Until my marks are gone, I want only to give. And only to you.") Björn then asked if he could sleep in Theddo's arms.

"And where would you like to do this? In the hall? In the street? In the enormous Winter Garden Room of the Grand Hotel? Any location that works for you is just fine with me!"

"Really? Do you mean this?"

"No, Little Yearning Björn. I am joking . . . but it *is* the way I feel."

"How do you feel? Tell me?"

"I feel . . . full of joy. And love."

"Love for *me?*"

"Mm hm."

"Did you feel love from the beginning, from when you saw me?"

Theddo, for all the bliss of his body, felt his mind go on alert.

"Not exactly. As I said in the bar, I *liked* you when I first saw you. Felt something special about you. Something I . . . do not fully understand, and am . . . not really prepared to explain at this moment. I will try to find the words . . . at some point. But, at this moment, it is difficult for me to speak. I know only that you have been so . . . tender, so *generous* with me this evening . . . you have made me happy, very happy. So, to the extent that I understand love, I feel love."

Björn sat on the edge of the bed. He put his hand on Theddo's knee.

"Would you want to stay here? In Stockholm? With me?"

Theddo sat up, pulling his bare knees to his chest.

"Of course. I would *want to*, Björn. I would *very much* want to. But of course, I cannot. You heard my speech to the conference. My home, my work, is in America."

Björn nodded, rested his head on Theddo's knees.

"Ya, I knew for pretty sure that you would say this. I am still happy that you would *want* to." He sat up, replicating Theddo's knees-to-chest position, smiling.

"I would like also for *you* to know something. Even if . . . if we never see each other again, that I would want this too. To stay together with you here in Stockholm. I would want this very much."

Theddo saw the tears start. He looked down, unable to deal with it.

"Please Thedd-doh. It is fine. I am not crying for sadness. I am crying only a little, and it is for feelings of caring for you. May I do one thing?"

"What is that?"

"May I sleep here? Not in the street or in the Winter Garden Room. Just here, in this room, in your arms. Just for tonight?"

"I will have to turn a light on, to get ready for bed."

"Yes. I understand. I can go in the dark to the toilet. I see in the dark. Like a kangaroo, somebody once told me. Then, when I come back, I will get under the duvet in the dark, and wait for you in the bed. And when you have washed, you can come to bed and hold me."

Theddo smiled. "You have this all arranged, have you?"

"No not arranged. I just propose a way for me to stay in the dark and also stay with you, yes? What I want most of all is to sleep in your arms and for you to hold me."

It seemed so small—and so touching a thing to want.

"All right, Little Björn, I think we can do this. I would actually like very much to do this."

"Little Björn. Do you know how to say 'little' in Swedish?"

"No."

"*Lille.* You say '*Lille.*'"

"*Lille.*"

Mister Axelsson Receives

Despite a number of mostly German or Japanese tourists in the narrow streets of the Old Town, business had been slow, so Baltasar Axelsson decided to close his shop and see who was new and pretty at the Emerald Pub.

He had just locked the latticed iron grille when he saw two enormous men running towards him. They were dressed entirely in black leather, as was he, as he always was. The only difference was that the two behemoths also wore black gloves and their faces were, except for eye and mouth holes, completely covered by black leather zip-up masks.

They were on Axelsson quickly. One, holding him by the neck, pushed his face, gently but firmly into the grillework. The other, to his amazement, unzipped and pulled down his pants. While one man stood watch, the one who had pants-ed him then threw him across a bent knee. The Watcher, still watching, held Axelsson's head down, facing the ground. The other man, having produced some sort of flat wooden object, proceeded to beat Mister Axelsson's bottom. Repeatedly and very hard.

As this was happening in dusky but quite clear light, with the streets full of people, and as he was yelping like an outraged Pomeranian, the stunned and smarting Axelsson did not understand why no one came to his aid.

There were two primary reasons.

1. Those who actually knew him did not particularly like him, and retreated in see-no-evil amusement.

2. Most passers-by, who did not know him at all, saw three men in leather and assumed it was some sort of Scandinavian S&M Street Theatre, and certainly not anything with which they should interfere.

Baltasar Axelsson's spanking lasted for little more than a minute (though it seemed considerably longer to *him*). He was then dropped onto the ground and the two assailants took off down the street and onto a T-Bana subway train.

Given a week to think about what had happened, Axelsson, who had never been on the *receiving* end of a paddling, was surprised to note that he found the experience, however painful, not uninteresting.

So it was with mixed feelings that he responded to what he assumed was the same two brutes waiting outside his apartment building late one night. Before he could decide exactly what he felt about it being after dark, and at his home, one man shoved a gun-barrel into his side and ordered him, in an unfamiliar accent, to "Just open the door, in silence, and you will not be hurt." He did as he was told.

Once inside the apartment, the man who was not toting a gun (or at least not using one on *him*) asked, in the same sort of accent as Gunso, "Where are Björn Nilsson's things please?"

"Björn? My God! Did *Björn* send you?"

"That is not your concern. Just get his things. Now!"

He did so. The clothes, knick-knacks and comic books of Björn Nilsson were placed in a green garbage bag, under the eyehole-scrutiny of the two large leatherfaces. When this was done, No-Gun said, "Right. Now. You are in no way to harm Mister Nilsson. Not at all. Not at any time. Or we, or others of our group will be back and it will be worse."

"Worse than spanking?" Baltasar inquired. He tried to smile, but he'd lost control of his mouth. His lower lip jerked twice to the right, and his nose twitched repeatedly like a cocaine-seeking hamster.

"No. Worse then this," the man replied before drawing back his fist and then punching Baltasar Axelsson full in the face, breaking his nose, sending a searing, blinding pain into his brain, spewing blood all over the Aubusson rug.

With leather gloves and masks in a yellow plastic shopping bag, the Mpumelelo twins, Jonas and Rupert, ran laughing towards the

T-Centrallen train station, throwing the charcoal grey water pistol from one to the other, taking turns shooting water into each other's mouth. High-fiving, African toy-toy dancing, exclaiming "yes!" in Xhosa, like the nineteen-year-olds they were, they passed the department stores, they wove back and forth across the wide boulevard until, breathless and still laughing, they stopped to lean on the concrete railing of an overpass.

Speaking Xhosa, the twins agreed that it had been good to punch a white man in the face. A white man who hurt boys. It would have been better if this white man had been Fredrik Van der Meulen, the Afrikaner man who had hurt black Soweto boys. The white man, now benignly dead of old age, who had hurt *them*. This was, Rupert said, *definitely* the next best thing!

It was sad as well, Jonas said. Sad that they had to do this beating and punching in Stockholm. Except for the man Doctor Gwangwe had sent them to punish, they actually liked the Swedes they'd met—particularly those at the *World in Colour* performers' workshops. And the Swedes were clearly friendlier to black people than most white South Africans (except for a few journalists and those in the ANC underground). Friendlier, for that matter, than the English white people in Brixton, where they worked for Oliver Gwangwe, doing dance workshops and "anything or anyone else that needed being done." Among black people in Brixton, they were known as "the Dee*Gee* Dee*Bee*," or "Doctor G's Dancing Bodyguards."

Doctor G. had done many good things for the black people of London. And he said this man Axelsson had to be punished. Said that he had physically hurt the boy dancer, Nilsson. This Axelsson, Doctor G. said, had also stolen some of Nilsson's belongings. The Mpumelelos had met Nilsson when they danced at the hotel. He was friendly, asking questions about African rhythms, and saying enthusiastic things about their dance. Doctor Gwangwe, who had seen Nilsson dance, said he was very talented.

Rupert said he wished they could stay in Sweden for a while. Jonas said that was impossible, that they had air-tickets for London. Doctor Gwangwe needed them. Doctor Gwangwe supported them. Doctor Gwangwe was a great man. Rupert agreed. The Mpumelelo twins got their suitcases out of a locker in the T-Centrallen station and took the shuttle bus to the airport.

Theddo had been back in Washington for three days, and was stretched out on the sofa in his living room drinking from an ice-cold bottle of Devon's Jamaican ginger beer (and thinking about Björn), when the phone rang.

"HeLLO, My friend!"

"Hello, Oliver."

"Did you have a good flight?"

"Yeah. Thanks. I'm still jet lagged . . . and a bit wistful, but otherwise all is well."

"It is better than that. The deed we discussed has been done. Rather creatively, I think. You want the details?"

"Please."

Everything seemed to have gone the way the two old friends had planned, with fairly wild nuances added by the Mpumelelo twins. Concerned about repercussions, Theddo hoped Björn had left, as he'd said he would, for his mother's in Gotland, on the island of Fårö. Björn's mother had married and divorced a second husband, and did not have the name Nilsson. In any case, Axelsson was unlikely to follow him to Fårö. It was, Björn said, a close and quiet island community, where a "Stockholm leatherman with head like an egg would really stick himself out."

Theddo had the Fårö telephone number, and had given Björn his home address and phone number. They had been sitting side-by-side on the oversized sofa in the Stockholm hotel room. After a second night of gifts in the dark, Björn wanted to ride with Theddo to the airport. This was, of course, impossible. Theddo, seeing a face full of hurt feelings, said, "Look, conference people are going to the airport in groups. It has all been arranged. It would be . . . difficult for me to explain the presence of a beautiful young Swedish man who was accompanying me."

"No. It would not be *difficult*. You just say, 'This is Björn. I asked him to come with me to the airport because I love him,'" Theddo laughed, kissing Björn in the centre of his forehead.

"Björn . . . you know I can't say that."

"No. I do not know this. Do you not have gay leaders in America?"

"Not very many . . . among my people. American acceptance is not like European . . . and black people have . . . other fights."

"You have also *this* one, I think. God! It is 1977! You should stay here, not live in American cupboard."

"Closet."

"Yes, that."

The discussion went round and round, as it always would. Björn did not want to fight with his new friend. Finally, he said he accepted that things had to be different with an American, with a black American. Especially when that black American, that so special new friend, had promised to get his things back from Axelsson.

He too made a promise; he promised he would go home to Fårö for a while.

"Well, if I cannot go with you, I want to go away right now, without eating the room-service food, because I will get too sad and I want you to think of me as happy. Because you make me happy!"

And he hugged Theddo, kissed him all over his face, hugged him again, and ran from the room.

Theddo ached with wanting to follow him, but stood stock-still. He felt abandoned. It was crazy, he thought, shaking his head—feeling abandoned by the boy he would not keep with him.

Two days after the call from Oliver, he got a call from Björn.

"Thedd-doh?"

He knew the voice immediately, that special pronunciation of his name. He was startled by the joy he felt. Like a teenager who had been waiting by the phone.

"Yes?" he said.

"Hallo! It's Lille Björn! From Stockholm."

Oh, *that* Lille Björn, Theddo thought, amused.

"Yes, I recognise your voice. It is good to hear it. How are you?"

"I am happy! I have heard this terriFICK t'ing! Thedd-doh, did you really beat Balti's ass and break his nose?"

Theddo laughed. "My *goodness*, Lille, of *course* not! How could I do such a thing? I was here, in Washington."

"I did not tell you *when* this happened."

"That's true, you didn't. Did you get your belongings back?"

"Ya! All things! My friend Per says that two *enormous* men pulled down Balti's pants and spanked his ass with a paddle right in front of his shop! In daylight!"

"Well, it was *twilight*, actually."

"Aha! You *do* know! Then you did this! Yes, yes you did! You are brilliant!"

"You are too kind."

"Vah? What?"

"Nothing. I was just teasing. How are you, Björn?"

"I am good. Happy. Like you say, TerriFICK!"

"*Where* are you?"

"As I promise you, I am in Fårö. In Gotland with my family."

"Good. Can you stay there for a while?"

"I can if you come to visit me."

"Oh Lille, I'd love to, but I just got back to Washington. I have tons of work."

"Can you not come for just a few days? It would make me so happy. I miss you."

Theddo booked a flight for a week later.

Far

Getting to the island of Fårö was no simple matter. Theddo flew from Dulles Airport in Washington, D.C., to Sweden's Arlanda Airport. Then came the shuttle to the Central Station and the commuter train to the suburb of Nynäshamn. At Nynäshamn he boarded a ferry to Visby, the medieval walled Island city that was the capital of Gotland. At Visby, cold, foggy and outside the walls of the reputedly exquisite Old City, there was a bus to Fårösund, where he took a damp, bone-cold ten-minute ride on an oversized flat-raft ferry, and was, finally, deposited on Fårö Island. After planes, trains, buses and ferries, plus a seven-hour time change, it was close to two in the morning when Theddo stood, duffel bag in hand, in the cold moist air of a flat and deserted island place.

There was only one tall steel streetlight and Björn was under it, a bright red woollen watchcap pulled over most of his burnished gold punky hair, his neck wrapped and re-wrapped in what appeared to be a hand-knitted very long matching wool scarf.

"Thedd-doh! I am here!" he shouted, vigorously waving a gloved hand, but remaining in his spotlight.

Theddo walked to him—smiling, bemused, looking about.

"Christ, Lille, where are we?"

Björn grinned. "We are in Fårö. *Min hem!* My home. Welcome!" He threw his arms around Theddo, hugging him. Theddo dropped his duffel bag and hugged in return, grateful to share both affection and body heat.

When they broke from their embrace, Björn picked up Theddo's bag saying, "Come. I have my mother's car. They knew you would be late. They are all asleep."

"I don't wonder. A good idea, being asleep."

"You are tired?"

Theddo pressed the back of his hand against Björn's cheek. "Mm hm. Tired and cold. Very glad to see you, Lille, but also very tired."

Björn took hold of the leather-gloved hand, quickly kissing the inside of the palm. "Well, I shall take you soon to your bed, but first I drive you to something you must see. Must see in the moonlight."

It looked like the first night of the world. There, on the beach, in the December air and lit by the moon, only metres from the sounds and smells of the sea, seemingly growing out of the sand, small stones, and patches of snow, were huge prehistoric rock formations. Lumpy, bumpy, and twice as tall as Theddo, their powerful dappled grey faces a mass of stone pustules.

"Good lord! What am I looking at, Lille?"

"*Raukar.* You are looking at *raukar.* They have been here, only here on Fårö, since forever. Tourists from many countries come in many buses to see them. Not so much now, when it is cold."

"And two in the morning."

Björn looked at his Jensen watch. "T'ree. It is now t'ree in the morning. Would you like to see a new dance I make with the *raukar?*"

"More than almost anything in the world, my darling. But not now. Now, I can hardly see at all. Let me first sleep and then I will rejoice to see your dance. All right?"

Björn laughed. "All right. It will be warmer in daylight. And I really need my music anyway. I show you my dance tomorrow. Now I take you to your bed."

As Theddo walked back to the white car, Björn, who was running on ahead, holding his scarf-ends out like blood-red wings, shouted over his shoulder.

"Sorry I ask to dance for you after your long journey! I forget how old you are!"

"Bitch!"

He laughed. "No. Bitch is woman. I am 'bastard.'"

"No. You are bitch," Theddo said, lifting the laughing Björn and swinging him around, watched only by the enormous Elephant-Man faces of the *raukar*, who, having seen it all since forever, were not at all surprised.

"What is your mother expecting? Who did you tell her I am? In your life, I mean," Theddo asked as they drove along the night-darkened little tarmac road.

"I told her you were an important social leader from America, and that we met when I performed at your conference. I lie only a little. Saying *performed,* instead of *observing.* I told her I observed also the other dancers. I told her that you said many good things about my dancing, so I invite you here to see the dance I make with *raukar.* I told her you had to be in Stockholm anyway, for a United Nations business."

"I see. *Is* there a 'United Nations business'?"

"I do not know. There *could* be, yes?"

"Yes. There could be. And . . . where will I sleep?"

"In the shed. It is not really a shed. It *was* a shed. My Uncle Erik, brother to my mother, is a carpenter of houses. He made it into a little *hytt*, with bed and chair and t'ings, for when my Aunt Anne, sister to my mother, and her husband come from Malmö to visit."

"Does it have *heat?*"

"Of course! It has a fireplace. Swedes are used to living with cold and having to make heat. Not like people from tropical places like Washington, D.C. . . . What does D.C. mean?"

"Damn cold."

"It does not!"

"Perhaps you're right. But it isn't *tropical.* Except in the summer, when it can be hot and humid as a jungle. The word used for that time is not *tropical.* It is *disgusting.*"

"Disgusting means it is very unpleasant. Very bad. Yes?"

"Yes."

The converted shed was, Theddo thought, charming. Made entirely of barn wood, with a straw-thatch roof in the tradition of old Fårö houses.

Against one wall was a dark-wood double bed, covered by a fat white duvet. On the tiny table alongside the bed was an oil lamp, which Björn lit with a wooden match. There was a light-wood rocking chair in a corner, a little wooden dresser and an armoire. Moonlight bounced off the criss-crossed squares of thin wire embedded in two double-glazed windows (one on each side of the room). Each window had open wooden shutters and long cream-coloured curtains that may have once been white. In the wall facing the bed was a stone fireplace, with logs, kindling and old newspapers stacked alongside. A black cast-iron pot hung inside the fireplace. There was an assortment of framed prints and photographs on the walls. On the back of the door were a couple of wooden clothes pegs and a wooden rack containing two towels.

"Do you know how to make fire?"

"Rub two stones together?"

"No, with matches and paper and wood."

"Yes, Lille Björn, I know how to make fire."

"Good. You make fire. I will bring washing-water for pot."

Theddo stood in the middle of the cold little room for a moment.

"I love this room," he whispered, though he was alone, "and I love this boy." This moment is a keeper, he thought. I will always see it. He blinked back tears. "Easy . . ." he said softly and set about making a fire.

"Good fire. Fine fire. First-rate damn fire," he mumbled.

Some moments later, his water-bearer arrived with a large pitcher, pouring its contents into the cast-iron pot. It burbled, bubbled, and boiled. Björn removed his boots, and then sat on the edge of the bed, swinging his grey-socked feet back and forth, looking as happy as a kid having a sleepover with a new best friend who was also a football star.

This boy, Theddo thought, this young man, who's been hustling himself since god-knows-when, has, if not *actual* innocence, an extraordinary *will* to innocence. All he needs is an excuse, and he is born again into his virginity.

Well, almost. Björn handed Theddo a small towel, which had been under one of the large towels. "Here, Herr Daniels. Your face towel and soap. You have *tandborshte?*"

"What?"

"Brush for teet'?"

"Yes, of course."

"Good. You should wash face and hands first. And bottom parts last. And brush teet' in the middle. So you can spit in pot."

"Thank you. Sounds like a good plan."

He took the little towel, dipped it into the pot of hot water, wrung it out, washed his hands and face.

"Now teet'."

Theddo dutifully brushed his teeth. And then placed his toothbrush and toothpaste on the mantel.

"Now bottom parts."

"Björn . . ."

"What? You have been travelling all day. Bottom parts have sweat and smell, yes?"

"Probably."

"Well then, take off panting."

"Pants?"

"Ya."

Björn went to the door-rack for a large towel. Returning quickly, he unhooked Theddo's belt and pulled down his jeans. Theddo kicked the jeans across the floor. Björn then fluttered his hands upward. Theddo, understanding the mime, raised his arms above his head. Björn pulled the white turtleneck sweater over his head, threw it on top of the jeans and, moving behind Theddo, pressed himself against his back.

"Are you still cold? I imagine yes you are. I rub you to keep you warm."

"Björn . . ."

"What? You do not like being kept warm?"

"Yes. I like it."

"Good."

Björn took the towel, dipped it in the water, and reaching around from behind, washed the front section of Theddo's bottom parts. He then resumed stroking the back section of these bottom parts. Theddo turned to face him.

"Björn . . .?"

"Yes?"

"Nothing. Not a thing."

They kissed, fully. The moment that Theddo had known he would remember became an hour—a pre-dawn hour in a wooden one-room house on a prehistoric Swedish island.

When Björn's gifts stopped being given, it was still night. In the light from the oil lamp, Theddo saw that the Axelsson scars were now all healed and mostly gone. He sought to reciprocate as giver, but was rebuffed, because "I want only that I give to you, because you are first-time guest in my home, and I am so very happy you are here."

Feeling too loved to argue, Theddo accepted this, and, shortly there-after, fell into contented sleep. Some time later, he groggily awakened because Björn, curled up fetally, loosely fisted hands clinging to Theddo's thermal shirt, was talking in his sleep. "Far," he said, "far."

"Yes," Theddo agreed, "far . . . a long journey. But I'm here now." He gently brushed Björn's hair away from his forehead. "Far," Björn said again, still in deep sleep.

Sometime later, Theddo felt his shoulder being shaken.

"Thedd-doh?"

"Mmm?"

"You sleep. I must be in my own bed when everyone gets up for morning. At breakfast, I will come wake you to come and meet my mother and the childrens."

"Thanks, Lille."

"You love me?"

"Mm. Yes."

Theddo felt his neck being kissed, and then felt the absence of the warm body that had been pressed around him, the long warm arm that had encircled his chest. He sank again into sleep, noting, as he separated from awakeness, that even with the smell of sex and body-heat, the room's strongest scents were of cedar and cinnamon wood.

It took a moment for Theddo to understand where he was. Then he saw Björn standing in the doorway holding a pale-yellow ceramic coffeepot and a white cup. He sat up, modestly pulling the duvet around him, smiling.

"Coffee?"

"Ya! Coffee. Is black okay?"

"You're asking *me* if black is okay?"

"No, I mean . . ."

"I'm teasing, Lille. Black is perfect. Thank you."

He gulped the hot and welcome first cup and Björn poured a second. Theddo noted his attire. Black corduroy pants, thin wine-red belt, pale blue cotton turtleneck sweater, white running shoes, and heavy white socks. He looked like a fresh-scrubbed schoolboy. How long, he wondered, *had* Björn gone to school? Had it been on Fårö Island? Had he been a closeted kid, as he, Theddo, had been, or an openly queer kid, as more and more young people had begun to be? At least urban white kids. He wondered if openly queer kids were only possible in cities, and not on prehistoric islands looked down on by . . . what were those things? Did he dream those enormous lumpy-faced grey stone men?

"What were . . . did we see . . . huge rock men?"

Björn laughed. It was his turn for teasing.

"Men? Rock men? You have had bad dream. Bad Swedish Viking monster dream!" Then he laughed, put down the coffeepot, took away the cup and hugged Theddo.

"*Raukar*. Yes, we saw *raukar*. Last night. And today we will all go there and I will show you my *raukar*-dance. But first you must dress and come to the house. Dress in warm things, for the beach. My mother has made you a terriFICK breakfast with *pannkakor* and *smor* and *sylt*."

Theddo had no idea what those things were, but if they weren't dead snakes and live bugs he did want to eat them. He was stomach-rumble hungry, having not eaten since the plane trip from Washington. He also wanted to meet Björn's family.

"Right. Thank you for the coffee, Lille. It was good. Strong."

"Swedes make fine coffee."

"Indeed. Now, could you please go to the house and tell them I will be there for my terrific breakfast very quickly, yes?"

"Yes. Are you happy, Thedd-doh?"

"I am."

"You look happy. Sleepy but also happy." And he was away, slamming the door behind him.

The room was warm, with a fresh fire in the fireplace. In the night, illuminated by the moon and an oil-lamp, Theddo had found this room beautiful. In full morning light it was still a pretty room—neat, well made and well appointed. To his surprise, however, it also reminded him a bit too much of the well-tended and well-preserved slave quarters he had seen on a tour of such places in Charleston, South Carolina.

They were waiting for him, as polite and deferential as a remote tribe waiting to be photographed by an anthropologist.

"*Goo Morrronn*, Fru Nilsson!" Theddo said in the best of his limited, conference-based Swedish, having, in the moment, forgotten what he already knew about Björn's mother's name.

The plump and round-faced woman, with two deep dimples and goldy-blonde hair as frizzy as her eldest son's was straight, ran a stream of Swedish at Björn, both of them laughing.

"*Min mor*, my mother, says good morning to you, Herr Daniels, but that she is not Fru Nilsson. My father died when I was baby. My stepfather, who no longer lives with us, was Mister *Lindqvist*. My mother is Fru Lindqvist. And these two, the little ones, are Lisa Lindqvist and Marius Lindqvist."

The Little Lindqvists, auburn-haired with Björn's round blue eyes and their mother's dimpled smile, looked up at the huge dark man before them and, at just about the same moment, said "*Hej!*"

Theddo had noticed the "hej" business during the Stockholm conference. There was something warming in this word, which sounded exactly like the Southern American greeting "hey."

"Hey!" he replied, smiling.

Breakfast was pancakes, butter, jam and coffee. The jam, a golden-orange colour, was new to Theddo, and he loved the taste.

"What is this jam?"

"*Yoortron*."

"Do you know what that is in English?"

"Yes. Cloudberries. Arctic cloudberries."

Both Björn and his mother seemed to take pleasure in Theddo's enthusiastic appetite, nodding at each other and smiling, as Mrs. Lindqvist and Theddo offered each other small phrases in Swedish and English that Björn would translate, thoroughly enjoying his usefulness.

The Little Lindqvists managed to eat their fill without dropping a forkful, even though they did not for one moment take their eyes off the extraordinary creature in their kitchen.

After breakfast, Theddo tried to help with clearing the dishes, but quickly saw he was just underfoot and in the way. At Marius Lindqvist's urging, he joined Björn and the Littles outside, kicking a soccer ball around in the yard. Despite the fact that, as with most Americans in the 1970s, he knew little about soccer, Theddo quickly got the hang of it, and, having the biggest head, knees and feet in the group, played rather well. Then everyone, softly fattened by layers of clothing, piled into Mrs. Lindqvist's car, Björn driving, and headed off to the wintry beach to see the new dance.

The beach, with its enormous sclerodermic rock men, was less of a moonscape in daylight than it had been by night, but was nonetheless unlike any place Theddo'd ever seen. Easter Island by Giacometti.

It was, he noted, certainly damp, but not nearly as cold as Minnesota in December. The winter light was the palest mauve-grey, under a sky speckled with clouds, and above a turbulent dark sea. Theddo, in leather bomber jacket, white turtleneck sweater, jeans and boots, jammed gloved hands into his jacket pockets.

And almost immediately had to unpocket them and put them to use. There was a zigzag flurry of family activity. Mrs. Lindqvist opened the car's trunk, handing Theddo blankets and a picnic basket filled with thermoses, sandwiches and fat cinnamon buns. Björn, removing an enormous black boom-box radio from the recesses of the trunk, turned and shouted something to Marius and Lisa, who ran to take a cluster of cushions from him. Their kiddievoice babble and laughter bounced off the rocks of a small hillock as they arranged the cushions, arguing good-naturedly about placement.

The designated audience each sat on a cushion assigned by Marius, who got to practise his school-English.

"Mister Danielss, you need to sit on the biggest pillow!"

"Thank you. I think."

Following Mrs. Lindqvist's hand gestures, accompanied by the words "Ya, ya, ya," the group huddled together, and she covered them with blankets, folding the ends snugly under their feet as if tucking them in for bed, making Theddo feel, for an amused moment, like an enormous four year old.

He watched as Björn, with total concentration, arranged the boom box and speakers between two large but less face-like rocks, pulling each speaker as far as possible to the left or right of the music machine. This done, he removed his jacket, scarf and gloves and placed them behind the rocks. Then, looking at Theddo, he grinned, winked, pulled the bright red watchcap over to one side, keeping both ears covered.

He knelt down and pressed a button. Within seconds, unfamiliar and elegiac-sounding violin music filled the patch of beach. Björn, between the two rocks, stood stock-still, listening. He then swayed a bit, allowing his upper body, neck and head to follow each extended arm and bare hand, first left, then right. Then he wove himself once around each rock, in time to the violin music, coming to rest again in his original position, hands resting on his thighs, still.

For all Björn's talent, there was something ludicrously earnest about a pale slim boy flailing about on a beach. Theddo looked discreetly at the Lindqvists. They seemed proud and attentive. Theddo decided he was being a City-Snob, insufficiently grateful for this creative merging of art and nature. He modulated his sense of the absurd and gave Björn his full attention.

The music then changed, sharply, loudly, insistently. Hands, or boards pounding in rhythm. Theddo laughed, recognising the music, and the pun.

"We will, we will ROCK YOU!" The Queen anthem, which had been heard all over the U.S. earlier that year, seemed to be sung by gargantuan Swedish rocks. Björn ran and leapt, quickly reaching the largest and most powerfully anthropomorphic of the *raukar*. His dance turned sharply angular, his eyes, as at *Klubb Kul,* simultaneously staring somewhere beyond his audience, and somewhere inside himself. Geometrical arm and leg movements sharply echoed the staccato of the music. Then he wove around the long neck of the rock. This was followed by his climbing and stroking that neck, turning neck into phallus. Björn's intention seemed unmistakable. Furtively, Theddo looked again at Mrs. Lindqvist, who was sipping hot coffee from a plastic cup and beaming at her boychild. This reminded him of a show he'd seen at a Harlem New York high school a few years earlier. It had featured a fifteen-year-old girl dancer who was honouring the late Josephine Baker by doing an incredibly suggestive dance, wearing nothing but a banana-skirt and black bra. Theddo, not knowing quite where to look, had stared self-consciously down at his programme, only to be nudged to attention by the woman sitting next to him. "That's my baby, Mister Daniels!" the woman shouted proudly, before turning to make sure the row behind also had the information.

"That's my baby! Right there! Jonelle Sanders! She's gonna go downtown to Juilliard. Got herself a scholarship!"

As with Jonelle Sanders' mom, a white Swedish mother, who didn't even know she was instructing, was now instructing Theddo to get his mind out of his pants and watch the talent of the dancer. And to join in the pride a family took in that talent. Nodding graciously, he accepted a cup of black coffee, and passed two buns and cups of cocoa to The Littles.

He returned his attention to Björn, who had moved to another, slightly smaller rock. The music also changed; still Queen, it had gone from "We Will Rock You" to the ballad-tempo pride and wistful disappointment of "We Are the Champions." The new rock-partner seemed more feminine, as did Björn's entreating, more balletic movements. He then ran, leaping and tumbling, towards his mother whose face he touched, circling it lovingly with his hands. He did the same with The Littles, and with the startled Theddo (Oh Lord, Theddo thought, he's going to kiss me. When this did not happen, he felt both relieved and disappointed).

Oblivious to his lover's anxiety, Björn dashed back to the "lady-rock" and, climbing its stem, tenderly replicated the face-caressing gesture. He then dropped to the cold sand, bent his knees, and, as if spring-loaded, did one of his gravity-defying high leaps, before crouching down, eyes wary. The harsher percussive tones of "We Will Rock You" began again. Björn, now standing at attention, repeated the earlier geometric arm and leg moves. He was turned away from his audience, facing the largest "male" rock, arms and hands raised in entreaty, angrily shouting something. Theddo could not hear exactly what word or words were being shouted. Then the music stopped, and, kneeling down, arms and head reaching skyward, Björn shouted a single word, four times.

"Far! Far! Far! Far!"

Far. The word he'd murmured to Theddo in his sleep.

"Marius," Theddo asked, "does the word *far* mean anything in Swedish?"

"Ya, Mister Danielss. It means 'father.'"

Theddo looked over at Björn, who was scurrying about, closing down his radio and speakers.

Far. Father, Yes, Theddo thought. He knew that was part of it. How could it not be? He knew, but he hoped. What he hoped for was something more equal. Something that might come with time. Or might not.

When they returned to the house, Mrs. L. heated a large pot of vegetable soup. There was also butter and some supermarket white bread. Björn oven-toasted and buttered about twelve slices.

"Lille," Theddo whispered, "do you think I could have a bit more of that jam from this morning the . . . arctic cloudberry?"

"Ya, sure."

The soup, inexpensive to make, tasty, easy to stretch, reminded Theddo of his childhood, when almost all meals were built from the previous day's food. Each thing was the base for something else. Probably true of everything, he thought, and then laughed. There you go, Mister Daniels. Always on the job! You can offer it up at the next rally. "Everything you do can, *must* become the base for the next thing you do!" Ain' nobody gonna argue with that. It can be true or meaningless. *Perfect* for large gatherings.

"What are you laughing at, Thedd-doh?"

"Nothing, Björn. Just my own self."

"So. My dance. You liked it, yes?"

"Yes. I told you, but am pleased to tell you again. I loved your dance. You have great grace and originality."

"*Tack*. Thank you. Your words mean much to me."

After the late-afternoon meal (lunch? dinner?), Björn went outside to try teaching The Littles how to leap straight up in the air. Theddo watched them from the kitchen window, while Mrs. Lindqvist, with whom he'd periodically communicate in hand signals, loud English and a smattering of semi-ersatz Swedish, watched him.

Having exhausted The Littles who went off to their room to sleep, Björn returned to the kitchen, helping himself to more soup.

"How long can you stay?"

"I must leave tomorrow, Lille."

"*Tomorrow?* That is too soon!"

"I agree. But I'm not supposed to be here at all. I have meetings and commitments. I'm sorry."

That night, Theddo, having built his fire and washed himself, lay in bed looking up at the beamed ceiling, hands cradling the back of his neck, waiting for Björn. Who did not come to him. Finally, he rolled over and went to sleep.

Shortly before first light, he was awakened—being kissed, caressed, given to. It was time, past time, for him to give back, but when he tried, Björn pulled sharply away, saying, "No! Please!" Theddo couldn't see his face, but he sounded frightened—very frightened.

"What is wrong, Björn? I only wanted to . . . to love you, I . . ."

"No. For me that is not love. For me is love when I give to you. When you hold me. When we kiss. All other is . . . is . . . I do not want to speak about it now. Now I want you to hold me. To hold me close, because you are leaving me soon and I want to be able to sleep inside the remember of your holding when you are not here. Please."

"Of course, Lille. Come, I will hold you."

Björn slept. Theddo did not.

The two of them stood waiting for the flat ferry. Björn said again that he had hoped, *expected* that Theddo would be able to stay longer.

"I truly wish I could, Lille. Not just for you . . . although *mostly* for you. I like your family. They have been warm and welcoming to me. But I do have an important meeting. The dates could not be changed. I did try, before I left Washington, but there were too many people involved. I came here because you asked . . . to show you that you mattered to me."

"Then let me come to you. To Washington."

"I would like that . . . but cannot figure out how to do it in a way that . . . won't cause problems."

"For you?"

"Yes. And for InterAfrA. And for *you*. Let me think about it, try to work something out."

Björn's face toughened up, as it had at moments during his dance. "It is all right. I am glad for the time we have had."

"Don't shut me out, Lille. I mean what I say. I will try."

"Okay. My mother gave me this for you. The jam you liked. She makes it herself. The cloudberries grow here."

"Tell her *tack så mycket*, please."

"I will. I also must leave here soon. It is good to be with my family, but I cannot keep making ice-cold dances on the beach! My mother has some pensions and government money, but it is not much. I need to earn my own money, and to send some to her also. She never asks, but I know she needs. And the childrens need also."

"I understand. Can I give you some money for them?"

"Yes."

Not even a pause for breath. Just yes. Yes, of course. Yes, American man with money. Of course you can give money to me for them.

"I will send a cheque when I get back to Washington. I don't have a lot of actual cash, InterAfrA has money, and they take care of my work expenses . . . but I never touch that money for . . . personal matters. This trip, to see you, was from my own money. Can you get more dance work in Stockholm?"

"I don't know. It is hard. Balti went around to many clubs where he is a patron, telling them not to hire me. I will try to find other places."

He will try, Theddo thought. He *will* try. There would not likely be an enormous need in Stockholm for solo dancers. For a solo dancer who's been barred all over town by the slimy sonovabitch who'd once gotten him work. He would, in all likelihood, get the work he was getting when Theddo first saw him. Work gotten on the ferry dock across from the Grand Hotel, along with those other boys and young men. Helpless, sad and full of love, he hugged Björn as hard as he could, then turned and boarded the ferry.

As the early morning outsized raft lazily crossed to Fårösund, Theddo its only passenger, Theddo waved, shouting at the slim and still figure standing on the winter-grassy shore.

"I'll call you, Lille!" he shouted. "As soon as I'm back in Washington! And please, if you leave here, make sure to let me know where you are, Yes?!"

"Ya! Sure!"

Björn turned, ran to his car, gunned the engine, and was off down the hill.

Ya. Sure.

Mister Daniels Takes a Decision
Ydra, Greece, 1995

Theddo watched the tiny yellow-orange cat take off down the hill and then sat heavily on a whitewashed stone step of the Hotel Melissa, lost in thoughts of Björn. Thoughts of love and wonder. Thoughts of impossibility, helplessness and pain. And, as the clear Mediterranean light began to shine through the filmy grey remains of night, he took a decision. The decision meant that he needed to talk to Johnny Reed. If he waited another hour or so, Johnny would be starting his shift at *Sto Kéndro*.

But Johnny was not at *Sto Kéndro*. Thanassi, his employer, said that he'd asked for the day off, that he had something he needed to do.

The "something" Johnny Reed needed to do was to sit on one of Ydra's few tiny spits of sandy beach, up over the hill to the right of the port. Theddo Daniels had, innocently enough, opened up a complex chunk of Johnny's history. Opened up memories of things set aside, things locked away. Things that not even Soula, with her talent for knowing the unspoken, fully knew.

Soula did know that her husband's American past, both historically and in its personal particulars, was complicated for him. She felt, always, that she and Marilena were truly loved, and knew their daughter felt this also. She knew her husband was happy living on the Island. She knew that all would be told when Johnny was ready.

Johnny, staring out at the sea, was *not* ready, but, ready or not, his head was filled with what he'd told Theddo, and with the whole goddamn rest of it!

Some of the Whole Goddamn Rest of It
Los Angeles, 1978

When Johnny returned from the funeral and rally, wearing Uncle Carl's blue jacket, a taxi took him from L.A. Airport to Hillside Hacienda. He opened the burglar's-dream wooden door, dropped his black duffel bag onto the static-riddled "Dynel" Halloween-orange shag carpet and called the ActorFoneWest answering service.

"ActorFone, Kelli Anne speaking, how may I help you?"

"Hi Kelli Anne, it's Johnny Reed. Have I any messages?"

"Oh *yes*, Mister Reed, you have *tons!* Were you away?"

"Yes."

"Well, you coulda used the toll-free. Do you have the toll-free? It's 800 . . ."

"Thanks, Kelli Anne. I *have* the toll-free. I just didn't have time."

"Oh. Were you on location?"

"No. I was at a funeral."

"Oh. I'm so sorry. My *deepest* sympathy. . . . Do you want your messages now, or would you rather call back?"

"No, I'll take 'em now, thanks."

"Right. Okay. Have you got a pen? There really are *lots!*"

There were indeed lots.

Rose Golden called.

Chad, the second assistant director called, with Johnny's new audio-recording time.

Shari, the film's still photographer called, asking him to call ASAP.

Claude Martin called.

His mother called. Twice.

Various magazines, both black and Caucasian, and three supermarket tabloids called. One of them five times.

Dorrie Stockwell called. Four times.

He called Dorrie. She was not in. He called ActorFoneWest again, and left a message for Dorrie to call him. He called Chad's answering service and said he'd be in the studio for his recording call the next day. He called his mother, said he got home safely, said he loved her too, said he'd call again.

He walked across the crackling rug, receiving prickly shocks. He cursed the rug, spraying it, and his clothes, with Static Guard, knowing the carpet would be sparkle-shooting again in less than twenty minutes. He got a bottle of beer from the fridge, opened it, sucked on it twice, lay down on the sofa and fell asleep, waking in the middle of the night to wash the beer and airport food out of his mouth. "Oh, man" he muttered, "You can be woke up by your own breath!"

He stumbled back to the bedroom, watching the rug make minute sparks in the dark. He removed his clothes, hung Uncle Carl's blue jacket in the closet and crawled onto the king-sized bed. Naked, he sprawled on his back under a bright orange bedspread he called Ray Charles Floral, assuming no *sighted* person could possibly have made it ("and even Brother Ray wouldn't want to *touch* the thing").

With his body still on East Coast Time, or maybe it was film-shooting time, he awakened at five in the morning, had a hot shower and brewed a pot of coffee. The bread had turned to doorstops, speckled with petrified blue mould. He threw it out and ate a couple of Multigrain Wheatcrisps, which, he thought, tasted like thinly sliced cartons, and would grow stale and die some time after Keith Richards, cockroaches and those bigassed Hungarian actresses. The phone rang.

"Hey, Reed. I called the minute I heard, but you'd already gone. Want me to come over?"

"Yes, please."

"I'll be there in fifteen. Unless there's traffic in Laurel Canyon . . . in which case I'll be there tomorrow. On my way."

"Thanks, babe."

"Reed?"

"Uh huh."

"Nothing I can say is enough, but I'm really sorry. About your Uncle Charles."

"Carl," he said, but Dorrie'd already hung up.

Half an hour later she stood in the doorway, wrapped in her ancient Burberry trench coat, pale yellow hair loose, long and shiny. They looked into each other's teary eyes. He pulled her inside and they hugged for a long time. When they broke from that, Dorrie looked around, then back at him. Touching his cheek with the palm of her hand, she shook her head.

"Really ugly rug, Reed."

The love they made was less about sex (though the sex was a sweet and full release) than about nearness, warmth and trust. Afterwards, they slept, gently entangled, until the middle of the afternoon. Neither of them spoke of Marty Rachman, who was, in this same time-period, speaking of *them*.

The following day, Johnny was at Westwood Recording, redoing various lines from *Brotherz* ("Some problem with the body-pack mike during the art studio scene at the end of the film. Just a few lines"), when Ramon in the control room said he had a call. The last time he'd had a call while doing audio, it was about Uncle Carl. This time it was Dorrie. At the sound of her voice, he smiled, relieved.

"Hey, Reed."

"Hey yisself, girl. What's happening?"

"There's a party tonight. At Marina Di Martello's house. In Santa Monica. She's a super hostess, and it should be an interesting bunch. I think it would be good for you to come, good to not be all alone now. There'll probably be lots of people, but her place is big enough to find a quiet corner, if you want one. Please come, whaddaya say?"

"What about Marty?"

"I'll be there with Marty. When I suggested asking you, Marty said you could probably use a break, after the heavy stuff you've been through. Those were his words."

"I dunno . . ."

"Please come, Reed. It really isn't good for you to be alone now, y'know? If you hate it, you can split."

"I dunno . . . Okay, I will. I'll give it a try."

"I'm glad. Pete St. Pierre is also coming. He said he could pick you up."

"Pete?! That makes it *lots* better. I mean *easier*. What time should I be ready?"

"'Bout eight. It won't be a long night. The usual L.A. problem— some people are shooting in the morning."

"Cool. See you tonight."

Shooting. The word for film. The word for Uncle Carl. It was a new thought. He didn't like it. He hung up the phone, thanked Ramon, and walked back into the recording studio. Putting on the outsized earphones, he dropped back into his film character—a terrified kid brother with a mob of armed redneck homophobes outside the door.

"Who's there?!" he shouted over and over into the microphone, looking into his own frightened eyes on the screen in front of him.

"Who's there?!" he shouted. "Who's there?! Who the hell is out there?!"

No One Here Can

Johnny had expected working to be hard, with his heart and mind so filled with Uncle Carl. On the contrary, Robert MacKenzie, Andy Phipps, Pete—the whole cast and crew—were like a warm, safe room he could nest in, knowing he was covered, knowing he was valued. It was also good to be inside the character he was playing, a loving brother defending his older brother from danger. Defending in a way he could not defend his Uncle Carl. He felt a guilt about that, but knew there was no way he could have been there for his uncle. The people who want to do us in, he thought, are everywhere. No *one* person can be *everywhere*.

He heard the horn of Pete's black Toyota honking twice, then twice again. "Right down!" he shouted out the window. Having learned it was "all show-business, we never close" in L.A., he quickly checked himself out in the full-length mirror inside his bedroom closet. Black jeans, black leather gym shoes, beige-y pink Armani silk shirt. He looked okay. Nothing amazing, but he didn't feel amazing. He felt waterlogged with sadness and doing his best to keep his nose above the water line.

He ran down the building's glossy wrought-iron staircase.

"Hey, baby! You jump in the back. Keep Miss Rhodella comp'ny. I'll be your driver."

Johnny recognized her immediately. Rhodes Linton. She'd played Lena Horne in a mini-series, and was up for all the television awards. Although there had never been a woman in America better looking than Lena Horne, Rhodes Linton—who looked a lot like Miss Horne—was a serious contender for any beauty prize that might be available. Climbing in next to her, he inhaled her perfume, remembering the scent. Gina Bellini had worn it. Ysatis. Givenchy. Give-Entchy, Gina had called it.

"Hi. I'm Rhodes."

"Yes, I know. Good to meet you. I'm Johnny Reed."

She laughed lightly "Yes. I knew *that.*"

"Well, at least we've demonstrated that neither of us was brung up in a barn."

"Or without an occasional copy of *Daily Variety.*"

Marina Di Martello's house, a sand-coloured 1920s mansion with a turreted black roof, was floodlit in pinks and greens, and right on the beach. A young valet, his straight and sleek black hair in a low ponytail, opened the back door of the Petemobile, offering his gloved hand to Rhodes Linton.

"Good evening, Miss Linton."

Johnny followed behind. Pete opened and closed his own door, handing the valet his keys, in exchange for a numbered pink tag.

"Thank you, my man."

"Thank *you*, Mister St. Pierre."

Pete looked at Johnny. "How the hell did he know my name? I mean, the picture's not out yet and I haven't done diddly else out here."

"Probably memorized it from the Guest List. You know, coloured guy, Pete St. Pierre."

"Uh huh. How'd he know I wasn't *you?*"

"I dunno, man. I'm probably listed as light-skinned *skinny* coloured guy."

"You think?"

"Dunno. Could be I'm down as *incredibly good-looking* light-skinned skinny coloured guy."

This riff, accompanied by Rhodes Linton's laughter, got the trio to the huge, ornately carved, wooden door.

Pete knocked, and the door was opened by a tall, tuxedo-ed, handsome white-haired black man with one of those half-Native American faces, all almond eyes and cheekbones. Johnny thought his Uncle Carl would have grown old looking like this old gentleman, had the world chosen to let him grow old.

"This old gentleman" was reciprocally studying the young three-some. There was a flicker of friendly conspiracy, quickly replaced by formal neutral grace.

"Good evening. Welcome. Please come in."

"Thanks. I'm Pete St. Pierre. This is John Grandon Reed, and, of course, Miss Rhodes Linton."

"Yes, I recognised Miss Linton. A great job as Lena."

"Thank you. You're very kind."

As Rhodes gave her white cashmere shawl to the coat-check woman, she whispered, "I don't think you have to introduce yourself to the butler."

"Yeah, I do," Pete replied.

Rose Golden had told Johnny, "'Hollywood is filled with Famous People. Like Washington, D.C., it's a one-industry town. Film is Hollywood's industry, and fame its principal by-product." It did seem to Johnny that most of Hollywood was some degree of famous.

Movie Stars were another matter entirely. Almost otherworldly, with big faces that looked natural when, up on a screen, those faces were bigger still. On huge screens, in cities and towns all over the world, Movie Stars had sparkly white teeth and, male or female, lips as big and full as pillows, wide-open eyes, at once all-knowing and innocent—the descendants of the world's ancient mythic gods. A number of people were regularly airpumped by publicists until the repetition of their name and picture made them seem like Movie Stars. They weren't. They were good-looking Potemkin Villages, and had what theatrical agents and casting directors, with specificity-avoidance, called "an interesting quality." If you walked around behind these Potemkin Movie Stars, you might find a superb male or female ass, but not much else. From behind or head-on, there was no radiance, no Bhuddic bell-echo.

Movie Stars, real International Movie Stars, always surrounded, preceded and followed by their own radiance and the echo of a bell you could hear in your heart and feel on your skin—were, like true leaders, secular or spiritual—very rare. Marina Di Martello was a real Movie Star, and had been since before Johnny Reed was born.

The silver-gilded art deco mirrors lining the large entrance hall made it seem as if she were moving towards them, in multiplicate, from every direction.

"*Buona sera*. Good evening. Welcome to my home."

Her cascade of 1940s red-brown hair and opulent bosom cleavage were true to the legend. She was, however, smaller than Johnny'd expected, *tiny* really. He had watched her films since he was about seven, and knew she had to be sixty-something. Holding her unlined, warm little hand with its pale shell-coloured polished nails, looking at her baby-smooth face, into her chestnut-brown eyes, this seemed impossible. She did not look surgical, tightly pulled; nor did she look *young*. Simply age-less and exquisite. A Movie Star.

Embracing the hand of each new arrival, she then waved towards the noisy ballroom behind her, calling, "Giorgio! *Qui, per favore!*" in a strong but mellifluous voice. A short man with large teeth and white hair, plump-ness firmly contained within his tuxedo, appeared at her side, carrying a tray filled with glasses of red wine, white still wine, and Champagne. Pete and Rhodes each took a flute-glass of Champagne. Johnny, who wasn't going to ask Marina Di Martello if she had any beer, did the same.

"Good. Now you have drinks. Come, please, join the others. There is a buffet of food on the terrazzo, and, of course, more to drink."

"Fay*muss*, my brother! Seriously Fay-muss!" Pete murmured. Johnny wasn't sure if he meant Marina Di Martello or the entire ballroom. Either way, he was right. Even the reasonably well-known Rhodes Linton looked a bit stunned. Almost every face Johnny saw was one he had seen before. It was fairly certain that those he could not recognise were "power people"—behind the scenes star-makers.

One of whom was moving straight for him like a smiling land-shark.

"Hey pal! Good to see ya. Dorrie said she'd connected with you. Sorry to hear about your uncle. Poor bastard. Really sorry."

"Poor bastard" offended Johnny, but he knew that almost anything Marty Rachman might say or do would likely offend him. Poor bastard was probably just Rachmanese for deepest sympathy.

"Thanks, Marty. He was a special man, my Uncle Carl, he . . ."

"Right. I'm sure he was. Have you eaten? There's a *phenomenal* spread here . . . and I *am* talking about the food, though you could say . . ."

Dorrie popped up from somewhere behind them, in a sleeveless full-skirted pale green fifties retro dress that made Johnny think of a high-breasted, wasp-waisted pistachio ice cream cone.

"Hey, Reed! Glad you made it. Hi, Pete."

"Hello, Dorrie. Do you know Rhodes Linton?"

"No. We've not met, but I love your work. Hi, I'm Dorrie Stockwell."

"Thank you. For what you said about my work. Aren't you doing Phil Murphy's new series?"

"All day, every day," Dorrie laughed, shaking her head.

"Well, Phil's a friend. And he's been saying great things about *you*."

Marty Rachman interposed himself between the two women, throwing an arm over the shoulders of each.

"All right, girls. You're both my clients, so of course you're both brilliant. Now, stop stroking each other so this bereaved skinny bastard can get some food."

This *bastard* shit has to cease, Johnny thought, the smile stiff on his face.

"Food. Yes. Good idea. I'm gonna go do that. Anyone coming with?"

Marty did not relinquish his hold on the women's shoulders. Dorrie looked nervous. Rhodes seemed slightly offended, yet unwilling to wriggle out of her agent's grip.

"Women don't eat in this town. Let's do it, Bro'," Pete said. Dorrie and Rhodes laughed. It did not sound like real laughter. "You got it. Lead the way," Johnny mumbled, following Pete outside to "the terrazzo."

"What the fuck was *that* all about?"

"Rachman? We don't like each other."

"No shit! Is it 'bout Dorrie?"

"Not really. I'd think Rachman was a slimy showboating jiveass even if I didn't *know* Dorrie."

"Yeah, but you *do* know Dorrie. You two gettin' it on?"

"Dorrie is my best friend, man."

"That's not what I asked you."

"Yeah, I know. Let's eat."

"Uh huh."

Actors tend to appreciate free food in general, and the free food at Marina Di Martello's was particularly good ("Any place that has enough cold shrimp *and* enough oysters does *not* have a money problem," Pete noted. "We *like* such places"). They stayed out there on the terrazzo for a while. The food and drink were indeed abundant and fine, but both young men knew they were also there for other reasons. Johnny remembered his father explaining about how there had been, in the slave-holding South, coloured folks for the field and others who were accepted in the house. Relative to Marina Di Martello, her friends and her house, Pete and Johnny felt more comfortable on the terrazzo—in the field.

Through the large French doors, they could see Rhodes Linton. Surrounded by attractive, interested people, she was laughing, and making others laugh. Light was twinkling off her pale pink sequinned high-necked sheath. Glamorous, confident, Rhodes Linton was definitely house. Johnny wanted to be house too.

"Pete, we're gonna get fat out here. At least *you* will. Let's go inside."

As they re-entered the house, Marina Di Martello was in the centre of the ballroom clapping her hands for attention.

"Ladies and gentlemen, *per favore.* There is my favourite jazz trio downstairs in the *piccolo cabarettino* . . . along with more to eat and drink. You do not *have* to go to hear them, but they are truly *maraviglioso*, and I am going to hear them. I hope you will join me . . . you will not be sorry."

Accompanied by Giorgio the butler, Miss Di Martello headed down the stairs, followed by most of her guests, including Johnny and Pete.

The basement was indeed a miniature cabaret: round tables, small stage, large buffet of food and staffed bar.

Johnny recognised the trio as the old groovers from his first night out with Dorrie and Marty. They were playing "Blue Gardenia." The mellow, sweet sound warmed him. He also felt that the bridge from field to house would be better crossed if he could play the piano. When the trio took a break, he approached the piano player, a milk chocolate–coloured man with a thin moustache, processed hair and a wide, dimpled smile. He looked to Johnny like a shorter, pudgier Duke Ellington.

"Hi. Great set. I'm Johnny Reed."

"Thanks much. Ferdy Malverne."

"Good to meet you. I heard you play at that club in Malibu."

"*Jo-Jo's.* Yeah, I thought I seen you before. *Jo-Jo's* is our regular room."

"I play some piano. Do you think it would be okay for me to play a song or two during your break?"

"Oh, we can do better than that. Why don'cha sit in during the next set? Here, write your name down on my set list here. We can put you in between "Don't Get Around Much Any More" and "All Blues.""

"Ladies and gentlemen, we have a young man here who wants to play a couple tunes for you. Would you welcome . . . John Grandon Reed."

The crowd applauded, Pete and Dorrie a bit too loudly, Dorrie smiling, shouting, in that calm and confident way the rich-from-birth could do without sounding vulgar, "Go, Reed!"

He played one of his Uncle Carl's favourites.

"*Ev'ry time we say goodbye,*
I die a little.
Ev'ry time we say goodbye,
I wonder why a little . . ."

Dorrie moved to him, then turned and leaned against the piano, the thumb of her right hand resting on the shiny mahogany surface; four fingers slightly elevated and pointing at him, a tiny quartet of support and connection. Johnny was pleased to share the song with her. "*Every Time We Say Goodbye*" was one of their old *Teddy's ShowBar* standbys. Seamlessly, he kept on playing while Dorrie sang the bridge on her own.

"*How the gods above me, who must be in the know*
Think so little of me, they'd allow you to go . . ."

They finished the song as a duet:

"*When you're near, there's such an air of spring about it*
I can hear a lark somewhere begin to sing about it
There's no love song finer
But how strange
The change
From major
To minor
Every time
We say
Goodbye . . ."

They received strong applause, complete with cheering and

whistling. Dorrie bowed to the house, then to Johnny, and returned to her seat next to Marty Rachman.

Johnny, having honoured his murdered uncle, wished also to salute his father.

"Thank you, ladies and gentleman. This next song is by the legendary black artist, Bert Williams. Mister Williams had a character called Mister Nobody. Charlie Chaplin based his Little Tramp on Mister Nobody. This is Mister Nobody's theme song. Written in 1905."

"When life seems full of clouds an' rain
And I am filled with naught but pain
Who soothes my thumpin' bumpin' brain?
Nobody.
When I try hard an' scheme and plan
To look as good, as good as I can
Who says 'look at that handsome man'?
Nobody
I ain't never done nothin' to
Nobody
And I ain't never got nothin from
No-bo-dy, no time
And until I get somethin' from
Some-bo-dy, sometime
I don't intend to do nothin'
For Nobody
No Time!"

Again, the response was enthusiastic. Johnny stood, smiling, and bowed.

"Hey, pal" Marty Rachman shouted, "what say you commere and keep Dorrie's seat warm while she sings our favourite song?"

Dorrie looked at Rachman, her brows furrowed. "Please, Marty. Don't do this . . ."

"Come on, babe. I really want you to sing it." He leapt up and faced the crowd. "Hey people, wouldn't you love to hear Dorrie sing another tune?! She sings it for me a lot, and she really does it great!"

The energy in the room had somehow gone weird. Most people felt it, but they thought Dorrie Stockwell sang very well in her duet with

Johnny. They also knew that Marty Rachman was a Serious Power Person in town. Energy shifts were important in L.A. No one wanted to read it wrong. Collectively, they decided to risk endorsement.

"Yeah, Dorrie!" they enthused, and "Go ahead and sing!"

"Up you go, babe. Sing our favourite song."

Dorrie stood up, between the standing Johnny and the seated Marty. Looking like she'd been told to stand in front of a firing squad. She looked at Marty with a focused angry pain, then moved quickly to the tiny stage, sat at the piano, played a chord and, staring straight ahead, her face in profile, she began to sing. Her voice was soft, but the piano was miked and the song was heard by all.

"*Pack up all my care and woe,*
Here I go,
Singin' low
Bye,
Bye,
Blackbird."

Marty leaned in, close to Johnny's ear, stage-whispering "Did you really think you could fuck my girlfriend without my finding out about it?"

Johnny froze, gripping the rounded edges of the table. He was fairly certain that at least those seated near them had heard Marty's question. He kept his eyes on Dorrie, who was still in profile, still singing.

"*Where somebody waits for me*
Sugar's sweet, so is he
Bye,
Bye,
Blackbird.
No one here can love or understand me . . ."

Suddenly, Marty pressed his hand, hard, over Johnny's, and hissed, "I asked you a question, Blackbird!"

Johnny yanked his hand out from under Marty's and was up and heading for what he hoped to hell were the stairs that would take him from this newly vertiginous place. The sea air was a brisk and cleansing oxygen rush. He asked the valet to call a taxi.

The cab arrived at the same time as Marty, Dorrie and a ragtag gaggle came pouring through the huge door in varying states of blurry agitation.

Johnny could not hear all Marty Rachman was saying, but the tone was ugly, and he recognised the words *pal* and *bye-bye*. He wheeled around and drove his fist, over and over, into the marshmallow nest of Marty's stomach.

Someone, he thought it was Pete, pulled him away from Marty, who doubled over fetally on the ground, moaning and spit-vomiting. Johnny got into the cab and told the driver, "Larrabee, just above Sunset, please." Within minutes, he was headed out of Santa Monica and down the Ventura Freeway towards West Hollywood.

The pool at Hillside Hacienda was lit up for the night, turquoise and shimmering. Johnny stood for a moment at the edge. He removed shoes, socks, jeans and red jockey-shorts, and then took off his watch, stuffed it into his jeans pocket, and laid everything but the shoes on a white plastic, butt-pleating stringchair.

"Signor Armani has made this shirt in silk. Signor Armani say you must not, not ever let silk get wet" the Armani salesman had told him. "It will make the permanent stain."

"Long live the permanent stain!" Johnny shouted as he jumped into the pool.

When he hit the cool water, he thought of the song the choir was singing, with his mother conducting, when he finally reached the rally for his Uncle Carl. He swam back and forth, singing:

"*Steal away, steal away, steal away to Jesus*
Steal away, steal away home
Oh, I ain't got long to stay here . . ."

"Amen, brother! You have well and truly fucked up your good shirt!" Pete St. Pierre said, leaning on the wrought-iron pool-light pole.

"Not to mention your career," Rhodes Linton added from somewhere in the darkness.

"Hi, guys," Johnny responded, bouncing up in the water, grinning, feeling lighter, freer than he had since before his uncle's murder.

"Would you *shut the fuck up* down there?!" came a hoarse male voice through a screened window on the second floor. "*You people* think you can just sing an' dance at *any time* uvva day or night! It's two inna the fucking morning!"

"*You people?*"

"Let it go, Pete. Guy's an alky crank . . ."

"A *racist* alky crank, I'll bet'cha," Rhodes whispered, before melodiously shouting upward, "Sorry, sir! Truly sorry!"

She then walked to the edge of the pool.

"And, speaking of sorry, I will now look the other way while you get your sorry ass out of the pool, not that I ain't seen stuff just like the stuff you got."

"Oh, honey! I shared a dressing room with this man. He's got him some truly *un*sorry stuff."

"Will you two please stop" Johnny said softly. "My apartment key is in my jeans pocket. Could somebody, maybe, get my robe from room one-oh-one on the second floor? It's hanging behind the bathroom door."

"I'll do it," Pete said, extracting the key and bounding up the iron stairs.

In minutes, he was back at poolside.

"Your robe, Mister Reed."

Johnny, his crinkle-clinging shirt water-tinted a medium brown, climbed out of the pool. Rhodes turned her back. He removed the wet shirt and wrapped himself in the white terry robe—a gift of the Santa Monica Boulevard Health Spa, in which Andy Phipps had enrolled the whole *Brotherz* cast.

"I think we should go inside before Crankyass Peckerwood makes another golden-throated appearance," Rhodes suggested.

Rhodes didn't want to be "up for three days," so Johnny fixed apple-ginger tea, rather than coffee.

"What were you thinking? You can't just *hit Marty Rachman*."

"Yeah, I can. In fact, I damn *did!*"

"I'm hip you did. But this isn't just *about you*. It's about Andy and me and MacKenzie and the studio and . . ."

"Whoa up. Whoa up a minute. None of those other folks you named *touched* Marty Pigshit Rachman. I did. I alone. Johnny Reed. John *Grandon* Reed. And what, what *exactly*, would *you* do Pete, if you were at a Hollywood party and somebody asked your best friend to sing Bye, Bye, fucking Blackbird, while he asked you, while she was singing, so people could hear, if you fucked his girlfriend, who is a very close friend of yours, like I said, your *best* friend, and . . ."

"Did you?"

"Did I *what?*"

"Fuck her?"

"You already asked me that at Marina Di Martello's. And it is *still* none of your business."

"White pussy!"

Rhodes had been staring out the window, letting the males have their fight, so they were surprised, both by the angry sound of her voice, and by what it had said. It rendered them silent. A silence that Rhodes, though she too was surprised, decided to fill.

"What the hell is the story with black men? Everything is starting to happen for you, Johnny. *Everything* does *not* happen for black folks a whole helluva lot, but here you are and it's all good and you blow the whole thing off just for white pussy?! What *is* that? Is there something *wrong* with *black women?* You think we're *ugly* or somethin'? I've seen black men with some of the *ugliest* white women God ever made. Fat, flatassed white women. White women with nasty scabby skin. I am talking *seriously ugly white women!* But they, my black brethren, would rather be with those *hugely uglacious* white women than . . . I mean, why do black men have to have white pussy?!"

"I don't," Pete said brightly, hoping to put an end to what Andy Phipps called Razor-Blade Discourse.

"Thank you, Pete, but you don't count. You don't want *any* kind of pussy. But this little brother here does, and he not only wants white pussy, *he* wants the white pussy who belongs to a really mean motherfucker who runs half the town."

"I told you, she is a friend of mine. And the really mean motherfucker is *your* agent!"

"How do you think I know he's mean? He is also a *brilliant* agent. And if you stay the hell out of his private life, which, through diligence and intelligence, I have managed to do, you don't have to *do* Mean Motherfucker with him *at all.* Just Brilliant Agent. Was his girlfriend, his in*credibly white* girlfriend, the only place you could get some quim?"

"She is not *quim!* I told you, dammit, she is my *friend.* We went to acting school together. We . . . know each other. I'm not *from* here . . . I'm from . . . Wetherill, North Carolina . . . I . . . my uncle . . ."

And he was weeping. Rhodes, having said what she had to say, lit a cigarette and went back to staring out the window.

"Oh, Lordy," Pete said, but he too stood where he was. Johnny's crying subsided. He wiped under his eyes with the heels of his hands.

"I'm all right," he said softly, to no one in particular. "It's been a helluva lot of stuff. I think . . . I think I need to sleep."

"Cool. We just wanted to make sure you were okay. C'mon Rhodella, let's split so the man can sleep. I'll call you in the morning."

"Okay . . . maybe the afternoon would be better. And thanks for coming by."

Rhodes wrapped her creamy shawl around herself and, silently, preceded Pete out the door, trailing cigarette smoke.

When the phone rang, Johnny, thick as wet cement, looked at the bedside clock. Seven in the morning. "No way," he said, rolling onto his belly, pulling a pillow over his head. Two hours later, the phone rang again. He was still unwilling to pick up the receiver. A few minutes after the ringing stopped, the knocking started.

"What the f . . .?" He hauled himself out of bed, put on his robe, and fumbled through the shock-o-rama rug to the door.

All he could see was two huge round nostrils—what his father called "a sheep-drowner"—a nose so upturned and rifle-barrelled that if the nose-owner stood out in the rain, he or she would drown like sheep do when they can't stop looking up at a downpour.

I'm staring up somebody's nose, he thought, opening out his gaze to include the entire vaguely familiar face before him.

He'd seen it twice before, briefly. The doughy, yellow-white complected and almost lipless snouty face of Mary Margaret Mulligan—a face in which sat two large and startlingly green eyes.

"Mister Reed?"

"Yeah?"

"I'm Miss Mulligan. The manager?"

"Yes. I know. Good morning, Miss Mulligan. What can I . . . ?"

"There has been a complaint, Mister Reed."

"A complaint?"

"That's right. One of our other tenants said that you had friends

146

here last night and that there was a lot of noise, both here in your apartment and at the pool. Now, Hillside Hacienda has a noise policy and a pool policy . . ."

"Oh. Have I violated a policy? Two policies?"

"I'm afraid you have, Mister Reed. May I come in? The policies are on the laminated placard on the back of your door."

"Sure. Come on in, an' we can check out the . . . laminated placard."

Mary Margaret Mulligan jerked her head back quickly. Was he mocking her? He was not smiling. He was not *anything*. Except maybe groggy. She stepped inside the apartment, her backless lime-green slippers shooting sparks off the orange rug.

"Here, you see. Here is our policy about the pool. 'No children . . . no pets. Not more than two guests any time without written consent by the management . . . no pool or poolside guests *at all*, after midnight, . . . no music or loud conversations.' And here, about the apartment itself. 'No parties without written consent by the management.' And 'No loud conversations or other loud noises by tenants and/or their guests in the apartments after ten PM.'"

"Oh yeah. I see. I wasn't actually expecting those two friends. They stopped by without phoning. It won't happen again, Miss Mulligan, I promise."

"ActorFone. Kelli Anne Speaking."

"Hi Kelli Anne. Johnny Reed . . ."

"Oh Hi, Mister Reed. You've got lots. Gotta pen?"

"Uh huh. Go."

"Rose Golden called from New York. Three times. The last one was just a little while ago, and she said to call her right away, that it was *very* important. And Claude Martin called twice. Also very important. Pete St. Pierre called. Said call him when you feel like it. Andover Phipps called from New York. *The Hollywood Insider* called. Twice. And Robert MacKenzie's office called. Please call him at his home number—they said you had it."

"Yeah, I do. Anything else?"

"Dorrie Stockwell. She said not to call her, that she'd call you again."

Uncharacteristically, Rose Golden was shouting.

"Are you crazy?! What did you do?"

"What did you hear I did?"

"Punched out Marty Rachman."

"Yeah, Rose, that's what I did."

"You *are* crazy. Do you know how important he is out there?"

"Yes. Yes I do. Do *you* know that he asked me to leave *you* and go with *him?*"

"Oh Christ, he does that with everybody. They all do."

"Do you?"

"No, in fact I don't. But I'm the world's first—and last—Jewish saint in the artists' representation area. Is *that* why you hit him, because he asked if you wanted to change agents? *Think* before you answer."

"No, that wasn't why."

"Good. You can still think, if sporadically. Now, would you like to tell me why you hit him?"

"Because he . . . he got ugly with me."

"*Bye, Bye Blackbird?*"

"Look Rose, what with my uncle's murder and all the travelling and all the shit that's gone down here, I'm really wasted. Could you maybe tell me what you already know and I can fill in the blanks, okay?"

"Fair enough. Sorry, kid. What I heard is that you were sleeping with Dorrie Stockwell and . . ."

"Rose, I don't . . ."

"I don't care what you don't. You asked me to tell you what I heard. Well, I'm doing that. So shut up while I do that and then *you* can talk, okay?"

"Okay."

"Good. So, where was I? Oh yeah, you were sleeping with Dorrie Stockwell, who is Marty Rachman's girlfriend, and he humiliated you at Marina Di Martello's party so you put his lights out. How'm I doing so far? Is that about right?"

"Yes. Sort of. Dorrie is . . . or *was*, I dunno now, my best friend . . ."

Rose's tone softened. "I know that, John. She brought you to my office, remember? She was, actually, my client before Rachman poached her. I like Dorrie. That does not change the fact that she is now Rachman's girlfriend, and that you knew this and . . . enough. Enough of this. I called MacKenzie's office. He says you've finished shooting, finished looping, and done your photo call. He agrees it would be good if you got out of L.A. while things settle down. He says you should go home for a while."

"Home? My mother sold the house. She's in Daytona. I suppose . . ."

"No John, not back down South. Here. To New York."

"I don't have a place there. I was in Actors' Playhouse student housing and then . . ."

"I know that. I've spoken with Andy Phipps. He's going to London next week for the West End production of *Brotherz*. So are Pete and Helena. We finally set the deal this morning. Pete tried to call you. The actors' union over there insisted on an English black actor for your part. We tried, but British Equity wouldn't budge on it. If the play gets good reviews over there, Pete and Andy will be in Europe for the summer. So Andy said you were welcome to stay in their loft downtown . . . if you will water the ficus and feed the cat."

"Ficus?"

"It's a plant. Please, Johnny. Pack your stuff and get your ass out of there ASAP. We'll sort everything out when you get here. Please?"

"Yeah. I think you're right. I'll get things straightened out with this apartment and with Claude and stuff and call you back later, okay?"

"Good. You have my number at home? With the time difference, it might be after office . . ."

"Yeah, I've got it . . . Rose?"

"Yeah?"

"Thanks."

"Don't thank me yet. I still don't know what size shovel this shit's gonna take. Talk to you later. Oh, re 'talking,' don't do any interviews until we've sat down together, okay?"

Johnny packed his clothes, vitamins and miscellaneous softish stuff in a large suitcase and larger duffel bag. He ran down to Turner's liquor store on Sunset for a couple of boxes. These he filled with whatever kitchen and bathroom gear he'd bought, plus two ten-pound barbells. Then he went downstairs and knocked on the door with the wooden sign that read "Manager."

Mary Margaret Mulligan said there could be no refund on his security deposit "until after damage and paint inspection," but that, subject to her approval, he could sublet to a friend for the remaining three weeks of his "current rent-month." Johnny said he'd try to find someone. She said she hoped he wasn't leaving because of her reprimand, that he was usually a good and quiet tenant, that the man who'd complained sometimes had a bad temper about other tenants, and that anyone could make a mistake.

Johnny thanked her, assured her that she'd not caused his leaving. Said he had a theatre job in New York. She smiled, saying, "Congratulations. Good luck . . . I mean *break a leg*, right?"

"Right."

Nobody knew exactly how old Claude Martin was. The rumour-range went from sixty to eighty. Whatever his age, he was a tall and handsome man with one of those accents that might have once been English, and a full Shakespearean head of snow-white hair. In recent months, he had also grown a bushy but neatly shaped salt-and-pepper moustache. The actor Cesar Romero, his long-time friend, said that Claude was his secret twin.

Gracious as ever, he asked Johnny if he'd like "a bit of fresh coffee or tea."

"No thanks, Mister Martin, I . . ."

"*Claude*, please. *Mister Martin* makes me feel a hundred and four, which not even the most evil bitches in this town have accused me of being. Please, John, have a seat. Be comfortable." He leaned into the intercom on his desk. "Nikki dear, please hold my calls. Tell everyone I'm in a meeting, and will ring him, or her, back very shortly. Ta' my love."

Claude walked around his desk and behind Johnny to a silver booze-trolley.

"Right. No tea, no coffee. That leaves the Glenlivet. Mellow unblended Scotch whiskey. Yes, John? It's within bounds—four in the afternoon. I'm having one."

"Yes, please. I'll have one too."

"Good, excellent. Why don't you sit on the sofa? It will give us a place to put our drinks."

John moved from the burgundy leather chair to a suede couch the same colour as Mr. Armani's shirt—the *dry* shirt. He seated himself in one corner. Claude placed the two drinks on the coffee table and sat down at the other end of the couch, crossing his legs. Johnny took up his drink. Claude clinked glasses with him.

"*Sip* this, John, sip it slowly. It's the only way."

Johnny nodded, smiling awkwardly. Feeling the slightly medicinal bronzy-coloured alcohol warm his belly, he discreetly regarded Claude Martin. Crossed legs. Hyper-polished tasselled black loafers and black silk socks, perfectly creased grey flannel trousers and the palest of pink shirts, open at the neck to reveal a triangle of charcoal grey tee-shirt. One elegant gent, Johnny thought. He laughed inside, realising that this gay man reminded him of his "watch your ass with the fruits" Uncle Carl. Some people came by their grace naturally. No sweat, no strain. Duke Ellington. Nat Cole. Uncle Carl. Claude Martin.

"Well, John, we do have a bit of a kerfuffle here with this Rachman business."

"How bad is it?"

Claude smiled, showing a row of heavy white teeth. "Oh, somewhere between really bad and utterly doomed. The problem is that Rachman, who is a dreadful man, is also the most important 'packager' in town. Just this morning, we lost two very good roles. Roles for which you were the first choice yesterday."

"The Bert Williams thing."

"Afraid so."

"Oh sh . . . 'Nobody' was my father's favourite song. I *really* wanted that."

"Yes, I know, and the people at Lumina really wanted *you*. Until this morning. Rachman controls too many people attached to the project. And he was prepared to pull all of them if you got anywhere near the thing."

"Damn!"

"Indeed."

"What's the other one I lost?"

"Well, it isn't green-lighted yet, but it's about Garvey and the 'Back to Africa' movement. They want Poitier for Garvey. And Rhodes Linton for the female lead. Rhodes Linton is . . ."

"Marty Rachman's client."

"Exactly. As is Calvin Fisk, who has been asked to direct."

"He, Rachman, can really do this?"

"Oh yes. Does it all the time."

Johnny pursed his lips, blowing out a breath. He sipped the Scotch, which helped thaw the cold fear he was feeling.

"What do we do now?"

"Not much we *can* do in the short term. Rose Golden told me you spoke this morning. I concur with her view. Go to New York. Find a play to do. Some television. Bob MacKenzie says you're really fine in the *Brotherz* film. When it's released you should get good reviews, and, given the passage of time, it will increase your chances for quality work here. That and the fact that none of Rachman's romances seem to last more than six months. Mind you, the fact that you coldcocked the creep could last a long, long time."

From Major to Minor
New York, 1979

Johnny pulled on his jeans and a grey sweatshirt. Taped to the bathroom mirror was a bright-yellow piece of paper with his initials, JGR, at the top.

Hey Little Brother—

There's food in the fridge, freezer and cupboards (eat it <u>all</u> if you want—you never gain any weight anyway!). The cat, who is probably hiding, is named Joe Louis (Jolo). He's big, black and scared of strangers, but, once he gets to know you, he's a pussycat (Sorry. Couldn't help it). The Ficus Benjamina (tree by the window in the living room zone) is called MacDougal (Mac), because we found him on MacDougal Street and nursed him back to health. Food instructions for cat and tree are on the fridge, between the "Queer Nation" and "Beautiful Barbados" magnets. Towels, sheets and other bed stuff are in the large armoire next to the bed. The super for the building lives on the first floor. Her name's Luba. She's cool. A painter. Russian. She's been a woman for about a year now. Was just like one before, except for the dick. Assuming dick. Never seen by us. Anyway, her number is also on the fridge, under the "Bed-Stuy is for Lovers, Motherfucker!" magnet.

Our London phone numbers are under the red double-decker bus magnet. Or you can call Liam Halloran (my agent at Arts International—his secretary is Debby) or Rose Golden (Pete's . . . and yours).

As to the whole upfuckment in El Lay, This Too Soon Shall Pass.

Lotsa Love,

Andy.

PS. I've seen a rough-cut of "Brotherz." You're perfect! Wish you could be here in London to do the play with us. The only way to bring you was to give up Helena. Helena is 72 years old (and brilliantly playing the "glue" that holds the story together). She has always wanted to see England. You will see England in time, Little Brother.

XOXO

A.

The phone, somewhere in the loft, was ringing. Johnny darted from place to place, tracking the sound. "Keep ringin'," he shouted, "keep ringin' and you shall be rewarded by . . . aha!" He threw himself across the enormous bed and pulled the gold-and-white phone out from under the bedtable.

"Good evening. Phipps-St. Pierre residence."

"Hi, Johnny. It's Marcia at the Golden Group. I have Rose Golden for you."

"Thanks." He waited.

"John?"

"Yeah, Rose. How are you?"

"I'm fine, John. How's Andy and Pete's place?"

"It's good. I haven't really explored yet. Sort of dropped my stuff and went for a walk. Great neighbourhood . . . if you're rich. Found a quiet place to read the newspaper and have coffee. There's a cat somewhere in the loft, but he's hiding. He'll probably show up when . . ."

"John?"

"Yeah. Sorry Rose. Didn't mean to babble at you."

"Not to worry. Listen honey, I have some news."

"News? 'Bout what?"

"About *Brotherz.*"

Apparently, Johnny was, as Andy had written, "perfect" in the film.

Apparently, Robert MacKenzie, who also thought Johnny was perfect in the film, had final cut.

Apparently, Robert MacKenzie was Marty Rachman's client.

Apparently, Robert MacKenzie's next film was to star two more of Marty Rachman's clients. Rachman told MacKenzie he'd pull those, as yet unsigned, clients, upon whose "attachment" the whole deal hinged, if MacKenzie did not cut John Grandon Reed's part in *Brotherz* down to nothing. Robert MacKenzie was a respected director, with two Academy Awards. He and Rachman had a huge fight. There was a standoff. Andover Phipps said Johnny was "brilliant, and a key component in the heart and soul of my story." Marty Rachman said "*Bend-over Phipps* has no power in Hollywood" and that he wasn't "gonna give an inch on this." Finally MacKenzie, already signed and in preproduction with the new film, caved.

"Bob MacKenzie is sick over this. I know him, Johnny. It isn't the usual Hollywood crocodile sympathy—he is truly sorry. And angry. Feels Rachman is making him hurt *his* film. Says he's in a corner. There's no way he can insist on your having full coverage without winding up in court for a long time. In which case, neither *Brotherz* nor the new project will see daylight until the lawsuit or law*suits* resolve. Says to please forgive him, and give it a year or two. He promised me he'd make it up to you. He also says that, even with the role . . . reduced, you are, to quote him, a great camera presence, and . . . John?"

The kitchen appliances seemed amazingly loud. Johnny let the hums and pings turn to music. Afro-Indian, he thought.

"John?"

"I'm here."

"Do you want to come over to my place? Have a good Jewish meal? . . . Hello?"

"I'm here."

"Well, why don't you come uptown? Meet Herb, my husband? Have some soup and pot roast?"

"Umm. Could I tomorrow . . . I need . . . to find the cat."

"Are you sure?"

"Yeah. Can I come tomorrow?"

"Of course . . . no, wait. I have to see a client in a bad play. I have to do this, you don't. What about Saturday brunch? We can show you around the Upper West Side. You like bagels?"

"Bagels?"

"Yeah. The best bagels in the world are . . . Oh, screw the bagels. I'm just talking bullshit. I'm worried about you."

"It's okay, Rose. I'll be okay . . . I'd really like to come to brunch on Saturday. And thanks for the worrying. It matters."

He put the phone on the bedtable, replaced the receiver and stood very still for a while, his right hand over his mouth. Then he walked to the window that faced Prince Street. He looked out at the night, the lights, the blur of people coming and going. The green neon sign across the road said *Bistro Bellini*. He wondered if Mister Bistro Bellini knew Gina. He knew *Bistro* wasn't a first name. But it *could* be, he thought, it fuckin' *could* be. He remembered the newspaper article he'd read that morning in the *Cupping Room Café*. About a little kid, little nine-year-old white kid. From Broken Bow, Oklahoma. He'd shot his sex-abusing stepfather. Shot him ten times. When the police asked him why he'd shot the man so many times, he answered, "I wanted to kill him more than but once."

The Baltimore police had wanted to kill his Uncle Carl more than but once. And, as he was starting to realise, Marty Rachman—with or without a gun— wanted to kill *him* more than but once. He did not know how many times Marty Rachman would kill him before he was believed to be fully enough killed. He imagined it could be a while before he'd be left alone, Rachman-free, to do Hollywood film work, possibly film work anywhere in America. Possibly television too. Theatre? Possibly. These thoughts both frightened and froze him. He stood at the window for a long time.

He turned because he was being stared at. A huge, black, yellow-eyed cat was watching him from across the room.

"Hey, Jolo? How you doin' man?" He moved towards the cat, who turned, revealing quite large testicles, and took off for wherever it was that he hid.

Johnny shouted after him, "Walkin' away from me, are ya?! Friend of Marty Rachman's are ya?! You got bigger balls!"

He had rarely smoked as a teenager, and never at all since his cigarette-addicted father died, but he wanted a cigarette. Better still, he thought, would be a joint. He knew that Andy and Pete liked to wind down with marijuana.

There had to be a joint somewhere. He opened the drawer of the bedtable and was staring at an enormous bright pink dildo.

"Well, it *is* a joint." Which caused him to laugh until tears came. Manic laughter and boil-lancing tears. He fell back onto the bed. He lay there for a while, staring at the glitzy silver stars pasted like a Las Vegas constellation on the deep-blue ceiling.

Finally, he sat up and slapped his thighs.

"Right. Feed the cat."

As soon as he began opening the tin of cat food (worst damn smell in the world, he thought, breathing through his mouth), Jolo appeared. Johnny spooned the food into a white plastic bowl, giving the cat time to watch him. As expected, Jolo approached. Still mouth-breathing, Johnny diced up the burger-coloured blob. Jolo rubbed against his leg, purring.

"Oh sure. *Now* we get the 'hand fulla gimme an' the mouth fulla much obliged.'"

Putting the bowl down next to the fridge, he then refilled the adjacent water bowl. Jolo ate, purring. Johnny thought about petting him, deciding against it. He put on his black-and-white high-tops and shoved the loft keys and a twenty-dollar bill into the zippered chest-pocket of his sweatshirt.

He walked west to the highway, not knowing what time of night it was. There was a fair bit of suburban and upstate-destined traffic. He zigged and zagged across to the river. He could see New Jersey on the other shore, speckled with the square geometric jigsaw of light from within apartment windows. A hulking grey ship was moored to his left. It looked military. And deserted. The black water was streaked with yellow undulations from streetlamps and Jerseylight. Johnny knew, from having looked at this Hudson River by day, that it was filled with condoms, turds and floating bits of junk. He had always wondered if that water had anything to do with New York tap water.

He didn't know where L.A. water came from, but it tasted lousy and absolutely no one in *the film industry*, as it called itself, drank it. Ever. L.A. had twenty or thirty different kinds of Designer Water—with or without bubbles. Andy Phipps got the *Brotherz* cast drinking a bubble-free one from Fiji.

Johnny, staring into the Hudson, wondered if they had Fiji Water in New York. He wondered if they had it in London. He wondered if he should drop himself into the water, sink to the bottom, stay there. The answer was no. It was actually Fuck you, Rachman, but no was what it meant. He walked back to the loft, stopping at a corner store to buy a few bananas and a bottle of San Pellegrino water. Italian. With bubbles.

Cat-Love
New York, 1979

The cat was curled up on the white leather couch. He squinted at Johnny.

"Hey, Jolo."

The cat closed his eyes and went back to sleep. Johnny showered, scoop-strained hard little turds from the litter box into the toilet, using the pancake-flipper Andy and Pete had provided for the purpose. Then he washed his hands, brushed his teeth and checked out the stuff in Andy and Pete's medicine cabinet. Found the marijuana and a packet of "Rizla" papers. He put on Andy's white silk pyjamas, rolled a joint and replaced the little plastic bag behind the "Nice Ice Herbal Botanical" mouthwash. He then poured his bubbly Italian water into an enormous wineglass and got into the huge bed, under the aptly named comforter. He had a few puffs of the joint. He'd smoked very little grass (his father had been so militantly, and publicly, opposed to it—"Stoned black people—the world doesn't need any more stoned black people"). It stung his throat. He coughed a few times. Then mellowed, then slept, dreaming he was swimming towards the light in a dark river filled with condoms, turds, tires and the severed head of Marty Rachman. He was trying to find Dorrie.

He awoke in the dark because the cat was standing on his chest, purring.

"Hey." He scratched Jolo behind his ears. Jolo purred. Then he stuck his pink sandpaper tongue inside Johnny's left nostril.

"Yuck! That is *so* disgusting, man! That is *completely* out of the question," he said, turning his head, and body, to the side. Jolo slid off his chest, made a squeaky little noise of complaint, butting his head against The New Human's back. After a bit of this, he accepted the redistribution that was offered and curled up in the bend of pulled-up legs.

With the morning light, Jolo uncurled himself, purring, and rubbed against the comforter-covered form. Receiving no response, he walked up to face level and licked Johnny's chin. Johnny opened his eyes, then held the cat aloft.

"G'morning. Lesseat."

He headed to the kitchen space, followed by his New Best Friend. He put dry cat food and fresh water in Jolo's bowls, and fixed himself some cornflakes with sliced banana. Jolo finished eating and circled his chair a few times, before curling up under it. "We big, we black, we bad," Johnny said. He spent the morning in the loft, reading Andy's ten-year-old first play, *Can You Tap Dance?* and goofing with the cat, who, having eaten the unsmoked part of the joint, would periodically jump straight up in the air.

Marilena Reed, Real Estate Agent
Ydra, Greece, 1995

Theddo, having covered all Johnny's known harbour haunts, decided to see if he was at home. Halfway up the hill, he encountered the youngest Reed, who shouted with joy.

"Mister DanYELLSS! Iasou! Hello!"

"Hello, Marilena. It's good to see you."

"It is good to see you also, Mister Danyellss."

"How come you're not in school?"

She smiled that smile of Polite Child Dealing with Stupid Grownup.

"It is SAVVato, Saturday, Mister Danyellss. There is no school on Saturday."

"Ah."

"Are you looking for my baBAH? He is not at home. I am going down to Fano's to find him."

"He isn't there either. Perhaps we can look for him together? If you wouldn't mind stopping at Kosta's for a *koulóuri?*"

"Could I have a sweet instead? *Koulóuria* are for the morning."

"Of course, you may have a sweet. And they will probably sell a *koulóuri* to a foreigner."

"Oh yes, they will do that. If there are any *koulóuria* left after the morning."

There were *three koulóuria*. Theddo bought all of them, and two white-sugar-covered crescent-shaped cookies for Marilena. As they walked towards Fano's, she licked at the sugar and talked about the weather.

"It is getting colder now. My mana wants me to wear more heavy clothing. I will do this very soon. For now, I am good with red sweatshirt and blue jeanaki. Are *you* cold, Mister DanYellss?"

"Not really. A bit damp. I'm always more damp than cold on an island. Because of all the water."

"Yes, Mister DanYellss. That is why."

Johnny was still not at *To Kósmo Tou Fanóu.* Or *Sto Kéndro.* Or *Ydróneira.*

"Why are you looking for him?"

"Well, I have a new book to write, and I've decided that I would like to stay and write it here. I think Ydra . . ."

"Reeeally?! This is very good. I believe baBAH will be happy to know this. We are all, the entire family, very happy to know this."

"My thanks, Marilena, to you and to the entire family."

"Will you live at our house?"

"No, I don't think that would be fair to your family. And I need my own little place to write. Need to be by myself for thinking. It is the way I work best. That's why I was looking for your dad. Thought he might know an apartment or a small house."

"Ah. *I* know an apartment! I know one! Do you know Dina, who has the café in Kamini?"

"Yes, I do, in fact. Had lunch with your father there."

"Well, there is an apartment on top of the café. Christo, who is the son of Dina, used to live there, but now he is in Limno, doing his military service, so his rooms are, I think, free. We could go there now, to Kamini, and ask Dina. Would you like to do this?"

"I would very much like to do this. I do appreciate your help, Marilena."

"It makes me good to help."

"It does that. It makes you very good indeed."

The apartment—two small rooms, plus an even smaller kitchen and a white-tile toilet with a shower attachment in the wall and a drain in the centre of the floor—was, as Marilena had thought, newly available. It also had a working telephone (which could take forever to get, had one not been in place) and a balcony with two white-metal chairs and matching table. Every room but the toilet offered a superb view of the water and the epic Ydrioti sunsets. The rent, 50'000 drachmas a month, seemed fair, and Theddo agreed at once. This, he realized too late, had disappointed Dina. As in the Arab world, he had been expected to haggle. He resolved to haggle at the next opportunity.

Marilena and Theddo were crossing the harbour square when Johnny's voice boomed out at them.

"Hey guys, wait up."

"Aha! Just the man we were looking for. Where've you been?" Theddo asked.

"I had some things to . . . *Marilena. pou EEnay tin DzaKETTA sou?"*

"BaBAH, why are you speaking to me in Greek? It will be better for Mister DanYELLSS if we speak English."

"Okay. Where, in English, is your jacket?"

"It is at home, BaBAH."

"Well, it's too chilly for your jacket to be at home . . . and you know it."

Theddo downwardly patted the air with his palms, signalling for a truce.

"Easy. I can give Marilena my jacket."

Johnny shook his head. "No, man. The idea is to keep *her warm*, not to make *you cold.*"

"I won't be cold, John. I'm wearing a warm sweater *and* thermal underwear. I'm toasty. Here, Marilena, put this on."

"You really shouldn't do this, Theddo . . ."

"Yes, I should. This young lady is my real estate agent."

Marilena, wrapping herself in the enormous leather jacket of her favourite non-family human, grinned, first at Theddo, then at her father.

"She's your *what?"*

"My real estate agent. I've decided to stay here for a while—don't know how long exactly—until InterAfrA calls me home—and work on a book I have in my head. My agent is waiting for a new book, and I finally know what I want to write about. I'd like to do this work here, on Ydra. I was looking for *you*, to ask about that, and, luckily, encountered Marilena, who knew that Dina in Kamini had some rooms. They are perfect for me. We have a deal and I'll move in tomorrow or the next day."

"Wow! That's great! I mean *really* great! We should celebrate! Let me call Soula, find out if she's cool with our having dinner together tonight."

"No. This is *my* celebration. I want to take you all to dinner. Is there anyplace with a view?"

"Not this time of year. It's just past the tourist season. The food's good at *Apollo Taverna,* but it's fluorescent light, television and neighbours. The best view I can offer is from our house."

"All right, but I'm buying . . . and I'm cooking."

"You're on. I'll call Soula—give her the news and get you some kitchen clearance."

Gay Sand

Johnny was very happy. Then Marilena got on the phone and she was happy too. Theddo Daniels was also happy. He wanted to celebrate by buying food and cooking dinner at the Reed house. Soula accepted his offer of food and wine, as he wanted so much to contribute these things, and there were no celebration-foods in the house. Cooking was another matter. He did not know her kitchen, she said. It would be easier and better if he let her cook. They debated this. Finally, she said, politely but firmly, "Please, let me cook for us in my kitchen and, after you are in your own kitchen in Kamini you can make us a meal *there*. I believe this would be best. And we will get to celebrate two times!"

Turf, Theddo thought. Clearly, it was important to her to do the cooking in *her* kitchen. He understood this—he was the same in his Washington house. "That will be, fine, Soula," he said. "And I look forward to cooking for all of us in Kamini." It was agreed, and Theddo went off with Johnny and Marilena, in search of chicken breasts, vegetables and wine.

Soula poured the last glass of red wine that remained in the bottle from the previous night's dinner. She went to the balcony. The sunset was starting. She sat watching it, sipping the wine.

Her husband and daughter were so pleased that Theddo Daniels would be staying awhile on the Island. Soula was not *dis*pleased. She liked Theddo Daniels very much.

She was, however, also worried. The idea of him handling things in her kitchen terrified her. She did not believe Ifighenia Kallifatidou, who said you got the AIDS from sitting on beach sand after *poosti* had been sitting on the same sand.

That had been a joke for Johnny. *POOSTIkoh ammo*—gay sand. He would examine the sand; smelling, sifting, holding his ear to the ground, saying he was listening for the sound of *The Village People* singing "YMCA." Finally, he would find a "safe" piece of beach for them and they would put down their three towels. That was ten years earlier, in 1985.

Soula never knew anyone with the AIDS. Johnny had lost people he loved to the AIDS. Mister Phipps. Mister St. Pierre. Mister Martin. Soula had seen pictures of these people. Two handsome black men and a very dignified-looking old white man. Johnny had left her and the four-year-old Marilena on Ydra for almost six months, to go and care for Mister St. Pierre when he was dying in New York. She had feared that Johnny would catch the AIDS, and then bring it back to the Island. She was afraid for herself, and for other Ydrioti, but mostly, she was afraid for her daughter. He had assured her that there was no way that Marilena could possibly be harmed by her father's going to his friend. She understood that Mister St. Pierre was like a brother. She understood that Johnny had to go to him. Still, she would imagine ways the Island could be made sick. She hid these thoughts—or tried to.

When Johnny finally returned, they sat together late into the night, Marilena asleep in her room, and she asked him what felt like a hundred questions. He knew much and answered everything. She could not remember all of it, but had a pretty clear idea. He said that he had been very careful in caring for his friend, that the AIDS was "really hard to catch," that he'd had an AIDS test before leaving New York (and for her sake, would have one a year, in Athens, for the following three years). The testing stopped when the Athenian doctor assured Soula that her monogamous, non-drug-using heterosexual husband was most unlikely to have the AIDS.

Johnny also got her some books and pamphlets about the AIDS, in English and Greek. One of the things she learned from reading was that you could get the AIDS from blood if a man who had the AIDS cut himself, and you also had an open cut and his blood went into your cut. Or into your mouth. Or, maybe, into your food. She believed this was true, was correct. And this cutting and exchanging would certainly be possible with kitchen knives. And she knew that Theddo Daniels was *omofiLOHfilos*—homosexual. She also knew, in the moment when he asked about using her kitchen, that he had The AIDS. Johnny had not told her any of this. He might not even know. He always said that she knew things before other people. She knew Theddo was sick with the AIDS—and she was afraid.

The Spazzmaynoids

The fruit and vegetable stand was outside the grocer's. Theddo commented on the colours, and on the scent of mandarin oranges and tiny bananas. The zucchini were enormous. He refrained from commenting on these.

It took three shops to accomplish the desired dinner menu, including wine. Theddo suggested things and Johnny did all the requesting. He did this entirely in Greek.

"I'm impressed," Theddo said as they walked through the twilight square, each one carrying two white plastic shopping bags.

"With what, Mister Danyellss?"

"With your father's Greek. He got us all this fine food and wine without a word of English."

"Of course I did, man. Greek is our language too. We live here. This is our country. You think I'm a Spazzmaynoid?"

"A *what?*"

"Follow me. I'll show you. Marilenamou, would you please carry these two bags home so Mana can start dinner."

"Can't I stay with *you?* I want to watch you show the Spazzmaynoids to Mister DanYELLSS."

"You see the Spazzes every day, Marilenamou. And your mother needs to start preparing the food. We'll be home right after Mister Daniels sees the Spazzmaynoids. Tell Mana we're on our way, okay?"

Marilena shrugged, accepting, but not pleased. She looked up at Theddo.

"Okay. I must first give to you back your jacket."

"No, Marilena. You keep it on. We really will be at your house very quickly. I'm warm enough."

"Are you sure, Mister DanYELLSS? I would not want . . ."

"Marilena! *Go!*"

"Okay, okay, BaBAH, I am going."

Theddo watched the slim, agile teenager sprint up the hill. Seeing her in his too-large jacket made him think of Björn. He sighed, realising that *most* things made him think of Björn. This particular trigger, however, surprised him. Sensing him watching her, Marilena turned, halfway up the hill, and waved. He waved back.

"She's a beautiful girl, John."

Johnny grinned. "Yeah. *We* like 'er."

There were six of them: five men and a woman. They appeared to be somewhere between forty and sixty years old. The woman, wearing a nubby, shapeless floor-length garment in a riot of colours, was what doctors and fitness freaks called "morbidly obese" (Johnny would later describe her as "late Orson Welles, and a *mean* drunk"). The men were slim to gaunt. One was poet-handsome, with prominent cheekbones, overly bright eyes of "contact-lens blue" and close-clipped blond and grey-flecked hair and beard. He wore jeans (as did all the other males) and a black sweatshirt. A peachy-coloured chiffon scarf was knotted around his slightly scrawny neck. A blue-black Greek fisherman's cap completed the ensemble.

He was being intensely spoken at by a man with a low, curly, silver-grey ponytail. Ponytail's jeans were complemented by a black turtleneck sweater and matching leather vest. Everyone was in running shoes. They were all white, and unmistakably not Greek.

Johnny and Theddo were standing far enough away to look openly and speak freely.

"There they be. The Spazzmaynoids."

"Americans?"

"Mostly. Chris Dennison, the one in the fisherman's cap, is English. Which hasn't prevented him working on the Great American Novel for about twenty years. Came here originally, I'm told, with a really good-looking American girl who left him for the son of one of the rich Greek shipping families. He's actually a pretty good poet. Also gets laid a lot. They say he meets the ferry every day in summer. Likes young stuff. Chris is probably Ydra's major non-Greek KaMAHkist."

"KaMAHkist?"

"Yeah. *Toh KaMAHki* is a Greek expression. It comes from Poseidon's trident. To do *toh kaMAHki* is to spear a girl. It generally refers to tourist girls."

"And who's the guy bending his ear?"

"That's Freddy TziKAHgo. Freddy Colluzzo. His father was a big mobster in Chicago."

"Sal Colluzzo?"

"Right."

"Wasn't he shot by his wife?"

"Uh huh. That would be Freddy's *mother*. Cecilia."

"And then the mob shot *her?*"

"You got it. Your command of white American history is impressive."

"Yeah, well, that one was in all the papers. For months. About twenty years ago."

"Freddy came to Ydra about a month after I did."

"What does he do here?"

"Paints naked ladies. From memory. I don't think he sees naked ladies much anymore. He also came here with a girlfriend. Tonina. Sicilian. Long, black hair. Looked like a movie star, only from the seventeenth century. He did lots of paintings of her. She left him for a German singer. A German *girl* singer. Freddy took it hard. Been sort of a hermit since. The bald man next to him is Shelly Weiss. He also paints. In the Chagall/Picasso palette—lots of turquoise, red, orange and yellow. Yorgo, our local gallery owner, says this *exact* colour scheme and style is favoured by almost every American ex-pat painter anywhere in Europe. The very large woman is Ellen Dink."

"Dink?"

"Uh huh. She's from Arkansas originally. Came here with a tiny husband nobody remembers. *Mister* Dink. About thirty years ago. Nobody knows where Dink done gone. Ellen says he went out to take a shit and the cats ate him. Ellen has done very well here, Dink or no. She rents and sells properties to foreigners. If you'd run into her before you found Marilena, you'd be spending twice as much money for half the space. They sit in *Ydróneira*, at that same table, just about every afternoon. There are also two or three other Spazzmaynoids."

"All right. What the hell are Spazzmaynoids?"

Johnny laughed.

"Oh, it's just a word I made up. Comes from *SpazzMAYno*—the Greek word for broken."

"That doesn't make it any clearer, John."

"Right. I will elucidate."

"Please."

"Every one of that bunch has lived on this island for at least ten years. They hang out only with each other. They do not, and in some cases *can*not speak a word of Greek. Until something gets broken. Then they'll pull it together, as if by magic. The language of the land rolls out of them—well, maybe not *rolls*, exactly—until one of the local people, whom they see as indigenous labour, fixes whatever is broken. SpazzMAYno. Then, when the Spazzmaynoids have to *pay* for the work, they lose whatever Greek words they know and pay as little as possible. To be fair, this *is* a haggling culture. They call it *bazari*. From the word *bazaar*. And Greek waiters and workers usually charge English-speakers and tourists more than they charge other Greeks. They don't do it when, ex-pat or not, you become an active part of the community and recognise that this is a *country* and not a theme park."

Theddo nodded. "Ah, theme parks. I've given speeches about cultures treated as theme parks."

"Yeah, well. That's the basic riff of the Spazzmaynoids. We're civil. They always say hello to me and invite me to join them. Americans in Europe like to be seen talking to black people. They think it shows that they're not racists. They don't seem to get it that treating the Greeks as a subgroup in their own country is . . . is . . ."

"The same shit?"

"You got it. So they do all this 'Hey man, how's it hangin'' stuff,' in loud chummy voices, and I say, 'Hello. A splendid morning!' They aren't talking like them and I'm not talking like me. White Nobody having a non-conversation with Black Nobody. They piss me off! Greece is a *country*, not a large hotel. I won't hang with 'em, anymore than I'd hang with black people who don't respect our heritage."

Which is what I thought *you* were when I saw you camping around on the job, Theddo thought. He looked at his new friend. That first day in the square seemed a long time away.

"Take it easy, John. If you don't want to hang out with these fools, *I'm* certainly not gonna ask you to." They laughed, and the Spazzmaynoids looked over at them.

"They really know how to have a good time," Ellen Dink whispered. "That's somethin' I miss from Little Rock. The sound of coloured folks havin' a good time."

Uncle Dag
Washington, D.C., 1978

Bringing Björn to America was, for Theddo, joyful and worrying in equal measure. That he was coming was the joy part. The worry part was figuring out exactly what this young blond male person would be coming to America *as*. "Hi, I'm Björn Nilsson, the teenage white lover of your completely closeted black civic leader" was the sentence that kept running through Theddo's head. A definite non-starter. And the truth. What was needed, what was *essential* was a solid, believable, supportable . . . lie. Theddo had a week to find this lie.

"Dag Ekstrom," he said aloud, in the middle of a meeting about funding for after-school arts workshops.

"You want me to get Senator Ekstrom on the line, T.D.?" Darla asked.

"Uh, yes please. Could you ask him to call me, here at the office, after four today?"

"Will do."

Dag Ekstrom, the tall white-haired seventy-two-year-old Senator from Wisconsin, was a civil rights activist long before it was either fashionable or a vote-getter. In fact, until the sixties, he was probably elected in spite of it. He radiated quiet dignified justice to such a degree (or at least looked like the MGM version of what those things would look like) that the Good Folks of the Land O' Lakes voted him in, figuring he was probably right even about those things that made them uneasy. The more discomfited voters did their best to go along with, or to ignore, the Senator's interest in "Negroes." Then, in 1974, his adored wife, cardiologist and health activist Kristin Holm Ekstrom, died of cancer, and that same electorate ignored the fact that their senator would very occasionally drink himself into a stupor. Dag had always drunk a lot. When Kris was alive, he could hold his liquor. Somehow, his boozometer, and the equilibrium it governed, were buried with her.

He was, however, sober when working (or seemed so), and one of Theddo's best allies and favourite people. As he stood behind his heavy oak desk, extending his right hand, it felt, as always, that the respect and affection were reciprocated.

"*Mister* Daniels! Good to see you, sir. How goes the battle?"

"Oh . . . uphill, Senator, with an occasional plateau."

"Indeed. What are you drinking? I'm having a shot of frozen Swedish vodka."

Theddo laughed. "Well sir, you are . . . more skilled than I. Which is a polite way of saying that a shot of frozen Swedish vodka would put me flat on my ass in the middle of the afternoon. Is there any white wine?"

"You know there is."

Senator Ekstrom crossed the room to a copper-coloured mini-bar fridge, fixed their drinks, and gestured for Theddo to have a seat in the large black leather chair in front of his desk. He then hitched a buttock-cheek onto the edge of the desk and sipped his drink.

"Ah," he said, "first of the day."

"Here's to . . . many more," Theddo replied.

"Hold that thought, my son, it's a good one. Any others?"

"Others?"

"Mm. Other thoughts. How may I be of assistance?"

Dag Ekstrom had been to the barricades with Theddo on numerous occasions. He was also one of about four people in Washington who knew from Theddo's own lips that Theodore Daniels preferred Danny to Annie (he kept wanting to introduce Theddo to this or that "lovely and intelligent young lady of my acquaintance"; finally, out of respect for the depth of their friendship, something had to be said).

The determinedly inclusive Senator was not entirely comfortable with the information, choosing to go around it, in the same way his own constituents looked past his drinking. He had even, when troublemakers started nosing around Theddo's private life, regaled the muckhounds with tales of Daniels the Cocksman and various Luscious Ladies, swearing them to secrecy, lest there be "a whiff of scandal." The secrets would then be duly reported in various corridors, men's rooms and media outlets. Dag Ekstrom, having thus established himself as a good source of gossip, would never be named as the source, in order to protect possible future morsels.

What Theddo wanted this time, however—once he finally stopped circling the block and got to it—was, at the least, nervous-making. As he explained it, he cared deeply for a young Swedish dancer—a *male* dancer, naturally, whom he had met at a conference in Stockholm. After a number of years, in which because of work-related anxieties, he had only permitted himself brief and discreet liaisons, he found that this young man was someone he wanted in his life. The young man, a "Björn Nilsson," seemed to share these feelings, he said, and wished to come to America so they could be together.

"As you can imagine, Dag, it's a difficult situation. Obviously, the easiest and safest thing to do would be to simply tell Björn no. Tell him it's impossible. But the truth is . . . I don't want to lose him. Not without at least trying to make it work.

"Now, I have a lovely basement flat in my house. I usually rent it to students. That is what I'd like to do with Björn—give him the apartment, as an exchange student, here studying dance."

"Yes, well, that sounds fine. He would have his own apartment. Why don't you . . . do just that?"

Dag poured himself another drink, downed it and poured another.

"Well, Dag . . . he's . . . Swedish."

"Yes. You said that. You have something against my people?"

Both men laughed.

"Yeah, right. It was a good neighbourhood until the Swedes moved in. Actually, that sort of *is* the problem. Being who I am, and doing the work I do, I've always rented the flat to students of African heritage . . . *my* people. I feel it would be . . . conspicuous to rent it, or appear to be renting it, to this very blond non-American . . . unless he was . . . your cousin."

"My. Cousin."

And so it came to pass, on a cold January night in 1978, the same night as the funeral and rally for a slain black musician, that Björn Nilsson, Swedish exchange student and instant cousin to Senator Dag Ekstrom, arrived in America to study dance. He waved joyfully to his new relative, and to the handsome middle-aged black man who was smiling hesitantly and, discreetly he hoped, waving back.

"Hey, Uncle Dag!" Björn shouted.

"Oh God." Dag Ekstrom muttered in response.

Mrs. Theodore Daniels
Ydra, Greece, 1995

"The Minoan Minotaur of Crete is a mythic ancestor of today's bull."

Marilena sat propped up in bed, completing her homework assignment—Animals in Greek Mythology. Using her glue-stick, she pasted a coloured picture of the Minotaur to the bottom of the left notebook-page, alongside one of "today's bull." She then leaned over and placed the notebook on the floor next to her bed, leaving it open so that the pages would not be stuck together the next morning.

Hanging over the bed, she smiled at the big brown Minotaur head. Large-eyed, with flaring nostrils and a slight smile (or so it appeared to Marilena), the animal-god reminded her of Theddo Daniels. Everything reminded her of Theddo Daniels. She tore a blank page out of her notebook and placed it on top of her mythology book.

On this blank page she wrote:

Κυρία Θέντο Ντάνιελs

Mrs. Theodore Daniels

Mrs. Theddo Daniels

Marilena Daniels

Seeing her own first name actually next to Theddo's last name made her face feel hot . . . and her brain feel really stupid. Mister Daniels was probably old enough to be the baBAH of her baBAH. By the time she, Marilena Reed, was old enough to be Marilena Anything Else, he would be either very old or dead. Or both.

In her dreams they were happy. They walked, played football, danced and laughed, telling each other stories. In these dreams, he knew the answer to every question she asked, and he would look at her, smile at her, and answer in his beautiful deep voice.

From when she could first read, the family bookshelves had books he had written. Books about people who had travelled into the rest of the world from Africa. People like her baBAH . . . and like the *mávri* half of herself. No, she thought, not *mávri*. Not just a colour. Mister Daniels wrote that she and her father were part of what he called the African Diaspora. *Diaspora*. A Greek word. Meaning, as she told the class in her previous year's heritage report, dispersion, scattering—and also related to *diaspro*—to separate with violence, rupture. Diaspora was the word that tied Greece to Africa. Tied her mother to her father. Tied her to Theddo Daniels. Her Dream Boyfriend.

"*VlahKEEAH Éenay . . . VlahKEEAH EEMAI!*" she said, giggling. "It is stupid . . . *I* am stupid. This is only for dreams!"

She threw off the duvet and got out of bed, crumpling the name-filled paper in her hand. Rummaging in her top dresser-drawer, she found the green plastic lighter she used for her red candle when there was an electrical failure. She lit that candle and then carried it, along with the paper, to the *toulétta*.

Quietly closing the door, she held the paper and the candle over the *toulétta* and burned the evidence of her stupidity.

Please, my God, she thought, let the real one who comes be more near to my age, but just exactly like Mister DanYELLSS.

On his second day as a resident of Kamini, Theddo arranged his blank paper and electronic typewriter on a rectangular wooden table in front of the parlour window. He'd work, he decided, from morning to sunset. He would prepare his afternoon meal at home. The thought made him smile. Mister Theodore Daniels is at home, in his sweet seafront apartment, in Kamini, Ydra, Greece. At night, Mister Daniels will dine out.

Johnny had lent him a radio/cassette-player, along with some rehearsal cassettes of the Rembetiko Brotherz. Viky's plaintive Greco-Turkish wail filled the room. He was alone. No one to be leader of, no one to be butch for.

The knot he usually carried between his shoulder blades gradually untangled. He turned the cassette to its other side, and made a cup of mint tea and some wheat toast. From his suitcase he extracted a carefully bubble-wrapped jar. The hand-lettered label read *Hjortron Sylt*—arctic cloudberry jam. Jam that Björn's mother always sent him at Christmas, and for his birthday, every October seventeenth. The orange, seed-filled preserve brought him, already opened by the music, to where he needed to be. The new book would go back to his childhood in Baltimore and Washington and forward to Ydra, but it had to begin with Björn. And, to Theddo's amazement, with hushpuppies.

Hushpuppies

Theddo and Björn's first year in Washington had its inevitable problems—mostly the slow and clumsy adjustments and accommodations of two people who are newly together. The elder, the supposedly more experienced of the two, had never lived day-to-day, night-to-night with anyone but his mother and sister. And, for two long-ago childhood years, with The Stepfather. At forty-two, Theddo was having only the third major relationship of his life (though this one was, if possible, even less publicly acknowledged than the first two had been).

In those early days with Björn, when at home and feeling safe, Theddo would watch with pleasure, as this creature from another world gradually inhabited his house and his life. Björn seemed to love *everything* about the Washington, D.C., neighbourhood he called Thedd-doh-land: he loved the little rowhouses of East Capitol and the sounds of black American girl-children jumping rope like leaping dancers and shouting their poem about "Little Sally Walker." He loved the big-faced cats that roamed the streets, stretching and purring when you scratched them behind the ears. Loved his little white-walled basement flat ("My first for just me") with its tiny windows and shutters; loved the bright red-and-black Persian rug in the living room; loved the large black beanbag chair ("It's sexy, I think, this chair. One, or two, can flop on it *anny*-where! I show you!").

He particularly loved the garden, with its huge old oak tree, which he could sit under or dance around, making what he called a Druid tree-dance (though he promised not to be naked or painted blue until an actual public performance).

He also loved going to the Eastern Market every Saturday morning, eating apples and grapes and three or four of the spicy fried balls of corn-meal and flour called hushpuppies ("These are the *best* market-food, I think. Yes. The best!") while Theddo bought big dark green vegetables, which he would later boil with bits of pork fat, insisting that they both drink the bitter green vegetable-water.

"Pot-likker. It heals anything. Heals stuff you don't even know you've got. Drink it."

"It tastes . . . *nah*sty!"

"Drink it fast then. One gulp. When everyone around you has a cold and feels spindly and poorly, *you* and *I* will be strong as bulls!"

And they *were* strong, that first year, the old bull and the young bull. Theddo helped Björn fill out an application to apprentice with David Schoenfeld DanceWorks. Schoenfeld had given a concert in Stockholm. Björn had attended, and very much admired the work of the American dancer-choreographer. Like his own dances, Schoenfeld's work seemed to fuse the ancient world with religious music, world-music and hard, driving rock n' roll.

Björn was invited to audition. This audition, in front of David Schoenfeld and two assistants, was rigorous. It consisted of an original dance, plus a lengthy test of Björn's ability to execute specific instruc-tions and respond to choreographic suggestions. Björn's shakiness with American-type English, coupled with Schoenfeld's heavy New York accent, made that component particularly difficult, but he did his best and hoped for the best.

A week later, the letter of acceptance arrived, which Theddo said was really fast. "They must have liked you a lot."

Waving the letter in the air, reading a few words aloud ("We would be pleased" . . . "they would be *pleased!*"), Björn whirled around the basement apartment; leaping, laughing, flinging his arms about. Theddo, seated on the couch, would be periodically kissed on the top of his head, as the euphoric Nordic dervish would shout, "He *took* me, Thedd-doh! *Schoenfeld took* me! He took *me* for his *Clahssess!*"

They celebrated with an enormous meal at Theddo's favourite restaurant, *The Drinking Gourd*. Theddo told him the meal was called Soulfood. It had come originally, he said, from the African slaves who were brought to America. Rice and beans, root vegetables, greens, the spicy sauce-covered ribs of pigs . . . and more hushpuppies. Such a funny-sounding word, Björn thought.

That night, after Theddo was asleep, Björn went downstairs to find his battered little Swedish dictionary.

"*Tysta-valpar. Tysta valpar?* Make quiet your little baby dog?" Could the food be called that? Was it once dog food? Food for the dogs of African slaves? Did eating it quieten the little dogs? Did they shove hushpuppy balls into the mouths of the dogs? It was crazy, American English, Björn thought. Americans could call something *anything*. It did not have to make sense anywhere else in the world. When you're powerful, you are allowed to call anything or anybody whatever you like.

Björn headed back up the stairs to the main house. He walked into the bedroom on his toes, quietly as he could, but Theddo opened his eyes anyway.

"What's up? You all right, Lille?

"Ya," he whispered, trying not to awaken Theddo any more than necessary. "I was looking for something in my Swedish wordbook."

"What? What were you looking for?" Theddo whispered back.

"Hushpuppies."

"Hushpuppies? Were they there? In a Swedish dictionary?"

"I'm not sure. I don't think so."

"Tell you about 'em tomorrow. Come to sleep."

The next morning, Björn, who was propped up in bed, watching through the open bathroom door as Theddo shaved, asked his etymological question again.

"So, where does it come from?"

"Where does what come from, Lille?"

"Hushpuppies. In Swedish it is to make quiet the little dogs? Is it dogsfood?"

Theddo laughed, shaking his head. He had noticed before that Björn, when he wanted to know something, would not let go of it until he had his answer. A terrier. A Swedish terrier. An un-hushable puppy. This was good, he thought. The Baltasar Axelssons of the world, however many of them there might have been, had not killed his curiosity. Theddo did not know *how* many there had been. He did not *want* to know. Björn, on the other hand, wanted to know absolutely *everything* about Theddo. Theddo told him about Billy, about Tafiq, about the Gypsy boy from the Porte Portese market. In answer to endless questions, he told him about his family, his work, his friends. He told him about everything but the one childhood thing that, he was almost certain, joined them together before they met.

"Hushpuppies, Lille, were poor folk's food. Also, in the old times, soldier's food. Fried cornmeal with flour and spices. And, as you know, very tasty. During the American Civil War, the Confederate soldiers would eat these things, and they'd throw a few to the dogs so the dogs wouldn't bark. Eating the cornmeal balls would "hush the puppies," which made them quiet. Keeping the dogs quiet was important. If they barked, then the Union soldiers would know where the Rebels were hiding."

"Rebels?"

"The Confederate soldiers."

"Were the . . . ConFEDerATTS the side that was trying to free your AHNcestors?"

"No. Those were the Union soldiers."

Throwing the duvet off his naked body, Björn walked to the bathroom door. His face was so gravely serious that Theddo, his own face still half-covered in shaving cream, turned, concerned, to face him.

"What, Lille? What's wrong?"

"I did not know this, Thedd-doh. I did not know that the hushpuppies were the food of the people who hurt your AHNcestors. I am so sorry! I will *never* eat hushpuppies in my life again!" And he threw his arms around Theddo, pressing his face against his chest.

Theddo couldn't help it. He laughed. Björn, eyes wet, looked up at him indignantly.

"You t'ink it iss funny that I do not wish to betray your people with my eating?"

"Well . . . yes, a little bit . . ."

"*Fin! Bra!* Good! I will eat hushpuppies all day!" He tried to pull away. Theddo held him by the upper arms.

"Lille, listen to me. I do not think it is funny that you care about black people. I do not think it is funny at all. What is funny is tying our oppression . . . or our salvation, to *hushpuppies.*"

"You are laughing at me, no?"

"No. I'm laughing at that crazy word. Hushpuppy *is* a funny word, yes?"

Björn giggled quickly, and then regained his stern face.

"Ya. *Iss funny word* . . . but . . ."

"Listen, Lille. Our side, the side of my ancestors, the Union side, the Yankees, *won* that war. And some of us, black and white, have been trying to build on that early success ever since. This building goes way too slowly . . . but the hushpuppies have damn-all to do with any of it. I swear to you. Black folks eat hushpuppies all the time. They are not . . . a political statement. Not in *any* direction. It's just poor folk's junkfood. This coming Saturday, at the Eastern Market, if I can do it subtly, without looking like I'm taking a census, I will point out to you all the black people eating hushpuppies. All right?"

"You think I am silly?"

"No. Not at all. I think you are in a new country . . . and want to be loyal to . . . people you care about. You want to do the right thing."

"Yes. Yes, I do."

"And this is good. This makes me happy."

Björn smiled, more shyly than Theddo'd seen since he first praised his dancing. In Stockholm. At *Klubb Kul.*

He reached again for Theddo, and they hugged. He had been the first to initiate the embrace, and was first to break from it. He walked back to the bed, then turned to Theddo again.

"Thedd-doh, if hushpuppies are not enemy-food, why don't *you* eat them when we go to the Eastern Market? Why is it only me eating them?"

"Lille, the reason I do not eat hushpuppies is that hushpuppies are fattening as hell! *You* stay slim, no matter *what* you eat. Whereas *I* pork up if I even *look* at hushpuppies. Listen, next Saturday, I will eat a hushpuppy, just to show you that I do not think they are a betrayal of my people."

"So. You truly do not think I am silly?"

Theddo lightly stroked Björn's cheekbones with his index fingers.

"Absolutely not. Concern about other people is *never* silly. Now, the fact that your hair is full of shaving cream, *that* is silly."

Theddo was late to his meeting at InterAfrA. He said he had been consulting with A White Outreach group that wanted to better understand black history. He did not say it was a group of one.

Transient Dancing

Björn's apprenticeship was not going as well as he had hoped. David Schoenfeld, a fine and innovative modern dancer, was also what dancers sometimes called The Breeder Minority—a heterosexual married dancer and the father of two little boys. Having danced since childhood, he was tired of the clichés about "sissy" dancers. While there were two gay male lead dancers in the David Schoenfeld Dance Company, they were expected to, as Schoenfeld put it, "dance male." The dances performed by the muscular and somewhat stocky Schoenfeld, as well as anything he choreographed, stressed masculine strength, and were, some said, a bit heavy-footed.

For the lithe and leaping Björn Nilsson, this new style was awkward and difficult.

"No, Byawn! Not so much hainds and awms. A smawl leap! Like Frank's. You are leaping *togethuh* heah. The two leaps should be the same size. Watch Frank. You don' have to hit the ceiling. SIMpluh moves! Less drama, Byawn, it is not a tragedy! It's about buying a girl a lemon ice cream, fuh Chrissakes! Stawt again. 1-2-3-4-5-6-7-8, and 1-2-3-4-5 . . . stay nearuh to the ground, Byawn, watch your back haind, it looks a bit like 'Swan Leak' . . . *And,* 1-2-3-4-5 . . ."

At the end of the day's work, Björn was assigned a back-row chorus part (as were all the apprentice dancers except one—a tall blonde girl). Typically, he took it all personally. Schoenfeld *hates* me, he thought.

That night, when Theddo returned home, he could see Björn through the largest of the basement windows. He was dancing. The door wasn't locked. He let himself in and quietly watched. There was a cassette playing; a gravel-voiced man singing in Italian. Björn stood in the centre of the red-and-black rug, swaying slightly to the music, eyes closed, elbows slightly bent as he moved his arms, first to the right, then the left, instructing himself in what sounded to Theddo like the Swedish version of a nasal Brooklyn accent: "No, No, Buh-yawn! Ya *caint* fling yer awms aout awll the way like that, Yull hit the persson nexta ya! 1-2-3-4." Still swaying, he opened his eyes.

"Hello, Lille. I could see you dancing, and the door was . . ."

Björn sank, in one clean, seemingly boneless move, down to the rug. Theddo threw his bomber jacket onto the couch and sat beside him. Björn looked at him with huge sad eyes. The same look which had, only a week earlier, accompanied his pledge to never again in his life, eat another hushpuppy.

"Oh THEDD-doh, it wass OH-full. *I* am oh-full! Mister Schoenfeld thought everything I did was . . . was too *flicka*, too *bög!*"

"*Flicka? Bög?*"

"Yah . . . too girly, too faggy."

"He said your dancing was *faggy?*"

"No. He said it wass *Nelly.* I did not know this word. So, in the dressing room, after the work, I ask Frank, another boy dancer, what means Nelly, and he, Frank, tells me Nelly means faggy, which iss a word I learn even in Stockholm. It is like the Swedish word *bög* . . . not masculine. Queer."

"Niggerish."

Björn shook his head emphatically. It seemed he had also learned *this* word in Stockholm.

"Oh no, Thedd-doh! Nothing like that!"

"Yeah, *something* 'like that.' It's the same shit! Look, Björn, there are lots of dancers, lots of schools, we can . . ."

Björn shook his head again, and spoke very softly.

"No, Thedd-doh. Absolute no. I *know already* how to dance like Björn Nilsson. I must learn also how to dance like David Schoenfeld. And how to dance with other dancers."

He grinned. "You see, David Schoenfeld can *not* dance like *me*. Not *ever!* His body and his feet are too tied to the earth. But, if *I* can learn his dancing, then I will be . . . be . . . earth *and* sky! I will be *all* of it, together!"

Theddo knelt on his knees and, taking Björn's face in his hands, kissed the centre of his forehead. He then pulled back and looked at him, smiling, shaking his head.

"Oh my! You can be such a Drama Queen sometimes, and then you say something like . . . like what you just said. I love you."

"Really?"

"Mm hm."

After a week of watching Björn come home from dancing all day and then continue dancing for two hours more, Theddo felt this diligence deserved a reward. He called Dag Ekstrom.

Dag owned a cabin-like log house in the woods just outside of Little Washington, Virginia. When Kristin Ekstrom was alive, they had gone there almost every weekend. After her death, however, the Senator found it painful to be in the place alone. So, he usually invited others to join him. Theddo had occasionally been one of those others—usually with Senator Callie Hodge, who was widely regarded as Theddo's long-time girlfriend. Keisha Dixon, who was *Callie's* long-time girlfriend, happily went along with all this. Tall, model-thin and glam, with a headful of Jheri-curls, Keisha's job as fashion editor for the weekend magazine of the *Washington Post*, was not threatened by questions of sexual orientation, but "you guvmint types" as she teasingly called Callie and Theddo, "have a whole nuther bag of situations."

Dag would always put Theddo and Callie in a twin-bedded room, where they would talk, read, sleep.

Theddo, knowing that Dag, while certainly not gay-*negative*, was gay-*awkward*, had not considered asking if he might visit *Woodhue* (as the house was called) with Dag's so-called Swedish cousin, Björn Nilsson.

The two men had years of honest exchange between them. No harm in giving it a try, Theddo decided.

"With Callie as well?" Dag asked, after a slight hesitation.

"It's up to you. I'm fine either way. I want Björn to meet Callie. But if . . ."

"Good. Let's do it that way then. You and Callie and Björn. I'll see

Callie on the Senate floor tomorrow, and find out if she's available this weekend."

"Thanks, Dag. Thanks a lot. Björn has been dancing his feet to a nubbin all week. Did you know he was accepted as an apprentice by David Schoenfeld DanceWorks?"

"That's great, Theddo! Give him my congratulations," Dag replied, having no idea what David Schoenfeld DanceWorks was.

Björn, who found American homosexual secrecy both peculiar and insulting, was delighted.

"Oh, at *laahhst!* Going somewhere together, other than to a marKETT, or a sometimes-restaurant! And with other persons too! PerFECT! Will we take a plane or a train to Uncle Dag's?"

"No, no, Lille. It's only about an hour and a half outside Washington. In the state of Virginia, which is next door to Washington. Dag or Callie will pick us up, in a car, on Friday night."

"I have clahssess on Monday. Will we be back on time?"

"Oh sure. We *all* have work on Monday. We'll drive back Sunday night."

Theddo dispensed this information as he stood at his kitchen counter, tossing a salad with two wooden spoons. Björn embraced him from behind, resting his head against Theddo's back.

"So, this Callie. How old is she?"

"Callie will be thirty-nine in April."

"You celebrate her birthday?"

"I do."

"And she is your girlfriend, yes?"

"Mm hm. For years."

Björn came around to alongside Theddo.

"Really? Really your girlfriend?"

"You know the answer to that question."

"Ya. I only want to hear you say it. I want to hear you say that she is not your girlfriend. I want to hear you say that *I* am!"

"Well, you're not my girlfriend either. Here. Take this bowl of salad to the table. I'll open the wine."

As they ate dinner, Theddo explained that he and Callie had begun working together years ago. Callie, as the third-ever black Senator, was a critical, and a more than willing professional ally. Between them, they'd gotten a lot done, particularly in the areas of decent affordable housing and a food programme for Washington schoolchildren.

Callie was also, as Björn knew from earlier discussions, a lesbian. It made things easier, in the mostly closeted world of Official Washington for them to appear to be a couple. From time to time there were rumours and "tabloid garbage" about both or either of them, but nothing ever stuck.

"People, white and black, like the *idea* of Callie and me. They *want* to believe it. So they do."

"What is she like?"

Very smart, very socially committed and hardworking, very funny . . . and very pretty."

"Pretty. Prettier than me?"

"Good God no! *Nobody on the face of the earth* is prettier than you!"

"I am serious."

"That's what I was afraid of. Actually, Lille, I've no idea if Callie is or is not prettier than you. I'm not in love with Callie."

"Aha! And you *are* in love with me, ya?"

"You know that."

"Ya. I do. I just like to hear it a lot."

"I've noticed."

"Do you dislike this? That I like to hear this a lot?"

"No. Not yet. I think it's enough times for tonight, though."

"Maybe one more. Later?"

"Possibly. Now eat your pasta or it will coagulate."

"Co-argue-late?"

"Mm hm. Turn into a cold ball of rubber gunk."

"Hey, hey, Uncle Dag!" Björn shouted, as he flung Theddo's large duffel bag into the trunk of Dag Ekstrom's ancient maroon Volvo. Seeing Dag wince, Theddo got into the passenger seat beside him, saying, "I need the room for my big legs," but thinking, 'Björn knows he makes Dag nervous and if he decides it would be funny to suddenly squeeze his knee, we'll go right off the road!

"Callie, meet Björn Nilsson; Björn, this is Callie Hodge."

To avoid rush-hour traffic, which, in the area comprising Washington, Virginia and Maryland, was, in Dag's phrase "one of the uglier circles of hell," they had left their journey until eight in the evening. The drive to Virginia was pretty in daylight, but all you could see at night were highways and dark roads, with occasional Main Streets of little towns.

They were on a back road when they came to a large, floodlit wooden sign, at the foot of a hilly one-car path that led to a resort hotel. Dag stopped the car.

"Ah, we have come, at last to the Arborial Urinarium. You will, excuse me for a moment, ladies and gentlemen," he announced, in his most oratorical voice. He then got out and went into the woods, off to the left of the sign. Theddo, who knew this ritual, smiled, as did Callie. Keisha giggled.

"What iss happening?" Björn asked.

"It's all right, the Good Senator has just gone to relieve himself."

"Relieve?"

"He's having a piss, Lille. 'Arborial Urinarium' is what the Senator calls his pissing place. He always does that here. The light from the sign lets him see the way to his special spot in the woods."

"He does this always here?"

"Always."

"And we wait?"

"We do . . . unless you want to have a piss too?"

"With the Senator?"

"No, Lille, not *with the Senator* . . . unless you want to scare him half to death."

They all laughed at this, including Björn.

"No, I do not wish to piss . . . or to scare Senator Dag. I will go to read the sign. To practise my English."

Björn stood in front of the sign, and read aloud:

"WELCOME TO BOUGAINVILLEA!

Gourmet Restaurant, Hiking

Horseback riding (English and Western)

Cross-country skiing (seasonal)

Canoeing, Bird-watching

Transient, Dancing."

Dag Ekstrom returned, saying "Old people. We have to do more of that sort of thing than you youngsters."

He got back into the car. Björn was still looking at the Bougainvillea sign. Finally, he walked to the car, and, still outside, pointed to the sign.

"Theddo, what, please, does that mean?"

"What does *what* mean, Lille?"

"That, here, *Transient Dancing?*"

Theddo looked out the window at the sign. He laughed.

"Those are two separate things."

"*What* are two separate things?"

"*Transient* and *Dancing*."

"But they are together on the sign. *Transient* and *Dancing*. What is 'transient'?"

"*Transient?* Well, 'transient' means . . ."

Callie, who'd been asking Björn questions about Sweden, enjoying his energy and curiosity, could see that this mattered to him. She jumped in.

"Transient means for a short time, Björn. It means momentary, passing—a temporary, impermanent thing."

"Ah! So *transient dancing* means dancing you do from place to place, for a short time. Temporary. That is what *I* do! In Stockholm, in Fårö, in Washington. Wherever I am. I am . . . a transient dancer!"

Callie nodded, smiling. "Yes, you could say that."

"Then I must have this sign!"

"Björn, it's late. We should just . . ."

"Please, Thedd-doh. This is *important!*"

Dag looked worried. "Theddo, could we . . . ?"

"Come on, Lille, we can take a picture of it tomorrow. With you standing next to it, okay?"

"No, not 'okay.' It is *my* sign. I take it now."

"Christ!" Dag muttered. "Theddo, please explain to him that if we're busted for stealing signs in the middle of the night . . ."

"Oh come on, you two old farts! Weren't you ever teenagers?" Callie asked, laughing, hopping out of the car, armed with her Swiss Army knife.

She and Björn worked together, twinkling like mad at one another. It only took about two minutes to remove the sign from its hinges and bung it into the back seat of the car. The thing was fairly large, so they stood it on its side on the car floor, flinging their legs over it, laughing, high-fiving and being generally obstreperous.

"Christ!" Dag said again. "It's like having a car full of bad kids! Can you imagine the headlines 'Two Senators, One Civil Rights Leader and . . .'"

"And one Transient Dancer . . ."

"Yeah, and one transient dancer arrested for . . ."

"Hey, Dag, is this 'Senator Busted' fantasy getting you off?"

"Getting me *off?* No, Callie, it is *not 'getting me off.'* I'm seventy-two years old!"

"So getting off is no longer an option?"

"That's not what I said. I just don't 'get off' from getting caught stealing other people's property."

"Must be a black thing then."

Dag was genuinely indignant "What?!"

"Easy, I'm kidding. Didn't you ever steal a stop sign, or a bus stop thing?"

"Sure, when I was . . ."

"About eighteen, right?"

Dag sighed. "I see your point. But we *still* could have been . . ."

"But we weren't. So let go of that and enjoy Björn having found his first piece of American folk art. Folk art about *him.*"

Björn looked at Callie as if she were his mother, and his mother had just turned into Nijinsky and Elvis, who were both a black woman.

"*Tack.* Thank you," he said softly.

"You're welcome, Björn. Any time . . . well, maybe not *any time,* but . . . 'evvy now an' agin.'"

And she laughed, and her laugh was so full, so musical to Björn that he wanted to make a dance of it. *Callie's Laugh,* A Dance by Björn Nilsson, Transient Dancer.

Dag parked the car by the side of a narrow, heavily wooded road. Then, after making sure the purloined signboard was securely locked in the trunk, the travellers grabbed various bags and, aided by their host's flashlight skills, made their way up a winding path until, in a clearing, they came to a log cabin.

Dag put down his bag.

"Hang in, troops, I'll go turn on some lights."

"It is perFECT!" Björn exclaimed. "Callie, this is little bit like Fårö, where I am from. We have such houses in Sweden. Not so much round wood, like this, but houses of flat wood. Here, I do that!"

Björn grabbed four bags and headed for the wooden door, as lights came on in the cabin.

Inside, Dag knelt in front of an enormous stone fireplace, rolling paper into balls, and shoving them under mounds of kindling and two large logs.

"I'm almost *dangerously* hungry!" Callie said, pulling off her black boots.

Dag lit the paperballs and fire-crackle began. He then headed for the kitchen, where he lifted a large woven picnic basket from the floor onto the table.

"I thought that might be the case. This hamper contains fried chicken, potato salad, bread and wine. Oh, and a homemade apple and raisin pie, courtesy of Missus Drennan, the mother of my secretary, Barbara."

"*Swedish* fried chicken?!"

"You think Swedes can't fry chicken, Mister Daniels?"

"*Anybody* can fry chicken, Senator. What makes me nervous is having it stuffed with herring."

"I see. Callie, could you and Björn set the table? Dinner for everyone. Bread and water for Daniels. *White* bread and water."

After dinner, Callie, the only smoker in the group, went outside to have a cigarette. She stretched out in the multicoloured Mexican hammock that was strung between two large maple trees, took a deep drag and blew the smoke up at the sky. Theddo, having done the dishwashing, came out to visit with her.

"Hey, Thedd. Grab a piece of tree. Where's the lad?"

The term made Theddo self-conscious—did she mean lad as in fella, or lad as in boy? He let it go.

"Watching television. *Silver Streak*."

"Good film . . . well, fun film."

"He loves Pryor. Says Swedish kids love Pryor. Says they all learned to say 'motherfucker' from Pryor."

"Well, that is certainly an important contribution from our people to the Nordic world."

"Björn says Pryor is *an absoLUTE Geeneeusss!*"

"I agree."

"Yeah. Me too." Theddo smiled. "He also says, Björn does, that he likes watching the film because seeing Pryor and Wilder together reminds him of the two of *us.*"

"He thinks he's Gene *Wilder?* Wilder is old enough to be . . ."

"His father? As am I."

"I didn't say it."

"I appreciate that. I can say it, or *think* it, enough for both of us."

"Does it worry you?"

"Not usually. Sometimes . . . but we both seem to be . . . where we want to be. Everything seems . . . clean and honourable between us. For me, it's like all this energy, all this *life* has . . . I've never . . . I don't usually . . . oh, let's just leave it there for now, and enjoy the night."

"Of course. I didn't mean to pry."

"You weren't. You never do. We wuz just talkin'."

"Indeed. And where is our host? He also watching *Silver Streak?*"

"No. Went upstairs with a pile of envelopes. Says he's got a heavy Monday."

"We all do. My Manila Monsters are in my suitcase. They'll keep until tomorrow. You bring stuff?"

"Nope."

"Actually, I have something I'd like to show you."

"Senate bill?"

"Yeah. College tuition and on-campus housing."

"Fine. Not tonight, okay?"

"I'm not touching *any* of it tonight. Tomorrow? Afternoon?"

"Terrific. Happy to."

"Thanks."

Callie sat up, swinging her legs over the hammock's side. She lit a second cigarette from the first, stamped out and shredded the first butt.

"You smoke too much, Callie."

"That's what Keisha says."

"Keisha smokes too much too."

"That's what I say back. She says I'm the one with the lousy family history. I like him, Theddo. Björn."

"Yeah. I could see that. And, now that you've shown your talent for both spontaneity and theft, he thinks you're a god."

"Dess."

"What?"

"God-DESS."

"Right, God*dess.*"

When Theddo and Callie returned to the cabin, Dag and Björn were seated across from each other at the heavy wooden kitchen table—discussing government-supported health care.

Dag, Callie and Theddo had long been fighting for single-payer health care in the U.S.—some version of the system that existed in almost every other so-called "developed" nation. Björn, who had lived his entire life in such a system, was telling Dag "it saved the life of my mother twice, and also my little brother when he fell out of window because of playing. Without national health, they both, the two, would be dead now."

Callie and Theddo, wanting to let this connection continue, stayed near the door, understanding everything, saying nothing.

"Listen, Björn, could you ask your mother to send you the most recent information about Swedish health care?"

"Well, my mother might not have much of written information, but my friend Per can get it. Or . . . another friend."

Stig Hanssons, Theddo thought irritably, and then corrected. Let it *be.* The man was good to him. One of the few, I'd reckon. And Björn is here, with me. Be cool, Mister Daniels.

"That would be very helpful, Björn," Dag said, rising from his chair and stretching. "I'd really appreciate it."

"I am glad to help."

He was grinning as if "glad to help" didn't begin to express his pleasure. As was Theddo. Grinning so fully that Dag felt the energy and turned around.

"Well, we are all assembled. Now, I don't know about you youngsters, but I'm pooped! I think we should all hit the hay, and, first thing in the morning, I'll do us all some pancakes, sausages . . . and, of course, herring for Daniels."

"All right, all right with the herring routine. The Swedish fried chicken was fine . . . if a bit bland . . ."

"Yeah, well wait till you try my Swedish chitlins. Now *that's* serious eatin'. Anyway, enough of this badinage. Theddo, you and Callie take your usual room and . . ."

Björn looked as if he'd been told to sleep outside.

"But . . ."

Theddo was quickly at his side.

"It's all right, Lille . . ."

"But . . ."

"Come outside with me for a minute." His voice was soft, but firm.

"But I want to . . ."

"*Now*, Lille, please . . ." As he said this, he gently led Björn out, grabbing his jacket, not looking at the others. He closed the door.

"Fuck! It is cold as fucking hell out here!"

"Here. Take my jacket. Don't shout."

"But Thedd-doh, Dag knows that we are . . . we are *together!* Why is he putting you to bed with Callie?"

"He is not 'putting me to bed with Callie.' We always have the same room here. It has two beds."

"But, that was . . . before there was me."

"Yes, Lille, that *was* before there was you. And Dag knows that. And . . . you are starting to know each other. It was a fine thing you did in there, about health care. He needs that information, and I know he was very glad to have your help, and . . ."

"What does this have to do with bed?"

Theddo laughed. "Oh Lille, it doesn't have a thing to do with bed. Not a damned thing. Except that Dag Ekstrom comes from a time and place where . . . where he would be uncomfortable putting two men in the same bed in his house. He knows what you mean to me. Remember, it was Dag who made it possible for you to come here. But he needs to go easy with . . . actual 'bed' matters. The next time we come here, we can probably have the room that Callie and I have always had."

"With the two beds?"

"With the two beds."

Björn grinned. "And if I came, in the middle of the night, into your bed . . .?"

"We . . . could certainly deal with that when the time came . . . but for now, to help Dag learn some new things, can we do it this way? Please?"

"Where will I sleep?"

"Let's go back in and find out."

Dag had dealt with "the awkwardness of the situation" by going upstairs to bed. Callie awaited them with full instructions.

"Hi guys. Dag said Björn gets the library bed, down here. It's a good hard mattress. I know. I've slept in that bed. The room has its own john . . . toilet . . . and, lots of books to read . . . and, if you're like me, you can also go to the fridge real easy in the middle of the night and get cold water and stuff. Come, I'll show you where everything is."

Inside their usual room, Callie turned to Theddo.

"Well, *that* was something new and different. How is he? Is he cool?"

"Sort of. Trying to be. I told him, outside, that all this about us, was, on a personal level, a lot of new stuff for Dag. And it's not just Dag who's having new stuff. I sometimes forget that Björn has never been in this country before. He's learning something new every day."

"So are you, I'd reckon."

"No lie!"

Sometime later, Theddo, who had been sleeping lightly and fitfully any-way, saw the door open. Slightly, quietly, letting a thin white stripe of light into the room. That light, from the wall-sconce in the corridor, bounced off Björn's yellow hair.

Oh God, Theddo thought, he is going to climb into bed with me. But Björn did not move. He stood in the doorway, looking at what he believed to be the sleeping figures of Theddo and Callie. He did not want to climb into bed with Theddo. What he wanted was for there to be a huge bed, with room for him to climb in between them. And sleep. Just sleep. He wanted this very much. He watched them for a few moments more, and then closed the door.

There are things that people can live their whole life without knowing. And, with many of these things, that is just fine. Many of these many things need not be known at all. On a Sunday in late March, in a log cabin in Virginia, Theddo Daniels was informed of one such thing.

Callie and Björn were in the woods looking for mushrooms, Björn having assured her that he had known, since he was a child, how to tell edible from poisonous ones.

Dag and Theddo were tidying the cabin in preparation for heading back to D.C. that night.

"I'm glad Björn will be able to help you with Swedish health care information," Theddo said as he sprayed the table with wood-polish and wiped it clean.

"Yeah, me too. There are so many false rumours about Sweden, about Canada, with regard to health care, it will be good to have as much as possible from 'the horse's mouth' when we bring it forward . . . yet again!"

"Björn told me how pleased he was that you spoke with him about it."

"Good. I don't know a lot of . . . young people, and don't always know how to relate to 'em. Please tell him . . . it was good to have him here."

"I certainly will. And Thanks a lot Dag, for this weekend. We both needed to get the hell out of D.C."

"Everybody needs to get the hell out of D.C. That's why I'll never sell this place. Want a shot of cold vodka?"

"No thanks, Dag . . . and if you're going to drive . . ."

"Callie's gonna drive. That's our deal. And I'm not gonna get loaded anyway, so don't worry. Just one. Maybe two."

He went to the refrigerator, filled a juice glass with vodka. And returned to the living room.

"Long live the potato!" he toasted.

"To the potato!" Theddo mimed in response.

"He's a good kid, actually, your Björn . . . though I *do* wish he wouldn't call me Uncle Dag. He loves to shout that 'Hey, Uncle Dag!' at me. I think he knows it gives me the drizzlin' willies. And I'm *not* his uncle. I'm not even his *cousin*, which is the bogus thing he's *supposed* to be calling me."

"Björn *can* be a bit of a smart ass. But I think he calls you Uncle Dag because . . . because he wishes you *were* his uncle. I've met his mother, and his little half-brother and half-sister. They live on the Swedish island of Fårö . . ."

"In Gotland?"

"Yes. Have you been?"

"Years ago. With Kris. Amazing place."

"Yeah. Those rock men. Anyway, Björn's family are, I think, very good people. But there was no adult male around, and I had the feeling that the rest of his relatives have not been . . . that good for, or to him."

"Well, I'm honoured that he wants me for an uncle. But it still would be . . . less awkward if he didn't bellow it at me in public."

Theddo was re-stacking logs alongside the newly immaculate fireplace, which Björn had cleaned out that morning, insisting that he was Cinderella.

"I will tell him. At an appropriate time. Mind you, one joyous greeting at the airport and another in front of my place hardly constitute massive public proclamation. As far as I know, he hasn't been down to the floor of the Senate, bellowing 'Uncle Dag.'"

"No," Dag agreed, lifting the mostly empty picnic hamper and placing it by the door with various bags. "But he has done it in the lobby of the Hay-Adams Hotel."

"Oh? I didn't know that. I'll speak to him about it. It won't happen again. Sorry."

Dag, a politician almost all his life, knew instantly that he'd said a problematic thing. He looked up. His friend was making words, but his voice had gone funny, thinned out. Theddo busied himself straightening furniture and restoring lap robes to the back of the outsized chocolate-brown leather couch. He knew Dag was looking at him and forced his tone back to normal.

"He's young. He's also a performer. He loves being looked at. I will talk to him about not *Uncle Dag*-ing you in large public venues . . . like the Hay-Adams Hotel."

On the drive back to Washington, Callie and Björn prattled away; Björn asked question after question about which were the good dance companies and where one found various types of music and clothing.

Dag, in the back seat beside Theddo, pretended to sleep and, fairly quickly, stopped pretending and slept.

Theddo only spoke when (rarely) spoken to, and mostly stared at the place where Björn's choppy hair met his neck. Thinking about what had happened a month earlier.

Hay-Adams, If Love Were All

Björn had returned home at two-fifteen in the morning. Theddo, in his own bed upstairs, heard his "tenant" let himself into the basement flat. He then heard the door opening at the bottom of the stairs and Björn bounding up into the bedroom.

"Hey, hey, Thedd-doh! You are awake! I am glad. Sorry for my being so late. After dance class, a group of us went for food together and, because we were talking about dancing, I lost the time!"

"I see. Did you all go to a club?"

Björn laughed, curling up next to Theddo, and kissing his chest.

"No, no. Sometimes it *is* good to do that, to just keep dancing, but I was too full of food to want to dance. Some others did go to a club. I wanted to come home." He looked up into Theddo's eyes, his own eyes newborn with innocence and wonder.

"I was afraid you'd be already asleep. I know I have ways to wake you, but I am glad you are awake." He sat on the edge of the bed, bending over to remove his running shoes and socks. Theddo, in the light of a bedside lamp, looked at his hair.

"So. You were at a restaurant all this time? Getting full of food. The Italian place?"

"No, not that one. A French place."

"French. Isn't that pretty expensive for your budget?"

"Allowance. Gabrielle from class says it is not called a budget. It is called an allowance. Anyway, she has a very large allowance. From her family in France. And she took everyone to dinner. Five people!"

He was standing in front of the dresser-mirror, looking at himself unbuttoning his yellow flannel shirt. And seeing Theddo, in the mirror, in the bed behind him.

"Björn, does it bother you that I give you . . . an allowance?"

He turned, leaning against the dresser. His voice was cool. The innocent wonder-filled look was gone. It was replaced by a neutrality that Theddo neither knew nor understood. There was no anger. Nor was there any love, any friendship, any anything. He could have been speaking, clearly and sensibly, to a wall.

"No, Theddo. Not at all. I had no money when you invite me here to live with you. I have told you that I will not borrow money because it makes enemies. I have seen this happen. I have also promised that as soon as I am working as a dancer, I shall stop taking this weekly money from you. This I promise you."

"And I believe you."

"Good."

"Why is your hair wet?"

"What?"

"I asked you why your hair was wet."

Björn shifted his weight, laughed lightly.

"That is a silly question. My hair is wet because it was raining when I walked home?"

"No, Björn. I've been working all evening. And awake in bed reading for the past hour. It did not rain."

Björn stared at him. Theddo felt . . . felt *what?* Dared?

"Oh you probably fell asleep during the little shower. There was a little shower."

"No, Björn. Wide awake. And even if I *had* dozed off, rain would have awakened me. You know I'm a light sleeper, and . . ."

"Ya! I am ah*MAYSSED* that you did not wake up for the sound of the rain."

Theddo's voice wasn't loud, but it had sharp corners.

"Björn, stop. I would simply like to know why your hair is wet. When you've been indoors for hours. And then walked home on a *completely* dry night. You also had wet hair last week, after coming home from seeing a film you had already seen, saying you had liked it so much you wanted to see it twice. Was there a shower in the movie theatre?"

Björn stood up, running his long fingers through his hair.

"Oh fuck! I do not believe this conversation. Are you making a study on my hair? What the fuck doess it matter if my hair iss wet?"

Theddo put his fingers over his mouth, blowing out a sigh. He got out of bed. He was naked. He *felt* naked. Clumsy and foolish. The anxious, petty, accusing middle-aged lover of a boy who had always lived off middle-aged lovers. He felt like poor, pathetic Stig Hanssons, the loyal old fool who would be anything to Björn that Björn would allow him to be. He *had* felt like the exception to all that. And now, in one evening, he did not. Because of what? Wet hair? He grabbed his wine-red silk robe and put it on.

"Björn, I am not making a study on your hair. And I know how petty and stupid I must sound. I do know. But I also know that on two occasions, less than a full week apart, you have returned home from dry places with wet hair, smelling of soap and cologne. And the other night I found this in your bathroom." He held out a tiny guest-soap. On it was written *Hay-Adams. Washington, D.C.*

"You are watching my fucking hair, taking my fucking soap?! Do you look also through my letters? My fucking dahnce bag? What else. Oh fuck it!"

"Björn, saying fuck all the time does not mean you're learning English. I just want to know . . ."

"I do not care what you want to know. I am going out now. To take a walk in the dry night with my wet hair! Was *that* all right, that English?"

He gathered up his shoes and socks and took off down the stairs.

I will not run after him, Theddo thought.

"I will not come back!" Björn shouted before slamming the downstairs door.

For three days, he didn't.

Theddo figured Björn would stay out all night—perhaps with a friend from the dance company—or with whoever the hell he was visiting at the Hay-Adams—and then come home the next day. While he was at work.

Theddo's workday was hectic, with meetings both in and out of the office. He told Darla to buzz him if he had a call from "my tenant, Mister Nilsson." His tenant Mister Nilsson did not call. And nobody answered when he called home. Four times. Between meetings.

"Right. We have a problem," he said to himself as he walked home. It wasn't just that he *wouldn't* look for Björn; he *couldn't* look for Björn.

There's no way, he thought. I mean, exactly who is it I say I am, and why am I looking for my tenant? Did he fail to pay the rent? Well, in that he doesn't *pay* any rent, you *could* say that—but you *can't* say that because he's never been *asked* for any rent. He is *not* your tenant, turkey! He is your *lover*, and you have pissed him off so profoundly that he has walked out. And there's the true thing—an' what'cha gonna do about it, Mister Daniels? Oh, nuthin', I reckon. S'pose I'll do nuthin'. Except ache and be scared and worry my guts out.

When Björn had been missing for two days, Theddo called Callie.

"Yeah. He's been here. This afternoon. Walked into my office and told Alicia, my secretarial apprentice, that Dag Ekstrom's nephew, Mister Nilsson, wished to see the Senator."

Theddo laughed in spite of himself.

"Balls of a brass monkey."

"I'll take your word for it. He is *seriously* pissed at you. What happened?"

"Meet me. I don't want to do it on the phone."

"Cool. *Hawk and Dove* at seven PM."

"Uh-uh. Don't want to do a bar. Your place?"

"Keisha's here. And she's got a flu-bug. Let's do *Hawk and Dove*. We'll get a corner table, and call him Brigitta."

"Brigitta?"

"Something. Some girl-name and some other guy. It's good for us to be seen together anyway. The guy from the *Post* is always there during Happy Hour, looking for a few inches."

"What?"

"Column inches, dingbat. Stuff to fill his gossip column. So *Hawk and Dove* at seven. That's my final offer."

"Sold . . . Cal?"

"Uh huh?"

"I appreciate it."

"As you should. Don't worry. It'll sort out. See you at seven."

The Hawk and Dove, a popular East Capitol hangout, was only a few blocks from Theddo's house. So, after leaving his office, he stopped to check for any signs of Björn having been home. There were none. His clothes were still there in the basement bedroom closet. Theddo, seeking good omens, took this as a good omen. The huge Transient, Dancing sign stood propped against a chair.

He changed from his black corduroy suit to black jeans and a white turtleneck sweater. He rarely got to wear it when Björn was in residence, because Björn loved it too, and wore it almost always.

As Theddo pulled the sweater over his head, Björn's smell surrounded him. "Oh please God, let him come back. We can solve this," he said aloud as he headed out the door.

Brigitta and Brigitta's Friend

Callie was already there, at a corner table.

"Hey, love," she said, standing and kissing Theddo on the cheek. "How's your day been?"

"Yeah right. How're the kids? Did you fix the car? Worm the cat? Bury the buzzard?"

"Bury the buzzard?"

"I can't do small talk right now, Cal. When did . . . Brigitta come to see you? And what did he, *she* say?"

"She said that . . . the man she was living with didn't trust her. Is that true?"

Theddo ordered a beer, and another white wine for Callie.

"Is Brigitta not allowed in the Hay-Adams?"

"Of course she's allowed in the Hay-Adams. This in not about segregating the Hay-Adams."

"No Swedes allowed in the Hay-Adams!"

"Stop, please. I can't be silly now."

"You're the one who said bury the buzzard."

"Yeah, I know. Look, the problem is . . . is that . . . Brigitta's lover . . . damn, this is hard . . . *Brigitta's* lover first met Brigitta at a fancy hotel, a Hay-Adams-like hotel, in Stockholm, and he was, *she* was . . ."

"Working the hotel?"

"Yeah, something like that."

"And why would she need to do that now?"

Theddo grabbed a handful of beer nuts from the wooden bowl in the centre of the table, chewed them, and, ignoring the glass that had been provided, washed them down with a swig of beer straight from the bottle.

"He doesn't *need* to do it now, but . . ."

"She."

"What?"

"She. *She* doesn't need to do it now."

"Right. *She* doesn't need to do it now. But it might be . . . reflexive. From what . . . I know, that sort of thing has been a part of her life for a long while."

"She told me that she loves . . . her friend, and doesn't need anyone else, but does need to be trusted. She said she was in the Hay-Adams because she met the father of a classmate there. A diplomat from Paris. The girl's name is . . . Danielle."

"Gabrielle?"

"Yes. You know her?"

"Not sure. I met a group of dancers one night. In an Italian restaurant. She may have been among them. Björn, as well as Brigitta, has mentioned her to me. Oh God, Callie, do you think she's telling the truth? Brigitta?"

"I don't know, Theddo. What I *do* believe is that Brigitta does love her friend. Love is complicated for Brigitta . . . people learn love from those who love them."

"Axelsson."

"What?"

"Nothing. What would you do, Cal . . . if you were Brigitta's friend?"

Callie put her elbows on the table, cradling her head in her hands.

"I'd trust her, Thedd. Trust Brigitta. *I* think that if she sees she's trusted, she will try, hard, to live up to that trust."

"Do you really believe that? You're not just being 'Rosie Scenario'?"

"Yes, I do believe it. I believe it's at least worth a serious try."

"Yeah. Me too. So, where is he?"

"Dunno. We went to lunch and then he took off. Wouldn't tell me where to. I *did* ask. Brigitta said, 'I *cahnt* tell you.'"

"Did she say she'd come home?"

"Nope. Only that she wanted to. And that she loved her friend. I'd . . . tell the friend to wait it out. I think she'll show soon."

Callie stood, brushing beer-nut skins off her dark green wool skirt. "Listen, I've got to get some honey and lemons for Keish . . . for *my* flu-ey friend. Call me tomorrow evening and let me know how things are progressing, okay?"

"Mister Daniels, there's a gentleman here with a stack of papers from Senator Hodge. He says his instructions are to see you personally."

"Does he? Well, Darla, send him in."

Björn stood in the doorway, one foot crossed over the other. He was in the jeans, yellow shirt and denim jacket he'd had on when he fled the house. Around his neck was wrapped, no, *flung*, a long red mesh scarf, covered in little bits of silvery metal. His eyes and smile were soft—half-sure and half-tentative. This, Theddo thought, was the person he most wanted, and most wanted to see, in all the world.

"Hello, Lille."

"Hello, Thedd-doh."

Neither man moved from where he stood—Theddo behind his desk, Björn in the doorway.

"The scarf . . ."

"Callie bought it for me."

"It's . . . wonderful. Crazy and wonderful."

"Like me?"

"Close the door."

Björn closed the door.

"Yes. Like you. Come home."

"I have. Can you come there with me now?"

"No. I have one meeting. I will be there in about two hours."

"May I . . . cook food for us?"

"You cook?"

"Ya, yes."

"Why didn't you tell me before?"

"I was afraid you would make me cook."

And Theddo laughed, then Björn laughed, then they held and kissed each other and, for each of them, the embrace held all the love and hope imaginable.

Two hours later, as he passed Darla's desk on the way out, she looked up.

"T.D.?"

"Uh huh?"

"Does that kid really work for Callie Hodge?"

"Uh huh. Sometimes. He's Dag Ekstrom's cousin."

"Couldn't she find someone *whiter?*"

"He's . . . good on race, actually. Dag needed to find an apartment for him. He's my tenant."

"I see."

Theddo thought it was entirely possible that Darla, who'd been working with him for ten years, did indeed see, but he was so suffused with happiness that, paranoid as he was in such matters, he could not bring himself to worry about it.

Björn had prepared perfectly spiced fried flatfish, with a butter, lemon and leek sauce. There were boiled potatoes, as well as sautéed broccoli florets and mushrooms. There was a huge lettuce and shredded carrot salad, and a bottle of quite decent Chilean red wine.

Where did he get the money for . . . no, trust Brigitta. Brigitta's friend trusts Brigitta, Theddo said to himself.

"A splendid meal, Lille. Truly. I thank you for it . . . and promise not to make you cook."

"Good. I only enjoy cooking when I can offer it. Do you wish coffee?"

"I wish *you.*"

"Too much food. First coffee, then me, yes?"

"Yes."

It had never been discussed, not even by inference, but for all the tenderness between them, they still had their *original* problem—the one they'd had since Stockholm. Björn loved to "give" to Theddo, but apart from being embraced and kissed, would not do anything he understood as receiving.

After Björn had given to Theddo as completely as ever he had, they lay side by side, each with a relaxed hand on the other's chest.

"Lille . . .," Theddo said softly.

"Ya?"

"I am very happy that you are here."

"Ya. Me too, very happy."

"Lille . . . I love you, and I love what you . . . do for me."

"*With* you."

"Yes, *with* me . . . only . . . you have always insisted that you only wished to 'give,' but *not to* 'receive.' When you care for someone, you also want to *give* to them. Otherwise . . . otherwise it feels like . . . like you are a little bit . . . my slave."

Björn sat up. "No, it iss the *precise* opposite. Slave-making people always want to *do things* to a boy. But like this, like we do, I am man and you are man. Do you understand?"

"Trying to . . . okay, if we are both man, both equal, why does it matter who does what, if it brings pleasure?"

"It will not bring pleasure. It will bring bad memories."

"I don't want to bring you bad memories. Not ever. Could I . . . try to give a little, and if you do not like it, I will stop."

"It is important for you?"

"Yes."

"All right. We try."

Within moments, Björn was weeping and crying out "No, *slutta! Slutta!*," which Theddo thought meant slut, but which meant stop.

He stopped.

"Oh, Lille. I'm sorry. I only wanted to . . . hold you in my mouth."

"I know. I cannot. When you, as you say, hold me in your mouth, it is not, for me, love. It is . . . business. Are you angry?"

"Not at all. I am happy because you are here. The rest will wait. Come here, come and let me hold you. Not in my mouth, in my arms."

"Yes. I like this."

"I know."

Björn fell asleep almost immediately. Theddo did not, staring up at the ceiling and wondering "Who did this to him? It *has* to have been the stepfather. It has to have been very early. It has to have been . . . like my stepfather."

The next morning, a Saturday, Theddo awoke before Björn, who could sleep through a high school band practice (and was, in fact, doing so). Wrapping himself in his silk robe, he padded to the kitchen, where he made a pot of strong coffee. Then, staring out into the garden, he thought about Brigitta and Brigitta's friend.

The question "Where did you stay for three days?" could not be asked. If Björn wanted to tell him, he would tell him. There was something surreal about not asking this question. But if Callie was right, what needed to happen was trust. Proof of trust. He would try.

"I smell coffee, yes?"

"You smell coffee, yes. Black, two sugars?"

"Precisely. Thank you."

Theddo filled a large blue mug with coffee, then added the sugars. Björn put both hands around the mug and drank.

Right, Theddo thought, what do you discuss *instead* of "Where did you go? Who were you with?"

He poured himself a second cup of black coffee.

"So, how are classes going?"

Björn scrunched up his face.

"Oh, *clahhssess!* I don't know. I am learning many things, and I like some of the other dahncerss very much . . . but I have this little chorus part in the dahnce that will be performed next month. I need to be making my own work. To be dahncing bigger t'ings. You know, Thedd-doh, sometimes I do not understand the world at all. But there is one thing I always understand—I'm a *dahncer!*"

The Rest of the Whole Goddamn Rest of It
1978–1981

"I'm *an actor!*"

Rose Golden poured another coffee for Johnny, putting more tiny pastries on his plate, even though he'd taken only one from the first batch.

"Yes. I know that. I'm your agent, remember? What can I say? This Rachman problem is . . . pervasive. I've been trying for half a year, and all I can come up with is . . ."

"Nickel and dime television parts; thirty-seconds-worth of generic black badasses I wouldn't play when nobody'd seen me do *anything*. Look, Rose, even with my part in *Brotherz* cut all to ratshit, I still got some good reviews. And those reviews got me the movie-of-the week thing, which *also* got me good reviews, and then . . . nothing. Stone flat nuthin'. Is Marty Fuckin' Rachman, excuse my language, the *entire* American film industry?"

Rose emptied a cluster of vitamins onto an espresso plate and downed them all at once with a gulp of coffee.

"No, Johnny, he is not. He *is*, however, a very large turd in this particular punchbowl. And when he wants to make a stink, it is a stink of some size. When he saw the TV film, *and* the good reviews, he hit the roof and called in whatever markers he hadn't already used to make you unhire-able. So, what was already lousy is now . . ."

"Worse?"

"You got it."

"What do I do, Rose? Leave the country?"

"Not exactly. There *is* something. Something that could be interesting."

Johnny always had amazing focus when he listened. On hearing the word *something,* applied to his newly "nothing" career, he began listening to Rose Golden so hard that the inside of his head pulsed.

"Interesting? What?"

Rose pulled her white-metal kitchen chair closer in under the table, almost as though being overheard, on a Saturday in her own apartment, would somehow get back to Marty Rachman and kill a deal that had not yet been signed.

"You know that Andy Phipps and Pete St. Pierre love you and feel awful about what's happening here?"

"Sure I do. I saw Pete and Andy last night. We talked about it."

"Yes, I know. That's how Pete got the idea. You know he's rehearsing this Broadway thing of Andy's about the drag queens and the Stonewall riot?"

"Sure. *Stonewall Divas!* I saw the script when Andy first finished it. Unless he's changed it since then, there aren't any parts for me. There's only one major black part. The drag queen, Anita. Pete's part."

"Uh huh. You know Manny Kalscheim?"

"Yeah, he's producing *Stonewall Divas!* He came to *Brotherz,* and was really nice to me backstage."

"Well, Pete spoke to him this morning, and we can get you the standby for Pete, and . . ."

"What, *understudy?*"

"Don't get grand, John. You need to work. It's a super role to work *on.* And, as you said, Manny thinks you're good. It's *standby,* not understudy. Which means you don't have to play any bit parts, or even come to the theatre very often, once you know the role. It's better money than understudy. Well-known actors do it. All you have to do is phone the theatre at half-hour and once the curtain goes up. And—this is the beauty part, Pete has agreed to let you *play* the matinees."

Johnny couldn't help it; he laughed.

"Pete *hates* matinees! He was the biggest buttpain about matinees during *Brotherz,* he . . ."

"Did you hear me, cutie, I said you get to *play?*"

"Yeah, I heard you. Let's do it. Let's *absolutely* do it!"

So, in November of 1978, John Grandon Reed, Standby for Mr. Pete St. Pierre, joined the cast of Andover Phipps' first musical, a big camp celebration of gay pride called *Stonewall Divas!*

The musical was based on a famous 1969 downtown New York riot led by spontaneously militant drag queens, who, tired of having their bar-hangouts hassled by payoff-seeking police, went wild. Arrests and trials followed. What was done by what Andy Phipps called the Camp Commandettes changed forever the bar-life of American gays, in New York and other major cities.

Johnny Reed had sung well all his life. He had, however, only done this as a "mannish" person.

At his first rehearsal, the thirty-member company was not in attendance. Only Andy Phipps, Pete St. Pierre, director Melanie Roth, music director Purcell Gerard and choreographer Tommy Torres were witness to Johnny's first attempt at singing "her" big number, "A Girl Like I" as the drag star character, Anita Loosely.

Andy spoke first.

"A singing gym teacher in a dress," he said. He spoke for everyone.

"Come on, guys! I've never done this before!"

"No shit, Scheherazade! Baby, you a *ugly* drag queen. We gone hafta take you home an' find your Femma Nine Side!"

That night, Johnny arrived at the Phipps-St. Pierre loft. Jolo was pleased to see him. They rolled around on the floor for a while.

Finally, Pete said, "Up you go, babycakes, it's time to dress you."

In their bedroom, Andy and Pete put Johnny in an elaborate make-up, including a long Dolly Parton-blonde wig, a double-row of eyelashes and huge, high-gloss, tomato-red lips. The face that looked back at him from the three-way vanity mirror was a cross between his Uncle Carl and every woman his Uncle Carl had ever dated.

"Meet Bernice!"

Nothing had prepared him for Bernice. "She" wore what actors call a fat-suit—a one-piece light brown combination of tights and leotard/bathing suit, with enormous quantities of padded, rounded arms, legs, tits and ass.

Under instruction, and amid laughter and rude remarks, Johnny climbed into Bernice, then wriggled into a silky-feeling red-back-grounded floral-printed 1940s rayon dress.

"We'll wait for the high-heeled shoes. No point in having you break your fat bottom when you're so close to perfection!" Andy said, ushering Johnny to a full-length mirror.

Johnny Reed's ability to instantly accept what Ben Eisenglass at the Manhattan Actors' Playhouse called "the given circumstances" had been legendary. "You could tell Johnny here," Ben had said to the class, "that he was a house, a two-storey brick house by the side of a deserted country road, and he would start feeling and seeing the rooms inside himself . . . and listening longingly for the sound of an occasional truck going by. Now, most actors have to work their asses off to just believe that they are some other *person*. Not our Mister Reed! Our Mister Reed plays doorknobs, birdbaths and blades of grass. Fortunately, he also plays people!"

But nothing—no doorknob, no birdbath, no blade of grass prepared Johnny for Bernice.

There she was, looking right back at him from Andy and Pete's full-length mirror. She was big, she was black, and she was, no doubt about it, beautiful. Johnny had never dated a really big woman, but as he stood there, looking at Bernice, his reaction gave a whole new meaning to go fuck yourself.

"Sing, baby," Andy said softly, and Johnny, looking into the mirror, began:

"Hey lovers, hey brothers!
Hey, all you sons of mothers!
Hey, you guys
With thunder thighs
Surrounding priapoloozas of some size!
I'm here
To hold you near.
To make the situation clear—
I can take you, I can shake you
And when I make you
You will know where you have been!
So, come on in!

Let the party begin!
Once you enter my lair,
You will go to where
Hell and heaven, earth and sky,
Soul and bone
Find their ecstasy zone
In the worl'
Of a Supergirl! . . .
A girl like
I-I-I!"

For a Broadway musical, Johnny/Bernice's rendition of "A Girl Like I" was not very loud. It would get louder, and also be body-miked and/or stage-miked. (On the first day of rehearsals, Manny Kalscheim said, "Nobody just stands up and belts anymore. The Ethel Mermans have been replaced by these pretty little voices with mikes up their butts").

What mattered was that, from the moment John Reed clapped eyes on Bernice, Anita Loosely, Avenging Drag Amazon and Hot, Creamy Erotic Goddess, was alive and well. And would, through four weeks of rehearsals, get alive-er and well-er.

Johnny was re-manned, and Bernice placed neatly in a beige duffel bag. Then, the three men went out for a joyous celebration (Johnny's first since leaving Hollywood), involving Italian food and, there being no rehearsal the next day, a copious amount of red wine.

The following evening, Drag Queen class resumed chez Phipps/St. Pierre. Johnny was dressed in every aspect of Bernice but her wig and makeup. To the ankle-to-clavicles bodysuit was added a penis-flattening, buttocks-amplifying girdle ("Trust me—the girdle hurts less than tucking and taping," Pete said. Johnny trusted him), and extra-large no-run black pantyhose. Ankle-strapped bright red sandals, with their helpfully thick but nonetheless four-inch heels were a genuine ordeal. Johnny sat, strapped on the shoes, stood up, walked two steps and fell down.

Another benefit of Bernice-ness was that a fall was fully padded. Johnny stuck his Bernice-Butt in the air as he struggled to push himself to a standing position.

"Ooh honey!" Andy said, "I could get such *good* money for you right now!"

"Will you shut it, Phipps, and just help me stand up?!"

"Ee-ventually, sweetheart. I just want to take a Polaroid first!"

"Andy, when I get upright again, I'm gonna put your lights out."

"Never hit the playwright."

Pete, who'd gone to the bathroom, returning in time to hear this last remark, said, "Oh. I thought the rule was you can never hit the *producer*, you *shouldn't* hit the *director*, but you *can* hit the playwright because he doesn't have a strong union . . ."

"Finish it."

"No, that's okay."

"*Finish* it!"

"Right. And, of course, you can slap the shit out of an actor, as long as you don't do it in the theatre."

"*Thank* you!"

"Will you two stop doing your party piece and get me upright! If I don't start by *standing, walking* is *flat out of the question!*"

Johnny did learn to walk in the shoes, and to do it while singing, acting and vamping his heart out. High heels, however, remained his least favourite aspect of life as a woman.

Stonewall Divas! opened in late January 1979 and was a critical triumph, even more than *Brotherz.* The opening night party was, as per tradition, at *Sardi's* restaurant on West 44th Street. The producer and the company waited until midnight and then Jay Ganzer, the first assistant stage manager, went out for the first edition of the next day's *New York Times*, the only newspaper that could, on its own, make or break a Broadway show.

When Ganzer returned, Andy Phipps was hoisted onto a table to read aloud to the assembled: "*Stonewall Divas!* is a musical, a circus, a party, a burlesque show and a celebration of pride vanquishing oppression. Andover Phipps' first musical *Stonewall Divas!* adds a big, bright jewel to his crown as our foremost black playwright, and one of our very finest playwrights, period!" Pete was described as "A brilliant performer, an always dynamic actor . . . and a great woman!" All the principal actors received superlatives, as did music, dance, sets and costumes.

Johnny, while he ached to hear his own name in the roll-call, was thrilled for the show. As he told Rose Golden, who, as Pete's agent, was one of the celebrants, "I'm really happy to be a part of this, Rose. Thank you."

"It'll get good for you again, Johnny. You'll see."

His first public performance as Anita Loosely was a Saturday matinée, four days after opening night. He'd already rehearsed twice with the entire company, who supported his maiden voyage with full concentration and love.

Pete, though not required to be, was backstage, walking Johnny through costume changes, entrances and exits. He would later describe Johnny's drag debut as the "Bambi" version, because of Johnny's still-wobbly legs in the Joan Crawford Fuck-Me Pumps (as all high-heeled shoes were called by the entire cast). There were significant differences in each actor's characterisation. Pete's Anita was a brassier, gutsier interpretation. His/her moments of pain were the howl of a wounded animal plunged into sudden darkness. Johnny's was a younger, sweeter Anita, with a heat-seeking sexiness and a fierce though girlish hope that, as she said, with deep investment in the line "Some day my Prince *will* come, you lump of shit, and he'll kick your donut-eatin' white ass clean into Jersey!"

After his third performance, another Saturday matinée, Johnny was in Pete's dressing room, where he dressed when playing Anita. The clothes, body and cascading blonde mane of Bernice had been put into a closet or onto a wig-stand, though he was still in full makeup. He had scooped up a handful of lard-like makeup remover when an announcement came over the speaker: "John Reed. You have a guest. John Reed, you have a guest at the stage door."

It was odd that Declan, the stage-door man, did not give the *name* of Johnny's guest. Perhaps, as was frequently the case, Deck couldn't pronounce it. ("A Mister Manderella, a Mister Nelson Manderella to see the company," was Pete's favourite fantasy version of Declan's guest-announcements.)

Dressing room number one (Pete's) was practically next to the stage door, so Johnny didn't bother picking up the intercom. He wiped the makeup remover off his hand, wrapped himself in the black silk dressing gown Pete had given him when *Brotherz* first opened, and, not expecting anyone, went to see who had come to visit him.

"Hey, Reed."

Johnny's first thought was Go away, Dorrie! If Rachman knows you're here, he'll call Kalscheim and I'll be back on the street.

He didn't say that. He didn't say anything. He just looked at her.

And *she* looked at the bathrobed body of her old friend, on top of which was the short-haired head of a garishly good-looking black woman with enormous fire-engine-red lips.

Dorrie spoke first.

"You were brilliant, Reed. You always are. You made me cry with the song about your twin who died."

"Thanks."

"No, thank *you*. It's . . . good to see you. I mean *sort of* see you. I mean, I don't know this fantastic lady-face, but I do know that you're in there."

"Yeah. Somewhere. You working in town?"

"No. My baby sister Nini just got married. I came in for the wedding."

"Oh. Was it here, in the city, the wedding?"

"No. Pound Ridge, a little upstate. His folks' place. They, his family, have a lovely English garden. Good for weddings . . . and flying insects . . . I'm going back to the coast in three days. The series has been renewed for another year."

"Ah. Congratulations."

"It's really hard work, the hours and stuff. But I knew that when . . ."

Declan (who Andy Phipps called "half-a-Deck," because he spoke really slowly and because, though English was his first and only language, his version of words never ceased to surprise and amuse) coughed, as he always did to signal that he was going to speak. He then spoke: "Ahem, ahem . . . Mister . . . Reed . . . I don't want to . . . rush you . . . but I have to . . . let . . . the janitarian girl in . . . to fix up Mister St. Peter's room . . . before . . ."

"Yeah, sorry, Deck. I'll clear out fast as I can. Look, Dorrie, I have to get this stuff off my face and get out of Pete's room. He plays tonight. Thanks a lot for coming back, and for liking the show. I hope . . ."

"I understand. Ben Eisenglass could never get us out of the Actors'

Playhouse building either . . . do you have time to have a drink?"

"No. No, I can't. I have to meet someone."

"Sure. Of course. Well, congrats again. It was terrific work. 'Bye." She put on the black leather glove she'd been holding in her gloved left hand, buttoned her long grey wool coat, looked up once and, smiling like an embarrassed child, turned quickly and was out the door. Johnny watched her go, from inside Bernice's face.

An hour later, he sat alone in his recently rented, tiny but "tastefully furnished" (as the ad had said) apartment, drinking a German beer and staring up at the full moon. I couldn't be seen with her, he thought, I just couldn't.

Four days later, he found a pale green envelope in his box at the theatre.

Very Dear Reed—

Marty threw me over a month after you split for New York. Not because of you. He met somebody else. Another tallish, thinnish blonde. Got her a series too.

I never loved him. I wanted to, but couldn't. I probably loved you. Didn't have the guts to deal with it.

Marty is still my agent. He got me the series, and just renegotiated my contract. I'm making money for him, he says, and he's making money for me. Unless it's something urgent, we speak now mostly through Joni, his secretary. Which is fine with me.

When Marty started doing all the bad things to you, I wanted to leave him, both as my boyfriend and as my agent. Again, I didn't have the guts.

I'm just not brave, Reed. Becoming an actor was the only time I ever went against my family's choices. Ever. Oh, and I suppose Marty a little, because he was Jewish. But he was also supersuccessful, which my parents understand. I was pretty sure my father could get me out of a contract with Marty, but if those two guys ever fought, there would be so much blood in the water. I hated the thought of it.

Ben Eisenglass said I was one of those Waspy-breedy blondes who work all the time. Except for the "work all the time" part, which no one can really know, I guess that's what I am. I don't think I'll ever do the high-wire, high-risk stuff that you do as if it were part of breathing. As I said, I am not brave. You are. I will always love watching you work. Always.

Somebody once said it was more important to <u>act</u> than be <u>acted upon</u> (this person was speaking of life, not the profession of acting). I've always been acted upon. I think that's true for a lot of us Waspy breedies.

I'm sorry about all the bad parts of what happened to us. Profoundly. Not about the good parts, which for me, is almost all of it.

I think I understand why you couldn't have a drink with me. (Your instinct was probably right.) Once Marty starts "getting even" he can't seem to stop, even though this isn't about me anymore. Maybe it never was. Men like Marty—and my father— sometimes do things just because they <u>can</u>. And they need to have the rest of us know that they can.

I wish you a great life, a great career . . . and a great woman. You are so absolutely worthy of all those things, and more.

Love, always,

D.

Johnny, at Pete's dressing table, put the letter back in its envelope, and began the transformation into Bernice.

A great life, he knew, could not be guaranteed. Marty Rachman, and the general situation for black actors in America made a great career an uphill climb—a climb in which, in the late twentieth century in America, he could not be seen drinking with a white woman. Yes, it was a *specific* white woman, but, he knew, without the *general* problem, the *specific* problem would not have life-support.

The "great woman" problem was, if a bit superficially, more easily solved.

That matinée afternoon, those who saw Johnny Reed play Anita Loosely got to witness, in fierce form and fine feathers, a great woman.

That was good for the audience, but What about me? Johnny wondered. He had been numbed into indifference for a while, both by the Hollywood Horrors and his subsequent involvement with becoming an onstage female, but was once again craving physical contact with a woman. Other than Bernice-Anita.

In the way these things sometimes do, this particular loin-longing coincided with a welcome backstage arrival after that best-performance-so-far matinee.

"Mister Johnny Reed, you have a guest at the stage-door. There is a Miss Dolores Feeney here to see youse."

Johnny took the intercom-receiver from the wall.

"Hey, Deck. It's Johnny Reed. *Who* did you say was here for me?"

Delia Farnham looked almost exactly as she had as Ophelia to Johnny's High School Hamlet. She was, to be sure, more grown up and citified, in a smart fitted burgundy suit and a single strand of pearls, a cream-white Melton wool coat over her shoulders. Her black hair was short and curly, with a few rust-orange highlights.

Her face, however, which had always reminded Johnny's father of the singer-actor Pearl Bailey ("Pearlie-Mae was a real beauty when she was young. She went into comedy, so people didn't always notice what a looker she was"), was the same; open, sensual, with large eyes, a small nose and a full kissy mouth.

"Deelie?"

"Uh huh."

They hugged, laughing.

"Oh man, is it ever *great* to see *you!*"

Delia, with multicoloured smudges of Anita Loosely's makeup on her cheek, replied, "Yeah. Good to see you too . . . to the extent that I *can*."

"Oh yeah, right. Lemme get my nat'chull self together, and we can grab some dinner. Can you do that? Have dinner with me?"

"I'd love to. I'll wait for you over by the 'Dolores Feeney' man."

He took her to *Sardi's*. It was not a place he usually went ("Blue-rinse crowd at night," Pete said, "and too much Bridge-and-Tunnel," which was shorthand for grey-haired persons and persons from the New York boroughs surrounding Manhattan). He thought Delia, new to the city, would enjoy seeing the whole circus of it, complete with autographed celebrity caricatures lining the walls.

And she did, whispering, "Oh look, there's a drawing of Sidney Poitier!"

"Uh huh. Amazing that you found Sidney so fast in all these pictures."

"It wasn't hard . . . he sort of . . . stands out."

"Don't he just! Good evening, Frank."

"Good evening, Mister Reed. It's good to see you."

"Same here. Can we have dinner upstairs?"

The upstairs of *Sardi's* was a gentler place. It had its own bar, which was always liberally leaned on by older actors (sometimes with very young dates) who liked a drink or two or five. Frank ushered Delia and Johnny to a table.

"Frank. Let me introduce you to Miss Delia Farnham. Miss Farnham is an actor from my hometown of Wetherill, North Carolina. We worked together in plays there."

"Did you? Well, well, well."

"Yes, we did. Directed by Johnny's . . . Mister Reed's father, Marcus Aurelius Reed."

"I see. And are you going to grace our fair city now?"

"I'm going to try, sir."

"Well, all the best, Miss Farnham."

Talking about Wetherill, and especially about Big Reed, was good. Johnny expanded from there, telling Delia story after story: stories about *Brotherz*, about Rose Golden and Claude Martin, about Andy and Pete, about seeing Bernice in the mirror, about wearing high-heeled shoes and being unable to stand up. Stories about everything and everyone except Dorrie Stockwell and Marty Rachman. As Ben Eisenglass always said, "When you find joy, roll into it, see where it goes."

It went to Johnny's little apartment, accompanied by Delia Farnham.

The next morning, he awakened, looked at the lovely face and soft warm body lying sleeping next to him and thought, I guess I'm gonna live.

After ducking metaphoric landmines and rat-holes for a while, it felt good to Johnny Reed to have a structured life, and to have that structure include a great role (twice a week) and a sweet girlfriend (about four times a week).

Girlfriend and Boyfriend were, for both of them, loaded terms. They agreed, and re-agreed that they were definitely not going together.

They were, they told anyone who asked, long-time friends from the same hometown.

As Johnny had done with the Manhattan Actors' Playhouse, Delia received a scholarship. Hers was with Olga Tchereskaya.

Madame O. was a scatty-seeming, orange-wigged and unusually tiny Russian woman, whose wine-red lipstick usually missed her lips by about a quarter-inch (to the left on the upper lip; to the right on the lower). She always wore layers of woollen garments, including two or three shawls and scarves (at any time of the year), in tones of dark, darker and darkest red, plus black wool tights and ballet slippers.

For all that she resembled a Georg Grosz drawing of a hundred-year-old gnome running from a burning building, her classes had produced a number of successful theatre and film stars.

Madame O. gave Delia a rough ride. The North Carolinian had been brought up to be polite, soft-spoken, deferential. For the Russian acting coach, this was "Constant aPOHlogy! Avry time ven you valk into ah rum, you are seeming to be saying 'I am sorry.' Vy are you sorry, DAYlia? Vy? Vot hev you done? You are not *vaitress*, you are *Ectress!* At least you are trying to be, but ecting all the time like little mouse!"

"She *hates* me," Delia moaned as they faced each other while taking a bath together in Johnny's enormous clawfoot bathtub (which was in the kitchen).

"She is *on* me all the time. Does she think being loud and rude is the only way to be a good actor? There's this girl in class, Melanie. She's fat and noisy and sloppy . . . and she's got this . . . body odour. One of the guys in class calls her Smellanie—not to her face or anything."

"Yeah, we had one of those stinkies at the Playhouse. And his actual name was *Cruddy*."

"*Really? Cruddy?*"

"I swear to you."

"Yeah, well anyway, Madame O. thinks this Melanie is just the *best!*"

Delia's prettiness and natural sweetness did get her work in commercials. She was proud to be earning and pleased that she could send some money home to her widower father in Wetherill.

The relationship continued for seven months, until Johnny was asked to take his Anita Loosely on the road.

Brotherz had been a success, both as a play and a film. While *Stonewall Divas!* was not likely to make it to the screen, as a live-theatre venture it was a "Monster Hit!" (to quote the ad copy, which in turn was quoting the *New York Times*). There were full houses for every performance, including those with John Grandon Reed in the lead role.

Manny Kalscheim decided that if doing capacity business on Broadway was a good thing, doing capacity business all over the country would be an even better thing. The performance of Pete St. Pierre was a key component of the show's success on Broadway. Manny had no intention of changing that chemistry. So Johnny, Pete's standby, was asked to head up the cross-America road company. Relishing an opportunity to both see the country and more fully develop Anita Loosely, Johnny didn't need much coaxing. Rose Golden only solidified his decision.

"This is perfect, John! It's a great role, the money is *faaabulous*, and, a year from now, when the tour is over, all the Rachmanshit will be history. The man may be petty and mean as a starving vulture, but he has an L.A. agent's attention span, and a helluva lot else to do."

The road company, a mix of people from the Broadway show and new people, rehearsed for a month, and on September 30, 1980, there was a huge two-cast party upstairs at *Sardi's*.

Followed by Johnny and Delia's party for two. He promised to write or phone whenever he could, saying also, "If something great happens for you, Rose Golden will always know how to find me."

It is said that there's no middle about theatre touring—you either love it or hate it. Johnny loved it. New cities, new restaurants, new foods, new clubs, new music and new women. He was travelling as the star of a successful Broadway musical, which meant having his picture in the papers and "talking trash" on radio and television. Which meant even *more* new women. Alicia Carpenter, the only actual woman playing a woman in the show was also giving him signals.

"Don't do it, man," said Gregg Beldon, his dressing room mate (and standby). "It's so hot while it's on, but then it's off, and you're still in the show together." So he didn't.

Six months into the tour, after Philadelphia, Boston, Chicago, Detroit, as well as Toronto, Canada (really cold, Johnny wrote his mother, very polite, lots of black people from the Caribbean), he was in

San Francisco, when Delia—to whom and *from* whom there had been fewer and fewer letters, postcards and phone calls—sent a Dear Johnny letter.

She'd made a lucrative career in television commercials, selling everything "from perfume to ass wipes," as Rose Golden put it, and had accepted a proposal of marriage from Chip Reiner, the most successful director of these commercials. She expressed regret: "You'll still be touring when we tie the knot. Twice! Once at his folks' place in Connecticut and once in Wetherill. He's a really good guy! I hope you two can get to know each other, and I thank you from the bottom of my heart for being so great to me when I first came to 'The Big Apple.' XOXO, Deelie."

If San Francisco was about Delia finding true love, it was also about Andy and Pete splitting up.

Pete called Johnny at his hotel. When he picked up the phone at about one in the morning (which made it three in New York), he heard:

"No matter what you hear, I'm cool."

"Congratulations. Who *is* this?"

"It's Pete, man. And no matter what people will say, and they *will say every friggin' thing*, I'm fine."

"I don't know what this is about. You and Andy having problems?"

"Not anymore. He got into a thing with a little cutie from the New York *Divas* chorus. It happened before. I mean, we were together for eighteen years, man. None of them ever lasted more than a week, if that long. This one, though, was hangin' in. I knew. I pretended not to know. He let me pretend. Finally I asked him about it and he told me. Said he was in love. Said we could try for some kind of *arrangement*, if I could look the other way. Shit, man, after eighteen years, there was no way I could *do* that. Some folks say that looking the other way is exactly what you're *supposed* to do after eighteen years, I just . . . can't. I believe we'll be all right, Andy and me. As friends and colleagues, I mean . . . I mean, he's my best friend, and I think that we will . . ."

Johnny had never heard a man cry. Not gutbucket wailing crying. Which was what Pete did next. Johnny just let him run it out, repeating only "I'm here, man. I'm here."

When the weeping stopped, they talked for a while. Pete was going to take two weeks off. "I'm gonna go to Paris. Fuck, man, I've never been to Paris. Even when I was in London. It'll be all over the papers by tomorrow or the next day, and I'd just as soon miss that."

It was not all over the papers the next day, but it was all over the *Divas* touring company. And, two days later, all over the supermarket tabloids. The story, and pictures, were stunners for Johnny:

Gay Sex Triangle

Three's a Crowd in a Closet!

And

Phipps Leaves Long-Time Boyfriend for Switch-Hitting Reed

He called his mother. Told her it was twisted, crazy, lying garbage. Told her the true story. Carlotta Reed, not exactly sure her son should be running around on stage in a dress anyway, said she believed him.

Then he called Rose Golden:

"Rose! What the fuck . . .?!"

"What do you think?"

"Rachman?"

"You got it. Not directly. He's too smart for that. Almost. Do you know who Joni Clayton-Deane is?"

"No. No, wait a minute; Rachman's secretary is an English black woman named Joni . . ."

"That would be our planter. She gave it to *The Investigator* and to Lily Shaw at *The News*, and the rest took care of itself."

"Did you see the pictures?"

"I've seen the whole ball of wax."

"Those pictures are just us horsing around in rehearsals, and at opening night parties and stuff. These two men are my friends!"

"I know that, John . . ."

"Pete and Andy *have* split up . . ."

"I know that too. Pete's my client. I've been on the phone with him for about a week . . ."

"Yeah, he called *me* last night. Said it was someone from the chorus of the New York company."

"Philip Brendan."

"Philip *Brendan*?! Philip Brendan has the IQ of a doorstop. Andy always called him Phyllis Brain-dead."

"John, he's young and pretty . . . and Andy is . . . at that age."

"Jesus. What's Pete going to do?"

"Pete is going to go to Paris."

"Yeah. He told me that. *Then* what is he going to do?"

"Then he's going to continue being a Broadway star in *Stonewall Divas!*"

"And what am *I* going to do?"

" You are going to be the star of the touring company of *Stonewall Divas!*"

"No, I mean . . ."

"I know what you mean. And here is what I suggest . . ."

What Rose Golden suggested was that Johnny continue doing dazzling work to sold-out houses in San Francisco. She also said, "The media is going to be looking for you. Low media, high media and everything in between. Let them find you. Don't duck them. Talk to them. Tell the truth. You have a good truth here, John, involving good friends. The best weapon you have is to just be . . . er, *straight*, if you'll pardon the expression."

"Okay, okay, I'll try . . . but what about L.A.?"

"What *about* L.A.?"

"It's Rachman-Land, Rose. I don't know if I can cut being there . . . and not killing the slimy bastard."

"Do not say *that ENNNY*where! A lot of people want Marty Rachman dead. If one of those many people decides to act on the impulse, the police will come lookin' for *you*. Which would be a terrible career move."

Johnny laughed—a dry little "hah!" "Right. Spoken like an agent. I feel . . . shook, Rose . . ."

"Will it be any easier if I fly out there for the L.A. opening?"

"I . . . don't know what will make anything easier with this, Rose . . . but I'd love it if you were here."

"Consider it done. I'll call Manny and get a ticket for the show. I'll be staying at the Hotel Soleil on Franklin. Sweet place. They have a pool."

"Oh, Rose. In L.A. the *gas station* has a pool!"

"Fine. *You* stay at the gas station. *I'll* be at the Hotel Soleil. See you after the show. Have a great opening, and call me if you need anything . . . John?"

"Yeah?"

"This *will* pass. It really will."

"Look, I can't explain this, and I know how paranoid it sounds, but I have the creepy feeling that it won't. Won't *ever* pass. Not for as long as that shitbag is . . . never mind. This phone could be bugged."

"That's not likely."

"Rose, *none* of this has been *likely.*"

The Los Angeles opening of *Stonewall Divas!*, like the Los Angeles opening of anything from laundrettes to pet cemeteries, was an overload of red carpets, anorexic interviewers (faces pulled so tight that they slept with their eyes open), sky-scanning lights and long cars designed by the human equivalent of the God Committee who did the camel.

Johnny was, as Rose had predicted, pursued by media, wanting to ask him about the Phipps-St. Pierre breakup.

He arrived at the theatre three hours before the curtain went up (he did this for any show, but the assembling of Bernice-Anita made it a necessity). Even at four in the afternoon, there was still a gauntlet to be run outside the stage door. And run it he did:

"Mr. Phipps and Mister St. Pierre are friends of mine. They always will be, individually or together."

"I have no comment on the nature of their relationship, as you put it. They can speak for themselves. One of them actually writes words for a living. Words I hope you'll enjoy this evening."

"I date women. I'm not sexually attracted to men. If I were, I would certainly send flowers to *you.*"

He had learned a lot, much of it from Andy and Pete, and was doing really well, until just before he went through the stage door.

"Look guys, I love women. All *kinds* of women. I love their company, the way they think, the way they speak, the way they smell, the texture of their skin. And I love them sexually. All of it . . . Now, I admit that *nothing* is quite as satisfying as sleeping with the girlfriend of an *impotent agent, who's got hair all over his back,* but, when I can't have that, I make do with all sorts of other lovely ladies."

"Oh God," Rose moaned when she saw and heard this on the local L.A. television news, "now this *will* last forever."

The reviews were raves.

The show was a hit.

Johnny got a standing, cheering ovation every night.

And neither Claude Martin nor Rose Golden could get him seen for anything. Not even for roles he would never agree to play.

Joshua Gunn, a black casting director, who knew the whole Rachman story, as did most of L.A. (thanks to Johnny deciding to be Mister Mouth), fought hard for him on two television movies. And lost.

Rose called.

"Hi, cookie. Wanna go to Europe?"

"You mean I've got to leave the country?"

"Not exactly. Kalscheim is putting together a world tour. What that means in human English is London, Paris, Berlin, Greece and Japan. He also wants to keep L.A. and New York running. So, if you say yes to this, someone, probably Gregg Beldon, will replace you in L.A. Want to see Europe and Japan?"

"I've wanted to travel since I was a kid. And my father really wanted me to. Yes, please. I will bring the tits and ass and heart and soul of Miss Anita Loosely to the whole world . . . and while I'm doing it, maybe MIStah Marty Ratfuck will fuckin' *die!*"

"You really have to stop saying that."

"I will when he dies."

Soula Meets Her Phoenician
Athens, 1981

Soula Damanakis sat at an outdoor table, in a little café in Syndagma Square, Athens, trying to explain what had happened without sounding either foolish or crazy.

She knew that Christina, her colleague at AthinaTours, tended to dismiss most things, thinking it made her seem more urbane. Having been born and raised in a mountain village on the island of Naxos, seeming urbane was very important to Christina. As expected, she made a little "tsk" noise.

"You are telling me *what?* That you were giving a tour and you met a *Venetian* from your *dreams?*"

"No, Christinamou, not a *Venetian*, a *Phoenician*."

"There *are* no Phoenicians, Soula. Phoenicia is a dead civilisation."

"I know that. That is what I'm trying to tell you."

"You are trying to tell me that you were giving a tour and you met a man from a dead civilisation?"

"No, that is *not* what I am trying to tell you."

"Well, I do not understand what you *are* trying to tell me."

"I see this. Let me try again."

And Soula, needing to share this magical destined thing, this thing that she had dreamt since childhood, and had regularly seen when her fortune was told from coffee-grounds, began again.

"I was giving a tour of the Akropoli. Just the usual tour. About twenty people. Mostly Americans, English and Germans. The two Germans spoke English, so I was showing and explaining in English. At one point, I turned from the Akropoli to face the group . . . and this man was there. He had not been there before. He was not part of my tour group. He was there by himself and heard me explaining in English, so he joined the group . . .”

“Oh, that happens all the time,” Christina said, lighting a cigarette. “These people who do not pay for a tour but attach themselves for free, so we get less commission!”

“Yes, I know. But *this* man . . . this man looked exactly like the man from my dreams. In one of these dreams, when I was about thirteen, the dream-man said he was Phoenician. So I have thought of him as ‘my Phoenician’ ever since.”

“And where is he *really* from, this re-incarnated ‘Phoenician’?”

“Wetherill, North Carolina. In America.”

“So, an American.”

“Yes. A *mavros* American. I have never seen his exact colour of skin before. Like . . . like bleached terracotta, except for his cheeks, which are like the reddish part from a peach. Oh Christina, he is *beautiful!* And his voice too. It is soft but rumbles from inside him.”

Christina stabbed her cigarette into the tin ashtray.

“A *mávros* AmerikaNOSS?! What if he is involved with drugs?”

“You mean the way all Greek Americans have restaurants with blue-and-white paper coffee cups? No, Christinamou, I talked to him. His name is Johnny Reed. He is an actor, and the *star* of a play in the festival at Irodio. He has invited me . . . and said I could bring a friend. It is tomorrow. Would you like to go?”

Christina, who had nothing to do during the following evening except wait another night for her married boyfriend to call, said, “Well, I was supposed to have dinner with someone . . . but I did not give a definite yes, and would like to see an American play at Irodio. Besides, I can protect you from Phoenician drugs!” They both laughed.

Soula stood in front of her bedroom mirror, wishing she had not cut her long black hair a month earlier. Men, she thought, liked long hair.

But her Phoenician had invited her to Irodio with the new look.

233

And everyone at AthinaTours said they loved her short tousled hair. Markos, the owner, who enjoyed speaking French, said she looked like *une vraie gamine,* which he explained meant something like a bohemian elf. He also said that the short hair made her eyes look *énorme!* Very big!

She wriggled into a stretchy black dress that showed her short, slim, compact body to good advantage, without, she hoped, looking vulgar. She then reached behind to clasp her gold chain, the one with the little open-work silver heart. Two thin bracelets, one gold and one silver, were, she thought, enough jewellery. Black pantihose with the black dress made her feel like a grandmother, so she pulled them off and put on the ones called Bronze Tan. Low-heeled black slingback sandals completed the ensemble. Nights at Irodio could be cold. She grabbed her long cream-coloured cotton sweater-coat.

Her mother was in the living room watching the national news.

"You are going out, Soulamou?"

"Yes, Mana. I'm going with Christina to see an American play, a play with music, at Irodio. She had an extra ticket."

Irodio—the Herod Atticus Amphitheatre, sat at the bottom of downtown Athens. It went back to ancient times. A large, roofless grey stone structure, it was frequently the site of Greek and international concerts, dances and theatre performances. The performances, no matter how opulent, skillfully staged or well performed, frequently had a moment where artifice was upstaged by nature.

At the back of the amphitheatrical stage were five fingernail-shaped archaic windows. At some point in the nightscape, indifferent to leaping dancers, declaiming actors or sky-rattling high notes of sopranos, the moon would meander laterally from one window to the next. When this happened, members of the audience would murmur like hypnotised bees, *"To féngari! Vlépis to féngari!*—The moon! Look at the moon!"

During *Stonewall Divas!,* a moon-moment happened as Calvin Chang, playing Corinna Goldenhole, was singing "Everybody Loves Me When I'm Walkin' Away!"

It was the end of the song, and Calvin, rolling a bodysuit-rump of plump globules, was undulating upstage. Each globule was rigged to roll sequentially, one after the other. As Calvin was facing the windows, he too got to watch the moon. (Years later, he would say: "The Greek Moon-Goddess blessed my song!")

Christina, seated next to Soula on the "best stone slabs in the house," suddenly exclaimed, to the amusement of the two men sitting next to her, "*Póosties!* This is a *Póosti* show!"

"This show, my darling," the older of the two men said to Christina in Greek, "is the biggest hit in America!"

"It's still a *Póosti* show," Christina replied, shrugging . . . and thoroughly enjoying the performance.

It was somewhat more complicated for Soula. What *she* was watching, after all, was the Phoenician Man of Her Dreams. And he was, suddenly, a fat blonde person. A fat blonde *female* person. This was not only not Phoenician; it was not *possible!*

Johnny had told her how to get backstage after the show. She felt unsure about doing this, but was persuaded by Christina.

"Come on, Soulamou. You told me you met a Phoenician man, and all I've seen is a fat blonde *mávri!* I want to see your beautiful man!"

The backstage area, outside Johnny's dressing tent, was filled with famous Greeks—actors, singers, politicians—waiting also to meet Soula's Phoenician. When Johnny finally emerged, a slim, handsome young man with skin the colour of bleached terracotta, his eyes scanned the crowd, looking for a woman with short, tousled black hair and enormous eyes.

They were like teenagers with nowhere to go. Soula lived with her mother and Johnny, to save money, was sharing a hotel room with Carston Young, his new standby.

So they walked around Athens holding hands, kissing in corners and doorways, dining after midnight (the preferred Athenian dinner hour).

And they climbed.

"Almost everything worth seeing in Greece is up a hill," Soula said. "Except you."

They looked down Lycabettus Hill.

"I am up a hill now. So are you."

Johnny was indeed up a hill. Having never experienced it before, he nonetheless knew almost immediately that he was, for the first time, in love.

He also knew he was leaving for Japan. He told Soula Japan was the last stop on the tour. He said that his contract was up after Japan, unless he renewed it. He said he wanted to give his notice and come back to Greece: "I want to . . . spend some time with you." Soula said she wanted this also. When the *Stonewall Divas* company left for Japan, Soula borrowed Christina's Honda and drove him to the airport.

Tokyo, which, for Johnny, was filled with seeming billions of people and cars and colours, was also the source of an extravagant long-distance phone bill.

"I miss you."

"Me too, I miss you."

"Only two more weeks."

"How is Japan?"

"Very crowded . . . with everyone but you."

"Shall I meet you at the airport?"

"Yes, please. Is it too much trouble?"

"Trouble. No, *this* is the trouble! What are you doing now?"

"Now? I'm going to sleep. It's late."

"Oh, it is a whole different time here. Too early for sleep. *OHneera GliKAH.*"

"What is that?"

"Sweet dreams."

"Well, the same to you, whenever it's the time for you to sleep."

Soula was twenty-three. Before meeting Johnny, she'd had two sexual relationships—one with love (and quick clumsy sex, two times) and another with a cartoonist from Marseilles who had taken her AthinaTour to Delphi (no love, amazing sex, three days). So she had known love and she had known sex. She felt that if she and Johnny could be alone together in some indoor place, she would know both with the same person. One thing was certain; they could not continue groping and kissing on hills like a pair of thirteen year olds.

Christina had a two-week holiday that started three days before

Johnny returned to Athens. She gave Soula the keys to her flat. That would give them ten days to find out if Greek girls and Phoenician *mávri* from America were sexually compatible.

Johnny'd asked her to find him a small clean hotel for a month. The "month" part made her feel loved. Nobody would want a hotel for a whole month just to have sex with a Greek girl.

She met him at Hellenikon Airport and, after a lot of hugging and kissing and collecting of luggage, they were off in the Honda, into the soft night air. When they got to Christina's, a two-storey stucco building in Ambelokipi, just outside the centre of Athens, Johnny said, "Are you sure this is a hotel?"

Soula grinned up at him as she turned the key to the outer door.

"I am sure it is *not* a hotel."

"Where are you taking me, woman?"

"To Christina's."

"And *Christina* is in a hotel?"

"Christina is in *Kríti*—Crete. It is her holidays. We have her place for ten days."

Sometimes, Johnny told Rose Golden by long-distance telephone, a thing looks like the real deal but falls apart if you get too near it for too long. "Soula and me, *we are* the real deal!" he shouted, causing Soula, lying beside him, to laugh. Real Deal? Was that the American equivalent of Phoenician dreams?

Each felt completed by the other—enough to want to do the rest of their self-completion with the other always nearby.

While Johnny was in Japan, Soula's grandmother died. She'd been ill for some years. It had been agreed that when Grandmother died, Soula's mother would move into her large house on the Island of Ydra. Soula, it had also been agreed, would stay on in the Athens flat until it was sold, and use some of the money from that sale to buy an Athenian studio apartment for herself. Feeling a strong possibility of new plans for that money, Soula asked Johnny to come with her to Ydra on the Flying Dolphin hydrofoil.

Ancestors

Mrs. Damanakis took one look at the smiling young people and knew she was seeing young love. She was less than pleased.

It wasn't that the young man was *mávros*. Not in the sense of "black" being a *colour*. Johnny was only a bit darker-skinned than Soula. And there were Greeks darker than both of them. *Greeks—that* was the point. The young man was not Greek.

As far back as Soula's mother could trace, from both memory and documents, the family, on both sides, was composed entirely of Greeks—with the inevitable Turkish accidents that are unavoidable during a four-hundred-year occupation. Somehow, this seemed important, seemed worth preserving. The Damanakis and Loukakis families knew their history, and that history was Greek.

To make matters worse, this "Tzonny," who seemed like a very sweet boy, did not seem to know where he came from. North Carolina, he said. But that was in America, which had, in Greek terms, a history of about four days.

"Where before that?" she asked.

"Africa."

"*Where* in Africa? What part?"

Johnny sighed.

"I . . . I don't know, exactly."

Mrs. Damanakis, who knew little of black American history, was puzzled.

"What do you mean? You do not know what place in Africa your *PROghonee* . . . what is in Engliss, Soulamou?"

"*Ancestors*, Mana," Soula answered. She knew more of black American history, and was afraid of this discussion.

"Yes, *ancestorrs*," Mrs. Damanakis continued, "you do not know what place in Africa your ancestorrs are coming from? How can this be?"

And Johnny Reed, son of Marcus Aurelius Reed and Carlotta Dixon Reed, who had grown up learning as much as he could about how this could be, sat in the opulent dining room of an old villa that had once belonged to seagoing merchants, and, as the huge red sun was devoured by the ancient sea of those merchants, he told the mother of the woman he loved as much as could be told in one sitting of African-American history.

Though Soula fidgeted a bit during Johnny's history-tale, her mother sat rapt with interest, rising only once to prepare after-dinner coffee. Soula thought to suggest that Johnny stop, but said nothing, smiling when he looked over at her for approval.

When Mrs. Damanakis returned with coffee, Johnny leapt up to carry the heavy tray. Soula took a bowl of fruit from a sideboard and placed it in the centre of the lace-clothed table.

"So, Tzonny, all you know is *Africa*, but the Americans mixed up families so that you cannot now find your . . . ancestorrs, yes?"

"Yes. Some, a few of us, *have* gone to Africa and found something . . . but mostly, even with those of us who say we found something . . . mostly it's that we *decide*."

"*Decide?* Marisoulamou, 'decide' is *apoFAHsee*, yes?"

"Yes, Mana."

"I do not understand, Tzonny. How can you do this?"

Johnny smiled shyly and then sipped from the little cup of slightly sweet black Greek coffee—which Mrs. D. said was one of the "Turkish little things that got into our Greekness." "We always call it *Greek* coffee . . . because of bad memories from the long Turkish rule, but our coffee is originally from the Turks."

"Greek coffee—that is something you decided," Johnny said. "*Our* deciding is more detailed. It has to be so, because more detail has been lost. Like the Greeks with coffee, we also have little things . . . from when we were slaves to the white Americans. Those little things make me this light colour. But we find our *heritage* in our *African* history. And we decide by looking at faces. African faces. Not just in Africa—in books, in magazines, in documentary films. Each place in Africa has faces that belong to different groups. If you look at them for a while, you get to know them, to recognise them. Some more quickly and clearly than others. I have never been wrong in identifying an Ethiopian face. Or a Somali face. Or a face from the Dan people.

"My father's family have Benin or Ashanti faces. From the place that is now Ghana. So I think my father's history is Benin and Ashanti. My *mother's* people are, I think, Yoruba. From Nigeria. And there is also some Seminole Indian from the American state of Florida, long before it was America. The Seminole were the original people from that piece of America. For thousands of years.

"So, I am an American of African heritage, whose ancestors are Benin, Ashanti, Yoruba and Seminole."

Mrs. Damanakis was smiling in spite of herself, the way she always did when she liked the *sound* of something.

"Say again, please Tzonny, the names of your people."

And Johnny Reed, smiling back at his future mother-in-law, said:

"Benin.

"Ashanti.

"Yoruba.

"Seminole."

Mister Daniels Has Two Visitors
Ydra, Greece, 1995

"Pasta. Flora."

Marilena stood in the doorway of Theddo's Kamin's apartment, her head haloed by an enormous Afro, through which the sun shone. She held a large plate in front of her. On it was what appeared to Theddo to be an oversized jam-filled Linzer torte—a double-cookie the size of a small pizza.

"Pasta?"

"Pasta *Flora*. It is a cake, Mister DanYELLSS. A gift from my family for your new home. Mana made it this morning, but she is working at the Women's Centre, so I asked if I could bring it."

"Well, Marilena, I'm glad that you have. And your hair looks extraordinary. Beautiful."

"*Ev hariSTOH*. Thank you. I have not done it this way for . . . a long time. I do it with the pick this morning to . . . celebrate your new apartment."

"Well, it's a lovely celebration, your hair. Please come in. As you see, I've set up my working space, but not much else. I have nothing to offer to go *with* your . . . pasta flora."

"Can you hold this please?" Marilena asked. Theddo took the plate of pastry. The girl then reached down to the ground beside the door.

"I have brought also two paper cups of *Dipló Métrio*—big-size Greek coffee, medium sweet. I hope that will be good for you."

Theddo and Marilena carried plate and Styrofoam cups to the little metal dining table that he'd placed next to the rectangular wooden one he'd designated somewhat ceremoniously, as the Writing Table.

"That will be *splendid* for me . . . but I think two big-size cups of Greek coffee might put me on the ceiling."

"Oh, the other cup is for *me* . . . that is part of the welcome. We have to make the welcome *together*. Just for a little time, and then I will go away and not bother your work."

"It's no bother. I *am* glad to see you, Marilena. You are, in fact, my first guest. But are you allowed to drink coffee?"

Marilena looked slightly indignant as she arranged their celebratory repast.

"I am *thirteen*, Mister DanYELLSS. I have coffee three times every week. Sometimes four. I *love* coffee! Where are your cake plates, please?"

Theddo was not exactly sure where his "cake plates" were, but rummaging in the little kitchen revealed all.

"Which utensils will we need?"

"Utensils?"

"Sorry. Knives, forks, spoons?"

"Oh, nothing of that. Mana said to be sure to tell you that pasta flora must be broken with the hands and eaten with the hands. It is a tradition."

"Well then, hands it is. I wish to honour your tradition."

"Tell me, Marilena," he asked later, as he washed their two plates, "do you ever wonder why you don't see more . . . *mávri*, I think that's the word in plural, here on Ydra?"

"Yes. That is the word. I think it is just that Greece is not a *mávro* country. But I do see many *mávri*."

"You do? Where?"

"On the CNN."

"You watch CNN?"

"Not at our house. We do not have the cable. It costs much money, the cable. But Litsa's family has it, so I watch the CNN at Litsa's house. Litsa's father says it is very important to watch the CNN."

"He does? Why is that?"

"Because the CNN always tells you when the Americans are dropping bombs. If they are bombing where you live, and you watch the CNN you can leave your house and go to live somewhere else and not get bombed."

"I see. Does Litsa's father think the Americans might bomb Ydra?"

Marilena smiled, pleased that she'd had the same thought as the smart and famous *mávros* from AmeriKEE.

"That is exactly what I asked him when he told me about the CNN. He said, Litsa's father, that, no, he did not think the Americans would bomb Ydra . . . but that they *do* bomb things . . . and that life has many surprises."

"Well," Theddo said, "I guess I'd better start writing then. Like Litsa's father, I don't think the Americans are going to bomb Ydra, but just in case, I do want to finish my new book."

"Yes, I will take our plate and go now. It was very good to have pasta flora with you, Mister DanYELLSS."

"It was *wondrous* to have pasta flora with *you*, Marilena."

"*Wunn-druss?*"

"Yes . . . I think the Greek word is *thávma*. Please thank your mana for making it for me."

"I will."

Marilena opened the door, looked for a moment at the sea, and then turned back to Theddo.

"Mister DanYELLSS?"

"Yes, love?"

"Your book . . . what is it about?"

"It is about . . . about how life is full of surprises."

"Oh? Does someone get bombed?"

"No. And yes. There are ways of getting bombed, Marilena, where there is no actual bomb."

"Bombed by an invisible bomb?"

"Not exactly . . . look, if I talk about it, I will not write it. I will just talk it away. But when it is done, I will give a copy to you and your parents, and you can all read it."

"That would be . . . *wondrous,*" Marilena replied, perfectly imitating Theddo's accent.

An hour later, Theddo was writing on his yellow legal pad when he heard the unmistakable sound of feline complaint. He looked around, and there in the kitchen was the little lion to whom he'd sung the blues in the rain. Blue eyes, pink nose and all. Theddo figured he must have come in when Marilena opened the door to go out. Because he was at that moment writing about Björn and the Lindqvists and the island of Fårö, and also nibbling at the jam-filled pasta flora, he remembered Mrs. Lindqvist's orange jam.

"Hello, Cloudberry," he said to the ginger-coloured furball.

Who responded with an even louder wail of dissatisfaction.

"Right. Sardines. I have a can of sardines. Will that do?"

The sardines did just fine. The cat lay on the couch after eating. Then he curled up under Theddo's chair. After a sleep, he came out slowly, stretching, then jumped up on the writing table and rubbed his head against Theddo's arm. Theddo scratched him behind the ears.

"Well," Theddo said, "life is indeed full of surprises."

For three days, Cloudberry was Theddo's writing and sleeping companion. And then he disappeared.

After twenty-four hours of cat-absence, Theddo put a plate of sardines on the balcony. These were eaten at some point, but Theddo, not seeing any sign of his little orange friend, did not know when, or by which cat. There were many cats on Ydra. The previous day, when he'd walked into Ydra town for some provisions, Pavlos the grocer had insisted that the Island had more cats than people. Although that seemed unlikely, it was true that, whether in the harbour or wandering up in the hills, Theddo saw quite a lot of cats. Of all sizes and colours, most were thin, and some clearly ill, with running eyes, dull fur and frothy mouths. Most, even the healthy ones, had the corner bitten off at least one ear. After a cat-filled walk, Theddo was glad he was feeding the bright-eyed and glossy-coated Cloudberry.

But perhaps it was too much. Perhaps the animal had been overwhelmed by the opulence and regularity of the sardines, and had wandered off in order to do what he knew.

A Carousel Horse
Washington, D.C., 1979–1982

"I have to do what I know. What I know is to dance. Danny will not let me do this in his company, except as a little "extra thing." Stig has found for me a job dancing on a tour of Sweden, Norway and Denmark. It will be with original music. I will be able to make my own dances! When the tour is finished, I will come back to you here."

Theddo had just poured coffee for the two of them, and was clearing the dinner dishes. All he heard was:

"Stig?"

"I knew you would do that. This is not about Stig. It is about my dancing. It is about earning my own money. It is also about seeing my family. I have not seen my mother, or Marius and Lisa, for over one year."

Theddo reached across the little wooden table and put his large brown hand alongside Björn's pale fine-boned cheek.

"Lille, I *do* understand. I just hate the idea of being without you. But yes, absolutely, you should take this job. How long will it be, this tour?"

"I am not certain. Two or three months. With a month to rehearse. And some time on Fårö with my family."

"Will Stig also be on this tour?" Theddo asked, knowing the answer.

"Of course. He plays flute in the symphony. Thedd-doh, Stig knows I am . . . with you. He is a very honest man. He will respect that."

"And will you be . . . sharing *living quarters* with this *honest man* while you're rehearsing? On this tour?"

Björn sighed, looking at his older lover as if he, the elder, were a querulous child.

"To save money, during rehearsals, I will stay in Stig's little extra room. As I have before. Without . . . romance. Once we are on tour, I will share rooms with the other dancers. You can ring me at Stig's. You can even ask him if he is sleeping with me, and he will tell you that he knows I am your lover . . . because in Sweden people are allowed to know this. Not like America."

Theddo decided to ignore the reference to the secrecy of their life in America, knowing he had no satisfactory response. He also dismissed the idea of asking Stig Hanssons, via long-distance phone whether he, Hanssons, was sleeping with Björn ("Hi, Stig. It's Theddo Daniels. I was just wondering, Stig, if you were doin' the nasty with my boyfriend? That is to say, are you having sexual congress with the young man I love, that is to say . . .").

He sat on the red rug. Björn came and sat beside him.

"Oh, Thedd-doh, you look so sad. Please do not look sad. The time will go fast. And you can come and visit me!"

"Where? At Stig's?"

"Of course not. When you come, you can take a hotel room, and I will stay with you there."

Björn's eyes were bright with excitement. He was a dancer, Theddo thought, and he wanted to dance. What sort of tight-ass would deny him that?

"Lille, I . . . know you should do this. I *want* you to do this. As to visiting, I can't go *anywhere* for at least two months. That school tuition bill is in the home stretch in Congress, and I have to see it through."

Björn smiled, resting his hand on Theddo's knee.

"That will work well. I need to listen to the music and decide the dances, and then make the dances and rehearse. By the time you come, you will be able to see what I have made. I am very much happy for this chance. Please be happy for me also, yes?"

Be gracious, be supportive. Smile, Theddo told himself as he stood in the doorway of the basement flat, giving a firm wave as Björn turned to look at him just before getting into the airport limo.

Good, he thought. You've managed this.

Sort of. Thoughts and mind-pictures of Björn would appear, unbidden, daily (and nightly), no matter where he was, no matter what he was doing.

The dances Björn created for the symphony were a success, garnering both critical and audience praise in Sweden and Norway.

Theddo had a conference invitation for Paris. It coincided with Björn's performance in Denmark.

He took an all-night flight to Copenhagen. An inability to sleep in the body-jamming hell of economy class left him a large broken mess of bleary jet-lag.

Björn called him at the Swan Hotel.

"Thedd-doh?"

"Hello, Lille."

"Hello, hello, hello! I am happy you are here!

"Me too."

"Me too also! Listen, I must rehearse on this new stage. The concert is at the Tivoli Gardens at twenty hours—eight o'clock in the night. It is only two streets away from your hotel. There are posters there, saying 'Odinsång.' There are black arrow-marks pointing to where is the stage. I have left a ticket with your name. Wait for me after, and we can walk back to the Swan or . . . ah, I must go, they need me to rehearse, see you tonight, very happy!" He shouted a stream of Swedish at someone and then hung up.

Theddo thought he would have a walk, look around. About fifteen minutes of this showed him that he could choose between lying down and falling down. He returned to his hotel room, left a wake-up call for five o'clock ("I think that is seventeen hundred hours, yes?") and slept, dreamlessly, until the phone rang at five.

The Tivoli Gardens, with nature, fairy-tale houses and restaurants outlined in little multicoloured lights, was a child's idea of an enchant-ed village by night. It sparkled and shone and made Theddo smile.

The smile changed to a gasp when he arrived at the tiny stage. Just behind the round stage, was an enormous old chestnut tree. There, naked except for a thong bikini the colour of his pale flesh, hanging upside-down from a thick branch of the tree, eyes closed, was Björn. A length of heavy rope tied him at the crossed ankles. His pale arms hung loosely, swaying slightly.

This must belong to the dance, Theddo thought, they cannot have lynched him upside-down. His mind knew that the hyper-agile Björn

247

was fine, yet could not bear to see him as a hanged man. He sat, still heavy with fatigue, and turned his attention to the orchestra, just to the right of the stage. Which musician, he wondered, was Stig Hanssons? He didn't remember what instrument Björn had said Hanssons played. The cellist was a tall broad-shouldered blond man, in the orchestral uniform of black cotton turtleneck sweater and black trousers. His jaw was the stuff of comic books, complete with Cary Grantian cleft chin. *Hanssons*, Theddo thought sullenly. This petulance was interrupted by that same cellist bowing his instrument. It was a long, mournful sound, cut through by Björn, loudly screaming a single word. To Theddo, it sounded like "Yailllpppaaaa!"

The twinkling Tivoli Gardens then filled with the sound of a male voice, deeper and older than Björn's, coming from two enormous speakers at each side of the stage. As the voice began its recitation, none of which Theddo could understand, Björn curled himself upward, and, holding to the tree branch with one hand, he freed himself and jumped to the stage. Theddo then realised that the stage was ringed by scalloped stones, each with a letter he recognised as runic. As the strange words and eerie polytonal rhythmic music continued, Björn danced with and around these stones, bringing each one, in its turn, to the centre of the stage.

He then placed himself, writhing, atop the stones, embracing them, arching and swinging his head, shouting other words, in the language of, and in counterpoint to, the recorded words. Lastly, he stood behind the stones and executed one of his flawless lateral-leg leaps. This was followed by his leaping, legs drawn up, *over* the stones. He raised his arms and chin to the sky. The music stopped. The audience, including Theddo, applauded and shouted. Björn bowed low, stood up, winked at Theddo and ran from the stage to somewhere in the darkness behind the tree.

"Thedd-doh, this is Stig."

He was at least sixty-five. Thin, with shoulder-length white hair, a gaunt, lined face. The eyes were young. The same bright blue as Björn's.

The smile was open and warm, showing strong, slightly yellowed teeth. He was the flautist, Theddo realised, *not* the lantern-jawed blond hunk who had played such a fine cello.

"Ah. Wonderful flute playing, Mister Hanssons. I'm glad to meet you," Theddo said, extending his hand.

"*Tack*. Thank you, Mister Danielss. It is also fine to meet *you*. I have heard so much about you."

Theddo's immediate, habituated thought was Oh God, you're not *supposed* to be hearing "so much about me." *Nobody* is, unless it's about my work, and . . .

Björn read Theddo's thought immediately, and interjected, a bit loudly: "Yes, Thedd-doh, I have told Stig all about your important work in America, and about my being able to help Senator Ekstrom and . . ."

"Yes, Björn is very proud . . ."

Björn, who hated the closet-covering babble, grabbed Theddo's arm. "So, did you like my dance?!"

Theddo looked at him. Björn's eyes were shining in that way they always did when he'd finished dancing.

"Of course. How could I not? It was . . . extraordinary."

"May we now celebrate? Just the three of us? Have a drink somewhere?"

"Oh, Björn, I would love to celebrate with . . . you and Mister Hanssons . . ."

"Please, call me Stig."

"Of course. With you and *Stig* . . . but I am so jet-lagged, I'm not sure I . . ."

Stig Hanssons nodded.

"Oh yes. You are in a completely different time zone. We are honoured that you made time in your important work to come and see our little program. Björn, you should walk your friend to his hotel. I will see you tomorrow."

Theddo searched Hanssons' face for irony, for sarcasm. There was none. Just one old guy knowing that a younger old guy was tired. And wanted to spend whatever coherent moments he could pull together with the person he had come to see.

"Thank you . . . Stig. I am sure that we will have a chance to celebrate . . . in time."

"Ya. In time. Come, Theddo, I will walk you home now," Björn said, sounding a bit like an attendant at the East Capitol Senior Citizens' Center.

Theddo and Stig shook hands again.

He seems a decent man, Theddo thought, it is good that Björn has his . . . protection.

In the two-block walk to the Swan Hotel, after making sure that Theddo liked Stig, Björn chattered excitedly about the dance he had made:

"It is about the most important time in the life of the Norse god, Odin, where he hangs from a tree for nine whole days, sacrificing his little personal self, to his greater universal *Self,* the Self of all things. At the end he finds the *runestenar,* the rune stones that are the first Nordic alphabet. It should have been an *oak* tree, and some say an *ash* tree, but there are no oak trees or ash trees in the Tivoli Gardens and . . ."

Theddo got his room key from the concierge and he and Björn entered the wrought-iron-and-glass birdcage elevator.

"The other dance, the one you won't be able to see because you will be in Paris, is a Druid dance. It is the complete dance of what I started to make in your back garden. I am, for this dance, completely painted in *blue* . . ."

Theddo opened the door to his room, gesturing for Björn to precede him.

"Perhaps, I will be doing that dance, the Druid one, when you can next come to Europe. If not, I will do it for you alone, this is a nice room I am thirsty is there . . .?"

"Lille?"

"Ya?"

"Please sit."

Theddo lay down on his back, shoes still on, and regarded Björn with bleary tenderness. Björn sat on the edge of the bed.

"Are you . . . all right, Thedd-doh?"

Theddo smiled, or thought he was smiling (it was more a twitch).

"Yes, Lille, I am fine. And very pleased to be here . . . and to see your remarkable dance . . . and I love you . . . but I am . . . almost *blind* with tiredness! I am so sorry . . ."

Björn pressed his fingers against Theddo's lips.

"Oh, Thedd-doh, please do not be sorry. I have travelled today, and then rehearsed and danced. I am also sleepy. I would like it very much if we only sleep, holding each other."

And they undressed, and held each other, and slept.

In the middle of the night, Björn, who could never eat before dancing, ate three candy bars and a bag of pretzels from the mini-bar fridge, washed down with a can of tonic water. He then brushed his teeth with his finger and returned to bed. Theddo slept through all of this.

The company had been invited to do a second tour: the United Kingdom, Ireland and France.

Of course, Theddo understood. Of course, Björn wanted him to visit as often as possible ("There's no way, in the schedule, that I can fly to America and also rehearse and dance").

He telephoned Theddo every week, bubbling with joy at "Dahncing! And people are loving it! I am soooo happy, Thedd-doh. It would be perFECT happiness, of course, if you were also here, but I will be home to you immediately after this tour! I do miss you, but I will return to you a stronger and happier person than ever before!"

Theddo *was* pleased by the pride he was hearing. Björn was earning decent money, for the first time really, solely based on his talents as a dancer and choreographer.

He did manage three more too-quick but loving visits during the two years that Björn danced his way through Europe.

And Björn returned to him as soon as the tour concluded.

Thanks to the choreographer of the Monster Dance, he did not, *could* not return as a stronger and happier person.

"Hey, Thedd-doh."

Even allowing for the fact that Theddo's joy at seeing him invested him with radiance, he looked extraordinarily beautiful.

The red-and-silver glittery scarf that Callie had given him was flung around his neck. His chopped-up haystack thatch of punky hair had grown long and straight. It fell over his right eye, affording an opportunity to occasionally toss it out of his eyes like a self-intoxicated drama student.

In those first moments, in the doorway, he did not toss his hair, but stood stock-still. He'd gotten a bit thinner, which brought into sharper focus his remarkable cheekbones and huge blue eyes.

It was in those eyes that the Monster resided. Björn's eyes were wide with shock. Theddo had seen such eyes before. In the faces of men, women and children who'd experienced sudden arson, sudden rape, sudden murder. What unexpected horror had Björn witnessed? Theddo wanted to know—to offer help, support, love.

Love. He knew from a lifetime of stiff emotional clumsiness that he might do it badly, but above and before all else, he wished to offer love. He embraced Björn, feeling too large, not wanting to injure. This too seemed strange. Björn had always been thin, but with the power of a dancer. Now, despite two years of dancing, he felt bird-boned, quivering slightly inside Theddo's embrace, while holding tight to him, kissing his neck, saying his name. Theddo, feeling a drop of water on his skin, held Björn away from him.

"What, Lille? Please, what is wrong?"

"I will tell you . . . the t'ings. Later. I am . . . happy to be back here, to be with you. Can we first just . . . be together?"

"Yes. Yes, of course." Theddo's voice, usually so dependable, would not come out. Startled and self-conscious, he accompanied his affirmation with head-nods.

"Frog in my throat," he half-whispered.

"We will free him," Björn replied.

It was a Sunday afternoon in May. Nobody had to be anywhere. Theddo closed all the curtains. Like adolescents whose parents were not home, they hurriedly removed clothing—their own, each other's.

Apart from one night, gracious but unspectacular, with an old friend from Chicago, Theddo had not touched a naked man for almost six months. The shock of warm skin, Björn's warm skin, the skin of the man—*man* not *boy* who personified his understanding of "I love," was almost dizzying. He laughed out loud, shouting "I have missed you so much!" They kissed deeply, then Björn sat up and pulled away.

Oh God, Theddo thought, we still have this "giving and receiving" business.

But it had become more complicated. Björn kissed Theddo again, and then whispered "Touch. Kiss. Hold. Nothing else. Just these things."

And they did just those things, erupting into orgasms that brought exultation, shattering both physical and emotional equilibrium. The rocketing, trembling, gulping reach of mouths and hands, of skin on skin, pushed and thrust through them, though neither was either pushing or thrusting. It was a more intimate, more loving engagement with another human being than either had experienced before—with one another or any other.

After, Björn lay, as he always had, with his head on Theddo's chest, kissing his skin, absently uncurling a chest hair and watching it bounce back into its tight coil. Theddo entwined his fingers in Björn's lank shiny yellow hair, now so long he could wind his fingers around it. He did this. Björn laughed softly, looked up at him.

"You like it, my new *classique* hair?"

He laughed again. And then started sobbing. Theddo held him. He cried for a while. Finally: "Talk to me, Lille, please. I'm here. Whatever it is, I am here. I am with you. Yes?"

"Yes."

He sat up in bed, facing Theddo, legs crossed in his Yoga-like way—naked and pale in the light from the bedtable.

"At first . . . it was just boys who disappeared. Some were from the Grand Hotel, from the ferry-place. Boys had disappeared before. Because they went away with someone, because they went home, because they were killed. When it was a killed boy, we would read about it in the papers. Sometimes right away, sometimes a year or more later. "Street Boy Killed, Remains of Boy Prostitute Found." You know. But these boys, these disappearing boys from these new times, some of them would first get very thin. I thought it was drugs. Heroin. But the thin did not look like drug-thin. It looked like pictures from concentration camps, from refugee camps, from war. Then, later, these war-boys would disappear.

"Four months ago, it happened to Per. You remember my best friend Per? He got the thin-ness. His doctor told him he had the Gay Disease from America. The doctor told Per that he would die of this because there was no cure. Per's man, the one he was with for three years, threw him out. I brought him to stay with me at Stig's. We took care of him, me and Stig. Stig had already seen this thing happen with two members of the symphony. I knew one of them. I thought he had gone to his home in Uppsala to take care of his old father. That was what he said when he left. But it was not true. It was the Gay Disease from America.

Some said it was the Gay Disease from *Africa*. The people who said Africa said it came from monkeys. From eating *monkeys!*

"Others said it came from dancing-club drugs. Inhalers. Per thought he got his disease in this way, because he went a lot to dancing-clubs and liked to do poppers and suck on handkerchiefs full of this amazing, chest-opening drug. Klora. A name like Klora, this drug. It made you feel so hot, so sexy. Per loved this drug, and thought it gave him the Gay Disease. After he knew he had it, we would go to the dance clubs together and suck the Klora handkerchiefs anyway. There were many there who had the disease. All dancing. I called it the Monster Dance because I could see the Monster who made the disease. He was invisible, the Monster, but I could see him making his dance, weaving through the dancing boys at the clubs. I could not see his face, just arms and legs, very long. One night, I tried to show him to Per, and he said, Per said, 'No. No monsters. Just dance' and he danced away from me like I was the Monster.

"Per got so thin, Thedd-doh. Like a beautiful little bird. And then like a not-beautiful little bird. His nose, which was not normally so big a thing, got looking very big and pink. And then he got these purple stains all over the outside of his skin, and, his doctor said, he had more of these blotches on the inside too. Two days before I left for the German part of tour, he went to hospital. He died there. I was with him in the hospital. Only me. If his father knew, he did not care. His mother was already dead, from when Per was little.

"Then, when I was dancing in Ireland, Stig, who was also in Ireland, playing in the orchestra, got very sick. I knew it was the same thing. We both got big drunk on brown beer and cried and cried. He went back to Stockholm. I was dancing in London when he died. I was actually *onstage*, and I knew. I cried out. People thought it was part of the dance.

"When I returned to Stockholm, Stig's brother, who hated Stig and always called him *bög*—queer, had taken the apartment and the house in the city and the house in Vaxholm and everything, so I took my things and stayed with someone else from the symphony.

"I went to the doctor. I have it, Thedd-doh, the Gay Disease. Well, not the disease. Not yet. First you get the germ. And then you get the disease. It can sometimes be a long time, the doctor said, between having the germ and having the disease. With Per and with Stig it was very fast. I do not know how it will be with me. Fast or slow. The doctor could not tell me. He said it is a little bit like being a carousel horse. You first go around and around with it, and then, later, you go up and down. He told me to say to you that you must go to the doctor."

Theddo, a gay man who was both American and African, had already heard about the new disease, had already seen his own cluster of disappearances. As with most personal matters that made him uneasy (particularly those that threatened to shine a light into his closet), he kept the information "somewhere over there"—somewhere where he did not have to look at it. I know you're there, he would think, but I am not promiscuous, I am careful. This has nothing to do with me. It is a bad and dangerous thing—a thing that is somewhere over there.

He also knew that Björn, the lover with whom he was not promiscuous, had been with scores of men. That truth, initially acknowledged, after the new disease came, was also kept somewhere over there.

Cautious, prudent and conservative in all but his social and racial activism, Theddo went to his doctor the following day. Ellis Robinson, also black and also gay, told him his tests were negative—he did not have what Björn had called "the germ." He also told him that promiscuity hadn't much to do with any of it. Yes, multiple partners increased the opportunities for the disease to attack, but one could get this thing from one experience with one person. Theddo, without mentioning name, age or country of origin, told him Björn's sexual history, to the extent he knew it, and, of course, his AIDS-status. Ellis gave him a paper with the rules for safe sex. He also gave him a box of condoms. He asked if Theddo wanted "your friend" to be seen by him professionally.

"No," Theddo improvised, "he has his own physician."

"Ah. Could you ask if he'd mind my having his doctor's name? In case we want to . . . co-ordinate?"

"I'll do that. Thanks, Ellis."

"Theddo, listen. I want you to see me every month for a while. We don't know enough yet about the incubation period for this sucker."

For a while, Björn was fine and Björn and Theddo were better than fine. They went to Dag Ekstrom's cabin almost every weekend, along with

Callie, or Callie and Keisha. Theddo said nothing to the others about Björn's condition. It was all too new and he did not want to alarm anyone. Both he and Björn, now knowing more, were careful about anything that could involve blood or bodily fluids.

A mutual tender protectiveness kept either of them from being irritable about all the cautions and caveats. Björn also relaxed into having a medical reason for the highly sensual but somewhat asexual loving he truly preferred.

Then the Monster changed the choreography. Björn got an AIDS-related pneumonia and was hospitalised. Theddo was at work. He called Callie Hodge, who had, at that point, been a secret sanctuary for two weeks. Afraid of pushing Dag Ekstrom too far, without first talking to him in detail, Callie took Björn to the hospital, telling the admitting nurse that he was a Swedish exchange student, her intern, and that she would be responsible for his expenses. When Theddo asked about this, Björn said, "I use Callie's name because she and Keisha are more like us than Senator Ekstrom." Theddo smiled. Björn had turned into a resourceful political thinker. And his germ had turned into what was called full-blown AIDS.

What a term! Theddo thought. Full-blown! It sounds so generous, so lush. And it means that the Monster and his crew are going to run at you from everywhere, with thin sharp knives.

The sharp knives came at Björn in a flurry: sore throats, cottage-cheesy stuff on his tongue and at the corners of his mouth. A bird-borne tuberculosis called MAI, headaches, eyeaches. He lost about twenty pounds. Then the flurry stopped, and the riot inside Björn was calm again. Shaky but calm.

"He's young, white, Swedish. He is . . . very dear to me. He is known here as Dag Ekstrom's cousin. He's had one hospital stay and has been going to a gay clinic in East Cap. I'd appreciate it if you saw him. I'll pay for everything."

So Ellis Robinson became Björn's doctor, and part of the secret.

Dag Ekstrom called Theddo at InterAfrA, asking to meet: "I'll come to your office whenever you're free."

Theddo said he was available after three that afternoon. At three-ten, Darla rang from the outer office.

"Senator Ekstrom is here for you, T.D."

Dag Ekstrom, who was an old man, had never looked like one. His height, ruddiness, mane of silvery-white hair—and those dark blue Swedish eyes—gave him a hearty appearance. On this day, however, to Theddo, Dag looked like a large sad old tree.

"You *have* to have something I can drink. Something other than wine."

"Uh hm. I 'ordered in.' Swedish vodka in the freezer."

"Bless you, my son."

Dag sipped his drink more slowly than usual. Theddo waited. Finally:

"Theddo. Is it true? About Björn?"

"Yes."

"Oh God."

The older man got up and walked to Theddo's bay window, looked down through bevelled glass at a prismatic street. With his back to Theddo, he said quietly, "He was in the hospital. Told somebody I was his damn uncle. I didn't even know he was ill, Theddo. You should have told me."

"I know. I know I should have. I . . . I was afraid. Afraid . . . that you'd be afraid."

Dag turned to face Theddo. "And you were *right*. You were *dead right!* I would have been afraid. I *am* afraid!"

"Dag . . ."

The Senator's face was angry. Theddo had seen this face when Dag was fighting for something in the Senate, or in a news conference. It was not a face that Dag had ever directed at *him*. There had been disagreements between them, but never anger.

"No! Let me get this out before it becomes like this crazy window and I can't see it whole!

"I took a chance for you, for Björn. Because *you* asked me to. Because we are colleagues. Allies. Friends. So, I took a chance. A helluva chance. I lied. I said that this boy, a boy I didn't know from a hole in the ground, was my cousin. And I stuck to it. Whenever Björn needed a 'cousin Dag,' *cousin*, not *uncle*, he had one.

"Don't you think that what I did for you both meant the two of you owed me something? Owed me having information before a blindsiding scandal rag called to ask me about it?!"

Now Theddo, in addition to feeling guilty, also felt afraid.

"Oh God. *What* scandal rag?"

"*Information for the Nation.*"

"What did they ask you?"

"They asked, it was a woman, *she* asked if 'your young *nephew*, the one who lives in Theddo Daniels' basement, has AIDS?'"

"She said 'lives in Theddo Daniels' basement'?"

"She did."

"Christ. What did you tell her?"

"What *could* I tell her, Theddo? I didn't *know* anything. I said he was a cousin, that I hadn't heard anything about AIDS, that he had been back in Sweden for a coupl'a years. Told her he seemed perfectly well when last I saw him."

"So, my not telling you gave you 'plausible deniability' . . ."

Dag's face grew red and he pounded on Theddo's desk.

"Don't you *dare* do that political shit with me. 'Plausible fucking deniability!' I listen to that doublespeak every day of my life. Sometimes I use it myself. But *not* with my friends, and *not* about a lethal disease! Now, are you gonna tell me what the fuck is *up* here?!"

So, as daylight leeched out of the sky and the red, green and yellow of traffic lights began bouncing off the carved glass of the windows, Theddo told his old friend what was up.

Dag listened quietly, filling his glass again. Theddo finished, saying "I, myself, am apparently negative—I don't have anything. It always has to be monitored, but, so far, I'm healthy. Björn is . . . *fighting* to be well, but the odds are . . . against him."

"I see. Why don't you take a shot of this vodka? *It* is very . . . soothing."

Theddo, who rarely drank hard liquor, agreed that a shot of very soothing Swedish vodka might be a good idea. Dag got another glass, poured, handed it to him. His eyes were no longer angry. Their signature bright gaze was soft.

"Theddo, I *am* sorry. I really am. I understand . . . how scared the kid must be . . . how scared *you* must be. I do wish you'd trusted me with the information, but I can also see that it's . . . a helluva lot of stuff all at once. I'll deal with the press, if there is any. And you may have to as well, because Björn is your 'tenant.'

"I also think . . . that we should not do the weekends for a while. Until I can get my head around all this, can learn a bit more about it."

"I understand."

That was not what he wanted to say. He *wanted* to say, "Look, I *have* talked to my doctor. I've read as much as is available on the subject. It is actually very hard to catch this thing. For *you*, it would be just about impossible. Björn and I are playing by all the rules. We are very careful. We would never put you, or Callie, or Keisha, or *anyone, knowingly* at risk."

But, looking at the weary bewildered face of a friend who had already put himself at considerable political risk, somehow "I understand" and the acceptance it signalled seemed the only appropriate response.

That Thursday evening, Björn asked about going to "Uncle Dag's." Theddo said Dag needed to have a working weekend by himself with lots of papers. Instead they wandered through the Eastern Market, eating hushpuppies and buying fresh fish and vegetables for dinner.

After dinner they had an argument about Björn wanting to go to a dance club.

"Well, if you worry so much, you come also, so you can watch over me."

"You know I can't do that."

"Ya. I 'know you can't do that,'" Björn said, mimicking Theddo's deep voice and American accent. "But I can. So I will."

And he did.

Theddo called Callie.

"Look, I know you took him to the hospital. And that he's been hanging out at your place. Thank you, Cal."

"No thanks necessary. He's our friend too."

"How much do you know?"

"Probably everything. He talks to me, talks to Keisha. When I drove him to the hospital and arranged his admittance, he asked me not to tell anybody that we knew what he had."

"Not even me."

"Especially not you, he said. He didn't want you worrying more than you already were. And he didn't want you to think he was exposing you to what he called 'scandal,' or taking advantage of us."

"I would never have thought that. As you say, you're his friends too."

"He *knows* that. He's just shook up. He's scared, Thedd."

"Yeah. So am I."

"I'm here for *you* too, you know, Mister Cool?"

"Thank you. I . . . tend to . . . keep my own counsel."

"Uh huh. Don't keep that counsel until it makes you crazy, okay?"

Three days later, Björn brought home a feral kitten, and he and Theddo had their huge fight.

He called Callie again. "Can you meet me at *The Hawk and Dove?*"

"Brigitta stuff?"

"Uh huh."

Brigitta Does the Caribbean

"Lille, would you like to go to St. Lucia?"

Björn was watching an old film on the large television in Theddo's living room.

"St. Lucia? The Christmas Saint from Sweden? She does not come now."

"St. Lucia is an island in the Caribbean. My mother's people are from there. It's a beautiful island. With a rainforest and amazing colours."

"And you want to send me there?"

Theddo sat down next to Björn on the couch.

"*No*, Lille, I do not want to *send* you there. I want to *take* you there."

"With you?"

"Yes, with me. And with Callie and Keisha. Just for a three-day weekend. I think we could both use a bit of sun. What do you say?"

Björn threw his arms around Theddo and kissed him all over his face.

"I say yes, yes, *yes!*"

St. Lucia set loose in Björn a constant exclamation of his favourite approval word.

The heavy, floral tropical air was *fantTAHstic!*

The rum and fruit-juice drinks were *fanTAHstic!*

Callie and Keisha in their bikinis were *fanTAHstic!*

The snorkelling in shallow water, watching schools of silvery, red-orange and electric-blue fish, was *fanTAHstic!*

Theddo had never been keen on the overuse of this word, thinking it camp, but seeing Björn so delighted with St. Lucia made fussy concerns seem absurd.

Björn received the rainforest, with its otherworldly flowers and iridescent multicoloured birds, as too fantastic for even that word, or, for a bit, any other. He stood speechless in the middle of it all—in faded cut-off jeans, a white tee-shirt that advertised the local beer, sandals, and that sparkly red scarf—opening his arms wide, trying to embrace the verdant world that was embracing him. He whirled around, and then closed his eyes as if feeling the forest on his face, listening to the birdsong and rustling of the trees, while the sun shot through the canopy of green fronds above him. He stood like that for a long time. Then he opened his eyes, smiled and bit his lower lip, sucking in his breath through his nose.

"Oh. Thedd-doh! It is *Paradise* here!"

"Yes. I know."

Seeing something on the forest floor, Björn knelt down. Squatting, he held it out to Theddo. It was a bird-feather; blue, red, green, yellow and white.

"Can *one* bird be these colours all at once?"

"It seems so, Lille."

He stood, winding and braiding the feather into his shoulder-length hair.

"How do I look?"

"Beautiful."

"Beautiful? I have not felt beautiful. I do feel so now. Thank you, Thedd-doh, for bringing me here. Could we be naked here?"

"I think, Lille, that our being naked here would be lovely. It would also startle the bejesus out of the tour group. We should probably try to find the others."

"If we cannot find them, if we are lost, can we live here?"

"No, unfortunately. Maybe some day."

"Some. Day. Yes. Come, we find the others." And Björn started running ahead, whirling and leaping. Theddo worried about the exertion but would do nothing to curtail rediscovered joy.

"I want to make a dance for this place! It is like another world. Like Fårö. I mean, it is *nothing* like Fårö, but it is, like Fårö, from another planet, ya?"

"Ya."

That evening, the foursome dined al fresco at a casually chic seafood restaurant in the harbour. Björn insisted that vodka and tonic was not in conflict with his medication. Theddo insisted that he would accept this medical opinion with regard to only one drink. Björn tried to pout, but was too happy to sustain it.

When the Soca/Reggae band started to play and sing, Björn and Keisha got up to dance. The glittering red scarf was bouncing light off the spinning mirror-ball in the ceiling above their heads

Callie leaned in towards Theddo.

"Would'ja look at that. 'Brigitta Does the Caribbean!' Do those two look hot or what?"

"They look glorious. This was a great idea. Thank you, Cal."

"*You* suggested it."

"Yeah, but you didn't let me chicken out."

"Well, you're the one with *roots* here. And you're the one with keys to his cousin's beach house."

"True. This would have been . . . harder to negotiate without that little house."

"Well, when Fred and Ginger up there have gotten their groove grooved, I think we should negotiate right to that little beach house, because watching my date dance with your date is turning me on."

Two hours later, Björn began breaking up like a rowboat on a rock. Voiding at both ends, seized by spasms of diarrhea and vomiting, he quivered and panted and cried out as the Monster tore through him. Theddo had seen him sick before, but nothing like this.

After an hour, he was empty even of bile. Kneeling in front of the toilet, his vision blurred, his mouth foaming, he looked at Theddo kneeling beside him and then passed out. Theddo ran upstairs, shouting for Callie and Keisha.

The women, in oversized tee-shirts, hurried down to the bathroom with him.

"Oh God, Theddo. Do you know a doctor here?"

"No. No, wait. I know a *dentist*."

"That's a start. Where's the phone book?"

"How do I know?! How the fuck do I know?!"

"Easy, Theddo. We're on it. Keesh, find the phone book and call the dentist. What's his name?"

"Grant. Aubrey Grant. I don't know him well . . . we played charity golf . . ."

"Doctor Aubrey Grant. Got it, Keesh?"

"Got it."

"Go. I'll stay with Björn."

They found the phone book and Theddo, fighting for steadiness, telephoned Doctor Aubrey Grant, DDS.

"Aubrey? Sorry to wake you at this hour, it's Theddo Daniels . . . Daniels. That's right, Theddo Daniels. I'm on the island. Listen Aubrey, we have an emergency. I'm here with Senator Callie Hodge, that's right, the black Senator. Listen, one of her . . . interns is seriously ill. Barfing, shitting, the whole nine yards. He's passed out in the john. No, he's not drunk, he's sick. He's *very* sick. Can you please come right away? It's 204 Hibiscus. The name on the door is 'Richards.' Bless you, Aubrey." He hung up and shouted down the hall.

"Callie! Keisha! Please get dressed! We're gonna be going to a hospital!"

Fifteen minutes later the black Mercedes of Doctor Aubrey Grant pulled into the drive.

Doctor Grant followed the smell, looked at the pale frail blond boy lying in the middle of his own reeking mess. "Jesus Lord!'" he said.

They cleaned Björn with cool wet towels, noting that he was both shivering and hot with fever. Keisha wrapped him in a white duvet, and the foursome got him out the door and into the back seat of the doctor's car, swaddled and stretched across the legs of Theddo and Callie.

Doctor Clyde Shelton was on call in the emergency room of the Castries Hospital. Aubrey Grant explained the situation. He said the older man, who had phoned him, was a well-known American civil rights leader, and that one of the women was a Senator. The boy apparently worked for the Senator.

They put a green hospital gown on the semi-conscious Björn, and then wheeled him into a room where he was medicated to stabilise his temperature and put onto a vitamin IV drip. Doctor Shelton then walked back to the corridor to talk to the Americans.

Callie took charge.

"How is he, Doctor? Is he dying?"

"I don't know. He needs a more complete work-up. He's very weak and quite sickly lookin'. Does he have cancer?"

"No. It's AIDS."

The doctor jumped back. It was a slight thing, but to Callie it was almost cartoonish.

"Jesus. I didn't . . . Aubrey didn't say . . . we don't have anything to deal with that here."

"We will take Mister Nilsson back to the States on the first available flight later this morning. I would suggest, however, that you start getting *things* to deal with that here, as this disease is gonna *be* here, Doctor. It's gonna be *everywhere*. In the meantime, we three will stay in the room with Mister Nilsson, and if he needs a doctor, we will call *you*. What is your name, Doctor?"

"I'm Doctor Clyde Shelton, chief of cardiology."

"How do you do. I'm Senator Calpurnia Hodge, Democrat, Maryland. The young man is my intern, Björn Nilsson. Can you do a chart on him? We'll need it in the States, how he 'presented' here and all that?"

"Certainly, Senator."

"Call me Callie, please. As I was saying, the young man, the patient, is Björn Nilsson. It's a Swedish name. I'll spell it. B-J-O-R-N, that's the first name. Second name, N-I-L-S-S—two esses—O-N. The first name rhymes with 'yearn.' Is there any coffee here?"

"There's a machine."

"Point me to it."

"I can take you there, Senator."

"No Clyde, you need to write up Mister Nilsson's chart. Pointing will suffice."

The first flight to the United States went to Boston. Theddo phoned the InterAfrA office there. When the plane touched down at Logan Airport, Doctor Lauren Greenberg was waiting on the tarmac.

Far

There could be no "winning" with the place Björn was. What there *could* be was support luck. In Lauren Greenberg, he had that.

Lying roped and wrapped on a gurney in the back of an ambulance, Björn opened his eyes, looked at Theddo, smiled lopsidedly through cracked lips and said, "Far?"

Far, Theddo thought—is he talking about the journey, or calling in Swedish for his father—or calling for *me?*

"I'm here, Lille."

"Thedd-doh . . . we were in a plane . . . I knew . . . by the sound. . . . We have travelled far?"

"Ah, far. Yes, Lille, we have travelled far. But we're all right now."

"We are where? In America?"

"Yes. Boston, Massachusetts, on the way to a hospital."

"We go . . . in a plane . . . from Paradise to here?"

"Yes."

"Callie and Keisha also?"

"Yes, but they have gone on to Washington. We will also go home, go back to Washington, as soon as they've got you good again."

"Is Doctor Robinson here?"

Lauren Greenberg, who had been sitting silently behind the gurney, came around and placed her hand atop Björn's.

"Hi, Björn. I'm Lauren Greenberg, your doctor here in Boston. I've spoken with Ellis Robinson, and we are working together. You're in Boston because we were the first destination flying out of St. Lucia."

"I was . . . big emergency, ya? I hear that word during an awake time. On the floor with the cold white stones."

"Yes. You were falling. But we caught you. Thanks to this gentleman."

"This gentleman, ya. He is *min* Thedd-doh. Hey, Thedd-doh."

"Hey, Lille."

Theddo had not believed it possible, but Björn, who had been so radiant so recently, looked awful—scrawny, pink, parched and broken, with eyes sunk deep into his head. He looked as he had described his friend Per, when Per was almost dead.

"Is he . . . close?"

"Yes. Probably. But not for sure. AIDS is weird. My brother had it; he's gone now. He rallied three times more than anyone expected. Including me, and I'm a medical professional who was loving him and cheering him on."

"Is that how you got into this? There are not many AIDS specialists, but Ellis Robinson tells me that you are one of the best in the country."

Lauren shook her head. She seemed uneasy about being singled out. Theddo thought he understood: look at my work, but not too closely at *me*. Was he projecting his own social guardedness onto her?

"I don't know about *best*. I am an immunologist and a doctor of infectious diseases. When Jamie, that's my brother, died, I decided to specialize in this work."

"What does Björn have? I know about the pneumonia, the bird-borne TB and the thrush. What else?"

"Pretty much everything at once. His white blood and hemoglobin cell count are quite low. No toxoplasmosis, but probably retinitis CMV—his eyesight comes and goes. No external Kaposi's legions—the purple blotchy things—but we found two internally, so that's started. We've medicated the MAI, the Avium tuberculosis, out of him for the moment, but you said he'd had it before, and it will probably be back."

"When can I take him home? To Washington."

"He *is* improving reasonably, within his limitations. I'd say in three or four days. Does he have family?"

"Yes. In Sweden."

"Can they come to Washington?"

"I will bring them."

Lauren Greenberg didn't ask what Theddo Daniels' involvement was. She had remained close with her brother's lover, who was an older business executive. Theddo was his darker mirror image.

He expected to see Callie and Keisha at Capitol General Hospital, and knew that Ellis Robinson would be waiting for his patient. He did not expect Dag Ekstrom. The old Senator towered behind the two women, almost as if they were shielding him, but not all that well.

"Hey, Uncle Dag." Björn, strapped to a gurney, tried to smile.

Theddo could see Dag take in the change the Monster had wrought in Björn's face. A career politician, he had fast recovery-time. He grinned.

"Hello, nephew. Very glad to see you. Doctor Robinson says you've had a helluva scare. Well, we have you now, and you're doing really well." He pointed to the two paramedics standing at the front and back ends of the gurney.

"Now, you let these good people take you to your room. We'll be in to see you after Doctor R. has done his healing work. Okay?"

"Ya, okay."

"Theddo, walk with me for a bit?"

As the two men walked back and forth in the corridor, Dag explained that he'd called "key members" of his family ("mother *and* father's side") and told them about Björn Nilsson, the new relative.

"You don't have to do this, Dag."

"Yeah. Yeah I do, in fact. You'd do it for me."

"Yes, I would."

"'Nuff said. Notification had to happen, in case the garbage-hunters called any of 'em. So, all the findable, relevant Ekstroms and Thorsbergs are now singing from the same page. Callie said you wanted to bring Björn's family here. She told me the family name. Lindqvist. Fårö. I called the wrong Lindqvist first, but he knew her. I got her number. She doesn't speak English, the mother, but my Swedish is passing fair. Her young son speaks better English than a lot of Senators."

"Marius. Terrific kid. His younger sister is Lisa. They're Björn's 'halfies.'"

"Well, they'll be here tomorrow. How *you* holding up?"

"I'm on the balls of my ass, but this ain't about me. I'll be all right."

"Don't fry yourself, Theddo. That won't help Björn. You have a team in place here. Let us share the weight."

"I'll try. I'm very grateful."

"Politicians like grateful. We bank it. I'm kidding. I'm here for a friend."

"Yeah, I know. I *do* know."

Dag also told him that somebody—Callie, Keisha or himself— would stay stationed outside Björn's room around the clock, so that Theddo could be in there without being ambushed.

"Dag, you guys all have day-jobs."

"Not Keisha. She's still got a week of vacation. Says she *likes* to do fashion layouts at night anyway. And Ellis Robinson has some friends from a clinic that is . . . used to dealing with this. They're also on call."

On call. Dire illness, Theddo thought, turns everyone that cares about the patient into a doctor. Knowing that nothing will make it right, you guess at what might at least make it better.

"You want water?"

"Can you eat? You should try to eat."

"Ice cream? Sure. I'll get you some.

"White blood cells up a bit from yesterday. That's *terrific!*"

"It's all right. I'll call the nurse and you'll be all clean again."

"Lean on me, put your arm across my shoulders."

"I'll take you."

"I'll get it."

"I'll find a nurse."

"I'll find a doctor."

And when the frail ravaged bird-boy slept, Theddo watched him breathe, wiping sweat from his face and white drool from the corners of his mouth, pushing away his own panic and horror.

He spent mornings at the hospital, and afternoons at InterAfrA. On one of these afternoons, Darla greeted him with good news. He'd gotten a victory in a university admissions case.

"We did it, T.D. Aaron Johnson and Fanita Crayne have made it over the wall into the Ivy League."

"Another stunning triumph for tokenism."

Not that he wasn't happy about the tokenism, and happy for the two tokens, calling each of them with congratulations before heading back to the hospital.

Dag, who had also fought for the two students, embraced him, patting him on the back.

"We did it, Theddo. Well done."

"Thanks, Dag. Back at'cha. How long you been here?"

"About twenty minutes. If you need to sleep, I'm good for a few hours."

"That's all right. Go do your life. I want to see him. How is he?"

"Had a barfing and shitting episode a few hours ago. Got into a babble. They think some of it was Swedish. Robinson's been here. Björn's been medicated. He's sleeping."

Theddo stood just inside the room, leaning on the closed door, looking at the sleeping Björn. His lank hair, in need of a wash, lay across his eyes. Under the sheet and blanket, his legs were pulled up fetally. Theddo crossed the room and sat in the metal-sided green-leatherette chair. After a while, Björn opened his eyes.

"Thedd-doh?"

"Yes, Lille. I'm here."

"I am happy you are here. Are you wearing a bumpy shirt?"

"Bumpy shirt? What do you mean, Lille?"

"I do not know the word. The underwear shirts you wear with all the bumps."

"Oh, thermal. Yes, yes I am. It was chilly this morning. It's warm now."

"Not for me. For me it is cold. Could I wear the shirt?"

Theddo laughed in spite of himself. "You really won't stop until you've stolen all my clothes. Of course you can wear it." He took off his bomber jacket and started unbuttoning his denim shirt.

"Now, it *will* be fun explaining to hospital staff exactly why I'm stripping off."

"Tell them you are going to get into bed with me."

"Yeah, that ought to work well."

Theddo gently pulled the thermal over Björn's head. The normally clingy garment hung off him like a waffled nightshirt.

"Ya. Warm. It smells of *you*. I like this!"

Pushing with both hands, he sat up in the bed, Theddo propping up pillows behind him.

And in came the Lindqvists.

Mrs. Lindqvist had been warned by Dag and managed to stifle her gasp, though Theddo could see the alarm in her round blue eyes as her fisted right hand flew up to her mouth.

Marius and Lisa, teenagers now, still with that open child-like gaze, stood silently, looking at this gaunt thing that had been their beautiful, magical, dancing brother.

Mrs. Lindqvist rushed to Björn's bedside, kissing him, saying words Theddo did not understand, trying not to cry.

Lisa, who had pressed herself against the wall, finally said, "Hey, Björn!"

"Hey, *min lille* Lisa!" Björn replied, which freed Lisa, crisply attired in a white cotton blouse and apple-green dirndl skirt, to run to the edge of Björn's bed, seat herself there, and bubble at him.

"*Björn! Jag har gjorde en dans för skolan, och vann et pris!*"

"*Undebart!*" Björn said, embracing his little sister, kissing her, laughing.

"What? What did she say?"

"She said she made a dance, Theddo, for school, and she won a prize! Isn't that good?"

"It's terrific. Congratulations Lisa—how do I say that in Swedish?"

"*Grattis, gratulera.*"

"*Grattis Lisa, gratulera!*"

Lisa looked shyly up at him: "*Tack så mycket.* Thank. You."

Marius, who'd been watching all this with a worried expression, asked, in English, "Would you all like to see Lisa's dance?"

Lisa jumped up, shaking her head, saying something in Swedish. Marius answered her, and then translated.

"Lisa says that she does not have her music. A cassette of a Swedish folk song. I have told her that I hear that song many times every night, when she was making her dance, and I can sing it."

Lisa was certain that Marius singing her dance-melody would be insufficient. Finally, Björn spoke.

"I want very much to see this dance. Please Lisa, could you do your dance for me? With Marius singing. Please." He then said this in Swedish, though Lisa had understood the English. If Björn wanted to see her dance, she wanted him to. She agreed, then conferred with Marius about the music, the two of them exchanging hums, Lisa showing the timing with her hands.

She moved the chair away from Björn's bedside, removed her running shoes and white socks, and then stood very still, with her head lowered, as Theddo had seen Björn do when assembling himself to dance.

Marius began singing in a sweet reedy voice. Theddo, of course, did not understand the words, but the melody was wistful and lovely, reminding him of the spiritual "Oh, Freedom."

Lisa lifted her head and began to move, slowly swinging her arms, first right and then left, following the trajectory of her arms with a sway of her head. Theddo saw at once that, despite obvious sincerity and a concentration of focus, she was an earthbound dancer, and if she had a special gift, as her elder brother did, it had not yet emerged. He looked over at Mrs. Lindqvist, who was watching her broken boy watch his sister. Björn was completely engaged with the dance, sometimes humming along with Marius, moving his hands and arms. Seeing Björn's obvious pride caused Theddo to smile at Lisa. Returning his smile, she executed a pair of slightly flat-footed leaps, and some twirling that caused her pale green skirt to billow around her. She then took a bit from the left and right ends of the skirt and curtsied low, rising proudly and without a wobble.

Everyone, led by Björn, applauded. Björn cheered, shouting, "Bravo, *min* Lisa! *Grattis*, bravo, ya, ya, ya!" Then, still smiling, but exhausted, he sank back onto the pillows, and Ellis Robinson walked in, accompanied by a nurse. The nurse wore bright yellow gloves and a facemask. Marius Lindqvist, who loved films about aliens, stared at her.

"Oh, why is that woman wearing . . . those things?" Marius asked.

"Some of the nurses are . . . afraid . . . that they will give germs to Björn," Theddo told him.

"Hello, young man. I am Doctor Robinson. The masks and gloves are not really necessary. Those who . . . have worked less often with your brother's illness feel more secure with the masks and gloves. As you see,

I do not wear them. Neither does Mister Daniels. And you do not need to either."

"But I like them. Sun gloves and Mars mask."

"We can get you some if you like."

"Oh ya, I like!"

"Ellis," Theddo said, "this young fellow is Marius, who is both vocalist and translator for the family. And this is Fru Lindqvist, Björn's mother. She has just arrived and doesn't speak much English. This little ballerina is Björn's sister Lisa."

Marius looked at Ellis, then at Theddo.

"Are you and Mister Daniels brothers?"

"Well . . . actually we are."

"Ah. I thought so. And the large man with the white hair is our family's American cousin?"

"Something like that. Now listen, Marius, will you explain to your family that your brother has been very sick and he is very happy to see you, but we have to do medical things with him now, so you must wait in the corridor while we do this. That includes you, Brother Daniels."

"Yes, Doctor," Theddo said, herding everyone outside as Marius explained everything in Swedish, and asked where he could get his sun gloves and Mars mask.

Dag Ekstrom was asleep in his chair, but opened his eyes when Theddo and the Lindqvists came trooping out. He stood, a bit abruptly and, dizzy, grabbed the back of his chair.

"You all right, Dag?"

"Never better. Just old age. Got up too fast. How is everything?"

"Well, we've just had dancing and singing, which Björn liked quite a lot. It's good that the family's here. It is also a bit of an exertion for Björn. If you can wait here for an hour, I'll take them home . . ."

"No, no, no. These are *my* relatives, and they are coming home with me."

"Dag . . ."

"This is not open to debate. We've already arranged everything, Missus Lindqvist and I. She believes, for the moment, that I am a distant cousin. We can sort it out tonight. In Swedish. A language *you* do not speak, Daniels. *Capeesh?*"

"That's Italian."

"So it is. And you don't speak that either."

He then turned to the Lindqvists, who were chattering amongst themselves, and explained, in pidgin-Swedish, that they needed to come home with him now, so that Björn could sleep and that he would bring them back to the hospital the following day on his way to work. Theddo thanked them again for coming, congratulating Lisa on her lovely dance, and Marius translated.

"*Din vacker dans,*" he said.

"*Min vacker dans,*" Lisa said softly, grinning.

The elevator opened, and the Swedish family, including Cousin Dag, piled in. The doors closed. Lindqvistless, and suddenly feeling his own exhaustion, Theddo slumped in a chair.

When Ellis Robinson came out of Björn's room, he looked less pleased than Theddo wanted him to.

"Something wrong?"

"No. Not wrong. He's sick, very sick. At the moment, he's happy and comforted that his family is here. He's also . . . weak as a baby. We had him on supplementary oxygen for a few hours. He didn't want to wear what he called 'things in my nose' when his family was here. I want him to sleep. Gave him a pill for that. He promised to take it, but wants to see you first."

Theddo pulled the metal-armed green chair alongside Björn's bed.

"Hey, Lille."

Björn, his head propped on two pillows, smiled and opened his eyes.

"Hey, Theddo. Did you like Lisa's dance?"

"Yes, of course. Did *you?*"

"I could not see it. I have not seen anything since this *ahf*ternoon. Even the doctor does not know this. I am good at pretending, yes."

"Yes, Björn, but is that a good idea, pretending to see? Doesn't the doctor need to know what is happening with you?"

"He knows what is happening with me. He knows that sometimes I do not see. I did not want him to know that at *this* time I did not see. I did not want him to tell my family. If he did that, then Lisa would know I could not see her dance. That would make her sad. There is enough sadness, yes?"

"Yes. . . . Can you see now?"

"Lillebit. Shapes. Colours . . . I am tired. Can you lie with me?"

"Lille, you know they don't allow . . ."

"Please, just for a little."

Not wanting to dirty the white sheets, Theddo removed his shoes and lay beside Björn on the narrow bed. They lay there silently. Björn, eyes closed, rested his head on Theddo's chest.

There was, there had been for a long while, something Theddo wanted to know. To at least *try* knowing.

"Lille?"

"Ya?"

"Your . . . first man . . . *my* first man was my stepfather. It was not good. I have always thought . . ."

"No."

"What 'no.'"

"No, I did not have sex relationship or any love or any touching with my stepfather. He was a fool. A drunk. He called me 'girl.' And he left my mother."

Björn, eyes still closed, placed his hand on Theddo's chest.

"My first man was American. Like you. A black man. Like you. He played piano in a jazz band visiting Stockholm. The Rex King Royals. Me, I fancied the saxophone player like mad. One night, to show off for saxophone player, I get up from the audience and make a dance in front of the band. Later, piano player, who is Rex King, leader of the band, asks me to come to his room. I go. He does things to me. Many things. Some for my first time. I am *tretton*. Thirteen. He says he will adopt me, that he will become *min far*, my father, and bring me to America. He does things to me for five days and then he is gone. I try writing him, to tell him that I still would like to come to America, that I would like him to be my father. All the letters come back. It was a long time ago."

"So. Your almost-father was a black man . . . does this mean . . . ?"

"No, *min* Thedd-doh, you are not my black father. When I first see you in Stockholm, I perhaps wanted that. Wanted father-lover. Both at once. But now, you are *min* Thedd-doh. *Min älskare* . . . my . . . lover."

Björn's voice had grown raw and barely audible.

"T'irst. Can you give me the bottle of water?"

Theddo placed Björn's hands around the plastic bottle. Drawing deeply on the clear plastic straw, he drained it. Theddo placed the empty bottle on the metal bedside table.

"Now is *my* chance for questions, *min* Thedd-doh. Please *you* tell *me,* how was Lisa's dance?"

"Her dance was wonderful, Lille. She's . . . a true dancer. Like you." Björn smiled.

"This is very good! She did leaps, yes?"

"Yes. Two."

"Two leaps. Ya, I thought so. How were they?"

"Magical. Not as high as yours, of course, but . . ."

"But they were magical?"

"Perfect. A bit like flying. One day, if she keeps at it, she will leap like Nijinsky . . . across the stages of the world!"

"Really?! Like flying?!"

"Yes. Like you do. Not yet, but one day."

"Oh, Thedd-doh, this is so fine! This is the best news!"

"Lille, I know you are happy about Lisa, but you must rest. Must sleep."

"Yes. Doctor Robinson says I am to take sleeping pill now. And also put oxygen t'ings in my nose. Will you stay in the chair while I sleep?"

"Of course."

Björn died in the night, in his sleep. Not in the pissing, shitting, vomiting frenzy that Theddo had so dreaded. His AIDS-frayed heart simply stopped struggling.

As his doctor had believed he could see, he died believing his little sister would carry on his tradition, would one day leap like Nijinsky across the stages of the world.

Theddo opened his eyes in the dark room. He reached to touch Björn's hand. The hand was cold. He turned on the bed lamp. Björn was a yellow-grey colour, his pale lips slightly parted. Theddo pressed the button that would bring a nurse, and ran to the door. There was a young black man in the 'vigil chair.' He looked up, and then stood up.

"Hello. I'm Kevin Jones from Gay Men's Care Clinic. Can I help?"

"Yes. Please call Senator Ekstrom, I will give you the number. Tell him that his cousin, Björn Nilsson, has died. Tell him that I am going to my apartment. I am Björn's landlord. I need to put his things together for his family. Tell the Senator that he will find me there."

Kevin looked at him, moved to touch him, felt the lack of permission and retracted his hand.

"Are . . . will *you* be okay?"

"Yes. I was . . . just helping the Senator. Please phone him now. Here's the number." He scribbled Dag's home and office numbers on a beige paper hand-towel.

"Will do." Kevin headed down the corridor to the pay-phone.

Ellis Robinson was running towards him.

"He's gone."

"Are you sure?"

"Yes."

The two paramedics, masked and gloved, who had responded to Theddo's buzzer confirmed this.

"Oh Theddo, I'm sorry, I . . ."

"I'm going home. There's nothing I can do here. Dag Ekstrom will be down, with the Lindqvist family. The family will want Björn's things. I need to put them together and pack them up. I need . . ."

"Theddo . . ."

"I really don't want to talk now, Ellis. You can get me at home if you need me. We will talk, but not now. Now just let me go."

The red glitterscarf hung from one of the white posts of Björn's wrought-iron daybed, its home when it was not on him. Theddo started packing socks, shoes and other clothing, knowing that some of it would fit Marius, and that he would grow into the rest.

He had wondered when he would cry. Dry-eyed, he had started to wonder *if* he would cry. At one point, thinking he *should* cry, he had tried to push it, but nothing came. Even his throat was dry. He drank a large bottle of Evian water and went to his dictionary, wanting to look up the word that had walked him home, the word that would not leave.

Desiccate—to dry up, exhaust of moisture. Yes. That was the word he wanted. He had never cried much, even as a boy. And, he had become, he thought as he lumbered through his house packing Björn's things, desiccated. Exhausted of moisture. Exhausted, period.

Not tired. Empty. Relieved to have an activity, he'd stopped at the liquor store around the corner and gotten four empty boxes. Packing, it seemed, would only require three.

He wanted to keep Björn's reviews, but realized that Mrs. Lindqvist—and Lisa—should have them. He took one, from London, with a picture of Björn. It was a theatrical shot, in three-quarter profile—Björn all pensive, hair in his eyes. He knew that Björn himself would like this picture, so he kept it, along with a Swedish review that he could not read. He also kept two glossy photos of the dancing Björn, leaving ten for the Lindqvists.

He stared at the enormous wooden hotel sign; the one Björn and Callie had liberated from the Bougainvillea Resort on the way to Dag Ekstrom's Virginia cabin. *Transient, Dancing*. Björn had recognised himself in that misunderstood description. He had wrenched the sign free as confirmation of his existence—proof that he was part of a group—the Transient Dancers.

Theddo did not want the sign, nor did he want to throw it out. The Lindqvists certainly didn't need to carry something so bulky to Fårö. He left it on the wall. He would offer it to Callie at some later point.

It had taken little more than an hour to sort and pack Björn's things. He was thirsty again, and out of mineral water. He drank a cold beer, sitting on the daybed, that was covered in a quilt made, years earlier, by his sister Dora. He took the glitterscarf from the bedpost. It smelled of Björn. He wrapped it around his neck and, certain it must look ridiculous on him, but equally certain that he was now its owner, walked slowly up the stairs to his bed.

Matters of Life and Death
Ydra, Greece, 1995

Once he had written about Björn, he found he could write about everything else: his long-gone stepfather, Billy Witherspoon, Tafiq Al Din—even the crab-lice boy in the Roman market. Dag Ekstrom had been dead for ten years and Theddo wrote in detail of his extraordinary support, thinking he'd ask Callie to read it before showing it to anyone else in Washington.

Callie. Less than a year earlier she had said, "I'll be your public girlfriend for as long as you want, but Keesh and I are ready to get out of the closet whenever you are. It's your call."

His call. His closet. His story.

Aware that the Monster could, at any time, choose to fast-dance with him, he wrote all day and every day, stopping occasionally to have a walk, cook a meal or dine with the Reed family.

From time to time, Marilena would come by after school and visit with him until he said, "I must go back to writing now." In saying this, he would also make it clear that he welcomed her visits, even if there were times when he shouted through the closed door that he could not be interrupted.

When the door was locked, signalling that he was at work, she would sometimes leave home-cooked food for him just outside. When roaming harbour cats ate the food, and returned, howling for more, Theddo started leaving the door unlocked while he worked. Marilena would look in and, if he was at his writing desk and did not speak, she'd place the food just inside the door, and, without a word, close it again.

Once, she also left something she had written—perhaps for school or simply for herself (or for him—he was not certain).

In a large clear longhand, on pale peach paper, it was about her hair:

"I love and hate my hair, usually at the same time. I love it that is red and brown. I love it that when I take my father's old 'Afro-Pik,' I can tease it out until it is a soft and fluffy thing that's like a huge earth-and-fire-coloured ball when the sun shines through it. I love it that all my friends, the girls, wish they had hair like mine. I love it that they all want to touch my hair.

"And those things, all the things I just named, are the things I hate about my hair.

"Sometimes, I really wish I had the same hair as my friends. Really wish I was not the only person in my school, on my island, who looked like me. Even my parents do not look like me.

"When I started school, when I was six years old, everybody always wanted to touch my hair. At first, this made me feel special, like a six-toes cat. Then it got boring and made me feel like a freak. Like a six-toes cat.

"Finally, I asked people not to touch my hair anymore. I had to fight a little to prove I meant this. I did not tell my parents. They were not bad ugly fights. No real hitting. Just pushing and shoving mostly.

"Now, sometimes, when a really good friend, like Litsa, stays all night at our house, or I stay at hers, I let her pick out my hair until it is enormous. I like this because it is like having your back scratched, which Litsa will also sometimes do. It feels good. As a reward for making me feel good, I let Litsa touch my hair. I also braid her hair, but it is not very interesting to do this.

"If there were other Marilena-haired people, we could start a club, like the ones at school for singing and football and racing."

And Transient Dancing, Theddo thought, as he put Marilena's essay in his briefcase.

In late January, the island weather, which had been cool and a bit damp, turned cold and rainy. Theddo wore two thermal shirts under his turtle-neck sweater and drank many pots of mint tea as he continued to work.

Cloudberry returned—cold, wet and demanding dinner.

Theddo was delighted. For over a month, part of his twice-daily walk had been to seek the animal—both in the town square and in the hillside brush between Ydra town and Kamini. At night, when he felt he could be heard but, mercifully, not seen, he would open his door and call *CLOUDberry* into the darkness, three or four times, along with the cat-traditional *psspsspsspss*. To no avail.

"Yeah, right. He knows his name, misses the hell out of you and will be along home presently," he finally muttered, closing the door.

But, came the nasty winter and there he was: a wet cat in search of food and warmth. Which Theddo was pleased to provide.

"Come in, my friend. You're just in time for sardines. And, if you'll give me a minute, I'll get the blow dryer and do something about that fur."

The blow dryer, left behind by Dina's son, was of no use to a short-haired black person. Carefully applied ("Not too close, or I'll burn your skin"), it worked wonders on a soaked cat. Within minutes, Cloudberry was dry, purring loudly and eating sardines from a blue bowl.

Having chosen his winter residence, the cat slept with Theddo, slept some more under the writing-chair, ran about the room chasing phantoms and, under an awning, catching bugs on the balcony; only wandering off occasionally, on sunny days.

Maybe he got a better offer, Theddo would think, always relieved when his roommate returned.

The writing continued until spring, when he knew he was expected by both InterAfrA and Doctor Ellis Robinson.

He and Ellis were in regular telephone contact. His health had remained stable, except for a bit of fever, which he had been able to nurse with soup, sleep and medication. Medicines were running low, but would last for about two weeks more. The pile of papers that would be his new book stood stacked on his writing desk next to the electronic battery-operated typewriter. Having only one copy made him uneasy, but Soula Reed offered the photocopier at the Women's Centre.

"When I get back to D.C., I am going to learn how to use a computer. It's time," he told her.

"Yes. Marilena is learning at school, but Johnny and I have no idea how they work."

It was feeding time, for both two-legged and four-legged residents, but there was no sign of Cloudberry. It had been a bright sunny day, all blue skies and glistening water. A day earlier, the sun set in a pink-streaked sky, followed by a night filled with low-hanging stars.

It's spring, Mister Daniels. You may have lost your roomie to his natural instincts, Theddo thought. This made him sad, but he knew he'd soon be leaving the Island and that the animal needed to retain his self-sufficiency.

He ate lightly, medicated, had a cup of mint tea and went to bed.

It was still dark when he awoke. "I finished it. I did it. I wrote it. The 'Big Bad Book,'" he said, happily, into the darkness, realising that he'd completed what had been, for him, an enormous undertaking—one that required him to push, hard, against his cautious and secretive nature. He also knew he had wiggle room; that he could still turn back, put the stack of words into a locked drawer and walk away.

He did not want this to happen, and thought he would be less likely to "chicken out" if he told somebody else. It was Monday morning. Johnny would be doing the early shift at *Sto Kéndro*. He decided to walk to Ydra town, watch the sun come up, and then tell Johnny Reed the news; tell him what the book was about. I should trap myself, he thought.

Soula and Johnny were awakened by the ringing of the phone. Marilena, in her bed, rolled over and pulled the pillow over her head. The caller was Fotini Karastamati, wife of Spiro the policeman. She was whispering.

"Soula?"

"Yes."

"It's Fotini. Spiro just telephoned. Keep Marilena at home. There will be no school. Not until the afternoon. After the last time, they want to be sure first that the square is clean."

"Last time? Clean? You mean . . .?"

"Like four years ago."

"Oh my God."

The light had turned to pre-dawn pearly grey. Theddo always loved this time. The Almost Time, he called it. Not day, not night; everything seemed possible.

He walked past the two sea-facing nineteenth-century cannons, nodding to the short stocky old man sitting on the bench just before the bend that ended in the town square.

The old man was almost always there, always wearing a dark blue jacket, black trousers and a grey-brown wool sweater. A blue-black fisherman's cap usually crowned his thin, gunmetal-grey hair, but on this particular morning his head was bare. Sometimes he'd be reading a Greek newspaper or a book, sometimes just looking at the sea and the traffic of people and animals. He had, Theddo thought, the quiet dignity of an elder. Theddo acknowledged this status with a respectful nod. The old man never spoke, but always nodded back, giving a tambourine-shake wave of his hand, palm turned inward. Theddo waved back as he rounded the bend.

It was like a lumpy patchwork fur rug, colours muted in the ghostlight, stretching from one end of the square to the other, fur rippling in the pre-dawn breeze. Here and there were bare spots, where you could see the marble. But mostly it was cats. Curled or sprawled, rigid with rigor mortis, eyes squeezed shut. Cats of every colour, every size.

At the far end of the square, men in dark clothes and yellow rubber gloves were scooping up the inert creatures and depositing them inside the open maw of the Island's large sanitation truck.

A man was running towards Theddo, waving his hands.

"Mister! Mister! Stay where you are!"

Theddo, still trying to apprehend what he was looking at, did not move. He'd had no thought of moving. The command made him realise that moving would be a complex act of navigation. Hopscotch in hell.

"What is this? What has happened here?" Theddo shouted back.

"GO. GO TO YOUR HOME PLEASE!"

"WHAT HAS HAPPENED HERE?"

Spiro was now weaving through the carpet of cats, thinking that the large *mávros*, DanYELLSS, was probably in shock. As the children had been, on their way to school, when this happened four years earlier. This time the ones who did it had done it in the deep night, knowing there would be fewer people, and no children in the area. They were right. There were, apart from those who were working with the problem, only two adult males, one a foreigner.

Spiro had called the heads of all schools. He called the owners of the early-opening cafés. His wife called various mothers, asking them to keep their children home. Each mother was asked to call others.

He put his hand on Theddo's shoulder. Theddo continued to stare at the cat-blanketed square.

"What . . . is this?"

"Someone . . . has poisoned the cats."

"Poisoned?"

"Yes. They eat the food, the cats. The people put food out all over the *PlaTEEah*, the square, and the food is mix with heavy poison, yes? Poison."

"Poison? Why?"

"Because . . . we have very many cats. Too many. The people who make the poison are not allowed to do this. It is against law to kill cats. But they do it before. Four years ago."

"Four years ago? Were they . . . caught?"

"The cats?"

"No. The people. The . . . poisoners."

"No. We had some investigations, but could not find them."

"Them?"

"Them. Him. Her. We do not know. Please. We must clean this square. Can you go to your home until later? The air is not good until we clean."

"The air?"

"Please. Please go home. I must help with the clean. You must go home."

"I need to find . . . my cat."

"Your cat?"

"Yes. Small. Orange."

"Please, mister. You cannot find *small* and *Ohranz* in all this cats."

"I need to look."

"No. Is not good here. Please. You must go home."

"Let me look from here. Just from here."

"From here?"

"Yes. From where I'm standing. Please."

"Only from here. Yes? Only from here. I must go back and help. You cannot go inside all the cats, yes? Understand?"

"Yes. Understand."

He tried to look from where he was, cat by cat. There were orange catballs and orange catsprawls, but they were all too large.

All at once, atop their tall metal posts, the halogen streetlights went out, signalling the arrival of morning light.

Then, in the middle of the square, next to the bank where he'd first met the minuscule lion that had become Cloudberry, he saw something that was both orange and small. It seemed to be stretching, reaching. He wove towards it, hearing Spiro shout.

"No, mister! You stay not close!"

"One minute," he shouted back, and then, not wanting to be a Spazzmaynoid, he produced the Greek.

"*Mia stigMEE.*"

Perhaps startled by the Greek words coming out of the black face, Spiro just shook his head and continued with the work of cat-disposal.

Pink nose with a black dot on it. White fur on back right paw and tip of tail. One fight-bitten tipless ear. He started to squat down, wanting to separate Cloudberry from the massacre. Then he remembered his Uncle Jory.

"Tularemia. Never pick up a dead animal, son. It'll give you tularemia."

He did not know what tularemia was—only that it meant lots of large needles and bitter medicine. Toxoplasmosis and HIV. Tularemia and HIV. Cats and HIV. He stood up.

And it all rolled out. From Björn's death. From before Björn's death. From his whole life from when he first stopped crying because sissies cried and sissies were a part of the danger zone. Standing in the middle of what he would later call feline Jonestown, he sobbed, letting the tears tumble out and down, dropping water on the tough little harbour cat who had hated being wet.

Spiro and the others heard the sobbing, but had too much to do. They let him sob.

He hugged his body, absently rubbing his upper arms. He was not cold; simply needing to be held. Finally, as the sanitation truck and the workers drew closer to him, he turned and wove his way back out of the square, still crying, more softly now, and fastidiously careful not to step on any creature.

The old man on the bench, who remembered what had happened before, and knew what had happened in the night, looked up at him, holding out his navy-jacketed arms, beckoning with his hands. Theddo stumbled into the man's embrace.

Human contact triggered another burst of weeping. The old man held him tightly.

Finally, he looked up and into the bright black-brown eyes of the man.

"Why . . .? Who could . . .? How could . . .? Does it *never end?!* Smash! Break! Kill! Kill the cats! Lynch the men! Rape the women and girls! Rape the boys! Beat up the faggots! Let 'em die! God wants 'em dead! Burn their houses! Bomb their villages! Shoot 'em, nuke 'em, knife 'em, poison 'em! Will . . . we *never, ever, EVER* get out of the *fucking CAVE?!*"

The man regarded him gravely, with concern and attention. He said nothing.

"I'm sorry . . . I didn't mean to . . . forgive . . . excuse . . . do you . . . speak English?"

The man did not reply, but touched Theddo's cheek and then tapped his heart three times. Theddo had seen that gesture before on Ydra, knew it to be one of both sympathy and solidarity.

His voice would not come, but he managed to croak out a soft "Thank you, *ev hariSTOH.*" He kissed the man in the centre of his forehead and stood.

"Thank you. Thank you. I'm . . . going . . . home now."

Michailoulaki, deaf since birth, had not heard a word. Nor did he need to. When he was born, in the north, his father believed it would be better if they drowned him. His mother refused. They hid in the hills. Then she took her silent baby to Ydra.

When Theddo staggered into his Kamini apartment, the phone was ringing. It was Oliver Gwangwe.

Spiro told Fotini; Fotini told Soula; Soula told Johnny.

"Jesus! He must be blown away. *I* was when it happened before."

"So was Marilena. It took her a year to stop seeing it. And Elly— Fotini and Spiro's Elly, still has the dreams."

"We should send Marilena to Theddo. He loves seeing her. It would help."

Marilena was angry.

"Why don't they catch these people, BaBAH?" she asked. "Are these terrible men going to do this every four years?"

"Terrible *men?* We don't know who did this, Marilenamou."

"Yes we do. Many do. But no one wants to name them."

"We can't prove anything, sweetheart."

"Spiro could prove something. He just won't. He is in the square at night, working. He always says *too many cats*. Elly told me." She ate a few more Kalamata olives—her "fish soup," her crisis food.

"Poor Mister DanYELLSS. The cat was living with him. He called him Cloud Berry. Not very big. Orange. I played with him. A sweet cat. I really . . . don't understand . . ." And she cried. Johnny held her. When she rested her head on his shoulder, all cried out, he asked if she'd like to be "an angel of mercy."

The door was locked. She knocked. No answer. She knocked again, shouting "Mister DanYELLSS, Hi! It's me, Marilena. I have some *kouraBYEDHes* . . . biscuits . . . cookies. They are for you . . ."

She heard him moving towards the door. It remained closed.

"Hello, Marilena. I need to . . . be by myself for a while. Finishing up my book. When I'm done, I'll telephone and come up to your house. Okay?"

"Okay . . . Are you okay?"

"I will be. Thank you . . . very much for coming by. I will see you, and your family, soon. Very soon. Okay?"

"Yes . . . bye-bye then. See you soon."

"Yes."

Marilena turned and headed away from the door. Then, at the start of the Kamini Road, she turned and ran back.

"Mister DanYELLSS?"

His voice came from further inside the apartment.

"Yes, love?"

"I'm . . . very sorry about Cloud Berry."

And then she turned and ran down the road, not wishing to make him feel he had to talk about it.

Goin' Home

"Chess Pie?"

"Yep. I know you Carolinians like it. Haven't made one for years. Hope it's all right."

Johnny took the pie.

"Come in, man. I'm sure it'll be terrific. You look good. Should this pie be in the fridge?"

"This pie should be eaten, is what it should be." Theddo smiled, more shyly than Johnny had ever seen him do.

"Definitely. Soula's at the Women's Centre and Marilena's still at school. I think we should wait for them, yes?"

"Absolutely. I'll bring my stuff in."

Theddo's "stuff" was a large duffel bag, his typewriter case and a beige canvas bookbag with a black, green and orange border design and the words *InterAfrA—Africans Everywhere.*

"What's all this? You leaving?"

"Yes. This has always been, roughly, my departure date. My colleagues at InterAfrA say it's time for me to be, as they say in the song, 'Goin' Home.'"

"Back to D.C.?"

"Not immediately. Do you know Doctor Oliver Gwangwe?"

I know who he is. Wasn't he at the Athens conference too?"

"That's right. He's an old and dear friend. He telephoned. His clinic in London has access to . . . a medical treatment that's having good results with . . . a chronic condition I have. He wants me to stop in London for a bit. See if it works for me."

Johnny was pretty sure he knew what the "chronic condition" was, and had read a few speculative articles about the new medical treatment in the anglophone newspapers.

"That's great. I hope it works."

Theddo nodded, smiling slightly.

"Yeah. Me too."

"It's brown and white?"

"Yes, Marilena, it's called chess pie. The design is like a chess board."

"It's pretty. Did you make it?"

"He did. And it tastes really good. If the saving-the-world business goes bust, Mister Daniels can always get a job as a baker."

"The saving-the-world business goes bust regularly, but I think I'll stay with it. Less fattening."

They helped Theddo carry his things to the harbour, and then seated themselves around a metal table in the dockside extension of *Ydróneira* café, waiting for the hydrofoil to arrive. On the balcony of the café across the lane, assorted Spazzmaynoids sat laughing and occasionally shouting in English.

"You know, Marilena, that essay you left," Theddo said, "the one about your hair, was very well done. I've kept it."

"Essay? Hair?"

"Yes, Soula. I suspect that Marilena has a talent for . . . personal social anthropology."

"Really. Howcum we haven't seen this essay?"

"It's just something I did for school, BaBAH. I gave it to mister DanYELLS. If you would like to see, I can show it to you when we go home. I have copies."

"Ah, copies. Thank you, Soula, for letting me copy my manuscript. I'm going to leave one copy with the Reed family. In case my plane goes down."

"No, Mister DanYELLSS! Don't say that!"

"I was joking, Marilena. I'll be fine. But I do want your family to have a copy of this. Particularly *you*, John. Could you read it and . . . let me know what you think? You know my other work, and . . ."

"I would be honoured, Theddo. Thank you."

Johnny took the paper bagful of manuscript pages.

"Here comes the Flying Dolphin," Marilena said, not very happily. They stood up, Johnny insisting on paying the bill for their three coffees and one lemon soda.

"Marilena. I meant it about the essay. I'll send you some forms. In your last year of high school, you can apply for a Fulbright Scholarship. When you get the forms, you could start thinking about what you might want to do, might want to study. Would you do that for me, have a look at the forms and the guidelines?"

"Yes, Mister DanYELLSS. Of course," Marilena replied, wondering what "guidelines" were.

And that other business. She knew that Mister DanYELLSS liked her, but full? Bright? Would these guidelines people, whoever they were, think she was full enough, bright enough? For Mister DanYELLSS, she would certainly try to be. And she had almost five years to work on it.

Theddo joined the pushing, luggage-laden cluster heading onto the hydrofoil; there was much hugging and promising to stay in contact.

The Reeds waved as the Flying Dolphin headed out, trailing spume behind it. They then walked up the hill silently, each with his or her own large thought-pile. Inside the house, Marilena cut a piece of chess pie, which she licked at more than ate, as she stared out the window and down the hill to the square. Soula kissed Johnny and started preparing the evening meal. Johnny sat in his beat-up old armchair, the one that had been in Soula's family for fifty years. He took Theddo's manuscript from the paper bag:

"Black/Out"
By Theddo Daniels.

Eight Headlines and Three Letters
November 1997

Daniels' New Book Reveals Secret Gay Life—*New York Times*
Civil Rights Leader Says "I'm a Gay Man'—*Harlem Sentinel*
Daniels D.C. Love Nest with Swedish Dancer—*National Informer*
Ekstrom and Daniels Bring Boy-Toy to Washington—*Keyhole*
Lover Died of AIDS; Daniels Comes Out—*GayWorld*
Theddo Daniels and Callie Hodge Exit Closet Together—*Gay Life*
**Daniels' New Book Thanks Dag Ekstrom ('He was braver
than I, and a friend to the end')**—*Washington News*
Theddo Daniels' New Book Rocks InterAfrA
—*African-American Journal*

London, England
5 March, 1998
Dear John,

*Hello from London, where I am working with Oliver at the
Brixton Clinic (and he, as you know, is working with me).*

*The part of me that hates <u>personal</u> (as opposed to issue-based)
attention (and that's still pretty much <u>all</u> of me) moved in London
just before the book hit the fan.*

*And the fan was righteously hit! I informed everyone at
InterAfrA months before publication. Some, of course, had known
for years, along with much of the media. I've come to realise that a*

number of people wanted to protect, if not me, then my work. This touches me.

There was, (and continues to be) nonetheless, a lot of heat about the book. Black males, many of us (including me) are complicated about gayness. Once, during an argument, Björn said that I belonged to two groups, but was only willing to fight for one. He was right. I never admitted that to him, and it took an awfully long while for me to admit it to myself. Now that I have, I feel both free and self-conscious as hell. I am hoping that, eventually, the self-consciousness will go, leaving only the freedom.

When I told the InterAfrans *about the book, I also offered to step down as chair, saying (truthfully) that I was proud to have founded InterAfrA, and of nurturing it, but that it was time for newer, younger voices to take up the leadership.*

After a courteous amount of nervous demurrers, it was agreed that I would resign, and that there would be an election. A strong candidate, Chris Varney was elected. He founded Brothers and Sisters, a good NGO, about ten years ago. He's smart, brave; husband of one, father of two. I admire and respect Chris, and believe he will do well. He's also interested in amalgamating Brothers and Sisters with InterAfrA, *which will create both a larger and younger lobbying base.*

I admit (only to you) that I'd hoped the other candidate Luanne Wills would get it—it's time for more women to be involved at the top level (it has <u>been</u> time for some time).

I <u>will</u> be able to work on that. It was unanimously agreed that I remain active as Permanent President Emeritus. I'm willing to wager that you have never before received a letter from a Permanent President Emeritus. Mostly that means I will continue doing conferences and other shit-disturbing activities, "at the pleasure of the president."

A propos pleasure, I am delighted that Marilena got the Max Cullemore Scholarship. As you know, the Cullemore required referee-letters. Both Oliver and I wrote sincere letters in praise of Marilena's project, but I was not otherwise involved in any way with the Cullemore committee's decision. Or with Marilena's. I simply sent her the information, along with info regarding other scholar-ships. She chose the Cullemore. Her project's concept and scope is also entirely her own.

I will (with great joy) come to Ydra in 2000 and, after visiting with everyone, escort Marilena to London.

Do you remember the story I told you in Ydra, about my sister Dora and her boyfriend Ezekial? Well, it seems to run in the fami-ly. Which is to say that I'm in a new relationship. Six months now. Ezekial (Zeke) is a doctor. From Ghana. He works with Oliver and me at the clinic here, and is setting up two clinics for us in Africa.

Africa. The AIDS situation in Africa, mostly women and chil-dren, is so vast that it makes AIDS #1 (North America and Europe) look like a seasonal flu bug. The white world tends to see it as "some-thing black, somewhere Over There"—which makes getting money and medicine damn near impossible!

Zeke, being a doctor from the region, knows who's true and who's on the take, which is critical to our work.

He's also HIV-positive, which makes the medical side of things easier for the two of us. He's a bright, funny, and compassionate man. Also tall, dark, and, I believe, handsome. I think you'd like him. I think Marilena will too.

John. Thank you again for all your written comments regard-ing the original manuscript of Black/Out. They were of enormous help.

Do you ever think of coming home? Working as an actor again?

There's a lot happening for African-American actors now. Darnell Collins is getting to do it all—serious acting, comedy, romantic leads—the whole package. A superb young actor, I think. And a gen-u-wine Hollywood Star. What I'm saying is that it seems there's more room now, if you wanted to give it another shot.

Further re Oliver: The "cocktail" (as it is called) with which he is treating me seems to have saved my life. And the lives of many other people with HIV-AIDS. The shame is that it came too late for so many—people who were, and always will be, beloved to us.

There are side effects: I've got a permanent lump on the back of my neck (and am extensive new collection of silk scarves!). Zeke has also suggested dreadlocks (I'm considering it). My belly's bigger and my legs are skinnier. A small price to pay.

Anyway, my dear friend, I will see you in less than two years. In the meantime, much love to you, to Soula and, of course, to Marilena.

Theddo

April 1ˢᵗ, 1998
Ydra, Greece

Dear Theddo,

Happy April Fool's Day from Ydra, Greece, where the holiday is not celebrated. At least not knowingly.

Great to get your letter. And to read that everything is so cool with you.

There's a <u>lot</u> of <u>pride</u> in the Reed household. Our daughter beat out over two hundred applicants! Of course, Soula is nervous as hell about her Little Girl going out into the Big World. Travel is complicated for Soula. On her <u>one</u> trip outside Greece, to London, two years before we met, she had a bad scene. It was only a one-time thing, but it convinced her that she should stay in Greece. Then, when she went to live on Ydra, she blossomed. Now, she doesn't even want to go to Athens. So, I've got this Island Wife and a daughter who is aching to see the world. And, to be honest, I'm a little nervous about it too. But Marilena is so blissed that we must, and do, support her joy. And she will be with the best surrogate parent I can think of—<u>you</u>.

I know that Marilena has sent you photos, but—and I'm not saying this as her father—you have NO IDEA! She is six feet tall and all the Spazzmaynoids and half the tourists keep telling her she could be "the next Iman." Chris Dennison calls her, in a rare attempt at Greek, "Imanóula." I have informed him (and I <u>am</u> saying this as her father), that if he lays a hand on my kid I will turn him into a soprano. And that all the Greek men on the island will help me.

Fortunately (for me and Soula, and, I think, for her too), she is not remotely interested in modelling. She wants to work with and for people. She gets this from my father and her mother—and from her great friend Theddo Daniels.

Naturally, all of Ydra knows about her scholarship—the result of my bragging from one end of the island to the other. When you come back to us, there will be a party for both of you at "To Kósmo Tou Fanóu." Fano and Viky say hello.

You'll be pleased to know that "Viky and the Rembetiko Brotherz" finally cut a CD. That led to being part of a World Music concert at the amphitheatre of Mount Lycabettus in Athens. And it looks like that might lead to a European tour. Soula and I have mixed feelings. We'd prefer to let the band be just a Greek thing.

Which brings me to your Hollywood question. When I was taking care of Pete, in 1984, I was in New York for months. Had long talks with my old agent (who has since died, at 83). She was a great lady and never lost faith in me. I appreciated this, and always will, but I'll tell you something—

I loved acting. Really loved it. And believe I had a talent for it. But I saw <u>some stuff</u>. <u>Really ugly stuff</u>. It's a great profession, but a terrible business. At least in New York and Los Angeles. And nothing major is gonna happen for an actor without those two places. I think the business is a twister for anybody, but lots worse if you're black.

You talk about Darnell. Darnell is an amazing actor. I saw his first film, in 1989. He had one scene of screen-time. I said, "There he is, The Next Sidney."

I'm happy for him, and hope he rides it long and well—hope they don't fuck with his head or with his life.

Me, I'm John Grandon Reed of Ydra, Greece. Husband of Soula, father of Marilena. I love my life. And my life loves me back. I have what I want. Very few people can say that.

Stay well.

See you on the island.

J.

14 May 1998
Ydra, Greece

Dear Mr. Daniels,

Apologies! I have taken <u>so</u> long to write! It's just that I've been <u>swamped</u> with school stuff (tests, projects, etc.—it's that time of year), and didn't want to write a quick 'blahblah' letter.

First of all, thank you <u>so much</u> for the fantastic red scarf with the little silver bits all over it. My mother thinks it's from the 1920s. Whatever it is, I love it! When I dance, or walk in the sun or stand under a tall lamp in the square, it really sparkles. All my friends think it's very cool— and they're right. I wear it <u>everywhere</u>. Not to school, where it's not allowed but just about everywhere else.

Getting the Max Cullemore Scholarship is the miracle of my life! And the letters that you and Doctor Gwangwe wrote, in support of my project, are amazing! I will work hard to live up to those letters, and to your belief in me.

Regarding other scholarships, I wasn't eligible for my type of Fulbright, because I don't know where I want to go to university. With the Cullemore, I can decide during my project. I understand that I must pick a university as a condition of the scholarship. I <u>want</u> to go to university, but just don't know <u>where</u> yet. Except for parts of Greece and one trip with my dad to Florida to visit Granny Carlotta when she was dying, I haven't been away from Ydra. Now I'll be going to London, Washington and South Africa. That is so fantastic!

I like it that Cullemore projects must deal with "the public good in relation to those of African heritage." I've thought a lot about that, and about you. I've now read all your books—including Black/Out (my parents finally agreed to let me. It was my mother who was nervous about it).

After reading Brothers—Black Men on Earth *(my father's favourite Theddo Daniels book), I told him I'd write a sequel;* Half-Sisters—Black and White Women on Earth. *I was teasing a little, but I do think there is a place for that book, and hope I will learn enough to write it.*

I know Doctor Gwangwe from your books, and his. That's how

297

I chose Health Care for People of African Descent in Three Cities: London, Washington and Johannesburg. *I will see and learn a lot. My plan is to then write about it, with specific proposals for improvements—not just talk, specific actions.*

It's great that I can stay with you in London and Washington, and with Doctor and Mrs. Gwangwe in South Africa. I think that's the main reason my mother finally agreed to let me go. She's still nervous, but my father and I are working on her. He, my father, says that my grandfather, Marcus Aurelius Reed, would be very proud of what I'm doing.

I want to learn about my paternal heritage. That sounds so formal. What I mean is <u>my people, on my father's side.</u> I'm proud of being Greek, but also proud of being African-American (my father read in the Herald Tribune here that African-American is our new name. I like it. Better than being named for a colour, and without a capital letter. Blacks are the only people with a heritage in lowercase. Even a German shepherd dog is a capitalised German). I want to learn more about what African-American means. For me, and in the world.

Can't wait to see you again. Please write when you can, and I'll do better at writing back. You said you were going online?! Bravo! My parents still can't do computers! When you are on the net, you can e-mail me at

   marilenar@argonet.gr

   Με πολλή φιλία *(With much friendship)*

   Marilena

   P.S. I have my <u>first passport</u>! My dad took me to Athens to get it. It's beautiful. It says, in Greek and English, "Marilena Marisa Reed, <u>Scholar</u>."

Wanderer Children—
Pigeons in the Underground
Ydra, Greece, 2000

The voice on the loudspeaker announced, in both Greek and English, that the "*Next stop will be Ydra, ladies and gentlemen. Ydra next. Please be certain that you have all of your belongings, and we thank you for choosing Flying Dolphin. Ydra next, Ydra!*"

The hydrofoil slid into place alongside the dock. The crowd, including Johnny, surged forward to meet visitors and returning islanders. Soula hung back, her eyes on Marilena, who was off to one side, waiting and watching, her long scarf sparkling in the sun.

Almost as tall as her father, with his slimness, she had slicked her hair into a long balletic braid that hung to the middle of her back. She wore a light red lipstick and had thickened her long eyelashes with a bit of mascara. Tiny silver hoops glistened from pierced ears. A simple, sleeveless pale yellow cotton dress and matching belt made her golden brown skin glow, or so it seemed to Soula.

Then she heard the scream.

She had thought about the scream before, but not since London, in 1979, had she heard it so clearly, so strongly. Not until Theddo Daniels came to take her daughter off the Island.

London, England, 1979

Markos Valoritis trained AthinaTour guides in London. He said it gave them a "better English. A proper English." This, he thought, inspired confidence in people taking an AthinaTour.

The London training centre was near to the airy, open Liverpool Street station. That station was also an entry-point for the grubbier and darker "tube"—the local London underground trains. AthinaHouse, Markos' other building, where trainees were housed, was in North London, in Kentish Town. The rooms were above a Greek restaurant, also owned by Markos, where trainees could take their evening meal at no charge, if they got there before ten in the evening.

Maureen, Soula's AthinaHouse roommate, had persuaded her to hear a band that was playing at an Irish music club near the office.

"The bass player is my brother's best friend. They're a terrific band! C'mon Sool'! You can't come to London and just speak Brit all day and eat Greek food every night! C'mon!"

Soula liked Maureen and loved music. She agreed.

The band played traditional Irish songs and original compositions, using electric rock n' roll instruments. Soula enjoyed the music. And the drummer asked her to see a film with him the following week, before the band went back to Dublin. She agreed.

By the time Soula and Maureen left *Pogue Mahoney's,* it was eleven at night.

"We've missed dinner," Soula said as they got their tube tickets from the machine.

"Yeah, well. I didn't want anudder heapin' bowl o' Stiffo annyway," Maureen grumbled nasally, her perfect English falling away, as it always did after class.

"Not 'Stiffo,' you crazy—*StifAHdoh*—Greek rabbit stew."

"Yeah, well. The bluddy *StiFAHdoh* is ev'ry bluddy night-oh. The Bombay place is open late. I t'ink we should go there an' have some curry an' stuff. Beery-Annie. I *love* Beery-Annie!"

"Me too. Biriani it is."

At Moorgate, they had to change trains for the Northern Line. Soula disliked the Northern Line. It was more beat-up and dirty than the other underground trains, and, after ten at night, had a funny energy. Something "not quite on," as Missus Oliphant, their English teacher (whose largeness had produced the obvious pun for each year's trainees) would say.

They were sitting on a bench at Moorgate Station, waiting for the Northern Line train when Soula saw the two pigeons swooping back and forth, high above their heads, over the tracks. Somehow, they'd gotten in and could not find the way back out. Then, while one was ricocheting among the waiting passengers, the other found a small hole and flew out. The remaining one dived down, and then swooped up again.

"Look!" Soula said, pointing, "that pigeon is trapped in here. With us."

"Wit' *us?* Poor bluddy bastard!" Maureen said as the train pulled into the station.

They'd been riding for three stops when the boys got on. There were five of them. Short, spotty-faced. Soula could not tell if they were indeed boys or just childish young men.

They were shouting at one another, very drunk. Both Soula and Maureen, in silent agreement, stopped speaking, placed their hands over the handbags in their laps. They stared straight ahead, pretending to be elsewhere. And then it started.

"WHERE *ARE* WE, D'YE THINK?" the shortest one, the one with the dyed fire-engine red hair shouted.

"ENGLAND! I *THOUGHT* WE WERE IN ENGLAND, MAN!"

"England?! ENGLAND, YE SAY?! Cahnt be bloody England! I mean *look* at THESE PEOPLE!"

All five boys laughed, jostling and pushing at each other, muttering or shouting "yeah" or "Bloody right!" or "Look at 'em!"

"BLOODY DARKIES!" Little Red shouted.

Soula looked across the aisle, as surreptitiously as possible. She could see two women in saris, a black woman with her young son, another woman whose hair and entire body below the neck were covered in black fabric. *Hijab.* She thought the word was *hijab.* A family from Morocco had come to Ydra one summer, while she was a teenager visiting her relatives there. The adult women wore these black garments. They kept to themselves. They swam in the black garments, wet, black, water-filled fabric ballooning around them. Soula wanted to know them, but felt they wished to be left to their own company. They spoke in Arabic and laughed a lot. They seemed to be enjoying Ydra. When Soula smiled, they would always smile back, and then look away. Her aunt said Moroccan people made a special music. She gave Soula a record. It was powerful, aching, yearning. Like Rembetiko.

Remembering the music and the women in the water, Soula smiled quickly at the woman across the aisle. The woman's eyes, as Soula's had moments earlier, went totally blank, trying to transport her spirit elsewhere.

"We should get off at the next stop," Maureen whispered.

"No," Soula whispered back. "I want to ride to Kentish Town. They've no right to run us off."

She had spoken very softly, but Little Red picked up her energy, and was suddenly in her face, all boozy breath and bad acne.

"And where are *you* from, DAAHHling?!" he hissed.

Don't panic, don't look in his eyes, stay blank, Soula thought, weaving her fingers tightly together over her handbag.

The train stopped. The black woman and her son got off the train, as did the two sari-clad women. The woman in the hijab remained seated, along with an old man, probably English, who had gotten on at the last stop.

Then Soula changed her mind about blankness.

She looked into Little Red's malevolent eyes. A soft hazel with greeny flecks. They'd be good eyes, she thought, if he were not the creature he was.

"Greece," she said, softly but definitely. "I am from Greece."

He grabbed her hair tightly, close to the scalp.

"Grease, eh? Bloody right! Greasy hair, greasy skin! England is filling with grease!"

Across the aisle, one of the other boy/men was slapping the old man, who looked to Soula to be about eighty and frail as a baby.

"Give me yer bloody money, ye fuckin' geezer! Now!"

The old man handed a billfold to his attacker, who riffled through it.

"Fuckin' nuthin'!" he said. "Ten fuckin' quid!" He took the ten-pound note and some coins and then tossed the billfold onto the floor. The old man looked at it, but did not move. At the next stop, he scooped it up and left the train.

I don't want to lose my money, lose my passport, Soula thought, but, with Little Red directly in front of her, she was afraid of attempting to stand and leave.

Then he let go of her hair, shouting, "Hey, lads! I'd like to have a piss! Anyone here like to have a piss?!"

The others agreed that they too would like to have a piss. Soula thought they were going to urinate on *her*, but they moved to a corner, just in front of the narrow door between the carriages.

They formed a semi-circle, standing shoulder to shoulder, a band of brothers.

Each one unzipped or unbuttoned his fly and pulled out his penis.

Then, pointing to someplace in the centre of their semi-circle, they all urinated. Having had a lot to drink, they did this for what seemed to Soula to be a long time.

The urine slowly ran in rivulets through the train carriage, over Soula's sandaled feet, wetting her toes, then around Maureen's running shoes, while another stream flowed down the other side, wetting the bottom of the Arab woman's black hijab.

At the next stop, the tormentors left the train, laughing and shouting. Three people got on, carefully stepping around the urine, which was pooling in corners or on the floor under seats, mixing with candy wrappers and other rubbishy things.

"I want to leave the train. Next stop, I want to leave the train," Soula said softly.

"Oh, fuckin' *brilliant*," Maureen replied, "*now* ye want t' leave the bluddy train! The little fuckers is gone an' *now* yiz wants to leave de bluddy train!"

"Please Maureen. I'll pay for a taxi!" Soula whispered urgently.

"Sure Sool, sure. We'll leave the train. C'mon. Here comes the stop."

Soula crossed the aisle. She spoke softly to the woman in the hijab.

"Excuse me. Would you like to share a taxi with us? We can take you to where you live."

She touched the woman's shoulder. The woman looked up at her. She screamed. An enormous scream. The train stopped

"Hey Sool, c'mon. It's Kentish Town annyways! It's our stop anny-ways! C'mon!"

They left the train. Soula stood on the platform. She was shaking. As the doors closed, the woman in the hijab was still screaming.

Ydra, Greece, 2000

There was a party for Theddo Daniels and Marilena at *To Kósmo Tou Fanóu*. Food, wine and Rembetiko Brotherz music. Theddo stayed with the Reeds. He and Marilena talked for hours about what she hoped to achieve, what he hoped to provide.

Then it was time for the hydrofoil to Athens, which would lead to the plane to London. And then, months after that, Washington, D.C. And after that, Africa. Everywhere adventures, Marilena said. New sights, new sounds, new people. And everywhere illness, Soula thought, because that was at the core of Marilena's project.

She stood on the dock, next to Johnny, waving at her tall daughter who was heading into the world. Marilena and Theddo disappeared into the hydrofoil, which coasted out into the open water.

Marilena is smart, Soula thought, it will be fine.

She could see the pigeon in the London underground, the one that got in but could not get out.

She could see the boy/men in the city she had always wanted to visit—the city that was so gracious, so civilised.

She saw herself in the train: "Greece. I am from Greece."

She felt the yellow-green urine rolling over her toes.

She heard the woman in the hijab.

She cried out, "Mari*LEHNAmou!*"

Johnny, having spent many nights walking with Soula, listening to her relive what had happened in London, moved behind her, wrapping one arm across her chest, his hand cupping her left shoulder. He lightly kissed her hair, murmuring "Easy, Soulamou, easy. She's smart. She's in good hands. What happened to you doesn't happen to *everybody.*" He said this knowing well that *something* happens to everybody.

Soula leaned back, into the comfort of her husband's body. Friends and neighbours had heard her cry, were watching her. She heard Viky say something about mothers and daughters.

Her second cry was not loud. She rocked slowly against Johnny, and, mouth open wide, softly keened—

"aaaaaaaaaaaaaaaaaaaaaaaa . . . ."

On the Flying Dolphin, Marilena said, "Come. If we stand on the connecting bridge they can see us."

They went out onto the short, corrugated steel deck that linked the main seating area to the café. The people in Ydra harbour were still individually visible, though the only sound that could be heard was the guttural churn of the hydrofoil skimming over the sea.

"Look, Mister Daniels. I can see Mana's mouth. She is saying *ya.*"

Theddo was surprised that "Ya," so Swedish to him, would be coming from Soula.

"*Ya?*"

"It's the short way for *iásou.* Remember that Greek word? It means hello *and* goodbye. Mana is saying her goodbye. Tomorrow, London will be my hello."

Acknowledgements

Given writing's solitary nature, it's surprising how many are involved in a writer's support. This intensifies if one cannot write fiction in the place one lives. I am one such.

Thanks to:

Sweden—First and foremost, the Baltic Centre for Writers and Translators in Visby, Gotland, Sweden. Gerda Helena Lindskog and Lena Pasternak create a work/living space where professional support intersects with the writer's self-sufficiency. Responsible adult support— a rare combination. Visby Centre friends and colleagues—particularly Pirkko Lindberg, Robert Kangas, Linda Boström, Lena Ulenius, Timo Lappalainen and Otto Lappalainen. Yvonne Petterson of Almedalen Library and Ishrat Lindblad of Stockholm University, for first readings in Sweden of both *Visible Amazement* and *Transient Dancing*. Françoise Sule and Denis Labrosse, as well as Jan Lindberg of Canada's Department of Foreign Affairs and International Trade (DFAIT) for arranging the Stockholm reading. CanLit Crusader, Heidi von Born, for including me in the ninth annual Strindberg Festival (along with countrymen Alistair MacLeod and David Staines). The Nordic Association for Canadian Studies (NACS), for their enthusiasm (particularly Keith Battarbee and Britta Olinder). Tomas Bolme and Gunnar Furumo, for answering questions regarding the Grand Hotel in Stockholm and the Fårö ferry. Thomas von Vegesack, for pointing me to the Swedish Writers' Union housing. Håkan Bravinger and the staff of SWU, for welcoming a wandering writer.

Denmark—Troels Munk, for showing me Copenhagen's Tivoli Gardens, and for information about Odin's tree.

Greece—Barbara and Grigoris Kotromagia, as well as Eva, of Pension Bouagia. Kosta, for *koulóuria* and kindness. Everyone at *To Steki*, for fine food and glasses of free wine. Niko Papandreou and Nikaiti Kontouri, for telephonic rescue from midwinter cabin fever. Ydra's feral cats, particularly Motoula, whose motorboat purr inside my jacket was part of winter-wet coffee mornings. Margarita Papandreou, for her determined, loving passion. Dina Vardamatou, for help with housing. Nontas Artemiou, and Giannis and Tassia Georgiades, for my long-time Athens home, The Athenian Inn.

London—As ever and forever, the Wise One, Martin Sherman, for providing a safe place for my book's hardest ride. I love you, dear Playwright. The Garden Court Hotel, Bayswater.

Canada—Peter Stephens of DFAIT. The Ontario Arts Council, Canada Council and DFAIT, for work-in-progress and travel grants. Sis Bunting Weld, for Hibiscus Cottage. Dr. Philip Berger, AIDS frontliner, for fact-checking and friendship. Susan Swan, for solidarity, as well as a writing-house, in company of the glorious Moses Ricci Swan-Crean. To Stuart Baulch of Toronto's Central Y, for providing "my" workroom and to Sophia Reid for having the idea. Holger Petersen, for Blooz Nooz.

U.S.A.—The Committee for Racial Equality of American Actors' Equity Association, particularly Harry L. Burney, Cooki Winborn, and Chuck Patterson. Gil Noble and "Like It Is" for leading me to the country within the country. The late Eddie Brown and the late Josh White, senior. Zenzile Miriam Makeba—my "X" is good, my "Q" not loud enough—but I sing your songs as best I can. Yours is the first sound I hear when someone says "music." Shirley Rich (her ethics, dedication and enthusiastic actor-support inspired Rose Golden—Rose is rounder and ruder—the homage, however, is to Ms. Rich).

Bookland—My publisher, Kim McArthur, for her unwavering support for and belief in my work. And to the "cast of thousands" at McA & Co—Janet Harron, Ruth Shanahan, Ann Ledden and Jim Palmieri. Susan Musgrave, whose clarity and passion makes any journey better. Linda Pellowe and David Szolcsanyi at Mad Dog Design for cover, graphics, and wading through punctuation. Copy-editor Pamela Erlichman for skill, patience and empathy. Marc Coté, for all of the questions and some of the answers. My agent, Jackie Kaiser, of Westwood Creative Artists, as well as Bruce Westwood who babysat me when Jackie had an actual baby. Ron Eckel, Amy Tompkins and, as always, Nicole Winstanley. Christine Wookey, for being a wisdomful reader. Thanks to all, for all—

G. Zoë Garnett, *April 2003, Toronto Canada*